knight

BOOKS BY TIMOTHY ZAHN

DRAGONBACK SERIES

Dragon and Thief*
Dragon and Soldier*
Dragon and Slave*
Dragon and Herdsman*
Dragon and Judge*
Dragon and Liberator*

QUADRAIL SERIES

Night Train to Rigel*
The Third Lynx*
Odd Girl Out*
The Domino Pattern*
Judgment at Proteus*

STAR WARS® NOVELS

Heir to the Empire
Dark Force Rising
The Last Command
Specter of the Past
Vision of the Future
Survivor's Quest
Outbound Flight
Allegiance
Choices of One
Scoundrels
Thrawn
Thrawn: Alliances
Fool's Bargin

COBRA WAR SERIES

Cobra
Cobra Strike
Cobra Bargain

Cobra Alliance
Cobra Guardian
Cobra Gamble
Cobra Slave
Cobra Outlaw
Cobra Traitor
Cobras Two (omnibus)
Cobra Trilogy (omnibus)

The Blackcollar
Blackcollar: The Judas Solution
A Coming of Age
Spinneret
Cascade Point and Other Stories
The Backlash Mission
Triplet
Time Bomb and Zahndry Others
Deadman Switch
Warhorse
Conquerors' Pride
Conquerors' Heritage
Conquerors' Legacy
The Icarus Hunt
Soulminder
Cloak
Angelmass*
Manta's Gift*
The Green and the Gray*

SIBYL'S WAR

Pawn*
Knight*

*A Tor Book

knight

A CHRONICLE OF THE SYBIL'S WAR

timothy zahn

TOR

A TOM DOHERTY ASSOCIATES BOOK

NEW YORK

KNIGHT

A Tor Book
Published by Tom Doherty Associates
175 Fifth Avenue
New York, NY 10010

www.tor-forge.com

Tor® is a registered trademark of Macmillan Publishing Group, LLC.

Library of Congress Cataloging-in-Publication Data

Names: Zahn, Timothy, author.
Title: Knight / Timothy Zahn.
Description: First edition. | New York, NY : Tom Doherty Associates, 2019. |
"A Tor Book."
Identifiers: LCCN 2018047502 | ISBN 9780765329677 (hardcover) |
ISBN 9781429946551 (ebook)
Subjects: | GSAFD: Science fiction.
Classification: LCC PS3576.A33 K58 2019 | DDC 813/.54—dc23
LC record available at https://lccn.loc.gov/2018047502

Our books may be purchased in bulk for promotional, educational, or business use. Please contact your local bookseller or the Macmillan Corporate and Premium Sales Department at 1-800-221-7945, extension 5442, or by email at MacmillanSpecialMarkets@macmillan.com.

First Edition: April 2019

Printed in the United States of America

0 9 8 7 6 5 4 3 2 1

knight

one

The metal wall section opened up, sending a blast of hot air into Nicole Hammond's face. Wading upstream against the flow, she stepped to the edge of the dark abyss. A moment later she was falling through the heat and blackness, her descent slowed by nothing more than a pair of giant butterfly wings.

The wings weren't hers, of course. And for once, the dark abyss wasn't very deep. She and the Wisp holding her dropped no more than ten feet before landing on some kind of metal grating. The Wisp unwrapped its thin, silvery-white arms from around her and stepped back, furling its butterfly wings onto its back. Squinting against the upward rush of hot air flowing through the grating, Nicole looked around.

They were in a large room, illuminated only by small ceiling lights that barely lit the area a foot or two around them and which seemed to extend to infinity in all directions. Unlike everywhere else she'd visited aboard the *Fyrantha*, the heat-transfer duct she and the Wisp had been riding seemed to end at the grating below her feet. Did that mean she'd reached the very bottom of the ship?

No, of course not—the fact that there was still hot air flowing upward through the grate meant something was still below her. The engines or motors, maybe, that powered everything aboard?

"Caretaker?" Nicole called, walking away from the duct and out of the updraft. "Ushkai? Where am I?"

Nothing. Maybe the *Fyrantha*'s hologram projector—or whatever it was the ship used to give her Ushkai's image—couldn't operate this far down in the ship's basement. Wiping the sweat off her forehead with her jumpsuit sleeve, Nicole fished a penlight out of her tool vest and flicked it on.

She'd been thinking about being at the bottom of the ship when she mentally tagged her location as the *Fyrantha*'s basement. Now, as she shone the light around, she saw to her mild surprise that she'd been closer to the mark than she'd realized. The damn place actually *looked* like a basement, or more specifically the unfinished basement at one of her old grade school friends' houses. There were pillars all around, running between the metal grating of the floor to the corrugated underside of the metal ceiling, like the ones she and Kamali used to grab when they roller-skated in endless circles around the stacks of boxes and other stuff Kamali's mom had stored down there.

Here, of course, as she'd already noted, the floor was a metal grating instead of a bumpy slab of concrete. Underneath the grating—

She frowned, holding the light closer to the grating. What *was* that down there, anyway?

It was a mass of dark brown, coming to maybe a foot beneath the grating, with tendrils of several different shades of lighter brown rippling through it. There was an odor rising from it, too; not a bad odor, exactly, but something that reminded her of the dank mustiness of Kamali's basement.

She leaned back a little, a sudden, horrible thought striking her. Could that be—? No. Surely not.

But there were people aboard the *Fyrantha*. A *lot* of people. Humans and aliens working to repair the ship; other kinds of aliens battling each other in a huge arena. People meant waste products . . . and waste products had to go somewhere.

But *here*? Sitting under a simple grate like an open sewer? Maybe some of the alleys in her old Philadelphia neighborhood were that way, but surely not here. "Caretaker?" she called.

Again, no answer.

"Well, *cra*—" She looked down at the brown mass under her feet and changed her mind about the word she'd been planning to say. So the Caretaker was lying low? Fine. There was more than one way to pop a clutch. "Wisp?" she called instead. "Come here."

The Wisp glided over, its black eyes and wide slit of a mouth expressionless as always. Nicole took its hand and squeezed the pale, silvery-white skin. *What's this brown stuff under the grate?* she thought toward the creature.

It's a part of the air system. The answer flowed across her mind. *Carbon dioxide and other unusable molecules are absorbed, fragmented, and converted into oxygen and other useful molecules.*

"Ah," Nicole said aloud, peering down at the brown stuff again. Vaguely, she remembered something in one of her grade school classes about plants doing that same job on Earth, eating up the carbon oxide stuff and spitting out oxygen. She'd never fully believed that—for one thing, if it was true, how come she'd never felt more awake in a park than she did when hanging around with Trake's gang? But the book said that was how it worked, and that was what the teacher had marked correct on the test, so she'd more or less accepted it.

There'd been something in that same class about why most plant leaves were green, too, but she'd forgotten what. The *Fyrantha* seemed to get along okay with brown stuff instead of green, so it probably hadn't been important. As long as it worked, things would be just fine.

Of course, that was the problem. The elephant in the room, as her grandmother used to say.

Because the ship *wasn't* working right. At least not all of it. That was why the Shipmasters had kidnapped a bunch of people from Earth, so that the ship could tell them what was wrong and they could fix it.

Of course, once it *was* fixed . . .

She shook her head firmly. One crisis at a time, as her grandmother also used to say. The *Fyrantha* had declared Nicole to be its Protector, for the most ridiculous reason imaginable. Nicole had tried to fix a plant in the arena, mostly because she'd been bored, and now the ship was looking to her to make sure it was properly put back together.

If and when she managed to do that, though, the Shipmasters who ran the place had some very nasty ideas on what they were going to do with it.

But that was the future. Right now, Nicole's crisis was to figure out her way around the ship she was supposed to be the Protector of.

It was more of a challenge than she'd expected. The *Fyrantha* was *huge*: two miles long, as near as she could figure, a solid half-mile wide, and ninety-six levels deep. In the past nine days she'd visited every one of those levels, but with only an hour on each one she'd barely scratched the surface. One of those nights, as she lay awake feeling her legs throb with fatigue, she'd guessed she'd seen less of the *Fyrantha* even than she had of Philadelphia.

Not to mention that so far she'd stuck exclusively to the right-rear fourth of the ship. Q4, Caretaker Ushkai had called it once, which she'd later figured out was probably short for Quadrant 4. If she wanted to *really* know the ship, she would have to take this same tour in Q1, Q2, and Q3.

She took a deep breath. One crisis at a time. First, she would get a handle on what was where in Q4. Then she would try to figure out how much work still had to be done back here. After that, she could see about the other quadrants—

She frowned, her thoughts suddenly stalling. Throughout her months aboard the *Fyrantha* she'd heard lots of background sounds from the ship: hums, drones, and whirrs, plus a whole range of different thuds, clunks, and bumps. But the soft thumping sound now coming from the darkness was something new. It was mostly rhythmic, but every few thumps there was a break in the pattern, as if the machine making the noise was occasionally freezing up.

It was also getting louder. Nicole turned her head back and forth, trying to figure out exactly where it was coming from. And why it sounded familiar . . .

She stiffened. Of *course* it sounded familiar. It was a set of footsteps.

And whoever was making them was coming her way.

Nicole's first impulse was to grab the Wisp, drag it back to the heat-transfer duct, and get the hell out of here. She'd had a couple of run-ins with the Shipmasters back when she was just a Sibyl, a relative nobody whose sole job was to relay the *Fyrantha*'s instructions to her work crew. Now, with the ship having declared her to be someone special and important, she'd lost that facelessness.

Anonymity had always been Nicole's best friend. It had saved her on more than one occasion, not just with the cops but also with whoever Trake or one of the others had been scamming or muscling at the time. Now that comforting darkness was gone, and she wasn't at all sure she liked that.

What she *was* sure of was that she didn't want to have her first meeting with the Shipmasters as Protector down here. Keeping her face toward the hesitant footsteps, she groped for the Wisp's hand—

And then, from the direction of the footsteps came a soft, weary birdsong warble.

She jerked in surprise. *Kahkitah?*

"Is someone there?" the English version of the birdsong whispered into her mind via the translator grafted to the side of her head. It sounded as tired as the song itself had. "Please. Is someone there?"

Nicole scrunched up her nose. It wasn't Kahkitah, she realized now—that wasn't his voice. But it *was* one of his fellow Ghorfs.

Did that mean an entire work crew was down here? She hadn't had much contact with other Ghorfs, but she'd never seen one on a job all by himself. The aliens were extremely strong, but like much of the criminal muscle Nicole had dealt with in Philadelphia they weren't all that well furnished in the brain department. Leave a Ghorf alone, and he was likely to forget what he was supposed to do, or just wander off and get lost.

Of course, in all fairness, she'd rarely seen one of the humans off on his or her own task, either. The Shipmasters seemed to like keeping their slaves in groups.

So what was a stray Ghorf doing down here?

It was a risk, she knew. Kahkitah was a decent enough person, but just like regular people she assumed Ghorfs had a whole range of personalities and mood types. It could be this one had run away from his team and gotten lost. It could also be that he'd gone crazy and been kicked out.

Nicole had dealt with plenty of crazies in Philadelphia. She had no interest in dealing with more of them here.

There was another plaintive bird whistle. "Hello?" the translation came.

Nicole sighed. *Protector* . . . "Over here," she called, turning on her penlight and shining it in that direction. "Follow the light. I'm over here."

The footsteps abruptly stopped, and for a moment there was silence. Then, the footsteps resumed, still shuffling but now much faster. Another whistle—"I'm coming," the Ghorf called. A shadowy figure loomed, and a moment later the alien stumbled into the light.

He wasn't in good shape. In fact, the closer he got, the worse he looked. His lumpy, a-thousand-marbles-poured-into-a-bag skin was pale and mottled, his squashed shark face seemed to sag, his neck gills were fluttering like a drowning man, his jumpsuit was so dirty that she couldn't tell what color it was supposed to be, and his gait was even more shambling than it had sounded. The creature had been through the sand sifter, and then some. He whistled—"Who are you?"

"I'm the—I'm a Sibyl," Nicole said. The *Fyrantha* might be ready to label her its Protector, but Nicole herself wasn't ready to take on the title. Belatedly realizing that she was hidden by the glare of the penlight, she turned it around and pointed it at herself. "I'm from the blue team," she added, though the color of her jumpsuit really should have told him that already.

"I'm of the gray team," he said, his thick paw-hands gesturing to his jumpsuit. "I was separated from the other workers and became lost. Have you any water?"

"Sure," Nicole said, glancing around as she pulled a couple of water bottles from her vest pockets. Most of the *Fyrantha*'s levels had supply closets at regular intervals, where food, water, tools, and repair parts were stored. Down here, with no corridors or walls interrupting the open space, the ship's designers had apparently decided such supplies weren't necessary.

And really, if all that was down here was the air filtration system, they were probably right.

"Thank you," the Ghorf said, stepping forward and taking the bottles. He twisted the top off one and downed it in a single, long swallow, then crammed it into his jumpsuit and started on the other.

"You're probably hungry, too," Nicole said, taking out her last two food bars. Kahkitah had shown a preference for a couple of the flavors, and she hadn't brought any of those with her. But different tastes apart, all the bars were equally digestible by both humans and Ghorfs.

"I am indeed." The Ghorf drained the last of the water and reached for the food bars.

And paused, his eyes running down her vest and jumpsuit. "But these are your last," he protested. "I cannot take the last of your food."

"There's plenty more right upstairs," Nicole assured him, pulling out her last water bottle as well. "Go on—eat."

"Thank you." Without further protest he tore open the food bars and dug in.

Nicole eyed him closely as he ate, feeling the same tingling on the back of her neck that she'd felt so often when Trake had put her together with Bungie for a score. Part of that was because Bungie's personality grated on her nerves, but mostly it was because Bungie's plans had a bad habit of going sideways. Her blue repair team had shared their cafeteria and medical facilities with the green and red teams, but only rarely had they run into someone from one of the other five groups. So even though she didn't recognize this particular Ghorf, it was entirely possible that he was who he said he was.

The problem was that she'd had the impression that all eight of their crews were working levels in the twenties and thirties, possibly the forties, but certainly no lower than that.

So how had this one managed to get all the way down here in the bottom nineties?

"What's your name?" she asked.

"I am Wesowee," he said, still chewing away at the food bar. One of the handy quirks of Ghorf physiology was the fact that their birdsong voices came from their neck gills, with their mouths reserved for eating. Nicole had occasionally wondered what her childhood would have been like if her grandmother had never had to scold her for talking with her mouth full. Maybe then she'd have stuck around longer instead of getting out the minute she could. "I am highly grateful for your generosity," he added.

"Yeah, no problem," Nicole said. "So how did you get down here? You said you got separated from your crew?"

"It's a little confusing," Wesowee admitted. "I was ordered to take a packet of large metal plates to the testing arena. Two of the—"

"Wait a second," Nicole interrupted. "The *testing arena*? A big chamber with high ceilings and a fake sky and sun?"

"Yes," Wesowee said. "Is that wrong?"

"Probably not," Nicole murmured. The testing arena was where the Shipmasters pitted two different groups of kidnapped aliens against each other, giving them weapons and threatening starvation if they didn't fight. If one of the groups demonstrated decent combat skills, the Shipmasters sold their planet's location to other aliens, who could then raid the world to grab slave troops for whatever wars they were fighting among themselves out there.

It was a scenario Nicole had seen way too often on the streets of Philadelphia. One gang would put their newest recruits in front in a fight, letting them get shot to pieces so that the bosses could see where their rivals had their shooters hidden. It was bad enough there, where it was just a few kids' lives down the

drain. Here, with whole worlds set up for slaughter, it was horrifying.

And Nicole may have played a part of her own in one of those
horrors. Though she'd gone into the arena hoping to save the lives
of the aliens trapped in what she'd thought was senseless fighting, her actions may have affected the Shipmasters' own decisions.

She didn't know that for sure. She probably never would. But
the thought that she may have helped condemn thousands or mil-
lions of aliens to death was a permanent ache in her stomach.

"Two of the Shipmasters were waiting," Wesowee continued,
"and ordered me to take the plates into the deep central channel.
I did so—"

"Hold it," Nicole again cut in. "A deep central *what?*"

"A channel," Wesowee said. "A deep hole in the ground running
the length of the arena."

"That doesn't—" Belatedly, Nicole broke off. She'd spent a *lot*
of time in the arena, and Wesowee's description wasn't even close.
The center wasn't a channel or even flatlands, but a ridge of hills,
some of them quite tall. There was no way the Shipmasters could
have carted off all that dirt and then dug a pit in the middle.

And *that* assumed digging was even possible. The *Fyrantha's*
levels were pretty uniformly flat, and very damn solid. Digging
through one should have taken far longer than the nine days that
had passed since she'd last been in there.

But when someone was pitching a lie, the dumbest move possible was to call him on it. People running scams needed to think
you were buying it, and it was never safe to poke a hole in their
balloon. They got angry *and* they got violent; and even a half-
starved Ghorf could probably punch her to death without trying.
"That doesn't sound safe," she amended.

"Truly, it wasn't," Wesowee said ruefully. "At one end of the channel was a downward-running conduit, and as I laid out the plates beside it I slipped and fell through. The conduit carried me into another chamber, also large but much smaller than the testing arena. When I finally was able to find a way out, I fell farther into a shaft carrying heated air upward. The shaft carried me here, and I've been searching for a way out ever since then."

"Wow," Nicole said dutifully, turning the story over and over as she searched for a good hole to call him on. It was dangerous to flat-out call a scammer a liar, but it was equally risky to look *too* gullible and accepting. Asking for a clarification or two was a good way to keep the right balance. "So how come you didn't break a leg or hip or something when you hit?" she asked. "It's a pretty long way down from the arena to here."

"I still had a hold on one of the plates," Wesowee said. "I was able to lift it over my head like a parachute, and it slowed me enough that I wasn't badly hurt." He whistled something Nicole's translator couldn't decipher. "Nevertheless, my ankles hurt for quite a while afterward. I don't think they're completely healed even now."

Nicole frowned. The Ghorf had been dragging his feet when he first arrived, but she hadn't noticed any actual limping. "How long ago was this, anyway?"

Wesowee whistled mournfully. "I don't know. Days, certainly." He stuffed the last bit of food bar into his mouth and gestured to his vest. "I had four bottles of water and six food bars. I consumed them carefully, but it's still been at least five days since I ran out."

He pointed to the heat-transfer duct behind Nicole. "I've seen many of these vertical shafts in that time and one very wide, very long one. But I haven't yet found a set of stairs with which I could return to my home and my fellow workers."

"Yes," Nicole murmured, a sudden memory cutting across the

cynicism about Wesowee's story. Back when the Caretaker had first declared her the *Fyrantha*'s Protector, hadn't he said something . . . ?

He had. He'd said the arena had once been a fighter-craft hangar, back when the *Fyrantha* had been somebody's warship. He'd said that some group called the Lillilli had taken out the racks and turned it into the testing arena. He'd then started to say something about other hangars.

Only Nicole had cut him off with a question. And somehow they'd never gotten back to that subject.

She beckoned over her shoulder to the Wisp still standing patiently behind her. The creature glided over, and Nicole took its hand. *Are there other testing arenas aboard the ship?* she thought at it.

There are three others, the Wisp replied.

Is one of them like Wesowee described, with a central channel?

Yes, in Q3.

Nicole nodded, feeling like an idiot. She already knew she'd barely scratched the surface of what the *Fyrantha* had to offer. She also knew that all of that scratching had been confined to Q4.

In other words, not only had Wesowee not been lying about his story, if he'd seen a bunch of heat-transfer ducts he'd clearly been wandering the ship for a lot longer and had covered a lot more distance than Nicole had realized.

She owed the Ghorf an apology. A big apology.

But since he didn't have the slightest idea of what she'd been thinking, an apology would probably only confuse him. "Okay, let's start by getting you some more food and water," she said instead. "After that, we'll figure out how to get you home."

"That would be wonderful . . ." Wesowee trailed off, his head swinging back and forth as he looked around. "But how can that happen? I see no stairs." He cocked his head. "How did *you* arrive here? Did you also fall?"

"No, I had help," Nicole said, turning to the Wisp. For a moment she wondered what Wesowee was going to think about what was about to happen, decided she really didn't care. As long as he got home okay, he shouldn't care how scary or befuddling the method was. "I need another Wisp," she said. She glanced at the Ghorf, noting his size. "On second thought, better make it two."

"What are these Wisps you speak of?" Wesowee asked.

"This is a Wisp," Nicole said, gesturing to the one beside her. As she did so, two more of them floated down the shaft, their descent slowed by the hot air rising against their butterfly wings. Their wings folded and they glided toward the Ghorf, their arms rising from their sides. "They'll take us to food, and then—"

She broke off at a terrified-sounding whistle from the alien. "No!" he pleaded, his hands extending outward, palms toward the Wisps, as he backed away. "Don't let them touch me! They kidnapped us from our world—don't let them now take me away from my friends here! Please!"

"Easy, Wesowee," Nicole admonished. "They're not going to hurt you. You must have seen them moving around the ship. They didn't do anything to you then, right?"

She might as well have been talking to the cafeteria's food dispenser. Wesowee continued to back away, whistling incoherently, his pawlike hands outstretched as if he was trying to hold back rush-hour traffic.

She already knew from her time with Kahkitah that the Ghorfs were strong and loyal but not particularly bright. Apparently, they were also easily spooked. "It's all right," she tried again, as the two Wisps passed her and continued toward him. "They're going to help you. You can't get up the heat duct without them."

Abruptly, Wesowee stopped, the frantic whistling fading away. He trilled a question—"We're going up the ducts?"

"That's the only way up," Nicole said. "Don't worry—they're stronger than they look."

"Their wings can lift both themselves and me?" he asked, looking back and forth between the Wisps as they came up to him.

"Two of them? Sure," Nicole said. "One of them is enough to carry me, and you're no more than, what, one and a half times my weight? Trust me. And trust them."

Wesowee still looked doubtful. But he remained silent as he followed the Wisps back to the duct. "I'll go first," Nicole said, stepping to her Wisp and touching its arm. *Where is the nearest supply closet to this heat-transfer duct?* she asked it.

Four levels up, it replied. *Thirty steps forward.*

Nicole nodded. *Four levels up, it is. Let's go. The other two will follow with the Ghorf. Keep it nice and smooth, okay?*

The Wisp wrapped its arms around her, and a moment later she was floating upward on the updraft. Too late, she realized she should have turned her head downward before the usual paralysis of this kind of travel set in, so that her eyes would be in position to watch Wesowee's progress. But she hadn't, and she would just have to hope he was doing all right.

She could still hear, though, and all the way up she kept her ears pealed for the distant thud that would mean the Ghorf had managed to break his own paralysis and the Wisps' grip and had fallen back to the air-purifier grating.

But the thud didn't come. She and the Wisp rode the upward wind four levels, the wall opened at the Wisp's unheard command, and a minute later she and Wesowee were once again on solid flooring.

"This way," Nicole said, heading toward the supply closet. "Or you can wait here if you'd rather."

"Thank you, but I'll come with you," Wesowee said, shambling his way to her side. "That was a most interesting experience. How did you discover that they would obey us?"

"Mostly by accident," Nicole said evasively. "And I'm not sure they'll obey *everyone*."

"Just you?" Wesowee gave another untranslatable whistle. "You must be very special, Sibyl."

"That's what my grandmother used to tell me," Nicole said with a sigh. For all the problems the two of them had had, she would give anything to be back in the old woman's kitchen in Philadelphia right now. Even if it meant eating her terrible soup. "So where exactly is your team located? You have any idea?"

Wesowee waved a hand vaguely. "I really don't know," he admitted. "All these areas look alike."

"Right, but you must have noticed the plates beside each of the doors," Nicole said. "Those give the room's location."

"So I was told," Wesowee said with a hint of embarrassment. "But I never learned to read them. I was told it wasn't necessary, because I would always be with my team."

Because someone in the group had decided to make sure their extra Ghorf muscle was always within reach? Probably. "Don't worry, we'll figure it out," she promised as they reached the supply closet. She popped open the door and beckoned for her Wisp. "There's the food—help yourself."

"Thank you."

The Ghorf grabbed two bottles of water and two food bars, eased himself onto the floor, and started gorging himself. The Wisp Nicole had called came up to her, and Nicole took its hand. *Do you know where the human work teams are in Q3?*

No. I am part of Q4 only.

So the Wisps were anchored to their quadrant of the ship? Ushkai hadn't mentioned that part. *Do you know where the human work teams in Q4 are?*

No. That is not part of our function.

Nicole scowled. It might have mentioned that in the first place. Getting information out of these things could be like pulling teeth.

Still, a lot of Trake's people had been that same way. Bungie, especially, had been a pain to get information out of.

But over the years Nicole had learned how to cross-examine them when she wanted to find out what they'd been up to or what they were hiding. She would figure out the Wisps, too.

Which still left the problem of finding a group of humans rattling around in a full quarter of a monster ship. Fortunately, there were ways to cut down the territory. In Q4, each of the work teams was headquartered in a group of rooms called a hive, each hive centered around a cafeteria and medical center. She would start by seeing if the Wisps or Ushkai could provide her with a list of cafeterias—

"But I *do* know how to find my way from the testing arena," Wesowee offered as he finished off his first food bar. "Can you lead me there?"

Nicole smiled tightly. And he might have mentioned *that* in the first place. "Yeah, I think I can find it," she said. "Grab some bars and water for the road and let's get you home."

two

The heat ducts provided a handy way to move up and down the ship, at least for Wisps and people the Wisps were willing to carry. For a while Nicole had hoped there would be an equally convenient way to travel front-to-back and side-to-side, but that hadn't panned out. She'd heard there were some horizontal tubes, but the Wisps didn't use them and she'd never gotten around to figuring out where they were.

Fortunately, getting to the Q3 testing arena was a simple procedure. Nicole led Wesowee along a half dozen corridors to the thick barrier wall that separated the Q4 areas from the central core of the ship, then walked forward along it until they reached the *lefnizo* section. On the other side of the wall was the long vertical duct that ran along the whole midline of the ship, separating the left-hand Q1 and Q3 sections from the righthand Q2 and Q4 sections. Another long duct went crossways, she knew, the two ducts isolating the four quadrants of the ship.

Fortunately, they wouldn't need to cross that latter duct today. She ordered the Wisps to open the hidden door to the front-back duct, then had them pick up her and Wesowee and ride the hot wind upward to level 32. Once there, the Wisp opened the wall on the far side of the duct and deposited the two of them on the deck in Q3 beside the curved wall marking the edge of the Q3 testing arena.

Through it all Wesowee remained mostly silent, trudging beside her as he worked his way through his supply of food and water. Only occasionally did he ask a question, and he never wondered—at least not out loud—if Nicole knew where she was going.

That made him either trusting, oblivious, or merely focused on getting back to his hive and his own bed. From what Nicole had seen of Kahkitah, she suspected it was probably all three.

"Okay, here we are," Nicole said as the wall closed behind them, cutting off the hot wind at their backs. "You said you can find your way from here, right?"

Wesowee whistled uncertainly as he looked around. "This doesn't look familiar," the translation came. "I must have been on a different side. There are other sides, are there not?"

"Yes, there's at least a front and a back," Nicole agreed, resisting the urge to roll her eyes. At least the Ghorfs were an even-tempered group. A lot of Trake's people had been just as slow-witted, but also bad-tempered, and they were rough to deal with. She never knew what might set them off.

On the other hand, the ones like Bungie who were bad-tempered but had a level of cunning and street smarts could be even worse. Especially the ones, again like Bungie, who thought they were smarter than they really were.

So now she and Wesowee had to get to the other side of the arena? Still, maybe that wasn't such a bad thing. This arena with a channel running through it was something she'd wanted to see anyway. Instead of trying to go around the huge room, they could simply take a shortcut straight through it.

She gazed at the curved wall in front of them, pulling up a mental picture of the area around the Q4 arena. Assuming this arena was similar to that one, there should be an entrance just around the curve. It would be locked, of course, but one of the Wisps could supply her with the access code. She turned around and beckoned.

To discover that all three of the Wisps who'd been accompanying them since they left the *Fyrantha*'s basement had vanished.

"Where did they go?" she demanded, looking up and down the hallway. Like its counterpart in Q4, one end of the passageway dead-ended fifty yards away, while in the other direction it stretched out most of the way to the rear of the ship. Neither direction showed any sign of their Wisps.

"They backed again into the opening before it closed," Wesowee said. "Should I have stopped them?"

"No, that's all right," Nicole growled, mildly surprised that he'd even noticed. "I doubt you could have done anything even if you'd tried." She looked back and forth one more time. There were no Wisps in sight. "Wisp?" she called.

Nothing. She tried twice more, with the same lack of results. "Perhaps they can't hear you through the wall," Wesowee suggested.

"There should be more of them over here," Nicole said.

"Perhaps these don't listen to you."

"Yeah, maybe not," Nicole conceded. "I guess we'll have to go around after all."

"Wait," Wesowee said, digging his big fingers into one of the pockets of his vest. "Our Sibyl—ah." Proudly, he withdrew his hand from the pocket and held out—

An inhaler.

Nicole stared at it, her stomach tightening. So simple a device. So innocent looking. So important.

So deadly.

"Our Sibyl uses them to hear the ship," Wesowee continued,

completely oblivious to Nicole's sudden change in expression and
mood. "That's how we know what needs fixing." He gave another
untranslatable whistle. "But of course you know that. You're also
a Sibyl." He edged his hand a little closer to her. "She asks me to
carry a spare one for her because she often runs out. You may
use it if you'd like."

Nicole winced. If Wesowee's Sibyl ran out of inhalant a lot, it
must mean she was using it a lot. Maybe Q3 had a lot of small
jobs, no more than an hour or two for each, forcing her to use
the inhaler four or five times a day. Or maybe she got confused
easily, or had a bad memory and had to keep asking the ship to
repeat itself.

But whichever it was, it sounded like she was using a lot of
the chemical.

Which meant she was dying even faster than she should.

"Sibyl?" Wesowee prompted.

"No, thanks," Nicole said, trying to shake off the sudden black
mood. It worked about as well as trying to shake off a hangover.
"Caretaker? Hey—*Caretaker.*"

Nothing. Like the *Fyrantha*'s basement, apparently this part
of the ship wasn't wired for holograms. "Wisps?" she tried again.
"Wisps! Come on, you guys—I need a couple of you."

Again, no response. It was as if by passing from Q4 to Q3 she'd
completely lost her new status as the *Fyrantha*'s Protector.

Maybe she had. Ushkai had warned her at their first meeting
that the ship had been fragmented into four different parts. It
had sounded a lot vaguer than just the physical split between the
different quadrants, and more like which parts of the ship could
talk to her. But maybe there was a physical aspect to it, too.

Of course, he'd also said the Wisps were all controlled by their
own part of that computer, which should mean they would be

under her control wherever she went. Either he'd been wrong, or else all the Q3 Wisps were off doing other things.

But whatever the reason, it looked like she and Wesowee were on their own.

She gazed at the curved wall, trying to visualize what she knew about the ship's layout. They probably couldn't get around the arena on this level—the corresponding one on Q4 was blocked on both sides. But it should be possible to take the stairs down a few levels, head toward the front of the ship, and get to the other side from underneath. It would be a lot of walking, but she and Wesowee should both be used to that by now.

Of course, that assumed Q3 had the same layout as Q4. That wasn't necessarily the case. Still, as long as she kept her wits about her they wouldn't get lost. And of course, there would be plenty of food and water along the way.

On the other hand . . .

She glared at the wall. The last thing she wanted was to take more of that poisonous inhaler drug into her lungs.

But damn it all, she *really* wanted a look inside that arena.

Abruptly, she reached out and snatched the inhaler from Wesowee's hand. "Fine," she growled. "Come on."

Spinning around, she stalked along the curved wall toward the door. "Did I do something wrong?" Wesowee asked anxiously as he hurried to catch up.

"No, you did fine," Nicole said sourly over her shoulder, squeezing the inhaler tightly. It wasn't his fault that she was a stubborn idiot. Anyway, Jeff had told her that a Sibyl would live for months with normal inhaler usage, and she certainly wasn't using the powder regularly. Not anymore. It would just be this once, just until she could figure out how to get the Wisps on this side to listen to her.

Or until she could just go back to Q4 and never come to Q3 again. Either way, it would be just this once.

The arena door was right where she'd expected, and was every bit as big and forbidding as the one in Q4. She planted herself in front of the keypad, squared her shoulders, and took a whiff from the inhaler.

The electrical junction in lefnizo-*one-four-three has a short circuit in the two-two-two-six dipple modulator,* the clear and ethereal voice murmured in her head.

"Not that," Nicole said aloud. "I don't want a list of what needs fixing. I want the code to get me into the arena."

The voice had already stopped. Biting back a curse, she tried the inhaler again.

The electrical junction in lefnizo-*one-four-three has a short circuit in the two-two-two-six dipple modulator.*

"*No,* damn it," Nicole snapped. "I'm not here to fix the damn dipple modulators. I want the damn access code." She lifted the inhaler.

And paused. This wasn't the way to do this. If hanging around Trake and Bungie had taught her anything, it was that if a plan failed the first time it probably wouldn't work the second time, either.

But what else could she do? The Wisps weren't coming. The Caretaker wasn't answering. Should she try punching in the last code she'd used with the Q4 arena? Unlikely, given that that code had been changed at least once before.

She tried it anyway. Sure enough, it didn't work.

She scowled at the door. She could always give up and try the long way around. That would at least get Wesowee home.

But she was tired, hungry, footsore, and not in any mood to give up.

"Can't you hear the ship?" Wesowee asked hesitantly.

"I can hear it just fine," Nicole growled. "It just isn't listening to *me*."

She frowned as a sudden thought struck her. She was hearing, but the ship wasn't listening. Could it maybe also work the other way around? Like if Ushkai could hear her, but couldn't answer?

It was worth a try. "Caretaker, I need the *Fyrantha* to give me the Q3 testing arena access code," she called. "I'm going to take this stuff one more time, and I expect to hear the code. Got it? Okay, here goes."

She took another whiff from the inhaler, wondering distantly how many days or years she'd sliced off the end of her life in the past two minutes. There was probably nothing really interesting in there anyway—

Enter the arena with the code two one five two two nine three.

Nicole snorted. *Finally.* Stuffing the inhaler into an empty pocket of her vest, she keyed in the combination.

With a click, the lock popped open. She grabbed the handle and pulled, and the massive door began to slowly swing open. "Give me a hand?" she invited.

"Of course," Wesowee said. He stepped behind her and got a grip on the handle above her hands, adding his weight to hers. A few more seconds, and the doorway was wide enough for them to get through.

"Okay; straight in and straight through, and we make sure the door's sealed first," Nicole said. She'd seen some of the aliens the Shipmasters had brought aboard, and while she could sympathize with their situation she also had no intention of letting them run loose on her ship. She stepped through, waited until Wesowee had followed, and together they pulled the door shut again.

She listened for the click of the lock and gave the door a final shove just to be sure. Only then did she turn around and really focus on the landscape stretched out in front of them.

Earlier, she'd groused that the arena probably didn't have anything worth looking at. Now, she saw that she'd pretty much been right.

The Q4 arena on the other side of the ship was beautifully landscaped, with wooded areas, plains, and a ridge of hills that started near one end and rose steadily to almost mountain height at the other. It had a wide variety of grasses, bushes, and trees, with streams and rocks and everything. The first time she'd seen it she'd been convinced that she'd found a door leading out of the ship and into some exotic location on Earth.

Compared to that, the Q3 arena was ridiculously boring. It was mostly flat, though there were a few small hills in the distance. There were a few trees, but only a few, and they were scattered and pretty short.

Mostly what she could see was grass. Tall grass, mostly waist high but higher than her head in places, colored a glossy tan, with tops that flared out like brown spiderwebs. The stuff started a few feet from where she and Wesowee were standing, filling the arena as far as she could see in all directions, looking for all the world like the Midwestern wheat fields she'd seen sometimes in movies.

Beside her, Wesowee gave an excited-sounding whistle. "This is the place! I can see where I am!"

"Great," Nicole muttered. Still, boring or not, they at least could cut through the arena now instead of having to go way the hell around it.

And all it had cost was three doses from the inhaler, and however much of her life she'd sacrificed to get in here. For a damn wheat field.

She took another look around. There were no signs that any-one else was here. Certainly there weren't any of the running battles going on that she'd had to contend with in Q4. Wesowee had said the Shipmasters were having him do work in here, so probably it wasn't ready to bring in players for their cold-blooded death games. "So where's this channel you mentioned?" she asked.

"That way," the Ghorf said, pointing straight across the arena. "Though, actually, since it goes across the entire arena, it would be anywhere you went in that direction."

Mentally, Nicole shook her head. Like dealing with a five-year-old, except that he didn't always ask *why* about everything. "Right," she said, frowning as a sudden thought struck her. "You *can* get up and down the sides, right? Otherwise we're not get-ting across it."

"No, no, it's easy to cross," Wesowee assured her. "Come—I'll show you."

He plunged into the grass, parting it in front of him like a ship going through a tan ocean. Nicole followed, noting that there was none of the crackling or rustling noise she had expected. Probably because the grass, for all its wheaty look, was really quite soft, more like upright strands of silk than any grass she'd ever seen. She peered upward as they walked, noting that the sky—the ceiling, rather, painted or whatever to look like sky—was also dif-ferent from the sky in the Q4 arena. Here, it was long gray clouds, with only a faintly glowing spot marking where the "sun" was. In the other arena, the sun actually moved across the sky. She won-dered if this one did that, too, or whether it just sat permanently in place behind the clouds—

She slammed straight into Wesowee's broad back as the Ghorf came to an abrupt stop. "Hey!" she snapped as she flailed her arms, fighting to keep her balance, and managing not to fall backward into the grass. Rubbing her chest where she'd bounced off Wesowee's bumpy skin, she started to go around him.

And stopped short as the tip of a sword abruptly jabbed into view, pointed straight at her stomach.

She froze, her eyes lingering for a heartbeat on the shiny point before lifting her eyes to the being holding the weapon.

The creature was like nothing she'd ever seen before. It was almost painfully thin, the kind of thin she'd seen in starving-children commercials, with equally thin arms and legs. Unlike the children in those ads, though, this creature was well muscled, with wiry bands rippling beneath its dark-gold skin. Its head was also thin, but it stretched backward over its short neck like one of the pterodactyl heads from the museum's dinosaur exhibit.

It was only as she looked back at the sword, noting that the hand gripping the weapon had six fingers, that she also noticed that the creature had four arms.

The thing made a noise like a DJ doing turntable scratching. "You will stand and not flee," the translation came into Nicole's mind.

Nicole's first impulse was to make a run for it. To bat away the sword and hope she could lose him in the tall grass and then get back to the door before he could find her. Her second impulse was to go into the helpless-female role that had gotten her out of a lot of messes back home.

Her third impulse was to decide she wasn't going to put up with this.

"Get that thing away from me," she snapped at the alien. "Do you know who we are?"

The sword wavered, just a little. More scratching—"You are the Shipmasters' workers," he said.

"That's right," Nicole said, feeling inexplicably irritated at the suggestion that she worked for the Shipmasters. As far as she was concerned, she worked for the *Fyrantha* itself, not for the manipulative bastards who were running the place at the moment. "And what were you told about threatening the ship's workers?"

It was a gamble, but a pretty safe one. She knew the Shipmasters had warned the fighters in the Q4 arena not to bother anyone in a worker jumpsuit, and it only made sense that they would have given the same instructions here. Still, she found herself holding her breath as the alien gave off more of its scratching.

Fortunately, she'd called it right. "We aren't going to harm you," the translation came.

"Right," Nicole said. "So get that thing out of my face."

The sword wavered; and then, to Nicole's surprise, steadied again, still pointed at her stomach. More scratching—"I'm sorry," he said. "But I have orders. Any newcomers to the battlefield must be brought before the Maven."

"What's a Maven?"

"She is the leader," the alien said. "She directs and guides our paths. She must make any decisions concerning you."

Once again, Nicole was tempted to make a run for it. Once again, she resisted the urge. This Maven probably just wanted to see what the *Fyrantha's* workers looked like. "What's your name?" she asked.

"I am Iyulik," the alien said.

"What species are you?"

"Pardon? What is a species?"

"I mean what do you call yourselves?" Nicole tapped her chest. "I'm a human. Wesowee is a Ghorf."

"We are the Thii," Iyulik said. His thin cheeks puffed out, then collapsed. "I don't know where we came from. Our arrival at this place was . . . confusing."

"Yeah," Nicole said. "Join the club."

"Pardon? What is a club?"

"I mean *everyone's* arrival was confusing," Nicole said, stifling a sigh. If she was going to have to stop and explain every other sentence, this was going to be a long day. "Can we get this over with?"

"Yes," Iyulik said, sounding a little uncertain. "Follow me—no; wait."

"What?" Nicole asked, frowning.

"If you follow me, you may flee," Iyulik said, his cheeks doing the puffing thing again. "But if I follow *you* . . . Do you know where the Maven is?"

"Of course not," Nicole said. "Just take us to her, will you? We're not going to run."

"Yes." Iyulik gestured with his sword. "This way."

He disappeared into the grass, leaving the thin stalks rippling in his wake. "Come on, Wesowee," Nicole growled, and followed.

Given the mostly flat terrain, Nicole had expected Iyulik to lead them straight toward wherever the Thii had set up shop. Instead, he took a winding path, weaving back and forth through the tall grass, mostly sticking to the waist-high parts but occasionally punching his way through one of the taller sections. Nicole could see no reason for the little detours, unless there were hidden rocks or pits the alien was avoiding. She thought about asking, but decided she didn't care enough to bother.

They were nearly halfway across the arena, as best as Nicole could estimate, when they reached the Thii camp.

It was a real camp, too, just like the kind Nicole had seen sometimes in movies. The aliens had flattened a circular section of waist-high grass beside one of the taller sections and rigged up shelters out of poles and pieces of heavy-looking cloth. In the center of the camp were piles of water bottles like the ones Nicole and the other workers could get from the ship's supply closets.

And there were weapons, too, laid out on top of empty water bottles where they would be up out of the grass. There were five swords like the one Iyulik was holding, plus a couple of small bows, and arrows.

A *lot* of arrows. There were three quivers full of them beside the bows, and Nicole could see another full quiver lying beside a sleeping pad inside one of the shelters.

Three more Thii were in the camp, sitting cross-legged on the ground beside the weapons stash. Two of them unfolded their legs and stood as Iyulik entered the circle, both of them picking up swords as they caught sight of Nicole and Wesowee. The third remained seated, and Nicole spotted a pair of thin blue bands on the upper-arm wrists.

It wasn't exactly gold chains or tooth caps. But it was decoration, and Nicole knew that the fanciest decoration always belonged to the boss.

"Greetings, Maven," she said as Iyulik led the way toward the others. "I am the Sibyl. This is Wesowee, one of the workers, and we have work to do. May I ask why we've been brought here?"

Bungie had always tried to get in the first word in confrontations like this. It never seemed to work for him personally, but Nicole had seen some of his friends and enemies use it to good effect, and it seemed worth a try.

Unfortunately, she was apparently as bad at it as Bungie. For a long moment the Maven just sat there, staring at Nicole's face with unblinking eyes. She spoke—"You are not to be harmed," the translation came.

Nicole let out a breath she hadn't noticed she was holding. Good—at least they were on the same page on that one. "Right," she confirmed. "So I'll ask it again—"

She stopped as the Maven went on. "The Ponngs also know this?"

Nicole looked at Wesowee, got a puzzled shrug in response. "I have no idea who or what the Ponngs are," she told the Maven. "But if they're aboard the ship, I presume they've been given the same instructions and warnings that you have."

"Just so." The Maven raised her two upper arms. The two Thii beside her took them and lifted her to her feet. "Let us test that thought."

"Hold it," Nicole said, warning bells going off in the back of her mind. "Whatever you're thinking, you can forget it. We're not going to fight for you."

"We ask not for strength of arms," the Maven said. "We ask only for strength of body."

Nicole frowned. "That makes no sense at all."

"It will." The Maven gestured with her lower arms. "Come and see."

three

The arena channel was just as Wesowee had described it: a wide ditch cut through the center of the open space, about fifty feet across at the top but tapering to less than ten at the bottom. The banks of the channel sloped downward on both sides, pretty steep but with hard dirt surfaces that looked like they wouldn't be too difficult to climb. The bottom itself was probably ten or twelve feet down, Nicole estimated. From the way the channel meandered through the arena, she guessed it had been designed to be a river in this particular ecosystem. There was no water in it, though, and from the cracks in the dirt down there it looked like there hadn't been any for quite a while.

What *was* at the bottom was a box: a cube three feet on a side, with a lever on one of the sides that faced away from the banks. On the near side was what looked like a dispenser tube that emptied into a removable bag, and according to the Maven there was a corresponding dispenser on the Ponng side.

And scattered all around the box were arrows like the ones Nicole had seen in the Thii camp. A *lot* of arrows.

"There," the Maven said, pointing through the line of grass stalks she and Nicole were crouched behind. "That's the source of our food."

"That, plus the one in your hive?" Nicole asked. It was the same pattern she'd seen in the Q4 arena: the Shipmasters gave each of the two sides a food dispenser in their respective living quarters, adjusting the output to be insufficient to support the group, then put an extra wild card dispenser somewhere else in the arena for them to fight over to make up the difference.

"By *hive* you mean the rooms at the edge of the grasses?" the Maven asked. "Those places are cold and metal. We don't live there."

"Ah," Nicole said. Not that she could blame them. The rooms in the human workers' hives were reasonably nice, with TVs and other comforts. The arena hive rooms, though, were mostly bare and pretty grim. "But there *is* food there, right?"

"No," the Maven said. "There is no dispenser elsewhere." She pointed again. "This is the one. The only one."

"You're kidding," Nicole said, frowning. So the Shipmasters weren't following the same pattern as they had in Q4.

But to feed two sides from just a single dispenser? Easing her fingers through the grass, she pried the stalks apart to try to get a better look.

And a second later threw herself flat onto her back as an arrow whistled past her head. "What the *hell?*" she snarled.

"Caution," the Maven reproved.

"Yeah, no kidding," Nicole bit out. "What the hell are they shooting at *me* for?"

"The Ponngs shoot at all movement," the Maven said. "The Masters provide all the arrows we wish, so there's no need for them to wait for a clear shot."

"Yeah, I got that," Nicole growled. The arrow that had nearly impaled her was wedged between a couple of stalks a couple of feet from her head.

She frowned. It had only gotten that far? At the speed it had been going, it should have punched its way through the grass halfway to the Thii camp. Keeping herself pressed against the ground, she stretched out and picked it up.

And frowned a little harder. No wonder the arrow hadn't gotten very far: it was lightweight, almost like the rubber-tipped arrows she and Kamali had used to shoot at targets in her basement. The arrows the Micawnwi and Cluufes had shot at each other back in the Q4 arena had been way heavier.

But unlike Kamali's toy archery set, these had real sharpened points. Nicole wasn't sure the arrow would have killed her, even if it had hit her square in the forehead like it almost had. But it sure as hell would have left a nasty hole in the skin.

Still holding the arrow, she carefully worked her way around and up again into a crouch. This time, she made sure not to ruffle the grass in front of her. "Okay; the food dispenser. Tell me how it works."

"At the third cycle of the morning, it delivers five measures of food," the Maven said. "If the lever is pointed toward this side of the ravine the food comes out the spout on our side and is suitable for us to eat. If the lever is pointed to the other side, it delivers five measures of Ponng food. That pattern will repeat three more times, at intervals of two cycles. When the fourth time is complete, the machine will no longer function until the third cycle of the next morning."

"How do you know when the payoff is due?" Nicole asked. "Do you have a clock or something?"

The Maven gestured, and one of the two Thii who'd accompanied them handed her his sword. "There, at the center of the hand guard," she said, pointing.

"I see it," Nicole said, nodding. There was a tiny clock set into the middle of the sword's hilt. It was an old-style clock, with hands and everything, except that these hands were both the same length.

And now that she had the weapon up close, she could see that the blade didn't seem at all sharp.

Carefully, she eased her thumb against the edge, then pressed a little harder. Nothing. The weapon might look like a sword, but it was in fact little more than a sword-shaped club. The tip, though, was pointed enough to draw blood.

Arrows and swords that could poke and hurt, but not easily kill. Whatever the Shipmasters were going for here, they'd sure given the fighters some strange weapons. "How big are these measures?"

"Each is enough to feed one person for a day," the Maven said.

"How many of you are there?"

"Twenty."

"And how many Ponngs?"

"We were told there are also twenty."

"Got it," Nicole growled, glaring across the ravine. So five rations delivered four times per day, for a total of twenty meals. One side could feed everyone while the other side starved, or else each side could go through a slow, half-ration starvation process. A little different from the system in Q4, but it had the Shipmasters' stamp of calculated cruelty all over it. "So you have to fight or you don't eat. Tell me your strategy."

"It's not so much a strategy as a necessity," the Maven said ruefully. "As the time approaches we send one of the young males down the slope to the machine. The timing is critical. If he goes too late, he risks being unable to win control of the lever from the Ponngs. If he goes too early, the enemy arrows will inflict severe injury on his body and again make it impossible for him to win the contest."

"Right," Nicole said, fingering the arrow. Though it would be hard to kill anyone with these things, she could see how a steady rain of them could raise enough welts and bruises and draw enough blood to incapacitate the victim. Especially when the victims were built as thin as the Thii were. "And I assume everyone else from both sides shoots arrows down at the other side's champion as long as he's in range?"

"That is correct," the Maven said. "We've tried sending more than one male down, with the second and third ordered to shield the first. But the result was to risk having three warriors incapacitated for the remainder of the day instead of one."

"And if you lose enough men early in the day, the Ponngs have easy pickings for the later feeding times," Nicole said, nodding. And of course, by giving both sides weapons that would only wound and disable, the Shipmasters had ensured that each side always had the same number of mouths to feed. "So it's a balance."

"Yes," the Maven said. "But now that balance has changed. The Ponngs will not dare to attack you. Thus, we will be able to turn our full force against their warrior—"

"Whoa," Nicole interrupted, holding up her hands. "Wait a second. I can't take sides in this."

"Why not?"

Because if I get involved the Shipmasters will have more evidence that humans can fight and they may put Earth on the chopping block along with whoever wins your damn little war here, that's why. "Because I can't simply allow the Ponngs to starve," she said instead.

"But you may allow *us* to starve?" the Maven countered.

"I don't want either of you to starve," Nicole protested. "I'm hoping to find a way to get both sides more food."

"How?"

"I don't know yet," Nicole said. "For starters, I need a closer look at the machine. I'll go get Wesowee and we'll head down there."

"Impossible," the Maven said stiffly. "Your companion will stay here in guarantee of your return."

So that was why the Maven had insisted Wesowee stay at their encampment while Nicole and the Maven made their little inspection tour. Nicole had assumed it had simply been because it would be hard for someone the Ghorf's size to get this close to the channel without drawing Ponng fire. "Sorry, but it doesn't work that way," she said. "He's my assistant. Where I go, he goes."

"Then neither of you goes," the Maven said, just as stiffly. "You will remain here until your own hunger forces you to comply with my instructions."

At other times and places, Nicole reflected, she might have gone into fear or defense modes. Here, faced with a threat from a bunch of spindly four-armed insects with blunt swords and toy arrows, her first reaction was to laugh.

So she did.

"You're not serious," she said when the laughter had run its course. "People who want to kill you are right across the channel. All I have to do is run across to them, and you'd be out of luck."

The Maven had a hunched, haunted look about her, the same look Bungie displayed whenever he'd backed himself into a corner. "Yet your companion is still with us," she tried.

"You're kidding, right?" Nicole scoffed. "Did you take a good look at him? He could break you in half without even trying." She leveled a finger at the alien. "Here's what's going to happen. You're going to send someone back to bring Wesowee here. He and I will then go down and look at that dispenser. Understood?"

"Yes," the Maven said, her voice sounding labored. "And then you will feed my children?"

Nicole frowned. Her *children*? "Are you saying these Thii are all yours? Seriously?"

"Of course," the Maven said. "When I became their leader, they became my children."

"Right. Whatever." Nicole had known women like that, women who thought they were mother to a whole neighborhood. Some of them had been good at it. Others had just used it as an excuse to yell and give orders.

She had no idea which kind of block mother the Maven was. She also didn't plan to hang around long enough to find out. "Just get Wesowee, okay?"

Five minutes later, the Ghorf had rejoined her. "There's the channel," he said eagerly, pointing through the grass.

"Yes, I see it," Nicole said, wincing in anticipation at the arrow that was surely about to zoom across the channel and bounce off his head or chest.

But no attack came. The Ponngs on the other side must be able to see enough of the big alien to recognize that he wasn't one of their enemies. "Was that food dispenser there when you brought in the plates?"

Wesowee whistled thoughtfully. "Is that what that is? A strange place to put food."

"The Shipmasters sometimes do things the hard way," Nicole said. Explaining how the arenas worked would take far more time than she wanted to spend. "So it wasn't here earlier?"

"I don't know," Wesowee said. "I delivered the plates to the far end." He pointed to their right. "I never came to this part of the channel."

And with the channel's meandering curves, Nicole realized, he wouldn't have been able to see very far in any direction. "Okay, it's not important," she said. "I want to go down and take a look at it. You're sure that if we do that we'll be able to get back up again?"

"I believe so, yes."

Which was probably as good a guarantee as Nicole was going to get without trying it. "Okay," she said. "Maven, how long until the next food drop?"

The Maven gestured, and one of the other Thii showed her his sword. "Approximately two-thirds of a cycle."

Nicole peered over her shoulder. Judging by how far the clock hands had moved, and assuming she was reading it right, they probably had a little over an hour. "Okay," she said. "Let's see what we can do. Wesowee? You ready?"

Wesowee gave a triumphant-sounding bird call—

And without warning plunged through the last line of grass stalks and ran straight down the slope. "Yes!" the translation belatedly came.

Bracing herself, hoping the Ponng archers still remembered the Shipmasters' warning about damaging their slaves, Nicole followed.

The slope was steep, but the dried dirt wasn't at all slippery. She took it carefully anyway, using the entire ten feet of flat area at the bottom to bring herself to a carefully controlled stop. Wesowee was already standing at the machine; with a quick look upward at the far side of the channel, Nicole joined him.

She'd hoped the box would turn out to be a variant of the food dispensers in the Q4 arena, which she'd already had a good look at. Unfortunately, there was no way to know whether or not that was the case. The outer shell was solid metal, with welded edges and no fasteners that would allow it to be removed.

"Hell," Nicole muttered, digging her hand cautiously up into the dispenser tube as far as it would go. Again, there was nothing her fingers could discover except more smooth metal. "What did they do, sit it down here and weld it shut?"

There was a whistle from the other side, and Wesowee's head popped up into view. "There are fasteners on the underside," he reported. "I can feel them. One at each corner and one at the center of each side."

Nicole reached under the box, digging a finger into the dirt at the corner until she could feel the underside of the metal. The Ghorf was right. Even better, the fasteners appeared to be the *Fyrantha's* standard triangle-head bolts. Easiest things in the world to remove.

Provided, of course, that you had a triangle-head wrench.

"You wouldn't happen to have a tri-wrench, would you?" she asked.

"No," Wesowee said, still feeling underneath the edges. "But I could go get one."

"I guess you'll have to," Nicole said, wondering what the hidden Ponng archers were thinking. Hopefully, they would assume the visitors had been simply working on the machine and allow them to leave without trouble.

But the Maven had tried to get her to do something to help their side. If the Ponngs suspected that, they might take exception to any attempt by Nicole or Wesowee to leave.

From above came a sound like a burning fire. "You," the translation came. "Come here."

Nicole looked up. There was nothing visible except swaying grass. "Excuse me?" she called.

More of the TV Christmas-special log fire sound. "Come up." There was a brief pause. "Please."

"Oh, well, since you said *please*," Nicole muttered.

Still, she and Wesowee were going to have to go up that side eventually if they were going to get the Ghorf home. And it wasn't like there weren't storage closets and tool kits on both sides of the arena. "Okay," she said. "No one shoot, okay?"

The slope was definitely challenging. But as she'd noted on the way down, the dirt was firm, and the cracks gave it a texturing that her boots were able to grip. Using her hands on the ground in front of her to help push, she headed up.

She was halfway to the top when an arrow slammed into the center of her back.

"Hey!" she shouted, wanting to turn around and glare at the Thii side but needing all her attention to regain her balance and keep herself from sliding back down. "Knock it off! *Now!*"

There was no reply. But there were also no further arrows. Returning her attention to the slope, she finished the climb without trouble.

Wesowee, who the Thii archer had apparently been smart enough not to shoot at, was already up and waiting for her when she reached the top. He held out a hand, she took it, and he pulled her effortlessly the rest of the way up. "Are you hurt?" he asked anxiously as they passed through the stand of tall grass lining the edge.

"No, I'm okay," Nicole assured him, trying to get a hand up to rub the tingling spot where the arrow had hit. Naturally, the damn thing had managed to land just out of her reach, from any direction. "They try it again, though, and I'm going to go back and kick their butts."

There was a fire sound from her right, and she turned to see a pair of short creatures coming toward her.

Really short creatures. The Maven and other Thii barely came up to her chin, and they had these things beat by at least three inches. The newcomers were wider, though, with proportions that were closer to human norm than the Thii's insect-like look. Even so, they seemed a lot less healthy than the Thii, with a sort of shrunken mummy look to them.

Or they would if mummies came with a layer of green moss on their heads, shoulders, and arms. "If you wish, we will attack them in response," the translation came.

"Don't bother," Nicole said, eyeing them. Between them and the Thii, the whole arena looked like it had been set up as a fight between the kids that were always chosen last for school games. "Who are you?"

"I am Moile," one of the aliens said. "I speak for the Ponngs."

"Call me Sibyl," Nicole said. "What did you want to say to me?"

"Pardon?"

"You called us up here," Nicole reminded him. "What did you want to tell me?"

"I did not wish conversation," Moile said. "Rather, I offer you a trade." His hand did a sort of circular pointing motion toward the channel. "Food, for servitude."

Nicole blinked. "Excuse me? Food for *what*?"

"Servitude," the Ponng repeated. "If you will provide for my people, I will be your slave." He did the gesture to the other Ponng beside him. "So will Teika, if you wish it."

Nicole looked at Wesowee. The Ghorf was just looking back, with no indication that he'd caught the significance and sheer awfulness of the offer. Probably he hadn't. "Thanks, but I'm not in the slave-owner business," she told Moile, trying to keep her voice steady. She had no doubt that the offer had been completely serious, which just made it worse. "What I need right now are tools."

"We have these," Moile offered, touching the sword at his waist and the bow slung over his shoulder. "But we have nothing more."

"That's okay—I know where to get them," Nicole assured him. "But you'll need to let Wesowee cross your territory to the door." She hesitated, knowing better than to promise something she couldn't deliver. But the look on their mummified alien faces—"If you guide him there and wait for him to come back, I may— I *may*—be able to get you more food."

"Then it is done," Moile said firmly. He gestured to Wesowee. "At your convenience."

Wesowee looked uncertainly at Nicole. "Shouldn't we both go?"

"No, I need to stay here," Nicole said. "You go get the tools. Just make sure at least one of them is the right size tri-wrench. Oh, and you'll need the code to get out and back into the arena."

"I saw the numbers you entered on the control board," Wesowee said. "Are those the ones?"

"Should be," Nicole said. "If the code lets you out, it'll let you in again. If you can't open the door, come get me and I'll find out what it's been reset to."

"All right." Wesowee still looked uncertain, but he nodded to Moile. "I'm ready," he said.

"Follow me," Moile said. A moment later, they had disappeared into the grass.

Teika took a step to the side, into the exact spot where Moile had been standing. "Is there anything I can do to assist you?" he asked.

"No, thanks," Nicole said. "I'm going to head along the channel and see what's at the far end."

"Shall I accompany you?"

"You can do whatever you want," Nicole said, feeling a flicker of anger. She could play the subservient, floor-mat role as well as anyone, and the game had saved her skin on more than one occasion on the Philadelphia streets. But these Ponngs were taking it *way* too far.

All the lectures about self-esteem and standing up for yourself that the teachers and special speakers had droned on and on about in school flashed across her mind. Here, she suspected, the platitudes would have even less impact than they'd had on her classmates.

Turning her back on him, she headed off through the grass.

It was slow going at first, but after a couple of dozen yards the grasses seemed to become a little less dense, and meandering lines of plain dirt appeared, almost like paths that had been built into the area.

It was, Nicole decided, something she should have expected. Ushkai had told her that the *Fyrantha*'s previous owners had planned the ship as a flying zoo, and from the way the Q4 arena had been laid out it had seemed likely they'd planned for visitors to be strolling through the various ecosystems.

She was in sight of the curved and disguised wall marking the end of the arena when she belatedly noticed that she had a shadow. Teika, having been given no orders to the contrary, had indeed decided to tag along, and was slipping silently through the stands of grass a few feet behind her.

Nicole's first impulse was to tell him to go back. Her second was that he would probably be hurt or offended if she did.

Her third was that she'd always wanted a pet dog, and this was probably as close as she would ever get.

Or if not a pet, maybe a native guide.

Because however long the Ponngs had been here, there was probably a good chance they'd thoroughly explored their half of the prison. "You—Teika," she said, beckoning him forward. "I'm looking for a control box of some sort. It'll probably be behind a plain door or panel. And it'll probably be camouflaged," she added, the whole approach suddenly starting to sound like a waste of time. Of course it would be camouflaged, and of course the Ponngs wouldn't have a hope in hell of spotting it. "Never mind," she said. "I just thought—"

She was interrupted by a burst of log-fire crackling. "Are you referring to the water-flow controls?"

Nicole felt her mouth drop open. Not only had they found the controls, but they'd even figured out what they did? "Yeah, that's them."

"Follow me." Eagerly, the alien brushed past and hurried toward the wall. Nicole, her mouth still hanging open a little, followed.

The control panel was positioned a few feet back from the edge of the channel, and it was indeed camouflaged to look like part of the wall. "How did you find it?" Nicole asked as she peered closely at it. There was no handle or obvious latch.

"We were seeking a way to escape," Teika said. "It opens here." He reached down to where the wall met the ground and dug his fingers into the dirt.

And with a metallic click the panel popped open. "We were trying the controls to see if they would open a door when water began flowing from a hidden pipe into the channel."

"I'll bet the Masters were just thrilled about that," Nicole commented, pulling open the panel. Inside, set back into the wall, were five switches protected by transparent flip-up covers. Beneath each switch was a slider control and a couple of lines of alien script.

"They were not," Teika said ruefully. "They came at once and ordered us never to touch the controls again." He seemed to brighten. "But they've not so ordered *you*, have they?"

"I'd like to see them try," Nicole said. Actually, given the weapons and equipment the Shipmasters had, she probably wouldn't. "Tell me about the controls."

"The two on the left bring water from two large pipes into the channel," Teika said. "We weren't able to try the others before the Masters came and ordered us to stop."

"What about the slider switches?"

"We didn't get to them, either," the Ponng said. "Some of our people suggested they might adjust temperature, aeration, or

mineral content. We were unfortunately unable to translate that script, as we've never seen it before."

"I have," Nicole said, swinging the panel partly closed again. "It's also used to mark rooms and other places on the ship. I don't know what any of these words are, though. How in the world did you spot the panel, anyway?"

"The light reflection from the edge is different than that of its surroundings," Teika explained. "A small difference, but noticeable if one is looking closely."

"Maybe to *your* eyes," Nicole said. So the channel had indeed originally been a river, and the water flow was still functional.

Which also explained the chamber at the other end, the big open area that Wesowee told her he'd fallen into. It was probably the collector for the water, either just to hold it or else a reservoir where the dirt or other stuff was sifted out before it got pumped back upstream for another run.

Of course, right now she had no idea what exactly she could do with such knowledge. But she was slowly learning that information was always a good thing to have. "Okay, so now I know," she said, pushing the panel all the way closed. "Show me where that release is and how to work it."

"It's here." Teika dropped onto his knees and pointed. "A small plate, which must be pushed down."

Nicole crouched down beside him and gave it a try. She felt the plate give, and the panel popped open. "Got it," she said, straightening up. "I guess we should get back and wait for Wesowee."

"As you wish." Teika hesitated, and when he spoke again the fire sound seemed hesitant and serious. "His offer was genuine. You *do* realize that, do you not?"

"What are you talking about?" Nicole asked as she set off back toward the center of the arena.

"Moile's offer of servitude," Teika said as he fell into step behind

her. "Any of us will willingly serve you, should you wish it. Or all of us, should you wish it."

The proposal had turned Nicole's stomach the first time she'd heard it. It didn't sound any better this time around. "We don't take slaves, Teika," she said.

"But you *did*, did you not, once upon a time?" he pressed. "Or was the Master incorrect?"

Nicole stopped short, spinning around and nearly causing Teika to collide with her. "What's *that* supposed to mean?" she demanded. "What were they saying about us?"

"I didn't mean to offend," Teika said hastily, cringing back from her. "The Master came to us shortly before you arrived today and told us you had once been slave-keepers. He suggested that we offer ourselves to you in exchange for your help."

"Oh, he did, did he?" Nicole bit out, glaring up at the ceiling. Somewhere up there, she knew, were hidden cameras that the Shipmasters used to monitor the action in their little war games. This had to be another of their stunts.

Only she couldn't for the life of her figure out what they were going for with this one. Were they trying to sour the Ponngs on any help Nicole might offer them by claiming she liked slavery? Were they trying to see how far the Ponngs would go to get enough food? Was it a test of Nicole, an experiment to see if she would be tempted by the chance to buy some free alien labor?

Or was it bigger than that? Was it a test of humanity itself?

In fact, that might be exactly what it was. Nicole had no idea how long the Shipmasters had been bringing humans aboard to repair their damaged ship, but it could easily have been a couple of decades. But despite having had people underfoot that whole time, it was more and more clear that the aliens didn't really know what kind of creatures their slaves were.

Up to now, they apparently hadn't cared. But thanks to Nicole's

bullheaded stupidity in the Q4 arena, they now knew that humans could fight, or at least that they could help other people fight. Maybe this slave game was part of their effort to find out just exactly how warlike the people of Earth really were.

Nicole had to make damn sure they didn't get the right answers.

"I'm sure he meant no harm," Teika said hesitantly. "I apologize if our words were insulting or hateful."

"Forget it," Nicole said darkly. "It's not your fault."

Wesowee was waiting when she and Teika reached the main Ponng area.

And he'd brought company.

"What the *hell* is going on here?" the newcomer snarled as Nicole and Teika came into view through the grass. He was a tall, thin man with receding black hair and a thick, bushy mustache.

"I'm a Sibyl," Nicole said. "I needed—"

"Yeah, I know what you are," the man cut her off. "Wesowee won't shut up about the wonderful Sibyl who saved his life. Are you the one who's making a mess out of our work schedule?"

"What the hell are you talking about?" Nicole countered, her anger at the Shipmasters starting to transfer over to this bag of noisy wind. "Who are you, anyway?"

"I'm Kointos," the man growled. "I'm *supposed* to be in charge of gray team." He waved a hand around him. "Except when all the Sibyls in the section suddenly pop off with new instructions and haul all eight teams to a single corridor in *lefnizo*-thirty. I'll ask again: Are you the one who did that?"

"What, you think suddenly all the Sibyls are listening to *me* instead of the ship?" Nicole demanded. "Since when has *that* ever happened?"

"I don't know," Kointos shot back. "All I know is that you show up, and suddenly everyone's working in the same area. We *never* all work in the same area."

"So what, you got claustrophobia?" Nicole scoffed. "Fine—you can work in here instead."

"*Claustrophobia's* not the word you're looking for," Kointos said scornfully. "And if you think I'm working for *you*, you're crazy. You're not my Sibyl. I don't take orders from you."

Nicole glared at him. They really didn't have time for this. "Fine—Wesowee and I will do it ourselves. Give me your tool vest."

"Look, *Sibyl*—"

He broke off at a harsh-sounding bird call from Wesowee. "Give her your vest!" the translation came.

Most people aboard the *Fyrantha*, Nicole had learned, herself included, didn't simply ignore an insistent, shouting Ghorf. Apparently, Kointos wasn't most people. "No," the man said flatly, folding his arms across his chest. "Not until I know what's going on."

With an effort, Nicole forced back the urge to tell Wesowee to strip the vest off the man, along with his jumpsuit and, if necessary, pieces of his skin. "There's a machine in the middle of the channel over there," she said. "It gives food to the Ponngs on this side and the Thii on the other side. It *doesn't* give enough for either group, so both sides are starving. I want to try to fix that. And they probably can't eat our food," she added as Kointos opened his mouth, "so don't bother suggesting we get them some of that."

For a couple of heartbeats Kointos just stared at her. Then, he gave a brief hunch of his shoulders. "All right, I'll play along," he said. "Show me."

Four

There was some rustling in the grass on the Thii side of the channel as Nicole led the way down the slope. She tensed in anticipation, but this time no one shot an arrow at them. "That's it," she said, pointing at the food dispenser.

"Who the hell puts a lunch wagon in the middle of a pit?" Kointos muttered as he walked over to it.

"It's complicated," Nicole said. The deadline for the next feeding was rapidly approaching, and she had no wish to be in the middle of a long explanation when the arrows started flying. "Can you get it open?"

"Sure." Kointos felt at the bolts, then pulled a pair of triwrenches from his vest and handed one to Nicole. "Here—make yourself useful."

Three minutes later, with the bolts removed, Kointos and Wesowee carefully lifted off the cover while Nicole maneuvered the dispenser tubes through the openings in the shell so that they wouldn't jam.

"Okay," Kointos said as he and Wesowee set the cover aside. "I gather you're familiar with these things. So what's next?"

Nicole scowled. She'd seen the insides of two of the *Fyrantha's* food machines back in the Q4 arena.

Unfortunately, this wasn't like either of those. Instead of the multiple tubes and colored-light mixing controls she was familiar with, the only thing inside the box were a pair of three-inch-wide conduits that came up from beneath the ground and disappeared into a complicated-looking mechanical box that then fed into the dispenser tubes. "I don't know," she said. "I was expecting a lot of input tubes and mixers and a control panel that could be changed. This one just seems to be a dispenser, with the mixing going on somewhere else." She tapped the mechanical box. "You have any idea what this is?"

"Looks like a limiter," Kointos said, turning his head to peer at the underside where the mechanism attached to the outside lever. "There's a counter under here that marks off how many liters or whatever come out."

"Can the counter be disabled?" Wesowee asked. "Perhaps both sides would be able to get more food that way."

"*Anything* can be disabled," Kointos said, running his fingers around the box. "The trick is disabling it to do what you want. You start messing with something you've never seen before—like this thing—and there's an even chance you'll wreck it completely."

"Meaning nothing would come out?"

"That's one possibility." Kointos cocked an eyebrow at her. "Though if we did that, I suppose you could use your magic Sibyl dust and find out how to fix it."

"*If* that's what the ship told me to fix," Nicole said. "It might not. Or if it did, it might just tell me how to put it back the way it is now."

"Well, in that case we're out of luck," Kointos said. "Looks like everything else comes up from under the deck."

"Or from inside the dirt," Nicole said slowly, frowning at the tubes coming up through the box's floor and trying to think.

Okay. The channel had been designed as a river—that much

was pretty clear. The inflow, according to Teika, was at one end, and the outflow, according to Wesowee, was at the other.

So why would the Lillilli who'd turned the *Fyrantha* into a zoo have installed these extra tubes here in the middle?

Answer: they wouldn't have. At least not for any reason Nicole could imagine.

Unless they were to feed the fish. But that seemed pretty unlikely. One of Nicole's teachers had kept a fish tank in the classroom, and they'd always just dropped the food on top.

Had dropped the food on top . . .

Nicole looked at the banks above them. Pet cats and dogs had food bowls, and she'd seen pictures of cows in the country going to feed troughs or bales of hay that had been put out for them. But out in the wild, if she was remembering right, animals usually had to go hunting for their food.

She reached into the box and carefully squeezed the tube coming up from below. It felt hard as a rock. "Have you seen this material before?" she asked Kointos. "I'm wondering if it's usually this stiff."

"Who knows?" Kointos said, poking at the tube. "I know there are plastics like this aboard that are pretty flexible. But there's no reason they couldn't also have a version that's stiff as a—*yowp!*" He broke off with a yelp as an arrow whistled over his head.

Reflexively, Nicole ducked lower. A Ponng had appeared at the top of the channel, she saw, a sword clutched in his hand, a thick clump of grass belted across his chest and other bundles on his forearms. There was a movement at the corner of Nicole's eye, and she looked across the channel to see that a similarly armed and grass-garbed Thii had appeared, except that he had a sword in each of his four hands. Both aliens began half running, half sliding down their respective slopes toward the food dispenser.

And as they did so the edges of the channel erupted in a hailstorm of flying arrows.

"What the *hell*?" Kointos gasped, pressing himself down into the partial cover of the food dispenser.

Nicole snarled under her breath. She'd thought they still had a few minutes before the next battle began. Clearly, she'd miscalculated. "Wait," she pleaded. "Everyone—wait. Please."

She might as well have been shouting at bad weather. The two fighters reached the flat section at the bottom of the channel and faced off, poking their swords at each other and swaying or jerking as the other side's arrows slammed into them.

Nicole had hoped the Ponngs and Thii could avoid any more battles. So much for that plan. The best thing she, Wesowee, and Kointos could do now was get away from the scene and let the two sides fight it out this one last time. Once the dust cleared, they could focus on finding a more permanent solution. If they could get those food conduits open—

"*Knock it off!*"

Nicole jerked violently. Kointos had risen from the shadow of the dispenser and was standing in front of the lever, towering over the two aliens, his hands outstretched toward them as if his presence alone could ward off the swords and arrows.

And to her amazement, it was working. Both fighters paused in their sparring, and even as Kointos filled his lungs for another shout the rain of arrows came to a slightly tentative halt. "That's better," he said in a more conversational voice. "The Sibyl has something to say." He lowered his arms and gestured to Nicole. "Go."

Nicole stared at him, a surge of stomach acid boiling up into her throat. *Go?* "Kointos, I can't—"

"You want them to stop fighting?" he countered. "You want

them to have food? You got a plan?" He gestured. "Then get on with it."

Nicole glared at him. Yes, she wanted those things. But she barely had even an idea, let alone a plan.

But he was right. If she didn't do something, the fighting and the starving would keep going until the Shipmasters decided to stop it.

She squared her shoulders. The *Fyrantha* had named her its Protector. Time to find out if the stupid ship had made a mistake. "You both want food," she began.

And immediately winced. A stupid comment—of *course* they wanted food. "I'm going to try to get it for you," she continued hurriedly, hoping they wouldn't notice.

"We *have* food," the Ponng said darkly. "It awaits us right here."

"It awaits the Thii, too," Nicole reminded him.

"It awaits strength of arms," the Thii said. "As it should be."

"Really?" Nicole countered. "What's your name?"

The Thii hesitated. "I'm called Sofkat."

Nicole looked at the Ponng. "And you?"

"Vjoran," the Ponng said briefly. "If you have nothing useful to say, then step aside and let us claim that which is ours."

"Really," Nicole said, feeling her nervousness fading into exasperation. It was like dealing with Bungie at his worst: the posturing, the impatience, the shooting off of his mouth. She'd had to put up with him way more than she liked, and she was *not* going to take the same nonsense from a half-pint alien with a toy sword. "Ten minutes ago your leaders were ready to become my slaves. Now you're not even willing to hear me out?"

"I apologize for his words," a voice came from the Ponng side. Nicole looked up, to see Moile and Teika standing at the edge of the channel. "Speak, Sibyl."

"Thank you." Nicole looked to the other side. "Thii?" she invited. "You ready to listen, too?"

There was movement in the grass, and the Maven stepped into view. "We will hear you," she said.

"All right," Nicole said. "Here's how it's going to work. The dispenser is about to allow five measures. Each of you will get two and a half. That should be enough—"

"Two and a half will barely feed a tenth of my children," the Maven protested.

"That should be enough," Nicole said, ignoring the interruption, "to hold you while we figure out how to tap into the system and bypass the machine completely. If I'm right about how it works, all of you will have all the food you need soon, and without having to fight for it."

"Do you think we fight merely for food?" Sofkat demanded, pointing toward the Thii side with his sword. "They have injured many of our people. That balance has yet to be redressed."

"The balance is indeed skewed," Vjoran said darkly. "But the scale of injuries rests to *their* favor, not ours."

"All right, let's try it this way," Nicole said. "You do as I say, each of you taking half of the next delivery and then helping me solve the problem; or I have Kointos here weld the lever to the box so that it doesn't give you any more food again. *Ever.*"

For a moment no one spoke, and Nicole held her breath. Bluffs were always dangerous, and she'd suffered more than her fair share of grief back home when one of them got called. She could only hope both groups of aliens were tired enough and hungry enough to go along.

To her relief, they were.

"The Ponngs agree," Moile called down.

"As do the Thii," the Maven said. "Who will operate the lever?"

Nicole looked at Kointos. "You, or me?"

"I'll do it," Kointos said. He pulled out a marking pen and pointed to Sofkat. "You—come show me on your bag where a full five measures comes." He shifted his eyes to Vjoran. "You'll do the same on yours. If one of you tries to cheat, his side will get a little less."

One at a time, the two aliens stepped up and marked their individual collection bags. As far as Nicole could see, the levels were identical. "Good," Kointos said. "You can both step back now. Sibyl, any idea when this one-armed bandit is due to pay off?"

Nicole frowned. "This *what*?"

"One-armed bandit," Kointos repeated. "Old slang for a slot machine. You never heard that before?"

"I don't think so," she said. "Sofkat, is there any signal?"

"A light appears above the lever," Sofkat said. His eyes were on his Thii counterpart, and the gaze didn't look friendly. "It will be very soon."

"Great." Kointos beckoned Nicole closer. "So what's the plan?" he asked quietly.

"These arenas were set up to be zoo-type places for animals to live," Nicole told him. "I figure—"

"Hold on," he interrupted. "Did you say a *zoo*?"

"That's what I was told," Nicole said. "I was thinking that maybe the way they set this place up to feed the animals would be to do it like you would a fish tank, dropping the food on top of the ground. Only instead of dropping it from the ceiling, I thought maybe they fire it up from the ground."

"Like a sprinkler system," Kointos said thoughtfully. "Only with food instead of water. That makes sense too—I'm thinking now that most of the mechanism in there is a kind of step-down depressurization setup, like the stuff is coming in under pressure. But why would they put it in the middle of a pit?"

"I don't think they did," Nicole said. "I think the Shipmasters tapped into the original system and ran extra tubes down here so that the aliens they bring in have a good place to fight over it."

Kointos shook his head. "I hope you realize this makes zero sense," he warned. "If I wasn't sitting here looking at it, I'd figure you were lying through your—oops. Showtime."

Nicole nodded as she saw that the light had gone on. "Make it as even as you can."

"No kidding," Kointos said dryly. "Here we go . . ."

The lever, it turned out, wasn't just an on-off thing, where any movement translated into a rush of food. A small movement caused a trickle of the multicolored pellets into the bag, while a larger movement made the flow increase.

Which made sense, Nicole decided, at least from the Shipmasters' point of view. They didn't want a given fight to be over too quickly, with the first side to reach the lever winning it all. They wanted the battle to continue as long as possible, going back and forth, each side having the chance to turn it around or gain some of their own food until that session's five measures total had been doled out.

And for that whole time, both sides would be doing their damnedest to injure or incapacitate the other side's fighter. No wonder both of them figured there were still scores to settle.

Kointos took it slow and careful, and in the end had the food divided up about as evenly as humanly possible.

"Now what?" the Maven called down as Sofkat and Vjoran headed up the slope with their half-filled bags.

"Now we find out where the Masters tapped into the underground food system," Nicole said. "Moile, you seem to have exceptional eyes, so we'll start on your side."

"And then?" the Maven asked.

"Take it easy," Kointos said. "Have a snack or something. We'll be over there as soon as we can."

A minute later, Nicole, Kointos, and Wesowee were on the Ponng side. "All right," Nicole said. "The original food delivery system would have been buried when the grass was put in. Sometime since then, the Masters dug down to one of the pipes, plugged in a new tube, and laid it underground to the middle of the channel. Your job is to find where the dirt has been disturbed."

"How long ago would that have been?" Kointos asked.

"I don't know," Nicole admitted. "I have no idea how long since the Masters redid the place."

"You can't ask the ship?"

"Not from here," Nicole told him. "There's some problem with communication from this side of the centerline."

"It's of no matter," Moile said confidently. "If part of the ground has been disturbed, no matter how long ago, we'll find it." He gestured. "You heard the Sibyl's orders. Go."

Nicole had hoped the Ponngs would be able to find the spot within the two-hour gap between food deliveries. In fact, it took them considerably less time than that. Less than half an hour after the searchers first fanned out, Moile announced that Teika had found it.

"Here," Teika said, pointing to the ground with his sword. "The dirt was disturbed at this point, with more digging in this direction." The sword tip traced along a path toward the channel.

Directly toward the food distribution box, in fact. "Are you sure?" Nicole asked. To her, all the dirt looked exactly the same.

"The soil in the underlayers has been untouched by the light for many years," Moile said. "Some of that soil was brought to the top, and there are materials in the mixture that reflect the light differently."

"Good enough," Nicole said. She still didn't understand this, exactly, but she was willing to run with it. "Start digging—here— right at this end of the trail. Teika, I need you to come with me."

"Where?" the young Ponng asked.

"We're going to the Thii side and find their junction for them," Nicole said. Turning, she headed toward the channel.

She got five steps before belatedly realizing that Teika hadn't moved. "Did you hear me?" she demanded, turning back.

"They are our enemies," Moile said stiffly. "They have injured many of us."

Nicole glanced at Kointos. "So?"

"So *you* may help them," Moile said. "But we shall not."

"Really," Nicole said, feeling a layer of disbelief rolling over her rising anger. Was Moile *really* going to play that game? "Okay, let's put it this way. You promised to become my slaves if I got you food. I'm getting you food. Now, you're my slaves."

The green moss on the top of Teika's head darkened visibly. "You said you didn't want slaves."

"I've changed my mind." Nicole leveled a finger at Teika. "So move it. Now."

She turned back around and started walking, not bothering to look and see if Teika was following. She'd reached the channel, gone down and then back up again on to the Thii side before she confirmed that he had.

Good. "Don't just stand there," she told him. "Find where the Masters buried the tube on this side. Maven?"

"I'm here," the Maven replied, stepping out from behind a clump of grass. She was flanked by two other Thii, both of whom held swords ready.

"This is Teika," Nicole said. "The food tube is underground, and he's going to find it for you. Teika, this is the Maven."

"And then?" the Maven asked.

"Then you'll dig it up, and you should have all the food you need," Nicole said. "Okay, Teika. Do your stuff."

This time, having seen where the Shipmasters had laid the pipe on the Ponngs' side, it took Teika less than five minutes to find the matching spot. "It's there," he said, pointing at the ground.

"Great," Nicole said. She gestured to the Maven. "Have your people start digging."

"What if he lies?" the Maven asked, her gaze steady on Teika.

"If he's *mistaken*," Nicole said, leaning a little on the word, "then he'll try again. Come on, come on—even with those swords this is going to take a while."

The Maven made an extra scratchy sound. "Swords? You surely joke." She gestured to one of the Thii at her side. "Dig."

And to Nicole's astonishment, he did.

Not with a sword, or with an arrow, or anything else. Instead, he dropped to the ground, balancing himself horizontally on his lower two hands like he was starting some break-dance move. Then, hooking his top two hands into claws, he started digging like a dog looking for a bone, throwing the dirt behind him in a steady stream. As the pile of dirt grew between his balancing hands, his legs bent at the knees and his feet scooped it farther away behind him.

For a moment Nicole just stared, not sure whether it looked more bizarre than graceful or the other way around. She looked sideways at Teika, saw what she was sure was an equally stunned look on his face.

Two minutes and ten vertical inches of dirt later, the Thii found the tube.

"That's it," Nicole said, feeling a sense of relief wash over her. She'd been pretty sure she was right, but there was a little uncertainty in everything. And she'd seen young men get shot when a deal like this went sour. "Let me go get a screwdriver or something from Kointos and we'll get it open."

"No need," the Maven said. "We can dig through that material."

"Okay," Nicole said cautiously. "The food inside is probably under a lot of pressure, though, so dig carefully."

"We will. Thank you." The Maven hesitated, then made a small gesture toward Teika. "Thank you, as well."

"You want to show your thanks?" Nicole asked as a sudden thought struck her. "I mean really *show* it, and not just talk it?"

All four of the Maven's hands twitched. "Explain."

"He showed you where to dig," Nicole said. "It would have taken forever without his help. On the other hand, you dig much faster than the Ponngs. How about giving them a hand digging up their pipe?"

"They are our enemies," the Thii standing at her side insisted. "They have hurt many—"

"And you've hurt a lot of them, too," Nicole cut him off. "You were hungry. *They* were hungry. Hungry people do what they have to. So how about returning the favor they've just shown you?"

"No," the Maven said flatly.

Nicole drew herself up to her full height—

"It's all right," Teika murmured. "We can manage without them." He made an untranslatable noise. "Not all are people of honor."

"I guess not," Nicole growled. But really, she should have known it would go this way. The gangs back in her neighborhood would rather have shot themselves than work together, too.

She'd hoped that people out here in the stars would be a little more classy. Apparently they weren't.

The Ponngs had made it about three inches down when she and Teika returned. "Don't worry, it's there," Nicole assured them. "Another six or seven inches, and then you get to figure out how to get into it without the food blowing out like an open hydrant."

"I've got some ideas on that," Kointos said, eyeing her curiously. "The other team already got to their pipe?"

"Yes," Nicole said shortly. "And I don't want to talk about it."

"Yeah, these guys are pips, aren't they?" he said sourly. "The whole bunch of them. I heard some of the ones on this side talking about going across the pit and starting a full-fledged war once everyone was up to strength again."

Nicole hissed out an exasperated sigh. She'd seen *that* brand of macho stupidity way too many times, too. "Some of the Thii would be happy to oblige them," she said. "Maybe we should go ahead and flood the channel. See how well they all swim with swords and bows in their hands."

"And then try to climb up out while someone on the other side stands there waiting to perforate them," Kointos said. "There was a reason people liked to build castles on lakes and rivers."

"I thought it was for the water," Nicole said. "Well, that's their problem. I just wanted them not to starve—if they still want to kill each other there's nothing we can do about it."

"Unless you want to rattle their skulls a little," Kointos offered. "I'd take a number six wrench against one of those swords any day."

"Not worth it," Nicole said, trying to sound casual. The last thing she wanted was for the Shipmasters to see Kointos and his buddies wading into battle with swinging wrenches. "Thanks for your help. As soon as you get the Ponngs into their food pipe, you and Wesowee had better get out of here. When the Ship-masters spot what we've done, they're going to drop a bucket of grief on everyone—"

"Sibyl!" a voice called distantly from somewhere across the arena. "Sibyl! I would speak with you."

It was the voice of Fievj. The Shipmaster who she'd tangled with before.

The Shipmaster who wanted to sell Earth into slavery.

Five

"Who the hell is *that?*" Kointos muttered, frowning.

Nicole swallowed hard. "It's the guy with the bucket," she said. "Never mind the pipe—they can get into it themselves. You two get out of here."

"What about you?"

"Sibyl!" Fievj called again.

"I guess I'd better go find out how big a bucket he's got this time," Nicole said with another sigh.

"You want Wesowee or me to go with you?"

"Better not," Nicole said. "I talked my way out of one of these before. I think I can do it again." She gestured. "You two had better get back to work before you get in trouble."

"You mean more trouble than we're already in?" Kointos asked pointedly.

Nicole wrinkled her nose. "Yeah," she conceded. "Sorry."

"No problem," Kointos said with a shrug. "Anyway, I don't mind a little trouble now and then. Beats the hell out of monotony."

"Sometimes," Nicole said. "Anyway, thanks."

She walked to the edge of the channel and looked around. No one was in sight. "I'm here," she called. "Where are you?"

"In the gorge," the answer came. "Meet me at the testing machine."

Nicole scowled. The testing machine. No doubt the Ship-masters' name for their fancy fight-or-starve food dispenser. "I'll be there," she called.

She worked her way down the slope and walked over to the dispenser. A moment later, from around one of the bends in the channel, the gleaming shape of the familiar armored centaur appeared.

Nicole watched as Fievj strode toward her, feeling her pulse pounding in her neck. That wasn't *really* some mythological creature inside that armor, she knew—only the front part was real, while the long horse body extending behind him was the Shipmaster version of a car trunk. The back legs were just there to hold up that end of the body, and though they mimicked the occupant's actual legs pretty well, now that Nicole knew what to look at she could spot the slight delay in their movements.

The armor and the sheer horse-like appearance would be frightening enough. But added to that was the fact that Nicole also knew what was kept in the horse-body storage.

Weapons.

Not the ridiculous toys they'd given the Thii and Ponngs. Not even the far nastier pikes and arrows they'd given the Micawnwi and Cluufes back in the Q4 arena. Nicole had gotten herself caught in the middle of that battle, and seen a *lot* of death and bleeding.

But the Shipmasters themselves didn't bother with such old-fashioned things. They didn't need to. They had something Nicole had dubbed *greenfire weapons:* four-foot-long black tubes that threw deadly green bolts like a science fiction movie's laser blasts. Nicole had seen them in action, and had no interest in ever seeing one used again. Especially not in her direction.

And that was just the weapon she knew about. There was no

telling what else they might have tucked away in their part of the ship.

Especially since the *Fyrantha* had originally been a warship. In every war movie Nicole had ever seen, people on warships *always* had weapons.

At least Fievj didn't already have a greenfire tube in his hands. That was something. Maybe he really *was* here just to talk.

Of course, it wouldn't take long for him to pop open the back of the horse and grab one out. Nicole would have to watch carefully for any sign that he was getting ready to do that. If he did, she would—

She winced. What she would do, really, was die.

Because there was no way she could make it up the slope in time. Aside from the dispenser itself, there wasn't any cover at all down here, and the greenfire weapon could probably shoot through the box anyway. Her only hope was to get out of the channel and into the arena's main ground, and she already knew she would never make it.

If Fievj decided to shoot, she was dead. She'd better make damn sure he didn't make that decision.

Still, because it was better than nothing, she took a couple of steps forward and to the side to put the half-disassembled food dispenser directly between her and him.

He came to a stop on the other side of the dispenser and for a moment eyed her in silence. Nicole braced herself—"Why are you here?" he said at last.

"I was summoned," Nicole said, feeling a touch of relief and another touch of annoyance. Of course Fievj hadn't just been standing there glaring at her in silence—he'd been talking to her in his own language, just like every other alien aboard the *Fyrantha*, and the delay had been from her brain-talking gadget waiting for him to say enough that it could start running the translation. The difference between him and everyone else was that she couldn't hear his original speech or see his mouth move through the armored helmet, which made it look like he was just staring at her.

"Summoned by whom?"

"By the *Fyrantha*," Nicole said. "Who else?" She cocked her head to the side. "How about you? What are *you* doing here?"

"What did the *Fyrantha* say to you?" Fievj asked, ignoring her question. "Tell me the exact words."

Nicole felt her lip twist. This was an old, old trick, one that had been tried on her over and over again. A guy who suspected she was lying would ask her to give a complicated or detailed answer to some question, then ask the same thing a little later, hoping she wouldn't remember what she'd said the first time.

Trake had been pretty good at standing up to that sort of thing. Bungie, with a mouth way bigger than his brain, had typically run into those tests head-on and, more often than not, had fallen flat on his face.

Nicole, whose own memory wasn't in much better shape than Bungie's after years of binge drinking, had learned to look for ways around such traps.

In this case, the back door was obvious. "That's not how it works," she said. "The *Fyrantha* doesn't speak in words. Not really. It talks in pictures and shapes, and kind of like feelings."

Which was a barefaced lie, of course. There was no way the ship could possibly describe the parts that needed to be fixed or replaced without using words.

But the Shipmasters couldn't hear the ship talk the way Nicole and the other Sibyls could, at least not as far as she'd been able to tell. She could tell Fievj that the *Fyrantha* talked to her in pictures of cats and he would have no way to prove her wrong.

Unless he'd already asked one of the other Sibyls the same question.

Sure enough—"That's not what we've been told by others," Fievj said. "Other Sibyls say that the *Fyrantha* gives its orders in words."

Nicole winced. *Damn.*

Now what?

The best defense, Trake had always said, was a good offense. Not that it always worked out, especially for lunkheads like Bungie, but Nicole understood the reasoning. If she could pull something out of her butt, maybe she could still get out of this. "Of course that's how it talks to normal Sibyls," she said, mentally crossing her fingers. "But I'm not a Sibyl anymore. Not *just* a Sibyl, I mean. I'm the *Fyrantha's* Caretaker."

Fievj actually took a step backward, the horse body arching a little before the rear legs caught up with the movement and straightened everything out. "*You're* the Caretaker?" he demanded.

"I am," Nicole said firmly, feeling her pulse pick up speed. Given how the Shipmasters seemed to feel about Caretakers, or at least how they'd talked to the hologram Ushkai the time she'd eavesdropped on one of their conversations, she'd hoped to keep her new position secret a little longer.

But this was the only way she could think of to get out from under the net Fievj had dropped on her. And from his reaction, it looked like it was going to work.

"Prove you're the Caretaker," he said.

Or maybe not. Unfortunately, Ushkai hadn't given her a badge or anything.

But there might be another way. "A couple of weeks ago, back when the ship was being attacked, there was something at the top of the ship that needed fixing," she said. "The Caretaker— the other Caretaker, I mean—told you a Caretaker had fixed it. That was me."

Fievj didn't take another step back this time. But Nicole had a feeling that he wanted to. "*You* fixed the shield cross-link?"

"Yes," Nicole said with a flicker of relief. She'd been afraid he was going to ask for details, and between her bad memory and the whole pile of other stuff she'd had to learn about the *Fyrantha*'s equipment she'd lost the exact name of the thing she'd replaced. "I swapped out a few of the components and got it started again."

At least, she assumed that was what had done the trick. She didn't actually know for sure. Still, Ushkai seemed to think she'd done it.

Assuming *he* knew what he was talking about. Given this was coming from a computer hologram that had promoted her to Caretaker based on a complete misunderstanding of a random action she'd taken, that might not be a good assumption.

"You must not interfere here," Fievj said.

So he wasn't going to argue any more about whether or not the *Fyrantha* had told her to come into the arena? Good enough. "I already told you I was sent here," she said. "The *Fyrantha* found a blockage in its food system and sent me to repair it."

"There's no blockage," Fievj insisted. "The test that's been set up here is vitally important."

Nicole felt her stomach tighten. So that was how he wanted to play this? Fine. She could play that game, too. "So is the ship's health," she countered. "The blockage is backing up a lot of pressure. We're looking at damage to several different systems if it doesn't get fixed."

"Nonsense," Fievj insisted. "The back pressure isn't nearly enough to be of any concern."

Right on cue, there was a muffled pop from the Thii side of the channel. Nicole looked up to see a spray of multicolored food bits flying up into the air, looking for all the world like someone had made a version of Old Faithful out of a piñata. Clearly, the Thii had made it through their pipe.

"There," she said, pointing. "See? Pressure relieved. The *Fyrantha* will be feeling much better now."

For a long moment—longer than a double translation should take—Fievj gazed up at the fountain. Then, he lowered his masked face again to Nicole. "I don't believe you," he said, his voice stiff. "I believe you're deliberately sabotaging our experiments."

Nicole snorted under her breath. So this was all just experiments now? Starving innocents and forcing them to fight was all being done in the name of science?

Yeah. Right.

"I am the Protector," she said, trying to sound regal. That never worked when Bungie tried it, but it was worth a shot. "My job is to guard the *Fyrantha* and the people inside it. That's what I'm doing."

"You said you were the Caretaker."

"I'm both Caretaker *and* Protector," Nicole said, silently cursing the slip. Identifying herself as Caretaker had been risky enough, and adding Protector to the mix could only put her higher on the Shipmasters' radar. But it was too late now. "The safety of the *Fyrantha* is my primary purpose, and I'll do whatever's necessary to that end."

Fievj gazed at her another long moment. "*Protector* is the Lillilli word for *warrior*. Yet you tell us humans do not fight."

"We don't," Nicole said. "The word is also translated as *caretaker*. Which I also said I was." She waved a hand. "And as one of the *Fyrantha*'s Caretakers, I need to get back to work."

Another long pause. Earth was in trouble, all right, Nicole thought bleakly.

And it was all her fault.

Plato had warned her and the rest of the repair team not to fight among themselves or show any other signs that humans were capable of combat or war. But Nicole had ignored him. She'd gone into the Q4 arena and helped bring the two battling alien groups to a draw. Worse, she and Jeff had both participated in that final fight.

Only later had Ushkai told her how the Shipmasters were testing alien races for combat capabilities, gathering information they could then sell to other races who were looking for cheap cannon fodder for their wars.

Nicole had spun Fievj a story about how she was an anomaly, that she wasn't like other people. But she doubted he'd believed her. Her only hope was that he hadn't been able to convince the other Shipmasters of that, or that they were concerned enough about losing their repair crews to sell Earth to anyone else.

But she'd dealt with people like Fievj back in Philadelphia. She knew his sort. He was stubborn, and suspicious, and he wouldn't give up until he knew the truth. All Nicole could do now was do her best not to add fuel to that particular fire.

No fighting, no aggression, not even any bad language if she could avoid it. If she behaved herself from now on, maybe Fievj's suspicions would blow over.

But then, maybe they wouldn't.

"Very well," Fievj said. "Return to your tasks. But be warned. Your interference will not be tolerated forever."

For a second Nicole was tempted to call his bluff and demand to hear exactly what he was going to do when the Shipmasters ran out of patience. But he might have an answer she didn't want to hear.

Anyway, it never paid to push someone into a corner. "That's up to you," she said. "But I must continue to do what the *Fyrantha* tells me."

"That's your choice," Fievj said. "But be aware that decisions have consequences. And not just for you."

Nicole felt her eyes narrow. "If you're threatening the Thii—"

She broke off, silently cursing herself. She knew better than to start a threat she couldn't back up with action. And no matter what tweaks she managed with their food supplies, their fate—as well as the fate of the Ponngs—was completely out of her hands.

"The Thii will soon no longer be your concern," Fievj said. "But there are others who your decisions may affect."

Nicole resisted the urge to look up along the bank. Hopefully, Kointos and Wesowee had already taken off and were safely out of the arena.

Besides, it wasn't like she'd asked Kointos to come in here. Wesowee was only supposed to get her a tool kit.

Maybe he'd misunderstood. Like Kahkitah, Wesowee was a little slow—

She froze. *Kahkitah. And* Jeff, *and* Levi, *and* Carp, and all the rest of her old team. She hadn't even thought about them.

For that matter, why was she thinking of them as her *old team?* Less than two weeks past, and they were already fading from her thoughts?

Not good. *Very* not good. She had a lot of ghosts from her past, but some of the worst were the memories of waking up with only the vaguest idea what had happened the night before.

Or the two nights before, or the three, or sometimes the whole week.

It had been bad enough back in Philadelphia, where Trake's knowing smile and Bungie's nasty comments had added a layer of embarrassment to the aches and nausea that usually came with the mental fog. But eventually the nausea would go away, and Trake's people would find something else to be amused by, and it would all be over until the next time alcohol got the better of her.

There, the result had been embarrassment. Here, surrounded by suspicious Shipmasters and warring aliens that might or might not obey their instructions to leave the repair crews alone, anything that dragged down her focus or memory could get her killed.

Speaking of which, being glared at by an armored centaur was probably not the best time to let her mind wander this way. "I can only do what the ship tells me," she said. It was dangerous to keep falling back on the same excuse, but it was the only card she had. "What happens next is not my concern."

"Perhaps," Fievj said. "There is mystery surrounding you, Protector. I don't like it."

"Really," Nicole said, resisting the urge to tell him that she really didn't care what he liked or didn't like. For one thing, antagonizing him would probably be a bad move; for another, she unfortunately *did* care what the Shipmasters liked or thought or did. As long as they were in control of the *Fyrantha*, she had to.

But right now, she mostly wanted them to do their liking and thinking and doing somewhere else instead of right in front of her. "But that's a conversation for another day," she said. "I have to get back to the *Fyrantha*'s business now."

Fievj didn't answer. Watching him out of the corner of her eye, Nicole started climbing back up the slope to the Ponng side of the arena. He didn't move as she climbed, and was still standing in the same place when she reached the top and looked back down.

Watching her? Studying her? Or was he just waiting for her to leave so he could call the other Shipmasters and seal up the holes the Ponngs and Thii had made in their food lines? Fix the holes, put the dispenser back together, and start the whole war thing again?

She scowled. Not if she had any say in it.

Moile and Teika were waiting at the top. "You are all right," Moile said, sounding relieved.

"Sure," Nicole said. "Why wouldn't I be?"

"We were concerned," Teika said. "The Masters are . . . fearsome to behold."

"They are that," Nicole conceded, frowning past them across the channel. After that first impressive geyser from the Thii side, the flow of food had disappeared from sight. Was that it? "What about the food? Did you get through the pipe?"

"We did," Teika said.

"And it's glorious," Moile added, waving both hands behind him. "Come and see."

The two Ponngs led her through the tall grasses to the hole in the ground. If they'd created the same kind of geyser as the Thii, it had been smaller and had already subsided. But there was still enough pressure in the line to drive the food pellets up out of the hole and into a sort of bubbling food fountain. The piles around the hole were already up to Nicole's shins, and the whole place was a flurry of activity as a dozen or more Ponngs scooped up the food with their hands and loaded it onto carriers made of tree branches and woven grass mats. When a given mat was full, the Ponng would drag it away, disappearing through the grass in various directions.

"Looks like you've got it down to a system," Nicole said. "How much have you gathered?"

"Vjoran?" Moile called.

One of the Ponngs turned, and Nicole recognized him as the one who'd been all set to fight the Thii for the food machine's output, and who'd seemed rather annoyed when Nicole and Kointos interfered with his moment of glory. "Yes?"

"Has a tally been made?" Moile asked.

"A full tally has not," Vjoran said, his eyes steady on Nicole. Still annoyed, she guessed.

"Has a *partial* tally been made?" Moile persisted.

Vjoran's eyes slipped away from Nicole's gaze. "We have food for some days to come," he admitted. "Perhaps five." He again looked briefly at Nicole, then looked away. "Perhaps more."

"With another four at least still ungathered on the ground," Teika added.

"At least," Moile confirmed. "You have saved us, Sibyl."

And to her surprise, he bowed low at the waist, his face nearly touching the ground. "We are at your service for the full length of days. Command us."

"Yeah, sure," Nicole said, wincing. Teika had said Moile's offer of servitude had been genuine. Clearly, he'd been right. "I don't need slaves, thanks," she said. "I'm just glad I was able to get you some food."

"We remain at your service," Moile said, still bowed to the ground.

"Fine," Nicole said with a sigh. "Get up. Come on, get *up*."

Moile—rather reluctantly, Nicole thought—straightened up again. "Okay," she said. "First: Did Kointos and Wesowee get out of here okay?"

"They left as you went to speak with the Master," Moile said.

"Kointos insisted," Teika added, "but I don't think Wesowee was fully pleased that you'd sent him away. He wished us to thank you further on his behalf."

Nicole shook her head. Between Moile and Wesowee, she was well on her way to building a starter slave kit. All she needed now was a plantation.

She looked around. Actually, this arena was already almost like a plantation, only instead of cotton it was growing grass.

And what every plantation needed . . .

"You want me to put you to work?" she asked. "Great. I've got a job for you, and after that you're done."

"We remain at your service," Moile said.

"You can remain wherever you want," Nicole growled, suddenly tired of this whole thing. "But once I leave here, you'll probably never see me again before the Masters send you home."

The two Ponngs exchanged glances. Maybe the Shipmasters hadn't said anything about sending them home. Or maybe they'd already concluded they would die here.

Maybe they would. She only had the Shipmasters' word that the test fighters were returned to their homes.

"What is this job?" Moile said.

"We're going to end your little war with the Thii for good," Nicole said.

"We're going to fight?" Vjoran asked eagerly.

"Nope," Nicole said. "Moile, Teika—follow me."

Nicole's memory and focus might be having some problems, but her sense of direction was working fine. Ten minutes later, they were at the control box for the channel water supply.

"Okay," she said, pointing at the controls. "Here's the job. You start the water, and you don't let it stop until the channel's at least half full. Got it?"

Again, Moile and Teika exchanged glances. "The Masters forbade us to handle these controls," Moile reminded her carefully.

"I don't think they'll bother you this time," Nicole said.

"Why not?"

Nicole hesitated. What should she tell them? What *could* she tell them? That this war had been staged to see how well the Ponngs could fight? That maybe, just maybe, giving both sides enough food had screwed up the Shipmasters' plans enough that they wouldn't care anymore if the two sides were kept apart by a flooded channel?

Or that it might already be too late? That every success or small victory the Ponngs had had against the Thii increased the chances that their whole race would someday be turned into war slaves under the rule of some vicious would-be conqueror?

No. A terrible and fearful future might await the Ponngs. There was no point in starting that fear any earlier than it had to.

Meanwhile, Moile was still waiting for an answer. "Because I'm the Sibyl," Nicole said. There was a lot of her grandmother's despised *because I said so* in that, but again it was all she had. "Remember, at least half full. Farewell."

"Farewell, Sibyl," Moile said, bowing to the ground again. "We will never forget you."

"Yeah," Nicole muttered under her breath. They'd remember. Maybe along with a curse.

six

She half expected one of the other Shipmasters to be waiting for her at the arena door. But maybe they'd all had enough of her for one day. She reached the door without incident, went through and sealed it behind her, and headed back toward Q4.

The trip through Q3 seemed shorter than it had the other direction. Partly that was because she hadn't known exactly where she was going the first time through, partly because she'd been saddled with a hungry and dehydrated Wesowee, who'd turned out to be even slower than the average Ghorf.

Still, it was a long way, and there were a couple of places where she wondered if she'd walked herself into a corner. She tried calling on the Wisps a couple of times, but they stubbornly refused to respond. Ushkai likewise remained silent.

It was like walking into an air-conditioned store in the middle of a Philadelphia summer when she finally reached the heat duct between Q3 and Q4 to find a Wisp waiting for her.

"Take me across to Q4," she ordered the Wisp as she backed into the creature's arms. "Where was everybody in Q3?"

The Wisp wrapped its arms around her. The familiar paralysis froze her muscles as the duct access door opened up—

Everybody? the Wisp said into her mind.

Nicole would have rolled her eyes if she'd been able to move those muscles. *I mean the other Wisps,* she clarified. *Aren't there any in Q3?*

What is Q3?

Nicole frowned. Or rather, tried to. *Q3 is the section of the* Fyrantha *we just left.*

We left from the edge of Q4.

It's also the edge of Q3.

I saw only the edge of Q4.

Nicole ran that one over in her mind. So the Wisp saw the right-hand edge of Q3 as the left-hand edge of Q4? *What about the corridor I was walking along when you first saw me?*

I saw no corridor. I saw you approach.

No corridor? What did you think I was walking on? Air?

We also walk on air, the Wisp said.

That's different, Nicole insisted. *We're riding on an updraft in here. There isn't anything like that out in the corridors.*

The Wisp seemed to consider. *You summoned me. I saw you approach. You came. We now travel across into the main part of Q4.*

And they were nearly there. *You really didn't see the other corridors?* Nicole asked, trying one last time. *Or the doors leading off them?*

I saw only the edge of Q4.

The door slid open in front of them, revealing the familiar corridors of Q4. *Have you any further orders?* the Wisp added as it floated Nicole out of the duct and onto the deck.

It opened its arms, and Nicole was able to move again. "Not right now," she said with a sigh. *Any further orders.* Ponngs and Wisps, all of them falling over themselves to please her. She wasn't the *Fyrantha's* Protector; she was the ship's queen bee.

Or its gang leader. Bungie and the rest of the group had treated Trake pretty much this same way. Not something she really wanted to think about.

She'd always assumed that the arenas on the two sides of the ship were mirror-imaged, with Q3 being directly opposite to Q4 and only a short duct crossing apart. But as she looked around, she saw that the Q4 arena was nowhere in sight.

Fortunately, the *Fyrantha*'s corridors and rooms were laid out in a logical pattern, and a look at the nearest room's identification plate showed that she was now about twenty corridors back from the arena, which put her about ten away from the hive. Picking one of the corridors she knew wouldn't take unnecessary twists and turns, she headed off.

The corridors were quiet as she headed toward the hive. With her thoughts still back with the Thii and Ponngs, she'd made it halfway before it suddenly dawned on her that the place was a little *too* quiet. She could hear no sounds of work being done, no voices calling back and forth, no footsteps or sounds of carts being rolled along the dark red flooring. Most of her team's work areas were between the hive and arena, but she knew one of the other teams had been working back here.

Was today a rest day? It shouldn't be, not unless the schedule had been changed. But that hadn't happened before, not in all the time she'd been aboard. Had everyone come down sick? Her history teachers back in Philadelphia had talked sometimes about plagues that had wiped out whole cities.

She took a deep breath. *Stop it,* she scolded herself. The violet and green teams had probably just been sent to a different level to work. As for her own team, by now the Shipmasters had probably gotten them a new Sibyl, and they were all back at their own tasks.

Nicole winced. Another Sibyl. Another innocent person dragged from her home on Earth to come here, take Nicole's place, listen to the *Fyrantha*, and die young.

A little knowledge is a dangerous thing. One of Nicole's

grandmother's friends had liked to say that. Nicole had never really understood what it meant.

But she knew now that a *lot* of knowledge could be a hell of a weight to carry, too.

There was no sign of her old crew as she reached the hive. Probably that meant she'd been right about a new work area. No problem—there was a pattern in the *Fyrantha*'s work orders, and the locations where those orders were carried out. A little thought and study, and she could probably guess where they were. Or, if she felt like cheating, she could find a Wisp and ask it.

But first, she needed to go to the medical center and check on Jeff.

The ghosts of faded memories—and the fading of more recent memories that never should have faded—came floating back. Jeff had been badly injured helping Nicole during that last climactic battle between the Micawnwi and Cluufes. She'd sent him back to the hive via the Wisps, figuring that Sam and Allyce would take care of him.

But with her focus on learning everything she could about the *Fyrantha*, she'd somehow never gotten back there to check.

That had been nine days ago. Had the doctors figured out how to treat the exotic wound he'd received? Was he on the mend, either here or in his room?

Had he died?

Wincing, she broke into a jog. If Jeff had died, alone, she would never forgive herself. She reached the medical center and slapped the control. The door slid open—

To reveal a deserted room.

She stepped inside, frowning. All the equipment was still there—the exam and treatment tables, the diagnostic equipment, the drug cabinets, and all the rest. But neither Sam nor Allyce was anywhere to be seen.

Which was *very* unusual. Normally during the day at least one of them was on duty in case of injuries on the job.

She could see Sam blowing off his duties here. He'd been accidentally snatched from Philadelphia with Nicole and Bungie and had never given up his anger at the fact that no one seemed interested in sending him home. But Allyce was a lot calmer, and she would never leave a patient hanging.

Really, the only time the center was unattended was at ship's night. And even then, there was a large glowing emergency button that a patient could use to call one of the doctors for treatment.

The button was still there, in the center of the panel nearest the door. But for the first time since Nicole's arrival it wasn't glowing. It was as if the medical center had simply been closed down.

Had the whole hive been moved? Picked up and moved to another part of the ship?

Was this what Fievj had meant by consequences?

Muttering a curse, she stepped back out of the room, letting the door slide shut behind her. Okay. No movement in the corridors might mean the crew was working somewhere else. No one in the medical center might mean some emergency had called both doctors away.

But the one place that absolutely had to stay in business if there was anyone still around here was the dining room. If and when they came back, that was the first place most of them would go.

Still no sounds of life as she approached the dining room door. Her heart was starting to pound now, the way it had that time her grandmother had been late getting home and Nicole thought she'd left her the way her mother had. She all but ran the last ten steps and slapped the release like it was her last hope of life. The door slid open—

"Oh!" Kahkitah gasped, jerking a little in his seat. "Nicole! You startled me."

"Sorry," Nicole apologized, her tension washing out of her. So they *hadn't* all run away and deserted her. "Where is everyone—?"

"I thought we would never see you again," Kahkitah continued, the time lag in the ship's translation running his words on top of hers. "I searched and searched, but couldn't find you. Where have you been hiding?"

"I wasn't hiding, exactly," Nicole said, looking around the room. Kahkitah was alone, with no indications that anyone else had recently been there. "Where is everyone?"

"You weren't hurt?" Kahkitah asked, his bird-whistling language sounding even more anxious. "When Jeff was brought in, I feared the worst for your safety."

"Yes, well, I think we've established that I'm all right," Nicole said, some of her relief at finding the Ghorf turning into irritation. Once Kahkitah got started on something, it was hard to shift him somewhere else until he ran out of bird calls. "I went to the medical center but Jeff's not there. Do you know what happened to him?"

"He was taken with the others," Kahkitah said. Abruptly, he stood up. "I neglect my manners. Are you hungry? Can I get you some food?"

Nicole's first impulse was to say no and get back to finding out what was going on. Her second impulse was that, after nine days of food bars, a proper meal sounded really good. "Thanks, that would be great," she said.

"Please—sit down," Kahkitah said, waving a massive hand at one of the other chairs at his table. "Sit, and rest. You must be very tired."

Nicole frowned. She *was* tired, but what had she said that could have given him that impression? "What do you mean?"

"You made a bargain with the Wisps to bring Jeff here after his accident," Kahkitah said. "If the cost for that bargain wasn't your life, as I'd feared, it must have been for additional work."

"Huh," Nicole said. She would never in a thousand years have come up with an explanation like that. Every time she started thinking of Kahkitah like he was just a weirdly shaped human, he would pop off with something like this and drag her back to the real world. "No, it was nothing like that," she assured him. "The Wisps . . . well, we have an agreement."

"Really," Kahkitah said. "That is most interesting. How did you manage it?"

"We can talk about it later," Nicole said. "Right now, I need to know where Jeff is."

"I already told you," Kahkitah said, sounding confused. "He was taken with the others."

"But you never told me where the others were taken," Nicole said patiently. "Or who took them."

"Oh," Kahkitah said. "Yes, I see. I don't know where they were taken. But it was that four-legged animal-shaped creature who ordered them to accompany him."

Nicole felt her throat tighten. "You mean Fievj? The same one who took Bungie away when you, Sam, Plato, and I went to get him from the room he was hiding in?"

"Yes, that was the one," Kahkitah said, brightening. "You're very good at these things."

"Yeah, I'm just terrific," Nicole ground out. There was only one reason she could think of why the Shipmasters might have taken the human team away but left Kahkitah behind.

Fievj suspected humans could fight. The rest of them either didn't believe it or weren't sure.

So someone had decided to make a test of it. To throw Nicole's team into one of the arenas, add some aliens, and see what everyone did when it came down to a choice between fighting or starving.

The food tray had appeared, and Nicole's stomach growled as the familiar aromas drifted through the air. But suddenly, she didn't feel like eating. "Come on," she said, standing up.

"Where are we going?" Kahkitah asked, sounding both surprised and puzzled.

"To find Jeff and the others."

"Do you know where they are?"

"If they're in an arena, they're either in Q2 or Q1. We'll start with Q2. Come on, come on—we need to move."

"But—" Kahkitah waved a hand helplessly at the tray.

Nicole hesitated. It really *did* smell good . . .

"We'll take it with us," she said. "I'll eat on the way."

She hadn't yet crossed the boundary into Q2, the section of the ship right in front of the familiar territory of Q4. But it was quickly clear that in some ways the situation was just like she'd seen in Q3.

The Wisps from Q4 who she summoned to take them across the heat-transfer duct delivered her and Kahkitah without trouble. But once they were across, a little questioning showed that, just like at the boundary with Q3, the Q4 Wisps apparently couldn't see the hallways and rooms stretched in front of them. They certainly weren't able or willing to accompany Nicole into that region. And again as she'd found in Q3, the Q2 Wisps—if there were any—ignored her calls for attendance or assistance. Ushkai was likewise silent.

Once again, Nicole was on her own. Only this time, at least, she had Kahkitah.

Not that he was likely to be very useful. The big Ghorf stood silently through her one-sided conversations with the Wisps, occasionally looking furtively around as if he was bored but trying not to show it.

He didn't speak until they were nearly to the Q2 arena. "Are Jeff and the others in danger?" he asked.

"I think so," Nicole admitted.

"The Wisps told you that?"

"The Wisps don't know."

"You've asked them?"

Nicole clamped down hard on a retort. "Yes, of course I've asked them. I asked the ones in Q4, anyway. That's the part of the ship we live in, the part we left when we crossed the heat-transfer duct. We're in Q2 now, and the Wisps here don't talk to me."

"That seems rude."

Nicole frowned at him. She hadn't thought about it that way before, but he was right.

And if that was the case, could their silence be because *she* was being rude to *them?*

It sounded ridiculous. As far as she could tell, the Wisps didn't have any emotions. She wasn't even sure they had their own minds, or whether they were just parts of the *Fyrantha*.

Still, it couldn't hurt to try. "Wisps?" she called into the low but continual rumbling that pervaded the ship. "Would one of you please come here?"

Nothing. She should have known it would be a waste of time—

And then, to her surprise, a Wisp appeared from a cross-corridor ahead and glided toward them.

"There's one!" Kahkitah whistled excitedly, jabbing a finger toward it. "It's coming! It's coming!"

"Yes, I see it," Nicole said, laying a hand on his arm to try to shut him up. Politeness got you nothing in her part of Philadelphia, and for the past nine days she'd gotten used to simply giving orders to the Wisps.

Her grandmother had always said *please* and *thank-you* were magic words. Aboard the *Fyrantha*, maybe they really were.

The Wisp stopped in front of them, its thin body towering above them, and opened its arms. Bracing herself, Nicole turned around and backed into its chest. The arms folded around her—

Welcome, Protector, the familiar voice came into her head. *How may I serve?*

Why didn't you answer me before now? Nicole asked.

The Shipmasters seek control over us, the Wisp said. *For a while they achieved it. Now, it is partially lost to them again.*

Nicole tried unsuccessfully to scowl. Terrific. Ushkai had warned her that Fievj and his friends were trying to take over the whole of the fragmented ship. She didn't realize they were that close.

And if they got control of the Wisps first, that would leave her with nothing. *Is that the situation in Q3, too?*

I do not know a Q3.

Just like with the Q4 Wisps she'd talked to. *Can you guide us to the arena in this section?* she asked. *Please,* she added, just in case.

Which door do you wish?

Door Three.

Shall I carry you there?

No, just lead. We'll follow. Thank you.

The Wisp opened its arms, releasing her. Nicole took a step away, and the creature turned and glided along the corridor in the direction they'd already been heading. The direction she'd already figured was the way to the arena.

So the Wisps didn't know about anything except their own part of the ship. Still, as long as they knew that and were under Nicole's control, that should be all she needed.

"Where are we going?" Kahkitah asked.

"To the arena in this part of the ship," Nicole said. "It's like the one you and Plato had to rescue me from a couple of weeks ago."

The Ghorf was silent for the next few steps. "Is that a safe idea?" he asked, his tone hesitant.

"Probably not," she conceded. "But there are only two places where the others might be, and that's one of them."

"Jeff was still injured," Kahkitah murmured. "I hope he hasn't been injured further."

"Yeah," Nicole said, a shiver running through her. "Me, too."

A few minutes later they arrived at the arena door. The Wisp stopped and stepped to one side, looking expectant. "Thank you," Nicole said, turning and again backing into its embrace. *Do you have the code to open it?*

No.

Does the Caretaker have it?

The Fyrantha *has it.*

Can you or the Caretaker get it for me from the ship?

No.

So it was going to be the inhaler again. Terrific. *Please alert the Caretaker that I'm going to ask the ship for the code.*

A pause. *I have done so.*

Thank you, Nicole said. *Release me.*

The Wisp opened its arms and Nicole stepped to the door, pulling out her inhaler. This had better not take more than one whiff. "Caretaker? I'm going to take this. Have the *Fyrantha* give me the Q2 arena door code. Please," she added belatedly.

No answer. Bracing herself, she held the inhaler to her mouth and sent a blast into her lungs. She coughed once—

Enter the arena with the code two zero zero four four three two.

"Thanks," Nicole said. She put the inhaler away and punched in the code. The lock snicked, and she grabbed the handle. Kahkitah took hold above her hands, and together they swung back the door.

The Q4 arena had been a diverse collection of hills, plains, trees, and creeks. The Q3 version had been flat grassland and a single winding river.

The Q2 arena was an impenetrable jungle.

Nicole felt her mouth drop open at the sight. Fifty feet from the door was a wall of close-packed trees, bushes, and thick bamboo-looking sorts of grass. The trees got bigger as they went back from the door, and the few hills she could see past the first line of trees also seemed to be covered with the same sorts of plants. There was a light breeze moving through the jungle, making the trees crackle like a fire in a fireplace as they swayed. The wind died and then shifted direction, bringing with it a sweet, flowery aroma.

Kahkitah gave a deep, untranslatable whistle. "Are Jeff and the others in there?"

"I don't know," Nicole said, a prickling sensation on the back of her neck. It had been bad enough trying to dodge the alien fighters in Q4, where there were only small sections of forest where they could hide. Here, she could walk straight into a spear before she even knew it was there.

"We must look for them," Kahkitah said firmly. "Which path should we follow?"

Nicole frowned. Overwhelmed by the view, she'd completely missed the fact that there were a pair of trails that started at the open area where they were standing and curved in opposite directions into the jungle. With trees on all sides of the paths it was hard to judge their size, but she guessed they were probably wide enough for even Kahkitah to pass without brushing the grass or bushes on either side.

Not that that was much comfort. Wide enough for a Ghorf didn't mean it was too wide for a spear. "I suppose—"

She broke off as a sudden series of doglike barks burst from the jungle, sounding like a whole angry pack was coming at them. She tensed, her eyes darting back and forth, but she couldn't see anything. "Are you our enemies?" a voice demanded in her brain.

A Ghorf bird whistle mixed in with the barks. "There," Kahkitah said, pointing up.

Nicole followed his finger. Clutching the top of one of the trees in the nearest bunch was a brown-and-gray creature that looked like a combination of a hockey goalie and a squirrel, with pale pink rose petals attached to its head and shoulders. Three of its four limbs were wrapped around the tree, gripping the bark with long, thin claws.

The fourth paw was clutching a gun.

Not like the gun Bungie had brought aboard with him. Definitely not like one of the greenfire weapons that had nearly killed Jeff. This was more like a long-nosed paintball gun, complete with a transparent tube hanging down in front of the trigger that held a lot of small yellow balls.

Up until this morning's encounter with the Thii and Ponngs, Nicole would have assumed that, whatever the gun fired, it was certainly deadly. Now, having seen the flimsy arrows and swords those other aliens had been given, she wasn't nearly so certain.

"Are you our enemies?" the creature demanded again. "We were told to expect enemies."

"Well, it's not us," Nicole said firmly. "So point that thing somewhere else."

The alien hesitated, then lowered his aim a little. "We were told to expect enemies," he repeated, sounding grumpy.

"Yeah, we heard," Nicole said. "A little tip: when they come, they won't come through this door. They'll come from across the arena from your hive."

"Our hive?"

"The place where your people are living," Nicole said. "Big metal rooms, laid out around a central area."

The gun snapped up to point at her again. "So you *are* our enemies," he snapped. "How else but by ploys and stratagems could you have learned of our home of exile?"

"Because we work for the ship," Nicole said with a sigh. "That's why we're wearing these." She gestured to her and Kahkitah's jumpsuits. "While we're at it, weren't you told that people wearing clothes like this were supposed to be left alone?"

The gun wavered, then lowered again. "We were told many things," he muttered, his dog barks changing to something that sounded more like a whimpering puppy. "We don't believe all of them."

"Yet you believe you have enemies aboard," Kahkitah reminded him. "Did the Masters tell you a reason for this?"

"Our enemies will try to take our food," the creature said, its whimpers changing to growls. "We must stop them if we're to survive. To do that, we must kill them."

"Obtaining food doesn't require killing," Kahkitah said, sounding confused. "Not aboard the *Fyrantha*."

"It does in some places," Nicole said sourly. So whoever the squirrel-people were, they'd apparently gotten here before whoever the Shipmasters were bringing in for them to fight.

Unless their opponents were already there, and the squirrel-people just didn't realize it. If the whole arena looked like this, there could be a small army hiding in there.

"That doesn't seem right," Kahkitah protested. "Why should one need to fight for food? Tell me, friend, who are you?"

The alien hesitated, then let go of the tree with its other upper limb and made some strange hand gesture. "We are the Ejbofs," he said, finishing the gesture and taking hold of the tree again.

"I'm Kahkitah," Kahkitah introduced himself. "My people are the Ghorfs. This is—"

"I'm the Sibyl," Nicole cut him off before he could say her name. Probably useless to hide her identity now that the Shipmasters had her pegged, she knew. Still, the habits of the Philadelphia streets would always be a part of her. "I'm a human. What's your name?"

The Ejbof snarled. "Do you mock me?" he demanded.

Kahkitah sent a startled look at Nicole, then looked up at the Ejbof. "Excuse me?" he asked,

"I asked if you mocked me," the alien said, sounding even angrier. "You know full well that I have no name."

"I do?" Kahkitah asked, sounding thoroughly confused now.

"No, actually, we don't," Nicole said. The Micawnwi did something similar with their children, she remembered, not giving them names until their fourth birthday. But the creature waving a gun at them sure didn't look or sound like a three-year-old. "Explain it to us."

For another moment the Ejbof glared at her, as if trying to decide if this was just another instance of mocking. "Our names were stripped from us when we were brought here," he said at last. "We must earn them back before we leave or face eternal shame and loss."

"Ah," Nicole said. That didn't make a single bit of sense to her— how could anyone call to someone else if they didn't have names? But she'd seen stranger things aboard this ship. "So what do they call you?"

"They don't call me," he said. "Nor will they."

"Fine," Nicole said with a sigh. She'd seen dissing games in Philadelphia, too, and they came off as just as stupid there. "Well, we don't want to keep you—you never know when some enemies will drop by. But really, they're going to come from the other direction. Trust me." She gestured to Kahkitah and started to turn back toward the door.

There was a snarling yip. "Stop!" the translation came. "I didn't give you permission to leave."

"We didn't ask for it," Nicole countered, turning back to glare up at him. "I'm the Sibyl, and you've been ordered to leave us alone. And we're leaving." She turned again—

And jerked as something slapped into the back of her right shoulder.

A piercing whistle split the air as she regained her balance. "Nicole!" Kahkitah screamed, and there was a sudden rustling of leaves and branches. Nicole turned around.

To find herself facing an extraordinary sight. Kahkitah had shoved his way through the undergrowth to the Ejbof's tree, wrapped his massive hands around it, and was shaking it for all he was worth.

It was a tall, thick tree, and Kahkitah was just one Ghorf, and there was no way he could possibly bring it down. But even as Nicole reached over her shoulder with her left hand she realized that wasn't what he was up to. At the top of the tree, where the swaying was the worst, the Ejbof was holding on for dear life, his gun all but forgotten as he clung to the bark. He gave a plaintive yip—"Stop!" the translation came.

"Drop the gun first," Nicole ordered. She let go of her shoulder, wondering if she was bleeding, and brought her hand around to where she could see it.

It was wet, all right, but not with blood. Smeared across her palm was a band of bright yellow.

She'd been right the first time. The damn thing was a paint-ball gun.

A second later she jerked back as something crossed her peripheral vision. But it was only the paintball gun, tumbling through the air as she'd ordered. For a second it paused in its flight as its shoulder strap hung up briefly on one of the tree branches, then it freed itself and fell the rest of the way to the ground. "All right, Kahkitah, that's enough," she said. "I'm okay—it's just paint."

"Paint?" Kahkitah repeated, frowning back at her over his shoulder as he slowed his shaking.

"Like marker dyes," she explained, looking up. With his gun hand now freed, the Ejbof was gripping the tree with all four limbs. "I don't know why the Shipmasters gave them that kind of weapon," she added to forestall the inevitable next question.

"They're for us to mark our opponents for easier sight," the Ejbof growled. He still sounded angry, but the anger was colored by more than a little caution. Clearly, he hadn't realized that Ghorfs could do that.

Actually, Nicole had been rather surprised by Kahkitah's action as well. Not that he *could* do something like that—she knew how strong he was—but that he *would* do it.

And especially that he'd take such a risk for *her*. After all, when he'd first charged in they hadn't known the Ejbof's weapon wasn't lethal.

"You'd better hope your enemies are more easily scared than we are," she growled back. "We're leaving now. Got it?"

"Yes." He hesitated. "Will you leave me the weapon?"

Nicole considered. She was hardly in the mood to do him any favors. But on the other hand, there didn't seem any point in going out of her way to be nasty.

Besides, getting caught with a gun would be the exact wrong message to send the Shipmasters. "This time, yes," she said. "You can come down and get it after we're gone." She pointed a finger at him. "But the next time you shoot at someone in a colored jumpsuit, I'll make you eat it."

He cocked his head to the side, and it occurred to Nicole that maybe that threat might not have translated accurately. But he seemed to get the idea. "Yes," he said. "We won't harm you again."

"Good for you," Nicole said. "Come on, Kahkitah."

And besides, she reminded herself soberly as she and the Ghorf sealed the arena door behind them, the Ejbofs were about to find themselves in a fight for their lives. Adding to their troubles would be childish.

"He seemed very fierce," Kahkitah commented. "His people should be formidable in battle."

"Maybe," Nicole said. "But I've seen plenty of guys who were all big talk until stuff went down. Then they melted like slush."

"I see," Kahkitah said, his whistling going quiet and thoughtful. "You think he may be that type?"

"No idea," Nicole said. "But that's his problem, not ours."

"I see," Kahkitah said again. "What of our problem? Where do we go next?"

Nicole pursed her lips, trying to work it through. So Jeff and the crew weren't in Q2 or Q3. She hadn't gone into the Q4 arena since that last battle between the Micawnwi and Cluufes, and there might have been enough time since then for the Shipmasters to have sent both alien groups home and rigged the arena for a new war game. They could have put Jeff in there.

But Nicole and Jeff were both familiar with the Q4 setup, and the Shipmasters knew that. If they were trying to figure out what humans were capable of, they probably wouldn't want them having any kind of home-court advantage.

In Q4 and Q2 Nicole had a certain level of authority, at least regarding control of the Wisps in those sections. In Q3 she didn't seem to have any control at all, but maybe that was just the lack of politeness. Anyway, she'd already checked out the arena there.

That left Q1.

Ushkai had warned her the Shipmasters had control over the *Fyrantha's* main functions. If all of that stuff was located in Q1, it was a good bet that they would have full authority over the Wisps there, as well.

Which made the Q1 arena the perfect place for Fievj to set up his experiment.

"We've got one more place to check out," she told Kahkitah with a sigh. "Come on."

From the arena door, it was just a short trip toward the *Fyrantha's* midline and the wide heat-transfer duct that marked the boundary with Q1. The Q2 Wisps again came at Nicole's call, though she didn't have the nerve to try summoning them without saying *please*. A minute later, they were standing beside the duct just inside the edge of Q1. Nicole ordered the Wisps to wait, and she and Kahkitah headed off.

Once again, as with the Q3 and Q4 arrangement, the Q1 arena wasn't directly across from its Q2 counterpart. If this was the same arrangement as with those two, she and Kahkitah needed to head toward the back of the ship.

The corridor that ran along the midline would be the simplest and probably the straightest. But it also might be a little too obvious if the Shipmasters came looking for them. Instead, she led Kahkitah two corridors farther in, to a somewhat more-twisty hallway, and headed toward the rear of the ship.

Once, back in Philadelphia, Trake had sent her and Bungie on a supply run across another gang's territory. Bungie had been super excited about the job, figuring it was his chance to show

Trake that he should be getting more jobs and a bigger cut of the pie. Nicole had been a lot less thrilled, figuring it was mostly her chance to get herself killed. In the end it had worked out okay, but there'd been a couple of tense moments. The whole experience had left her with two nights of drinking her fears away and a promise to herself to never again invade someone else's territory.

So now, here she was, walking in on the worst and most dangerous gang she could ever dream of.

"Where are we going?" Kahkitah asked as they walked down the silent corridors.

"Not so loud," Nicole growled, wincing. This part of the ship was as silent as Q4 had been. But if this was where the Shipmasters hung out, there probably weren't any work crews here. At least no human ones.

And anyone the Shipmasters liked hanging out with was someone Nicole definitely didn't want to bump into.

"Sorry," Kahkitah apologized, his whistling sinking to the Ghorf version of a whisper.

"It's okay," Nicole said. "We're heading to the arena on this side."

"To find Jeff?"

"Yeah," Nicole said. *Hopefully,* she thought.

There was a hint of movement at one of the cross-corridors ahead, a faint suggestion of shifting shadow. Nicole tensed, fighting back the urge to run back to where they'd left the Q2 Wisps—

From the cross-corridor a Wisp appeared.

Nicole felt herself wilt a little with relief. The Wisps here probably wouldn't obey her, but at least it wasn't Fievj or one of the other Shipmasters. The Wisp rounded the corner and glided toward them.

"It's coming toward us," Kahkitah murmured. "Will it obey you?"

Nicole shook her head. "Probably no—"

Right in the middle of the word a pair of arms slipped around her shoulders from behind and locked themselves across her chest. And once again, she found herself completely paralyzed.

Stupid, she snarled silently at herself. She knew how quietly the Wisps traveled. She should have kept an eye behind them for just this sort of ambush.

Only she hadn't. And now she was going to pay the price for her distraction. So far the Shipmasters had handled her like a gang handled a cop—not with any friendliness, but knowing not to push the line too far. But here in their probable stronghold, cut off from Wisps and maybe even Ushkai, who knew what they might be willing to risk? They could interrogate her, order her to back off, maybe even lock her up somewhere. Now that the Wisp had her helpless, it would be a simple matter of the creature turning to the right and taking Nicole down whatever corridors led to the Shipmasters' hive or headquarters or whatever.

Only the Wisp didn't turn to Nicole's right. Instead, it turned to her left.

Nicole tried to frown. To her *left?* But there was nothing in that direction. Nothing but the midline, and the Q2 areas beyond it.

And the heat-transfer duct.

And suddenly, she understood what was going to happen.

The Shipmasters weren't simply going to lock her up. They'd decided to go with a more permanent solution.

The Wisp was going to take her to the duct and drop her in. And kill her.

seven

No! The word screamed in her mind. No! Stop!

In her mind, but nowhere else. With her lips and voice frozen as completely as the rest of her body, she was utterly helpless.

She couldn't scream. She couldn't fight her way free. She couldn't even warn Kahkitah that they were under attack. The big stupid Ghorf would just watch, figuring that this was how it was supposed to be, right up to the moment when the Wisps dropped them.

Unless they hadn't bothered to grab him. He was somewhere behind her now, out of her limited range of vision. Were they just going to leave him here while they disposed of their main problem? Certainly there was no reason to kill him, and he was still useful to them.

So probably he would just get to watch, still not understanding, as the Wisp threw her to her death.

Wisp, stop! she shouted mentally at the creature clutching her to itself. Stop! I'm the Fyrantha's Protector. You have to listen to me. You have to obey me.

There is no Protector, the Wisp's voice came in her head. There is no Fyrantha.

What the hell are you talking about? Nicole demanded. This is *the* Fyrantha. *This ship—the thing you're standing in—is the* Fyrantha.

There is no Fyrantha. *This ship is the* Vengeance.

Nicole felt her heart sink. There was only one reason she could think of why the Wisp would refuse to obey her: the Shipmasters had already turned Q1 completely to their control.

And for them to have already renamed it the *Vengeance* meant Ushkai had been right about their plans. They were hell-bent on turning the one-time harmless flying zoo back into a warship.

Nicole was the *Fyrantha's* Protector. It was her job to stop that from happening.

Only she couldn't. She couldn't do anything.

Wisp, she called again. Hopelessly. Uselessly.

And then, with a suddenness that made her gasp through abruptly unfrozen lips the Wisp's arms opened and she was free again. She turned, opening her mouth to snarl at the creature—

To find Kahkitah standing behind the Wisp, his big hands gripping the creature's thin arms at the elbows, holding them open. "Kahkitah?" she breathed.

"Are you all right?" the Ghorf asked anxiously.

"Yeah, *now,*" Nicole said, her muscles starting to tremble from reaction as she saw they'd made it to the midline corridor. She'd been *that* close to dying. "Not so much a minute ago. The damn thing attacked me."

"Yes, I thought so," Kahkitah said, still holding the Wisp's arms. "What do we do?"

There was movement in the cross-corridor behind Kahkitah: five more Wisps had appeared and were coming toward them. A quick glance to the sides showed another five approaching from both directions along the midline corridor. "We run," she said flatly. "Back to where we came across. I told the Wisps to wait for us—let's hope to hell they did."

"And we must bypass these first?" Kahkitah asked.

With an effort Nicole resisted the urge to swear at him. Of *course* they needed to bypass these Wisps. Hadn't he been paying attention?

Only getting by them wasn't going to be easy. Already all three sets of Wisps had opened their arms wide, moving away from each other so that they mostly filled the whole corridor. She and Kahkitah would have to duck under their arms, or push them aside without getting grabbed, if they were going to get out without being trapped.

Two problems. She didn't know how well Ghorfs could duck, and she didn't know how fast Wisps could move.

But there was nothing to do but try. "Come on," she said. Turning toward the front of the ship, toward where they'd come across from Q2, she headed warily toward the Wisps.

And as she opened up to a slow jog, something touched her back.

She twitched violently away, her heart leaping. But it was only the outer arm of the Wisp that Kahkitah was still holding, brushing against her shoulder as he clumped his way past her and into the lead.

Apparently, she hadn't known how fast Ghorfs could move, either.

"I will lead," he called back to her, in case his burst of speed hadn't been enough of a clue. "Stay behind me."

"Okay," Nicole said, frowning. She'd always known Kahkitah was fond of her, but this sudden bravery seemed out of his usual character.

But then, he didn't know the full depth of what was at stake here. All he knew was that a few Wisps had gone rogue, and that Nicole needed to be rescued.

Though how he was going to pull this off she couldn't imagine. Kahkitah was charging full tilt at the Wisps now, still holding his captive, moving fast enough that Nicole was having a hard time keeping up. There wasn't any room between the Wisps—was he planning to let them capture him so as to let her escape?

Not as stupid or dangerous as it sounded, since they didn't need to kill him. But he didn't know that.

Of course, now that she thought about it, Nicole didn't know that, either. Not really. The Shipmasters didn't have any reason to kill him, but that didn't mean they wouldn't. She'd known plenty of guys who did stupid things in the heat of the moment when they weren't thinking straight. If Kahkitah helped Nicole slip through their fingers, they just might be mad enough to do something nasty.

Should she try to stop him? Or at least warn him? But there wasn't time for a full explanation, certainly not for someone as slow minded as Kahkitah.

She swore under her breath, her mind spinning as she tried to think. She was the Protector, and she had to survive. But did that mean she should let Kahkitah sacrifice himself if that wasn't necessary?

She glared at the Wisps blocking the corridor. No. Jeff had nearly died because of one of Nicole's crazy stunts. He might still die. She couldn't lose Kahkitah, too.

Besides, letting other people take the bullet for you was what people like Trake and Bungie did. She'd always hated that in them, and she wouldn't hate it any less in herself.

Clenching her teeth, she put on a burst of speed. If she could overtake Kahkitah and somehow get past the Wisps on her own,

surely the Shipmasters would understand that he hadn't done anything worth punishing him for.

But Kahkitah was still picking up speed, and with a sinking
feeling she saw that there was no way she was going to catch him
in time. He was almost to the line of Wisps—

Letting go of one of his captive Wisp's arms, he reached
down and grabbed its leg, swiveling the creature up into a horizontal position in front of him. He shoved his right arm straight
out, slamming the Wisp's legs into the Wisp in front of him,
knocking the blocker out of the line and sending it staggering
away, then turned and likewise slammed the arms and torso of
his captive into the one on that side, likewise throwing it off to
the side.

And suddenly the solid line of Wisps had a big fat opening in it.

"Come!" Kahkitah called, swinging his captive Wisp back the
other direction as one of the remaining Wisps tried to angle toward
him. This time he let go, hurling his captive against the other
Wisp and sending both of them toppling to the floor. A second
later he was through the line and heading down the corridor at
a dead run.

Nicole was right behind him.

"What do I do?" Kahkitah asked. His brief moment of initia-
tive was over, and he was back to the confused Ghorf again.
"Nicole? What do I do?"

"Just keep going," Nicole said, looking back over her shoulder.
The Wisps that Kahkitah had bowled over were back on their
feet, and they and the rest of the group were giving chase.

But unless they had a burst of speed in reserve that they were
holding back for some reason, there was no way they were going
to catch their targets. Nicole and Kahkitah already had too much
of a lead, and they were adding more to it with each step. "Back
to where we came in," she added, turning to face forward again.

What they had to watch out for now was the Shipmasters sending more Wisps against them from other parts of the ship.

But no new attack came. Either Fievj had been caught off guard by their escape, or he was content to just chase them away. At least for now. They arrived at their entry point to find the three Wisps who'd carried them across from Q2 waiting, just as Nicole had ordered.

"Great," Nicole said. "Come on, let's get out of here."

"Wait," Kahkitah asked, slowing down and holding out an arm sideways to keep her from running past him. "How do we know they're not like the others?"

"It's okay," Nicole assured him. "These are the same ones we left here when we came across."

"How do you know?"

Nicole shrugged. The Wisps all looked pretty much alike, and she still didn't know how she was able to tell one from another. All she knew was that she could. "I just do. Come on."

The Wisps waited while she and Kahkitah slowed to a trot, and then to a walk. "Take us back across," Nicole ordered, turning and backing into the first one's arms. The Wisp wrapped her in the familiar hug, the other two Wisps did likewise with Kahkitah, and the group turned to the access hatch that was even now opening into the heat-transfer duct.

A minute later, they were safely back in Q2.

It took Nicole a couple of minutes, sitting on the floor with her back to the Q2 arena door, to recover her breath and her composure.

It took Kahkitah considerably longer.

"Oh, my heavens," he muttered over and over. "Oh, my heavens. Oh, my heavens."

"Calm down," Nicole soothed, watching him closely. The Ghorf looked like he was high on some crazy street drug: sitting down beside Nicole for a few seconds, then bounding to his feet and pacing, then sitting down again, then fidgeting, then hopping up again. The whole time his hands were shaking, and once or twice during his rounds of pacing it looked like his legs were going to collapse beneath him. Whatever Ghorfs used for adrenaline, it delivered one hell of a punch.

Unless it wasn't adrenaline at all. Maybe Ghorfs just weren't equipped for quick action, even when their lives might be at stake. Nicole had heard that elephants and rhinos were so big that they didn't have any real enemies. Maybe Ghorfs were like that—so big and strong they never had to worry about getting attacked by anything.

Which put the whole Ghorf species pretty much off the table as far as the Shipmasters' war-slave plans went. Lucky Ghorfs.

Though Kahkitah would probably never realize that. Distantly, Nicole wondered if being strong and invulnerable made up for being stupid.

Back in Philadelphia, with danger pressing against her from every side, she would have made that choice in a heartbeat. Not to mention that being stupid would have spared her from recognizing a lot of the nasty comments people like Bungie liked to throw at her. But now, knowing what was hanging over her whole world, it was brains that were going to count.

And she'd better start using hers.

"Look, try to relax, okay?" she told Kahkitah, trying hard not to sound irritated. This guilt thing was eating up time they might not have. "We've got to figure out our next move."

"You don't understand," he warbled plaintively. He was back to pacing, and looking more agitated than ever. "This isn't how we do things. We don't move quickly. We don't decide quickly. We don't harm other beings." He stopped abruptly and leveled a finger at her. "It was you. *You,* Nicole Hammond. What have you done to me?"

Nicole felt her eyes go wide. *"Me?* What makes you think I had anything to do with it?"

"It wasn't until you arrived that I felt such . . . confusion," Kahkitah said, clearly struggling to organize his thoughts. "It must be you. Your influence—" He broke off, his trilling changing briefly to an untranslatable pulsing sound. "Your inhaler," he said, pointing toward her pocket. "You've used it several times while close to me. Could that have affected me?"

"I don't know," Nicole said, frowning. The inhaler was slow death, but until it killed her it was her window into the *Fyrantha's* computer mind. She didn't have a clue how Ghorf bodies worked, except that they could eat the same food humans could.

Was it possible that stray dust from the inhaler could have slowly brought up Kahkitah's IQ? "I suppose anything's possible," she said.

"Yes," Kahkitah whistled a murmur. "Though that would be strange."

"You have no idea," Nicole said, wincing. "But whatever happened, it happened just when I needed it. How come you knew I was being attacked, anyway?"

"You hadn't given the Wisp any orders," Kahkitah said absently, still clearly trying to work this through. "Always before you would give an order, or you would walk up to it and back into its arms. This time you did neither."

"Well, if it *is* the inhaler doing this, I'm damn glad," Nicole said. "I think it was going to throw me into the heat duct."

Kahkitah gave her a puzzled look. "You mean take you across? Get you out of that area?"

"No, I mean exactly what I said," Nicole said. "It was going to kill me."

Kahkitah gave a violent twitch. "But that's unheard of," he protested. "No Wisp has ever attacked anyone. Never."

"No Wisp has ever been fully under the Shipmasters' control, either," Nicole countered.

Though now, with the fear and panic fading, she had to privately admit that she didn't *know* that murder had been on the Wisp's mind. The Wisp hadn't said that. Fievj hadn't threatened that. Maybe Kahkitah was right. Maybe they were just trying to evict her.

She took a deep breath. No. Proof or not, however it was she could tell one Wisp from another, she knew the plan had been for her to die today.

"So Jeff and the others are lost," Kahkitah murmured sadly.

Nicole snapped her attention back to him. "What? Who says?"

"If we cannot go to them, they are lost."

"Who says we can't go?"

Kahkitah gave her a confused look. "But if the Shipmasters seek to kill you, we must stay away."

"A lot of people have wanted to do a lot of stuff to me," Nicole said, shivering at some of the memories. Most of the time she'd been able to avoid the nastier demands, either by playing one guy against another or just by being somewhere else at the critical time. The few times she *hadn't* been able to get clear . . . "The trick is not letting them." She hesitated. Clearly, he wasn't up to this. "But I can do it alone," she added. "There's no reason you have to come."

Kahkitah drew himself up to his full height. "I won't abandon you, Nicole," he said, his wavering and confusion disappearing. "I'll stand by you, and by Jeff and the others. But you must tell me what to do."

"I'll try," Nicole said. A whole quarter of a ship's worth of Wisps—not to mention the Shipmasters themselves—was a hell of a big order for two of them to tackle. But better two of them than just one of her. "Okay. I'm guessing the trick is to spend as little time as we can in the corridors where the Wisps have free run. We know the Q1 arena is set back from this one"—she rapped her knuckles against the door she was leaning against— "so we're going to head back along the corridor on this side until we get to a spot directly beside it. *Then* we'll get the Wisps to carry us across."

"Yes, I see," Kahkitah said slowly. "And you know where it is?"

"I think so," Nicole said. "I crossed from the Q3 arena over to Q4, and if it's the same distance up here, I should be able to find the access panel that's right beside the door."

"The same distance . . . ?"

"Between the Q1 and Q2 arenas as between the Q3 and Q4 ones," Nicole said patiently. "No, wait." She frowned as a thought suddenly struck her. "Maybe we can even do better. Never mind coming in outside the door—there was an access door *inside* the Q4 arena that led up to the top of the ship. If we can find one into Q1, maybe we can be inside before the Shipmasters even know we're there." Best of all, she wouldn't have to use her inhaler to get a door code.

She wrinkled her nose with disgust at herself. And if she'd thought of that earlier, she could have gotten into the Q3 and Q2 arenas without having to use her inhaler there, either.

The inhaler dust might make Kahkitah smarter, but it sure wasn't doing anything for her own brains.

"Then we should depart at once," Kahkitah said, again stretching to his full height. "Or as soon as you're ready."

"I'm ready," Nicole said, pushing herself back to her feet. Like *she'd* been the one they'd been waiting on while he worked through his panic attack. "Let's go."

———

Now that Nicole knew what to look for, the access panels into the heat-transfer ducts were fairly easy to find. Likewise, knowing how far she'd had to walk from the Q3 arena to their hive, plus the distance from there to the Q4 arena, was easy enough to work out. She and Kahkitah walked that distance; and, sure enough, there was the access.

The other entrance, though, the one that would hopefully lead into the arena itself, wasn't nearly so obvious.

"Are you sure it's here?" Kahkitah asked about the fifth time he and Nicole walked back and forth through the same area without finding anything.

"No, not really," she admitted. "The door I used was on the other side of the Q4 arena, the side farthest away from the midline. I just assumed there'd be one on this side, too." She shook her head. "Damn. Okay. Back to the main door, I guess."

"I have a thought," Kahkitah said hesitantly. "What would happen if we stood here and you told the Wisps to carry us across? Would they take us back to the other door, or use a closer one if it was available?"

"I don't know," Nicole said, frowning sideways at him. He was definitely starting to get into this thinking thing.

That, or as the inhaler dust slowly killed her it was also making her stupid. Jeff hadn't mentioned that part. Maybe he didn't know.

Or maybe he just hadn't wanted to make the bad news even worse.

"But there's nothing to lose by trying," she continued, pushing her fears and her annoyance into the back corner of her brain where she kept a lot of her experiences with Trake's group. "Wisp?" she called, raising her voice. "Wisp? Come here, please. I need you. Actually, I need three of you."

She paused, waiting. She hadn't seen Wisps very often when she was working with her team, but now that they were listening for her call they seemed to show up pretty quickly. She wasn't sure where they hid the rest of the time, but wherever it was—

"There," Kahkitah said, pointing over her shoulder.

Nicole spun around, tensing. Three Wisps were gliding toward them, their faces expressionless as always. She shifted her weight slightly, ready to make a run for it if the Shipmasters had gotten to them, too.

To her relief, they came to a halt a couple of yards away from her. She gave it another second, just to be sure.

"They seem all right," Kahkitah murmured.

Nicole nodded. "We need to go through there," she told the Wisps, pointing to the wall. "To the Q1 arena on the other side of the heat-transfer duct."

The Wisps didn't move. Nicole counted out three more seconds, just to make sure they weren't going to charge. Then, bracing herself, she stepped to the nearest one, turned around, and backed into it. Its arms enfolded her—

We want to go to the arena, she thought again toward the Wisp. *Can you take us there?*

The arena is behind us, the Wisp replied. *Do you wish to be carried the entire way?*

Not that arena, Nicole said. *The one past the duct, the one in Q1.*

The Wisp paused as if considering that. *Just past the duct is another section of the* Fyrantha, Nicole said. *I know you can't see all of it, but you should at least be able to see the first corridor or two, right? The arena should be right past the duct.*

Yes, the Wisp said. *I see now. Yes, we can take you there. Your companion, too?*

Yes, Nicole said. *The entrance should be somewhere nearby.*

Yes.

And to Nicole's relief a section of the wall opened up about six feet to her right, sending the familiar blast of hot air across her. As the Wisp turned and glided toward it, she had a quick glimpse of the other two taking hold of Kahkitah and also heading for the opening.

They were right on the edge of the duct when it suddenly occurred to Nicole that all the Shipmasters really had to do was let one of their Wisps duplicate the usual behavior pattern, and they could dump her into the duct before she had even a hint anything was wrong.

Fortunately, by the time that thought occurred to her they were already at the threshold, the Wisp gripping her had unfurled its wings, and they were floating up and across the flood of hot air blasting up from below.

Maybe it was because Nicole was still recovering from that latest flash of fear, but they were halfway across before it abruptly registered that while they were going across they were also going up.

I asked you to take us to the arena, she thought at the Wisp.

We are doing so, the Wisp assured her.

But the arena should be straight across from where we started.

There is no entry point straight across from that corridor, the Wisp answered. *We are instead taking you to the upper level.*

The upper level? As far as Nicole could remember, she'd never seen an upper level in any of the arenas. Was Q1 different?

She was about to find out. The Wisp had leveled off, and an access panel was opening directly across from her. Beyond, its image blurred and distorted by the roiling air, was some kind of room. The Wisp took her through the opening, lowered her gently to the floor, and opened its arms.

Nicole took a step forward, looking around. At first glance

the room seemed to be something like a wide balcony, with a waist-high ceramic barrier and a six-foot-tall transparent material above it that looked out and down into a brightly lit area. But a second, closer look showed her that there was a curve to the balcony, reaching out to both sides of the inner sky area and disappearing around the edges. A circular balcony, then, that completely surrounded the arena?

A soft whistling came from behind her. "An observation gallery," the translation came. A Ghorf hand stretched out over her shoulder, pointing. "And a recording studio?"

Nicole felt her throat tighten. Kahkitah was pointing at a pair of stands perched at the front edge of the balcony. On top of the stands were small rectangular boxes, their front faces angled downward. Several other pairs of stand-and-box combos were spaced around the balcony, she saw now, always two of them together, always angled to look downward. Beside some of them were what looked like full-face binoculars on their own stands, also angled downward into the arena. At regular intervals around the rim she could also see small control consoles with muted lights.

Aside from her and Kahkitah, the place seemed deserted.

Nicole turned back to the Wisps, who were still standing just inside the now closed access door. "Wait here," she ordered. "We may want you to take us somewhere else."

"Please," Kahkitah prompted.

Nicole pursed her lips. "Please," she added.

The Wisps didn't move, but Nicole had the sense that they were settling in to wait. "Okay," she said, touching Kahkitah's arm. "Let's see what the *Fyrantha*'s whipped up for us this time."

eight

Up to now Nicole had seen grasslands, jungles, and the mix of terrain types that she'd first found in Q4. But the Q1 arena topped them all.

It was the seashore.

A full seashore, too, complete with a rolling ocean that filled the right-hand third of the arena. On the left-hand section, closest to their current vantage point, there was a narrow beach with some scattered sticks that gave way to a mass of low, reed-covered dunes behind them. Beyond the strip of reeds were low hills with a mix of grass and short, wide-canopied trees. A rapid, white-water stream flowed down from a tall hill about midway across the land area, disappearing behind a tall, rocky bluff that jutted out of the beach, then reappearing as it emptied into the ocean. On the other side of the stream a second bluff rose from the beach, this one a little taller and even more rocky than the closer bluff. Nicole couldn't see much past the two bluffs and the stream's big hill, but it looked like there was another narrow stretch of beach on that side of the stream. The ocean ran right up to the base of the twin bluffs, with crashing waves that splashed another five or six feet up the rock with each surge of the surf.

"Is that a whole *lake?*" Kahkitah asked from beside her, his whistling sounding awestruck.

"More like a small ocean," Nicole said. Was that something moving among the low trees? "I don't think you get waves like that in a lake."

"Yes, of course," Kahkitah said. "Yet how are there waves in here at all? The ocean seems too small for waves to be natural."

Nicole snorted. "Nothing in this place is natural, Kahkitah," she said. "Look down there in the trees—there, just past the dunes on this side. Is that someone in a green jumpsuit?"

"Yes, I see him," Kahkitah said. "I think that's Iosif."

"Who?"

"Iosif," Kahkitah repeated. "He's part of Miron's green repair group."

"Right," Nicole said. Their own blue group hadn't had a lot of contact with the green group, and she'd never had a chance to learn all their names or faces.

But she remembered that the greens' usual work area was behind the blue's hive. If they were here, that would explain why that part of the *Fyrantha* had been deserted earlier when she'd traveled through it.

But what were they doing *here*? If Kahkitah was right about Jeff and the blue group being taken by the Shipmasters—

She tensed as it suddenly clicked. Up to now the Shipmasters' pattern—or at least the pattern she'd seen—had been to pit two different alien races against each other. But if they were serious about finding out if humans could fight, the easiest way to do that would be to throw two human teams at each other.

And it wasn't like they would have to fine-tune the Wisps and their teleporter gadget to find them, either. All they had to do was march them halfway across the *Fyrantha*.

"We have to get down there," she told Kahkitah, studying the area as best she could, trying to see who was where. But it was a waste of effort. The trees seemed reasonably short, but their leaf canopies were wide enough to block most of the area beyond the dunes.

Still, it made sense for the Shipmasters to split up the groups by people who already knew each other. If the green group was on this side of the stream, then Jeff and the rest of the blue group must be on the other side. If they were going to fight, there had to be a way to get back and forth between them.

Only she couldn't see any way to do that. The stream cut across the whole land area, from the hive end of the arena all the way to the ocean.

And it wasn't like any of the streams in the Q4 arena. Those were slow, lazy things, usually narrow enough to step over and equipped with small bridges where they weren't. This stream was a lot faster, spraying water and foam over the banks as it rolled down the cliff. It was also much wider, ten or twelve feet across, way too wide to step over. Unless there was a bridge somewhere between the two bluffs that she couldn't see from her position, it would be dangerous to cross.

"Look—there's a doorway back there," Kahkitah said, pointing past her face. "At the very back, below those tree canopies."

"Yes, I know," Nicole said, trying not to sound too irritated. Of course there was a door back there—those were the fighters' living areas when they weren't out fighting. "Forget that for now. We need to find a way into the arena."

"It's right there," Kahkitah said, sounding puzzled as he shifted his finger to point straight across the observation deck. "Those stairs."

Nicole frowned, peering across the balcony. All she could see was a coloring like more of the arena sky. "I don't see anything."

"You have to look past the reflection on the inside of the material," Kahkitah said, as if that was the easiest thing in the world.

"The material between us and the arena seems to pick up the sky colors, which makes it invisible from below—"

"Yeah, yeah, I got that," Nicole said, not bothering to hide her frustration this time. She'd already figured out that that was why she hadn't seen the similar observation deck in Q4. She'd always assumed the Shipmasters had hidden cameras up there; she'd never dreamed they had a whole wraparound room to hang out in. "You can see *stairs* over there?"

"Yes," Kahkitah said. "Come. I'll show you." He started off to the right around the edge of the deck. Taking another look at the arena, Nicole started to follow—

And for the second time that day slammed squarely into a Ghorf as Kahkitah abruptly stopped. "Kahkitah—" she bit out.

"Look," he said, his whistling sounding odd as he pointed to the wall. "Are those . . . ?"

Nicole looked where he was pointing, a shiver running up her back. Standing upright in a rack beside a desk and another of the consoles were six long, slender black tubes.

Greenfire weapons.

"They sure as hell are," she confirmed, forcing her voice to remain steady. The deadliest weapons she'd seen yet aboard the *Fyrantha*. The things that had made the difference between victory and defeat for the Micawnwi. The things that had nearly killed Jeff.

And here they were, six of them. Not locked up, not hidden away, not riding in the back end of a Shipmaster's centaur armor.

Ripe for the taking.

Because, really, what did it matter anymore? No matter what happened down there, the Shipmasters were bound to find out how well humans could fight. Nothing could stop that now. She didn't know what kind of gear Fievj would give them for their private little war, but a set of greenfire weapons would absolutely give Jeff the edge they'd need to live through it.

On the other hand, if she helped the blue group, it would mean hurting or even killing some of the green group. Did she have the right to take sides when it meant the lives of other people?

She felt her lips curl back in a snarl. Damn right she did. Protector or not, she'd started out as the blue group's Sibyl, and if it came to choosing sides that was where she would land. She'd taken Trake's side often enough when there'd been arguments within his group. Once or twice she'd even taken Bungie's side, though usually only when he'd already been on Trake's.

She was still eyeing the weapons when Kahkitah put a hand on her shoulder and shoved her to the floor.

"Wh—?" was all she managed before his other hand clamped over her mouth.

"Shh!" a barely audible birdsong whistled in her ear as the hand covering her mouth turned her head a little ways to her right. "Shipmasters!"

Nicole tensed as she peered over the balcony barrier. They were there, all right: Fievj and two others, wearing the kimono-and-sash outfits she'd seen them in once before when they thought no humans were around. They were striding in from a stairway she hadn't noticed before, leading off the balcony about twenty feet from the panel the Wisps had used to bring in her and Kahkitah.

The panel the Wisps were still standing in front of.

Nicole hissed silently between her teeth. *Damn.* What was Fievj going to think about Wisps just standing around their area? Especially Wisps that weren't from here in Q1? Or would the Shipmasters even have a way of knowing where they'd come from?

She bit down on her lip. Of course they would know. The first order Fievj gave—and was ignored—and the whole thing would blow up.

There was another soft whistle in her ear. "This way," Kahkitah said, gently pushing her head back out of sight below the level of the barrier as the hand on her shoulder urged her toward the stairway he'd pointed to earlier. Nicole took one last lingering look at the greenfire weapons—

"You!" Fievj snapped. "What are you doing here?"

Wincing, staying in a low crouch, Nicole let Kahkitah hustle her around the curve of the balcony, not daring to look behind her. Probably Fievj was talking to the Wisps, and hopefully none of the Shipmasters had spotted her or Kahkitah. But whether they had or not, this was no place to hang around.

The conversation behind them had shifted to something that sounded both puzzled and irritated by the time she and Kahkitah came in sight of the stairway. It was right where he'd said it would be, though how he could have seen it through the reflective layer she couldn't guess.

Getting from the barrier across the balcony was going to be the real trick. Luckily, either the Shipmasters were as bad at seeing through the glare as Nicole was or else their full attention was still focused on the wayward Wisps. She and Kahkitah reached the stairs without being challenged.

The stairway was similar to the one she'd used to get to the top of the *Fyrantha* once before: narrow, dimly lit, and curving around so that it was impossible to see how long the walk was going to be or where they were going to end up. Unlike the one the Shipmasters had used to get to the balcony, this staircase only went down.

Neither the length or the single direction seemed to matter to Kahkitah. He didn't hesitate, but headed immediately down the steps, rising from his own bent-waisted crouch only when he was far enough down that the deck would block any view of him from the Shipmasters at the far end of the balcony. Nicole, with nothing better to offer and with caution pretty much already out of the equation, followed close behind.

The stairway went down a *long* way, though considering how far above the arena floor they'd started that wasn't surprising. Still, Nicole had hoped the stairs would lead to another set of corridors where they would at least have a couple of options as to what to do next.

No such luck. They reached the bottom to find a single door blocking their way.

"This must lead into the arena," Kahkitah murmured thoughtfully. He ran his hands along the material, then gave a tentative push. The panel responded by swinging outward from the stairway, revealing a glimpse of sand beyond it. "Shall we enter?" he asked, holding it open a crack.

"Yeah, just a second," Nicole said, frowning at the door. She'd been all through the Q4 arena and had never seen anything like a door handle on any of the walls. If there wasn't an inside handle, and if they went through and let it close behind them, they probably wouldn't be able to get it open again. That would leave only the four main doors as possible exits.

Actually, there might only be *two* doors here. If this arena was arranged like the others, two of the usual doors would be positioned across the ocean.

Besides, those greenfire weapons were up this staircase. That wasn't an option she was ready to give up on quite yet.

On the other hand, even if they figured out a way to sneak in without Fievj spotting them from their eagle perch, a propped-open door would surely catch someone's attention sooner or later.

She started at the sudden sound of tearing cloth. She looked

over to see that Kahkitah had somehow torn a spiral strip from
his jumpsuit sleeve. "Here," he said, handing it to her. "Tie a knot
at one end."

She frowned, taking the cloth. What in the world—?

And then, she got it. Smiling tightly, she tied a double knot in
the end, then doubled it again just to be safe. "Ready?"

"Ready," Kahkitah confirmed.

"Okay." Taking a deep breath, hoping fervently that Fievj was
still talking to the Wisps and not looking into the arena, she
pushed open the door and stepped through.

She'd worried that they would emerge on the beach, completely
open to view from above. Fortunately, their door was farther back,
a little ways in from where the dunes met the trees, a spot that
should be fairly well hidden from the observation balcony. She
slipped through, held the door for Kahkitah, then dropped onto
her knees and set the strip of cloth on the ground with the knot
inside the stairway. Kahkitah had already taken hold of the door,
and now eased it shut, closing the strip into the crack.

Nicole peered up at the edge of the door. The cloth was thin
enough that it didn't block the door very much, though up close
like this she could see a tiny line where the panel didn't quite
close. Hopefully, that crack would be invisible from the Shipmasters' angle and distance.

Now came the real test. Getting a grip on the end of the strip,
she pulled it carefully toward her.

Perfect. The knot eased the door open—not much, just a crack,
but enough. A thin piece of something wedged in there, or maybe
even just the pressure of Ghorf fingers, should let them open it
the rest of the way whenever they wanted.

"It works," Kahkitah said.

"Sure does," Nicole said, letting the door close again and scoop-
ing a couple of handfuls of sand onto the cloth strip.

"Now we find Jeff?" Kahkitah asked as Nicole stood up, brushing the sand off her hands.

"Now we find Jeff," she confirmed. "Might as well start at the hive. Follow me."

The hive was laid out the same way as those in the Q4 arena: a large open door led into a round central area, with pie-piece-shaped rooms coming off the sides like spokes of a wheel. Nicole had expected to find someone on guard duty at the entrance, but there was no one in sight.

Nor did there seem to be anyone else present. Frowning, wondering if she'd figured the whole thing wrong, she started a search of the side rooms.

In the fifth one they tried, they found Jeff.

He was lying on a bed like the ones in their old hive's medical center, his eyes closed. There was a rack of equipment boxes on either side of him, with tubes coming out of them and feeding into his arms.

Kahkitah whistled softly. "Is he—?"

"Where the *hell* did you come from?"

Nicole spun around. Sam was standing beside a worktable, glaring at the two of them.

Sam. Dr. Sam McNair. The doctor Bungie had held up at gunpoint in the VA hospital parking lot, and who'd then been accidentally taken along with her and Bungie when the Wisps swooped in to take Nicole. Sam, who'd never forgiven her for having had his life snatched away from him, despite the fact that not a single shred of it was Nicole's fault.

"What do you mean?" Kahkitah asked, sounding puzzled. "Nicole came from Earth, as did you."

"Shut up, idiot," Sam bit out, his glare still on Nicole. "We thought you were dead. Fallen down a shaft or something."

"Sorry to disappoint you," Nicole said, silently cursing the slight quavering in her voice. Sam didn't scare her—not really—but he was probably going to take her reaction that way anyway.

Judging by the sardonic twitch of his lip, that was exactly how he was taking it. Damn. "Yeah, well, you can't have everything," he growled. "What I *meant*"—he shifted his eyes briefly to Kahkitah—"was where have you been hiding? You make a deal with the Shipmasters for this?" He waved a hand around them.

"Hardly," Nicole said. "This is the last thing I wanted for you."

"Yeah, I'll bet," Sam said.

"Leave her alone," Jeff murmured.

Nicole jerked her head toward him as an enthusiastic whistle filled the room. "You're alive!" Kahkitah crowed. "I was so worried when you were taken away."

"Yeah, nothing gets past *you*," Sam said sourly.

"At least Kahkitah cares," Nicole said, studying Jeff. His eyes were still slits, like someone with a hideous hangover, but at least they were open. His breathing seemed stronger, and there was a hint of a welcoming smile on his lips. "Hey, Jeff," she said.

"Hey, Nicole," he said in return. His voice seemed to be a little stronger this time. "Don't mind Sam. He's just worried about our little upcoming confrontation. What happened to your jumpsuit?"

"What?" Nicole touched her shoulder. "Oh, this? I got shot with a paintball."

"Who's running around with paintball guns?"

"It was in one of the other arenas," Nicole said. "What confrontation?"

"I think you know," Sam said. "We're going to have our own private little war. Thanks to you."

"Thanks to me?"

"The Shipmasters said you'd suggested it," Jeff said. "Which I naturally assumed was a lie."

"They didn't say she *suggested* it," Sam countered. "They said she *instigated* it."

"Maybe that's what they told *you*," Jeff said. "So what's going on?"

Nicole hesitated. The Shipmasters had been able to eavesdrop on the Micawnwi and Cluufe hives. But those bugs had been located with the food dispensers, and there was no dispenser in this particular room.

Outside would be better. But with Jeff hooked up to all those boxes that way, outside was probably out of the question.

She would just have to chance it. "Here goes," she said. "And you're not going to like it."

Jeff and Sam listened in complete silence while she ran through the whole thing. Kahkitah occasionally gave a low whistle which her translator didn't interpret, but otherwise he remained silent, as well.

The silence continued for several seconds after she finished. Jeff broke it first. "Unbelievable," he murmured.

"Yeah, in the original meaning of the word," Sam rumbled. "That has to be the most ridiculous story I've ever heard."

"But it's true," Nicole insisted.

"Who says?" Sam demanded. "The *ship*?"

"Why would it lie?"

"Why *wouldn't* it lie?" Sam countered. "It's a *ship*. Who knows *how* it thinks?"

"Plato believed it," Nicole reminded him.

"And Plato's dead, isn't he?" Sam shot back, his voice lowering ominously. "Some say because of *you*."

With an effort, Nicole forced herself to keep looking into his eyes. Bungie always said she looked away when she was lying, and she didn't dare let Sam get that idea lodged in his head. Especially since it was true. "What else could all this be for?" she asked instead. "They've told you you're going to fight for food, right? What other reason could there be?"

Sam snorted. "Give me a minute. I'll come up with twenty of them."

"Well, while you work on that, let's take Nicole's story as our working hypothesis," Jeff said. "Because it wasn't just Plato who believed that. All the other foremen did, too."

"Some urban myth passed down from one to the other?" Sam scoffed. "Right. If they all thought Elvis was alive, would you believe *that*, too?"

Jeff shook his head tiredly and turned back to Nicole. "So I gather our new strategy is to go out there and *not* fight?"

"Right," Nicole said, feeling a trickle of relief. At least Jeff believed her. "And not just us, but the other team, too."

"Yeah, that could be a bit tricky," Jeff murmured. "They're not going to be easy to reason with."

"Why not?" Nicole asked, frowning. "It's the green group, right? Kahkitah said he saw Iosif down there. Miron's in charge, isn't he?"

"He was when they were just doing repair work," Jeff said. "I assume he's still running things, though maybe he's turned this one over to Iosif. I always had the feeling Iosif had had some military training."

"Doesn't matter," Nicole said. "I've talked to both of them once or twice, and they both seemed reasonable enough."

"That was when they had plenty to eat," Jeff warned. "Who knows what they're like now?"

"I guess we'll just have to go talk to them and find out."

"I guess we will," Jeff agreed. "Sam? Get me out of this, will you?"

"Forget it," Sam said flatly. "You're not going anywhere."

"Oh, yes, I am," Jeff said firmly. "I need to see the kind of terrain we're working with."

"Everyone else is already doing that."

"That was when I thought we were going to fight," Jeff said. "*Not* fighting is a completely different tactical situation. Get these tubes off me, or I'll get out of them myself."

"Damn it, *listen* to me," Sam snapped. "Look. I didn't tell you this, but the only thing that's still got our little war on hold is the fact you're not well enough to fight."

"How do you know?" Jeff asked, frowning.

"The Shipmasters told us," Sam said. "Carp and me. I figure we can stall it another few days, maybe, but *only* if they don't see you walking around out there."

"And they *will* see you," Nicole warned. "There's an observation balcony running around the whole arena, and they're up there now."

"Are they, now?" Jeff said thoughtfully, pursing his lips. "Fine. They want to see a wounded warrior? Let's show them one. Sam, can you rig up one of these racks on rollers or something?"

"You mean like an IV rolling cart?"

"Exactly," Jeff said. "Only let's make it bigger and more impressive. Bells and whistles. Things like that always wow the gallery."

"You want to roll a cart through sand?" Sam countered, making one last attempt. "Because that's all that's out there. Sand, dirt, and rocks. You're not going to get five feet without bogging down or knocking off a wheel."

"Okay, then, skip the wheels." Jeff gestured to Kahkitah. "How about it, Kahkitah? You want to play corpsman?"

Kahkitah looked at Nicole, then back at Jeff. "I'm sorry, but I don't understand."

"I'm asking if you want to carry my life-support gear," Jeff said. "Maybe offer me the occasional arm for support while I hobble around out there."

Kahkitah gave an enthusiastic whistle. "Yes. I can do that."

"Great," Jeff said. "Get over here, Sam." He gave Nicole a tired grin. "Let's get busy and not fight a war."

nine

Nicole had hoped the other members of the group would stay away from the hive until Jeff was ready to go, giving her a little more time to figure out what she was going to say. Her days away from them while she studied the *Fyrantha* hadn't seemed that long to her, but from Jeff's and Sam's reactions—and, earlier, from Kahkitah's—it sounded like her vanishing act had seemed longer from their side of the street.

But as usual, luck wasn't with her. Sam had barely finished getting Jeff's tubes out and was starting to unfasten a couple of the boxes when the whole gang trooped in together.

It went about as well as she'd expected. Carp and Levi, the two men she'd worked most closely with, seemed genuinely happy to see that she was alive and well, though she could also tell that both weren't exactly pleased about her unexplained disappearance and whatever extra hassle it had caused the group. Tomas and Bennett had always blamed her for the continual headache that was Bungie after Plato attached him to the group, and they seemed ready to continue with that grudge. They were polite enough on the surface, though, maybe because Jeff and Carp were watching. Duncan and Joaquim, who had always kept pretty much to themselves, greeted her civilly, then retreated back into their individual shells.

None of them seemed impressed by her explanation of what was really going on behind the scenes aboard the *Fyrantha*. In hindsight, she decided glumly as she studied their stony faces, she should probably have let Jeff tell them about it instead of her.

"So let's say she's right," Carp said, looking at Jeff. "What then?"

"We do our damnedest to come off as complete wusses," Jeff said.

Duncan snorted. "You think Miron's going to go for that?"

"I think we need to persuade him," Jeff said darkly. "Matter of fact, that's where Nicole, Kahkitah, and I are off to right now."

"I don't like it," Levi said. "What if they jump you? They've already got an extra man. We can't afford to lose you."

"You missed the recount," Jeff said, nodding at Kahkitah. "We've got Kahkitah now, remember?"

"We do *now*," Levi said, eyeing the Ghorf. "But if this whole thing is about whether human beings can fight, I doubt they'll let us keep him."

"Which will be evidence enough right there that Nicole's story is on the money," Jeff pointed out. "Aside from all that, if the green group jumps me it'll just postpone the test, right? The Shipmasters already said I need to be healthy before we get started."

"All the more reason *for* them to jump you, as far as I can tell," Bennett said. "I can't see anyone really wanting to go through with this."

"So I just need to make sure they don't," Jeff said.

"Okay, but what if—?"

"Don't bother," Sam interrupted. "He's already made up his mind."

"Only because it needs to be done," Jeff said. Carefully, he swung his legs over the edge of the bed and sat up. He took a couple of slow, deep breaths, and nodded. "Nicole, get me my boots, will you? You ready, Kahkitah?"

"Yes," Kahkitah said. He stepped to Jeff's side and lifted the two boxes Sam had pulled from the rack. "I'm ready."

"Let's do it," Jeff said. He pulled on the boots Nicole gave him and stood up. "And keep an eye on the tubes—we don't want them pulling out along the way. The rest of you stay here and keep an eye out."

"And don't talk near the food dispenser," Nicole said. "The Shipmasters can listen in there."

"I've already warned them about that," Jeff assured her. "Come on, let's see what kind of mood Miron's in today."

The area around the arena hive, as Nicole had already noted, was mostly short, wide trees growing out of ordinary dirt. There was a wide path, dirt with some sort of half-seen rock underneath it, which she'd also noted, leading outward from the hive, presumably to the beach.

What she *hadn't* noticed on the way in was a similar, narrower path leading off the main one and heading up the rocky slope toward the distant stream.

"What's with the river up there?" she asked as she, Jeff, and Kahkitah walked slowly along the main path. "Is there a bridge or something you can get across?"

"Doesn't seem to be," Jeff said. "Joaquim and Bennett climbed up there a couple of days ago. They said the cliff edges are rocky right by the water—dangerous footing—and the river itself twists and turns a little. Lots of white water, too. They couldn't follow it all the way down, but what they could see didn't offer any way across."

"Seems kind of strange to have a river and no way across it."

"Agreed," Jeff said. "On the other hand, it's out of sight for a ways right between the two big bluffs at the ocean's edge. It's possible there's a bridge there."

"Though if it's where you can't get at it, what's the point?"

Jeff shrugged. "Granted."

"So how do you get from one side to the other?" Nicole continued. "Swim?"

"The waves make that pretty dangerous," Jeff said. "But no. The ocean seems to have a full tidal cycle, and at low tide there's a stretch of wet sand about twenty meters wide. Sixty feet. Or so I hear. I haven't been outside that room since we got moved here. You really think they're selling whole worlds' worth of slaves?"

"You don't?" Nicole countered. "Can you think of any other reason they're making people fight each other?"

"They're aliens," Jeff pointed out. "Who knows how they think?"

"No," Nicole said firmly. "This is what the Caretaker said it was. I know it. And we have to figure out how to stop it."

"That's what we're doing."

"I don't mean just stopping it for us," Nicole said. "Or even just for Earth. I mean we have to stop *all* of it. Get the Shipmasters off the *Fyrantha* and bring it back to . . . something. Anything except a warship."

"Can't argue with that," Jeff said. "Just be sure you don't bite off more than you can chew. Personally, right now I'll settle for saving Earth."

"And our own lives?"

"Oh, well, *that* goes without saying."

They passed the line of trees, and the mix of dirt and sand, and started weaving their way through the reeds and dunes. The sand was soft and squishy underfoot, dragging at Nicole's boots as she walked, and the reeds' outer surface had rows of tiny hooks that caught like sticky notes on their jumpsuits if they brushed against them.

For once Sam had been right. A wheeled cart would have been useless out here.

They pushed and slogged another fifty feet or so before the line of reeds thinned out and then stopped, leaving just the sand and the slogging. The roar of the ocean, which had been part of the background noise ever since they'd left the hive, was getting louder. But now Nicole could also hear the periodic wet slapping sounds as the waves hit the rock bluffs at the mouth of the river.

And the memories those sounds brought back weren't happy ones.

"You go to the beach much when you were a kid?" Jeff asked.

"What?" Nicole said. "No. Once. The . . . well, the salt water was yucky, and the sand was always too hot on my feet."

"I used to go all the time," Jeff said. "Or at least as often as I could. Mostly I swam in pools, but we got into the ocean a couple of times each summer. Tried snorkeling and scuba once or twice, but usually just swimming. Don't worry, there won't be any salt taste here—Bennett said it's fresh water—and without a real sun the sand shouldn't ever heat up too much."

"If it's okay with you I'll stay on the dry stuff anyway," Nicole said.

"Actually, it's the dry stuff that's the hottest," Jeff said. "Hardest to walk on, too. But that's fine." He shook his head. "A big flowing river feeding into an ocean with its own tides. I'd love to see the schematics for this place."

"The what?" Nicole asked, frowning.

"Schematics," Jeff repeated. "The plans for this area. How the rooms and wiring and ducts are laid out. See, they have to be recirculating the water somehow—"

"Yeah, okay, I got it," Nicole interrupted, peering ahead. They were close enough to the water to see the line of sticks she'd spotted from the observation deck. Now, close up, she could see they looked like thin branches and small pieces of tree trunks. "What are those?" she asked, pointing.

"Well, on a real beach, that would be driftwood," Jeff said. "Floating debris that came in on the tide. Don't know why it's here—there for sure isn't anywhere for driftwood to come from. Maybe to keep the beach sand from being washed away."

Nicole nodded. Or maybe it was there to give something like crabs or lobsters a place to live. She thought about telling Jeff how the *Fyrantha* had once been a zoo, decided this wasn't the time to get into that. "Maybe you'd better stay here," she said, eyeing the sticks. They were mostly laid out loosely enough to walk around, but a few of them were grouped into bigger tangles. "You don't want to trip and fall."

"I'll be okay," Jeff said. "Looks like the tide's already going out. See how far past the waves the wet sand goes?"

"What?" Nicole frowned at the sand. Then she got it: the waves weren't reaching as high onto the wet sand, which meant they'd been reaching higher earlier, which meant the water level was going down. "Oh—right. And you said it goes down another sixty feet?"

"The water only goes down a few feet, but dropping to that level opens up sixty feet of sand," Jeff corrected. "Or so I'm told. But one of the things they hammered into us in the Marines was always take intel with a light grip until you can confirm it yourself."

"So where down there is the extra food dispenser?"

Jeff's toe caught on the sand, sending him into a brief stumble. "I'm impressed," he said as he recovered his balance. "How did you know it was there?"

Nicole shrugged. "Where else would it be? You already said no one can cross the river."

"Well, *they* say that," Jeff murmured. "Like I said, I'm reserving judgment until I confirm it myself. But, yeah, the only reasonable place for the two sides to meet—and fight—is here on the beach. Nice bit of logic."

"Thanks," Nicole said, feeling her face warming. Getting a compliment from Jeff—especially on something that was just her thinking—felt better than she'd expected.

Trake had never complimented her on anything except how well she could use her body as a distraction during a job. Bungie's comments had always been more like insults than compliments. None of the rest of the gang had really cared one way or the other.

"So to answer your question, it's built into the bluff on the other side of the river," Jeff continued. "Only about a foot up, so it's underwater most of the time. I don't know if that's something the Shipmasters put in especially for their battles, or whether it was original equipment."

"Doesn't really matter," Nicole said. "The point is that the only time we can get to it, the green team can, too. Unless you can open it up underwater?" she added as that thought suddenly struck her.

"I don't know," Jeff said thoughtfully. "Definitely something we should check on. Okay, watch your footing—I don't know if the waves are uniform, or whether there might be sneakers."

"Right," Nicole said, shivering. She hadn't heard that name before, but she was all too familiar with that kind of unexpectedly violent wave. They reached the edge of the water; keeping one eye on the waves, she peered as far around the bluff as she could.

Which wasn't very far. The ocean was still coming at least three or four feet up the side of the rock, leaving the dispenser underwater and not giving her a view of anything on the far side. "I guess we'll have to wait," she said. "How long before it goes down far enough—?"

"Did you feel that?" Kahkitah spoke up suddenly. "Nicole, did you feel that?"

"Feel what?" Nicole asked, her skin suddenly crawling. Were there bugs out here? Had Kahkitah felt a bug land on him?

"A door opened," Kahkitah said. "A door like the ones we've traveled through many times today. I felt the warmer air come over us."

"What's he talking about?" Jeff asked.

"The *Fyrantha's* got a bunch of back doors," Nicole gritted out, looking frantically around. "Which door was it? Where?'"

"I think it was the one we came in through. Or another nearby."

So Shipmasters or Wisps, and either one was trouble. "You're sure it was *this* side of the river?"

"Yes." Kahkitah straightened up. "I'll protect you, Nicole," he said, his birdsong going dark and almost menacing. "They won't harm you while I live."

Which unfortunately wouldn't be very long if the Shipmasters had brought greenfire weapons. "Jeff—"

"I know," Jeff said. "Damn."

"We have to get out of here. If they get to me—"

"I said I *know*," Jeff said. "Can you swim?"

"Can I—? No."

"Well, you're going to have to learn, and fast," Jeff said. "But don't panic—the water's only three or four feet deep near the bluff, so there's no chance of drowning. The catch is that you're going to have to stay underwater as much as you can or they'll spot you."

Nicole looked helplessly at the water. The thought of getting in there—of putting her head right into it where she couldn't breathe—

"It's that or let them catch you," Jeff said. "You'll also need to keep your eyes open so you can see where you're going."

"I don't know," Nicole said, her voice starting to tremble. "I don't . . ."

"You want me to come with you?" Jeff offered.

"Or I can," Kahkitah added.

Nicole took a deep breath. "You're still injured," she told Jeff. "And *you're* still supposed to be helping him," she added to Kahkitah. "I'm the one they want. I can do this." She took another deep breath. "If they ask where I went—I don't know. Make something up."

Before either of them could raise another objection—and before she had time to think it through—she walked out into the ocean.

The first step, the one that brought the waves against her boots, was fine. The second—the one that sent the water into her shins, through her jumpsuit legs, and over the tops of her boots onto her feet—made her gasp with shock. The water was a *lot* colder than she'd expected.

But she couldn't stop now. She kept going, aiming for the edge of the bluff. The water reached her knees—her thighs—she gasped a second time as the cold slapped into her stomach—

"Go!" Jeff called from behind her.

Squeezing her eyes shut, Nicole bent at the waist, put her hands out in front of her like she'd seen divers do on television, and shoved off the ground into the waves.

She thought she'd been prepared for this. She was wrong. Not just for the shock of hitting the water face-first, but the wave of panic as it closed over her head and pressed up into her nostrils. For that first horrifying instant she was back at her one and only beach experience, rushing carelessly toward the surf, a sudden huge wave surging unexpectedly over her head and crashing her down as it filled her mouth and eyes with salt and sand. It was all she could do to keep from clawing her way to the surface and letting loose with a scream of terror.

But she didn't dare. Behind her were the Wisps, and the heat-transfer ducts, and an even more horrifying death.

Besides, in that first terrifying second she wasn't sure she *could* get out of this. Her waterlogged jumpsuit was weighing her down, dragging her into the depths of the ocean. She flailed her hands desperately, trying to remember what her grandmother had told her about swimming all those years ago—

It was yet another shock when she'd barely started sinking when her flailing hands hit the bottom.

And as suddenly as it had appeared, the panic vanished. Of *course* she was on the bottom—Jeff had already said the water was only three or four feet deep. She could stand up at any time and be clear of it.

And with that, she could finally focus on getting clear of the danger behind her. Bracing herself, she opened her eyes.

Like the ocean itself, it wasn't as bad as she'd expected. The image was blurry, and the water felt strange against her eyeballs. But she could see, and that was what she needed. Pressing her hands and feet against the bottom, she started pushing herself along.

At first, all she seemed to accomplish was to shove the sand out of the way. But the sand layer turned out to be only a couple of inches thick, with a more solid floor beneath it. Once she was pushing on that, she started making real progress, especially since the waves didn't seem as strong down here as they were on the surface.

But she wasn't in the clear yet. Her lungs were starting to hurt, and there was still the river mouth to get past. She thought about coming up long enough for a quick breath, decided that would be a good way to get grabbed, and kept going.

The river, when she reached it, was pretty intense. But like the waves, the turbulence seemed lower than she expected, certainly less than it had looked from the observation balcony. Maybe when the river hit the ocean and started spreading out it lost some of its punch. She got past it; and then there was only the second bluff between her and safety.

Her lungs were burning by the time she made it around the base of the bluff. She went as far past it as she could, then angled back toward the shore. The waves again started pounding at her as she came into the shallower water—

And then, suddenly, her head poked through the waves. She shook the water away from her face, puffed the last remaining air from her lungs, and took a shuddering breath.

She kept going, gulping in more air, staying flat and pushing her way through. She reached the beach and stumbled to her feet, slogging through more sand as she headed away from the water. Her wet jumpsuit dragged at her, and the sand now clinging to her boots and legs added to the weight.

But she'd done it. She'd done it.

At least for now. She couldn't see anything around the far side of the bluff—not Jeff, Kahkitah, or any Wisps. The question now was whether the Shipmasters were still watching from above her, and if they were how fast could they get themselves or more Wisps to this side of the arena.

Eventually, it would probably come down to getting caught or slipping out one of the arena doors. Which would probably only give her a choice of where else in Q1 she got caught.

One crisis at a time. She reached the reeds and wove her way through them, trying to figure out her next move. Her number one goal had been to escape from the Wisps, with everything past that a bit vague.

Still, if she could find Miron and Iosif and persuade the green group not to fight, maybe they could all sit down and figure out how to work together against the Shipmasters.

How she was going to get them on her side was another one of those vague future things she didn't quite have worked out.

But at least she was about to leave the Shipmasters' view. She passed the edge of the reeds and walked in under the trees—

"Gotcha!" a triumphant voice came in her ear as a hand closed around her upper arm.

Nicole twisted around, snapping her arm up to try to break her attacker's grip. But he knew that trick, and had a solid hold, and all she accomplished was to pull him briefly off balance.

At least it wasn't Fievj. That had been her first terrified thought before her brain caught up enough to realize that wasn't the Shipmaster's voice. Instead, her attacker turned out to be a black-haired man with dark eyes and a craggy face, dressed in a green jumpsuit, whose hand as he gripped her arm looked like it was twice as big as hers. "Oh, hi," she said, automatically dropping into the cheerful, friendly, brainless mode that she'd learned was the best way to greet a new and possibly dangerous face. "I'm Nicole. Who are you?"

He blinked. Apparently, that wasn't the reaction he'd expected. But he recovered quickly. "Who are *you?*" he demanded. "Where'd you come from?"

"I'm Nicole," Nicole said again. "I'm—well, I *was*—the blue group's Sibyl."

"The blue group?" the man countered, looking pointedly down at her jumpsuit.

"Yes, I—" Nicole broke off in bewilderment as she followed

his gaze. Her nice, blue outfit had somehow turned pure black. "I—*what?*"

"You got it wet," the man said, a little less belligerently. "Ours go pretty dark, too. I'm Gregor with the green team. What are you doing here?"

"I came to talk to Miron," Nicole said. "Could you let go? You're hurting me."

Gregor took a moment to think about it. Then, a little reluctantly, he let go of her arm. "Don't know if the boss wants to talk to *you*," he said. "But come on. Let's find out."

Nicole had spent a lot of time in the Q4 arena, and she'd noted that the two halves there were slightly different, with different layouts of trees and bushes and paths. It was the same way here in Q1, with more hills and less sand on the green team side of the river than on Jeff's. There were also two paths up the cliffs toward the river, instead of just one, both of them twisting and turning enough through the trees that she couldn't see more than a dozen feet along either of them.

There were three more green-jumpsuited men sitting on the ground near the hive entrance when she and Gregor arrived, all of them working on long, slender sticks with small rocks. All three looked up as Nicole and Gregor came into view through the trees. "Who's that?" one of them called.

"Nicole," Gregor called back. "Blue team's Sibyl." He gave a little snorting bark of a laugh. "She's here to see the boss."

"Oh, *this* I gotta see," the man said. He laid down his stick and rock and stood up, brushing the dirt from his butt. "This way, darlin'."

Nicole bristled. She'd always hated pet names like that, especially coming from people who barely even knew her. But this wasn't the time to make a fuss. Gregor led her through the door, and a glance over her shoulder showed the three others had joined up behind them. "Boss?" Gregor called as he led her toward the food dispenser room. "Got a visitor."

Nicole braced herself, hoping she would recognize Miron when he came out. There were few things more embarrassing—and dangerous—than getting a gang leader's name wrong or mixing him up with someone else. There was a shuffling of feet, and as they reached the door a man stepped out of the room into view.

Only it wasn't Miron or Iosif or any of the other green group members she could remember seeing. It was—

"I'll be damned," Bungie said, his surprised expression dropping instantly into a leer. "Look who finally came crawling back."

For that first agonizing second Nicole couldn't speak. She could barely even breathe. Bungie was the green team's boss? *Bungie?*

She'd thought he was gone from her life. She'd *hoped* he was gone her life. The last time she'd seen him had been when he'd tried to run out on Plato's death sentence. Nicole had helped with that, partly out of disagreement with Plato's decision, partly out of the fading nostalgia that connected Bungie to the world she'd been snatched from.

But his escape had been ended almost before it started when Fievj suddenly appeared and hauled him away. At the time Nicole had been too preoccupied with rescuing Jeff from the Cluufes—and was frankly just as happy to have Bungie alive but out of everyone's hair—to wonder what the Shipmasters might want with him.

Now, too late, it was obvious.

Plato and all the other foremen had worked hard to keep human aggression a secret from the Shipmaster. But Bungie didn't know about that. Even if he had, he liked bragging about his fights and scores way too much to keep quiet.

Which meant that in a single week—hell, probably in a single afternoon—Bungie had ruined everything.

"So you come here to beg, or what?" Bungie asked. His leering smile went all sly and knowing. "Or you got something else in mind?"

Nicole hesitated. She'd come here with the intent of talking Miron out of fighting. Even with a change in leadership she might still be able to do that, though her approach would have to be totally different.

But she couldn't do it here. Not in front of the dispenser room and the listening ear the Shipmasters almost certainly had there. "Let's take a walk," she suggested, nodding back toward the arena.

"Why, so that they don't hear the deal?" Bungie demanded, stabbing a finger at the other green group members. "You figure they'll all want a piece if they do?"

Nicole sighed. She should have remembered how obstinate Bungie was with anything that wasn't his idea. She would just have to go with the one way that always worked. She braced herself . . .

And spinning around, she ducked past the men behind her and made a dash for the door.

She probably could have outrun them. But that wasn't the point. She got through the door, continued on for a few steps, then stopped and turned and waited for them to catch up.

They came pounding through the door, Gregor and the other three crowded together in a bunch, Bungie bringing up the rear. The main group slowed as they saw that Nicole had stopped, but Bungie either didn't notice or didn't care. He charged straight through the pack, nearly bowling over Gregor as he passed. For a second, Nicole thought he was going to run straight over her, too, but at the last second he braked to a halt. "You think that was cute, bitch?"

"It's a nice day," Nicole said. "I thought we could get out in the sunshine for a bit."

"Don't pull that crap on *me*," Bungie snarled. "There's no *outside* here. Any idiot knows that."

"Ah," Nicole said. Which was pretty unfair, given that Bungie had been firmly convinced forever that the arenas were pieces of Earth. "Well, it's *sort* of sunshine. Look, what I wanted to tell you was that we don't have to fight. We really don't. There's plenty of food, and anyway I can get us out of here anytime you want—"

"What are you babbling about?" Bungie demanded. "What's food got to do with it?"

"The food," Nicole said, frowning. Hadn't he been paying attention? "The reason the Shipmasters want you to fight the blue group. There's another dispenser that you can get to when the ocean goes away—"

"We're not going to fight over *food*," Bungie cut her off. "What gave you that idea? The ship's got lots of food."

"I know," Nicole said, thoroughly lost now. "Then what— I mean, how did the Shipmasters talk you into this?"

"How do you think?" Bungie said with strained patience. "If we wipe out your side, they'll send us home."

A horrible feeling bubbled into Nicole's gut. "You mean back to the hive?" she asked carefully.

"I mean *home*," Bungie said, jabbing a forefinger toward the floor at his feet. "*Real* home.

"Earth."

ten

Nicole stared at him, her mind spinning like that park merry-go-round that had once made her sick. Was that possible? Plato had said it wasn't. He'd said so over and over. But Plato had lied about a lot of things.

After all this time, *was* it possible to go back home?

Once—a lifetime ago—she would have refused an offer like that. Life aboard the *Fyrantha* had been so much simpler and safer than the Philadelphia streets, and she'd actually begun to enjoy it.

But that was before she learned how she was being poisoned, and before the *Fyrantha* decided she was its Protector and saddled her with the job of taking the ship back from Fievj and his friends. Now, if she was offered the chance to go home, would she take it?

And then, she took a second look at Bungie's face. At his earnest, gleeful, smarmy, eager expression. Fievj had told him he could go home, and Bungie really, truly believed it, right to the center of his heart.

Only Nicole knew his record of believing things people told him, especially things that looked like they were going to bring him something he wanted. And she knew how seldom those offers and promises turned out to be true.

No, there was no going home. Plato had been right. The Shipmasters needed humans to repair the ship, and they weren't simply going to let them leave. A half-remembered image flashed through her mind: something involving Israelis and Egyptian pyramids and someone named Moses . . .

"What the hell did you get into?" Bungie broke into her thoughts.

Nicole blinked, the image of half-built pyramids vanishing. "What?"

"That," Bungie said, pointing to her shoulder. "What *is* that stuff?"

Nicole craned her neck. With her jumpsuit drying out, it was starting to change color back from black to its normal blue. As it did, the yellow of the Ejbof's paintball shot was also becoming visible. "It's nothing," she said, looking back at Bungie and that painfully eager expression. Fievj had simply figured out what Bungie wanted most, and fed him the right line of bull to get him to do what they needed. "Look—"

"Bungie!" A distant voice drifted out to them from the hive.

Nicole caught her breath. She knew that voice: it was the Oracle, the name the Shipmasters used when they talked to the people in the arenas. "Bungie! Speak to me!"

"Yeah, keep your shorts on!" Bungie called back. He swept a hand around the four other men, exactly the same way Trake used to pick out people for some job. "Watch her. I'll be right back."

He headed into the hive, hurrying even while he tried not to look like he was. The Oracle had summoned him, but he couldn't afford to let his men think he was being bossed around. Another of Trake's little quirks.

Mentally, Nicole shook her head. Trake had made this leadership stuff look so easy.

"Never seen anything like this," Gregor commented, stepping

closer to Nicole. He peered at her shoulder, then ran a finger gently across it. "Sure not a lubricant. Some kind of sealant?"

"I thought all the sealants were transparent," one of the other men said.

"They are in *our* section," Gregor agreed. "Who knows what they've got over here?"

Bungie had reached the dispenser room, and Nicole watched as he disappeared inside. "They're lying to you," Nicole said urgently to her companions, keeping an eye on the door. This might be her only chance to talk sense into them before Bungie came back and yelled or bullied them back onto his side. "There's no way back. Even if there was, they need us too much to let any of us leave."

"They're not going to let *everyone* go," another of the men said with Bungie's same strained patience. "Just the winners."

"To let *any* of us leave," Nicole repeated, leaning on the word. "You're being set up. We're all being set up. The Shipmasters—they like watching people fight," she said, switching explanations at the last second. The real truth would take too long, and this was close enough.

"Well, they should get a great show, then," Gregor growled. "That twerp—what's his name? Right—Carp. I still owe him for the time he shut down Ezana's music and threw us out of the dining room. Looking forward to taking that evening out of his hide."

"You're not listening," Nicole gritted out. "You can't fight. *We* can't fight. If we do . . . it'll be bad. Trust me, it'll be very, very bad. For everyone."

"Only for your side," Gregor said. "Bungie's told us some of the stuff he pulled in Philadelphia. With him in charge, we're gonna run over you like mice over cheese."

"I wouldn't believe everything Bungie says if I were you," Nicole growled. "He was more on the *getting* end than the *giving* end. Look, you've got to believe me. If we fight we *all* lose—"

"We're on!" Bungie's voice boomed. A second later he reappeared from the dispenser room, striding back toward them like he owned the whole ship. "Finally—they're gonna give us some weapons. Some *real* ones, not these damn stick things. Gregor, Bellic"—he pointed at Gregor and one of the others—"come with me. Cole, Fauke, you stay with her. And don't let her go—the Oracle said they're sending someone to pick her up. Come on— let's see what they've got for us."

Bungie and the other two headed off through the grass and trees, aiming toward the big door leading from the arena to the rest of the ship.

"Hope it's something good," one of Nicole's guards said. "Maybe one of those laser guns Bungie told us about."

"Dream on, Cole," the other—Fauke—said sourly. "I wouldn't trust most of us with even sharp knives." He raised his eyebrows toward Nicole. "Or was Bungie lying about *that,* too?"

Nicole braced herself, pushing back the reflexive annoyance. Why couldn't she get them to understand?

But this was her chance. Maybe her last chance. With only two of them here, and with Bungie gone, she might be able to get through. Once Bungie had weapons, especially if they were really *good* weapons, he'd be able to use threats as well as promises to get the green group to follow him down this road to hell.

And if she was going to shock them back to reality, she needed to tell them exactly what that reality was. "Okay," she said. "Here it is—"

She broke off. In the distance behind Cole and Fauke, moving into view from the sandy part of the arena, were a pair of Wisps.

Heading straight toward them.

Reflexively, she eased backward. "Hold it," Cole growled, taking a quick step toward her in response. "Bungie said you're to stay put."

Nicole clenched her teeth. Bungie had said that the Oracle was sending someone to pick her up. But she'd assumed that meant Fievj or another Shipmaster would be clanking his way in. Were the Wisps the ones who got jobs like that in this part of the *Fyrantha*?

Or were the Wisps running completely on their own?

And *that* was a very nasty thought. Ushkai had said that the ship was broken, with four separate parts where there should have been only one. He'd defined those parts as controlling the Wisps, the guidance system, the Sibyls, and Ushkai himself.

But maybe it wasn't quite as simple as that. Nicole had assumed that the Wisps in Q1 were under Shipmaster control, despite what Ushkai had said . . . but what if there was a broken part of the *Fyrantha* itself that was running them? In that case, it might not be the Shipmasters who wanted her dead, but this part of the *Fyrantha*.

She was barely staying ahead of Fievj. How in hell could she stay ahead of Fievj *and* a whole quarter of the *Fyrantha*?

Maybe she was jumping at noisy rats. Maybe all of Q1 *wasn't* against her, and those Wisps coming toward her were just following Fievj's orders.

But however it untangled, the fact was that they were coming for her, and she had damn well better be somewhere else when they got here.

And that was looking more and more like it wasn't going to happen. Even if she could figure out where to run, Cole and Fauke were big, strong men, and they were watching her like hawks.

Watching *her* like hawks.

Keeping her eyes focused on people in front of her while at the same time watching what was going on in the background was a trick she'd mastered early in life. Casually, she took a step to her right.

"Hey," Cole warned.

"Look, I'm not kidding," Nicole said. Sure enough, both Wisps had shifted direction in response to her movement. Not much, but enough to show that they were definitely aiming for her.

Now came the tricky part. "The Shipmasters want to see us kill each other," she said, easing her way back a bit to the left. "And just because Bungie makes it through okay doesn't mean you two will." She eased a little more to the left, watching the Wisps again shift in response.

"What did I just tell you?" Cole growled. He took a step toward her and grabbed her wrist. "Stay *put*, damn it."

"Do you *really* not get it?" Nicole demanded. The Wisps were almost on top of them, the faint sound as they brushed a couple of the reeds covered up by the roar of the ocean in the distance behind them. One of them had pulled slightly into the lead as the other fell back a bit. Maybe the Shipmasters or whoever was running Q1 had seen Kahkitah's maneuver and didn't want the Wisps to get knocked around with a single attack. "Bungie's just fine with getting the rest of you killed as long as he gets what he wants."

"Yeah, that's kind of what we figured," Fauke said. "He's already talking about hanging back—like a *real* general, he says—while we do all the fighting."

"Like we're going to let him do *that*," Cole added.

Fifteen feet to go. The Wisps raised their arms, getting ready to wrap them around Nicole and freeze her where she stood.

"Good luck with that," Nicole said. She took a small step to her right to line up the lead Wisp with Cole, making sure she didn't put any pressure on the hand loosely holding her wrist. The last thing she could afford was for Cole to think she was trying to pull away and tighten his grip. "In fact, good luck with *everything*—"

On that last word, with the lead Wisp's hands now two feet behind Cole, she twisted her arm up and against Cole's thumb, wrenching her wrist out of his hold.

He snarled something and lunged toward her—

And froze as the outstretched Wisp arms, aiming for Nicole, wrapped instead around the man standing in its path.

The other Wisp was still on the move. Nicole darted toward Fauke, who was staring wide-eyed in stunned disbelief at his friend and the Wisp, then ducked around his left side to put him between her and the other attacker. Fauke broke his paralysis in time to make a lunge for her.

And locked up in that position, the stunned expression likewise stuck midway on its way to anger, as the second Wisp grabbed him.

Nicole had no idea how long it would take for the Wisps, the Shipmasters, or the *Fyrantha* itself to recognize the mistake. She also had no intention of hanging around long enough to find out. The Wisp had barely settled into its grip on Fauke when she ducked around him and sprinted as fast as she could through the sand toward the ocean.

Toward the ocean, but not *to* it. There might be more of the green team in her way, and even if there weren't there might be more Wisps over on Jeff's side of the river. What she needed was a place to go to ground for a while and hope that the chase would die down.

And there was only one place she could think of that might offer her that chance.

She forced herself to pass the first trail that led up into the hills. The lure of a quick way out of sight was achingly strong, but she knew Bungie would think the same way and she had to at least try to throw him a curve or two. Fortunately, she reached the second trail without being spotted. Ducking between the two bushes flanking the path, she crouched low and headed up. Five seconds later, she passed the first curve and disappeared from sight.

At least she was no longer visible from the beach. Whether the Shipmasters watching from their sky perch could see her as she ducked under and around the trees she didn't know. But at least here among the trees, rock stacks, and other obstacles she would have a chance of dodging any new Wisps that Fievj might send after her.

Though dodging and quick maneuvering were starting to get more and more iffy. The terrain was getting harder as she continued upward. Some of the trees had branches at the bases of their trunks that edged onto the path, while the rock stacks along the trail were also becoming less firm, with chips and broken pieces of stone scattered across the ground and path. The noise from the river ahead was getting louder, rivaling and then completely masking the more rhythmic roar of the ocean, and Nicole was starting to feel occasional patches of cool mist against her face.

She remembered one of her teachers talking about how flowing or splashing water could break down rocks, sometimes hitting hard enough to turn them into sand. Maybe that was what was happening to the rock stacks here.

The noise was getting louder, and the path was getting steeper and rockier. The trees were crowding around her, making it difficult to walk, but at the same time providing plenty of branches she could use to pull herself up the slope. Above, the leaves on the intertwined branches were almost completely blocking the sky and, hopefully, the Shipmasters' view. Ahead, the path seemed to dip out of sight—

And suddenly, she was there.

For a long moment she just hung on to her last two branches, gazing down at the churning white water. She'd seen pictures of rivers like this in school, and some movies had had them, but she'd never seen one herself. Not up close. The roar in her ears— the spray of water on her face and hands—the violence of water being ripped apart by the rocks or whatever else was underneath the surface—it was fascinating and awesome and terrifying all at the same time.

Slowly, she raised her eyes from the roiling water to the opposite side. To the riverbank she had to get to if she was going to escape from Bungie.

The riverbank that was a good fifteen feet away.

Jeff had said the river couldn't be crossed. But he'd also said that he hadn't confirmed that for himself. Nicole, for her part, had assumed—or maybe just hoped—that the spot where the river emptied into the ocean would be its widest part.

Jeff had been right. She'd been wrong.

She couldn't see through the foam how deep the river was. But it hardly mattered. She *could* see how fast it was flowing, and unless it was no more than ankle deep there was no way she could wade through it without getting her feet knocked out from under her and falling in.

Her earlier ocean crossing had been bad enough. Getting dragged down the hills by thundering white water would be terrifying. If there were any kind of sharp rocks hidden under the surface, it might also be fatal.

She looked around, hoping there might be a cave or burrow or someplace where she could do some quick camouflage and disappear while she thought up a new plan. But it was all just trees and rocks and steep ground, good for ducking and dodging but not for hiding.

She clenched her teeth, looking at the river again. If it was deep enough, could she hide beneath the surface? But no. She'd need something solid to hold on to to keep from getting swept downstream to the ocean. There might be some rocks under the surface she could use to brace her feet, but there was no way to know where they might be without getting in.

Besides, there weren't any hollow reeds nearby, like people in movies always used to breathe through when they were hiding underwater.

But she couldn't give up. Not with an angry Bungie somewhere down there tearing up his side of the arena looking for her. Certainly not with Wisps who were probably already on their way.

If she couldn't cross here, maybe there was another spot where the river was narrower. Down by the bluffs near the ocean, maybe, where she and Jeff had guessed there might be a bridge?

Better yet, maybe up where the river came through the arena wall. There might be a spot either on the inlet pipe or on the wall itself where she could work her way across.

She peered that direction. The ground sloped upward at even more of an angle than she'd faced in order to get to the river in the first place, and the sight alone sent a fresh ache through tired arms and legs. No wonder the water was rushing as fast as it was.

But there was nothing else to try. Resettling her fingers on the branches she was gripping, wondering how close she dared get to the edge of the river before she risked slipping on a wet rock and falling in, she started upward.

She'd gotten three steps when a distant birdlike whistle seemed to weave its way through the roar of the water.

She paused, peering up the slope. Were there birds in here? She hadn't noticed any earlier. She looked downslope behind her, still not seeing anything.

And abruptly it clicked. *Birdlike?* She spun back around toward the opposite riverbank.

There they were: Kahkitah, Carp, and Duncan, standing well back from the river's edge, holding tree branches and waving their arms to try to get her attention.

Nicole waved back, a flood of relief flowing over her.

A relief that just as quickly disappeared. She was on this side, they were on that side, and there was an impassible river between them.

She was trying to figure out how to tell them that when Kahkitah reached his arm over his shoulder and threw something toward her.

Reflexively, she ducked, nearly losing her footing as her balance shifted. The object shot across the river in a shallow arc; and she had just enough time to notice that it was pulling a slender rope behind it when it crashed into the tree branches just over her head. She frowned up at it.

To find that what Kahkitah had just thrown at her was the top section of one of the medical center's crutches, and that the rope tied to it was the plastic tubing from one of the oxygen tanks.

She looked across the river again. *You're kidding*, she mouthed.

Either they couldn't understand what she was trying to tell them or else they didn't care. Duncan was busy pantomiming someone pushing something over and down, while Carp was pointing repeatedly at the tree beside her.

Nicole got the tubing between her hands and gave it a tentative tug. It was thick enough that she could easily hold on to it, and it certainly seemed strong enough to handle her weight.

But even if it was, she was no good at tying knots. How was she supposed to tie this to one of the trees without risking it coming loose?

Duncan was still jabbing his hand downward, and pointing to the tubing. Frowning, Nicole took another look at the crutch top. She'd used a set of those crutches once, and she knew how sturdy they were. She could also see that the tubing had been tied *very* securely around it by someone who knew what he was doing.

Duncan was pointing down. Carp was pointing at the tree . . .

She nodded as she finally understood. About waist high the trunk split into four parts, each of which then stretched upward with all the branches and leaves and stuff she'd already seen. Duncan and Carp were telling her to wedge the crutch top and tubing in where it wouldn't come out easily.

It took her two tries to get the thing set properly. She gave the tubing a good solid tug, proving to herself that it wouldn't simply break or untie itself, then gave a thumbs-up to the group across the river. Carp gave her a thumbs-up in return and then beckoned her toward them. Beside her, the tube went taut as Kahkitah wrapped the other end around his big hands and leaned backward, bracing himself against the side of another tree. Taking a deep breath, Nicole got a solid grip around the tubing and stepped into the river.

And instantly fell in up to her chest as the current knocked her feet out from under her.

Somehow, she managed to keep her grip on the tubing. Fighting for balance on the rocks below, feeling her feet and legs already starting to go numb with the cold, she managed to get back up on the riverbank. She unlocked her fingers from the tubing and looked across at the others.

She couldn't tell from their expressions whether they were relieved that she hadn't been carried off down the river or disappointed that she'd fallen in the first place. For a moment they held an inaudible conversation, and then Carp looked back at her and held his arm up, hooking the elbow downward as he pointed at the tubing.

Nicole made a face. But she still had to get across, and at least in that position she wouldn't have to worry about losing her grip.

Hooking her left elbow over the tubing and gripping her left wrist with her right hand, she again stepped into the water.

The current was as strong as ever, but this time she was ready for it and managed to keep her balance. She blinked away a sudden cloud of spray and started across.

She fell twice more before she reached the other bank, but both times she was able to get her feet back under her and keep going. Even better, with her higher grip on the tube the water only came up to her waist.

Still, she was shivering violently by the time Carp and Duncan grabbed her arms and pulled her up the bank. "You all right?" Carp shouted to her.

"If we get moving before Bungie gets here," she shouted back.

Carp's eyes widened. "*Bungie?*"

"Long story," Nicole said. "Come on, let's get out of here."

eleven

"I don't believe it," Jeff growled, once again stretched out on his bed in the makeshift medical room. "They put *Bungie* in charge of their squad?"

"Not sure it was their idea," Nicole said. "I got the feeling the Shipmasters pushed him on them."

"Well, if he brings the same effort to fighting as he does to *real* work, we've got nothing to worry about," Levi said.

"This *is* his real work," Nicole growled. "Or as real as work gets for him. Fighting and trying to con people are his big things."

"I assume he's mostly going to do the latter," Carp said. "So what do we do?"

"I don't know," Nicole confessed. "He seems to have everyone over there convinced he can win no matter what weapons they give us."

"*Can* he?" Jeff asked quietly.

Nicole swallowed. "I don't know that, either."

For a moment no one spoke. "Okay," Jeff said at last. "I think I convinced the Shipmasters that I still need a couple more days to recover before I can handle any serious exercise. We've got that long to come up with something."

"Can we convince them you need longer?" Carp asked.

"You were there," Jeff reminded him. "Did they *look* like they could be fooled more than a couple more days?"

"I wasn't thinking about fooling them," Carp said. "I was thinking more like if you happened to break your leg or something—"

"No," Nicole snapped. "Absolutely not."

"Not so fast," Jeff said, his tone thoughtful. "He might have a point. If I can't lead our side, they might forget the whole thing."

"No," Nicole said again. "They're here to make money off slave soldiers, and now they've got it stuck in their heads that they've had a whole crop of them under their noses this whole time. They're not going to give up the game just because they've lost one of their players."

"But not just one of their players, one of their *key* players," Jeff countered. "Remember, you and I are the only ones they've seen fight."

"You two and Bungie," Levi murmured.

"Actually, I'm not sure they've seen Bungie do anything but talk," Nicole said, frowning. An odd idea was starting to come together . . . "Jeff, remember Plato tried to convince them that you and I were different somehow, and that normal humans couldn't fight. Maybe we can still go that direction."

"I thought you said the green group probably wouldn't be willing to play ball," Carp reminded her.

Nicole braced herself. "I wasn't planning to give them a choice."

"Whoa," Levi said cautiously. "You're not suggesting we sneak over there at night and break *their* legs, are you?"

"I was thinking of something a little safer," Nicole said. "Like maybe putting something in their food."

"What kind of something?"

"I don't know," Nicole said. "Something to make them dizzy or uncoordinated. I don't know what kinds of drugs would do that."

"You think you could get it into their food?"

Nicole nodded. "I know I could."

"Into their food," Jeff said, "*and* into ours."

The others' mouths dropped. "In *our* food?" Levi demanded.

"You're not serious," Carp added.

"Think about it," Jeff said. "We all need to show the same symptoms if we're going to convince them that humans react like rabbits to the thought of fighting." He looked at Nicole. "This has got some possibilities. Let's follow it a second and see where it leads. Do you know what kind of drugs might be aboard and where they would be kept?"

"No, but I can find out," Nicole said. "One problem: I have to get back to Q4, and that means getting past the Shipmasters and Wisps on Q1. Maybe Q2, too, if they've figured out how to take control of that group."

There was a soft bird warble. "May I help?" Kahkitah asked, almost shyly.

"Of course," Nicole assured him, feeling a little ashamed of having ignored him through the whole conversation. When the big Ghorf didn't move or speak for a while, it was oddly easy to forget he was even there. "I might need you to kick more Wisps out of my way."

"You've been punting *Wisps*?" Jeff asked, frowning. "You didn't mention that one."

"It's a little complicated," Nicole said. "Right now, I need to know if you've run into any buckets around here."

"Buckets?" Carp asked.

"Or something else that can hold a lot of water," Nicole said. "This big yellow splotch on my shoulder makes me pretty visible. Getting the jumpsuit wet made everything turn black."

"Yeah, we noticed that," Levi said. "But they'll still recognize your face, won't they?"

"I don't know," Nicole said. "But I can't do anything about my face. I *can* make the jumpsuit color go away."

"How were you planning to get out of here?" Jeff asked. "Through one of the main doors?"

"That's probably what they'll expect me to do," Nicole said. "Luckily, there's another choice. Kahkitah and I came down from the Shipmaster observation balcony above the arena, which is where I left the Q2 Wisps who brought us over here. I'm thinking that's the way we'll go out."

"Assuming the Wisps are still there," Levi murmured.

"And assuming the Shipmasters aren't," Carp added.

Nicole winced. "Yeah, that could be a problem," she conceded.

"Well, either way, you don't want a bucket," Jeff said.

"I just told you—"

"Because if you're dripping water you'll be leaving puddles and wet footprints the whole the way."

Nicole stopped, feeling her face warming. "Oh. Right. Damn."

"That doesn't mean we can't get you wet," Jeff assured her. "It just means we don't completely soak you."

"Right," Nicole said. "So . . . just a spray from the water tap in the food dispenser room?"

"Or we could pat you down with a wet towel or something," Jeff said. "Levi, go see if you can find something she can use, will you?"

"Sure," Levi said. He straightened up from the doorway where he'd been leaning and headed out, turning toward the bathroom area.

"As long as we've got a minute," Jeff went on, "what are the Wisps doing that Kahkitah needs to throw them around?"

"Okay, but *just* a minute," Nicole warned. They had to get going before the Wisps tracked her down. "The thing is that the Wisps

in this part of the *Fyrantha* seem to be under the Shipmasters'
control. A group of them came at us as soon as we got here, and—
well, I'm not sure exactly what they were planning. But I'm pretty
sure they were at least trying to keep me from getting into the
arena."

"Or if you got here, to evict you as fast as they could," Jeff said
thoughtfully. "I assume you're going to take one of the side doors
out of the arena like the one you disappeared through back in
Q4?"

Nicole winced at the memory. She hadn't left through that door
on purpose, but the fact remained that her unexpected depar-
ture had left Jeff alone to face an angry group of aliens. "At
least this time you're—never mind. I was going to say that at least
this time you're safe. Only you aren't, are you?"

"Not so much," Jeff said with a wry smile. "But at least *I* don't
have the Wisps hunting me."

"Maybe not today," Nicole said. "I wouldn't make any bets on
tomorrow, though."

"Neither should they," he countered darkly. "You found something?" he added, his eyes shifting over her shoulder.

Nicole turned to see Levi reappear around the corner, holding
a smooth metal container in one hand and a folded towel in the
other. "Spare collector for the trail mix they've been feeding us,"
he said, lifting the container a couple of inches, "and a towel. Sorry,
the water's pretty cold—the drinking spigot was closer, and it
sounded like you were in a hurry."

"Can't be colder than that river," Nicole assured him, walking
over and taking the towel. "Let's see if this works."

"And while she's doing that," Jeff added, "see if you can scare
up another of those containers and fill it with water."

"You thirsty?" Levi asked, frowning.

"Not exactly," Jeff said, stepping to a cabinet along the wall and opening one of the drawers. "And I need it here by the time Nicole's finished," he added over his shoulder. "So hoof it."

It took more water than Nicole had expected to turn her jumpsuit black, though less than she'd feared. Levi did indeed make it back before she was finished, still frowning, with the container full of water that Jeff had requested.

Jeff accepted Levi's donation with a nod, then went back to whatever he was fiddling with. Nicole tried to see what he was doing, but the table he was working on was just out of her view and she didn't want to drip water any more than she had to.

Finally, she was finished. "How does it look?" she asked, a shiver running through her as she set down the towel and did a slow turn. Levi had been right about the water being cold.

"Good," Jeff said. "I can tell where the yellow splotch is if I look hard, but from any distance it should be invisible. You'd better get going before it starts wearing off."

"Right," Nicole said, moving toward the door. "I'll be back as soon as I can."

"Okay," Jeff called. "Be ready—with luck we'll be able to clear some of the Wisps and Shipmasters away for you."

Nicole frowned. "How?"

"If it works, you'll know," Jeff said. "If it doesn't, I guess you'll be on your own."

"Jeff—"

"We need to go," Kahkitah said, taking her arm. "Thank you, Jeff."

"No problem," Jeff said. "Good luck."

Nicole had been worried that the Wisps who came into the arena after her might have noticed and removed the cloth strip she and Kahkitah had used to prop the door open. But it was still sitting where they'd left it, and with a little effort they got the door open.

"What will we do if the Shipmasters are still in the observation room?" Kahkitah asked softly as they carefully closed the door again over the cloth strip.

"I don't know," Nicole said. She'd thought about removing the strip, but it had occurred to her that even if she and Kahkitah found another route into the arena they might still want to get out again this way. Taking out the strip now would make that impossible. "We'll just have to see what we've got and go from there."

He waited until she had the door set the way she wanted it. "There's still the rack of weapons," he reminded her.

Nicole felt her throat tighten. Yes: the greenfire weapons. Not just weapons, but weapons she even knew how to use.

But an open attack on the Shipmasters would be the absolutely worst thing she could do. "You heard what I told the others," she said. "We have to prove to them that human beings don't fight. Come on."

She started up the steps, but paused as Kahkitah put a restraining hand on her shoulder. "Perhaps *I* could try to fight them," he offered.

Nicole snorted. "You want *your* people to end up dead on someone else's battlefield?"

"The Shipmasters know we would make terrible soldiers," Kahkitah said. "We are . . . you know already. Strong, but not very clever."

"I don't think cleverness is what they're looking for," Nicole told him. "Doesn't matter. Neither of us is going to fight them. If they're there, we'll just have to figure out a way around them."

"And trust that they didn't chase away the Wisps from Q2."

Nicole grimaced. "Yeah. That, too."

There had been occasional times in Nicole's life—not many, but one or two—when everything had gone exactly the way she'd hoped or planned. Unfortunately, this wasn't one of them. She and Kahkitah were only halfway up the stairs when she caught the faint murmur of conversation from above. She put a warning hand on Kahkitah's arm, and they took the rest of the stairway at an even more cautious pace. They reached the top; motioning Kahkitah to stay where he was, she crawled over to the waist-high ceramic barrier that ran around the inner edge of the wide balcony and eased her head carefully up for a look.

They were there, all right: three of them, Fievj and the same two Shipmasters who'd been there before, standing together on the far side of the observation deck.

Nicole froze in place, wondering if she'd been seen. But their full attention was elsewhere, either on some of the instruments beside them or down into the arena itself.

She chewed at her lip, trying to think. Three Shipmasters, all of them between her and the door where the Q2 Wisps were hopefully waiting. The first quarter of that trip would be easy enough—as long as she and Kahkitah stayed low, the barrier would keep them out of the Shipmasters' sight. But as soon as they rounded the curve and came within sight of the trio, all bets were off.

Lowering her head again, she looked around. There were a few consoles around the outer edge of the balcony, similar to consoles she'd seen elsewhere on the *Fyrantha*, and a couple of them looked wide enough for even Kahkitah to hide behind if the Shipmasters weren't watching very closely. But getting to one of them would mean crossing a lot of open space, and unless the Shipmasters were really locked on to what they were doing there was no way they could miss that. Jeff had said he had a way to draw away the Wisps and Shipmasters, but she still had no idea what that plan might be.

No, she and Kahkitah were on their own. Somehow, Nicole needed to find a way to either distract them or get them out of here entirely.

She was still looking around for inspiration when one of the Shipmasters made a horrible screech.

Reflexively, Nicole dropped flat onto her stomach, her whole body shaking. If they'd seen her—and with that rack of green-fire weapons within easy reach of where they were standing—

"Look there!" the translation came. "Look there! *Fire!*"

Nicole felt her eyes go wide. *Fire?* Clenching her teeth, she eased her eyes back up over the barricade.

The three aliens were staring down into the arena, Fievj and one of the others leaning forward with their palms pressed against the transparent section. Fievj chattered something—"Call the Wisps," the translation came. "Send them in immediately. The fire must be stopped."

"How many?" one of the others asked.

"*All* of them," Fievj snarled. "Every Wisp in the arena area. *Hurry!*"

Nicole smiled tightly. So that was what Jeff had been doing. The stuff he'd been fiddling with must have been something he could use to start a fire, with the water jug he'd asked for standing ready in case the Wisps didn't get there in time to put it out.

Kahkitah was staring at her, his mouth hanging open, his eyes wide. Nicole held out a soothing hand toward him and crawled back. "It's all right," she murmured. "I think Jeff's started a fire as a diversion."

"He started a *fire?*" the Ghorf breathed. His face changed as he seemed to absorb that. "Is it working?"

"Let's see." Cautiously, Nicole raised her eyes above the level of the barrier.

And instantly dropped down again. "They're coming!" she whispered, grabbing Kahkitah's hand and pulling him toward the barrier. "Hurry—lie close to the barrier and don't move and they might miss us."

By the time she and Kahkitah were in position she could hear the slap-slap of running footsteps. She pressed herself against the barrier, wondering distantly what she would do if they spotted her.

To her relief, they didn't. The two Shipmasters charged past, heading for the stairway she and Kahkitah had just come up. Too late, she wished now she'd taken the cloth out of the doorway. Hopefully, in their rush to get down to the arena they wouldn't notice it.

Still, two Shipmasters down still left one to go. Worse, that one was Fievj, who knew Nicole by sight and probably wouldn't be fooled by a wet jumpsuit. She waited until the others had disappeared from view, then looked carefully over the barrier again.

Fievj was still there, standing between them and the far door. But instead of just peering down at the arena he'd moved to one of the binocular devices and was pressing his face into it.

And as long as he stood that way, with his vision blocked by the flanges of the binoculars, he was blind to anything happening up here.

It was a risk, but they had no choice. If she and Kahkitah were fast enough and quiet enough, they should be able to slip past him. She turned to Kahkitah, hoping he would understand her plan—

An instant later she had to stifle a gasp as the Ghorf grabbed her arm and headed around the balcony, all but pulling her behind

him. Apparently, he'd seen Fievj and come to the same con-
clusion.

Fievj never lifted his eyes from his binoculars. A nerve-racking
minute later, they were around the edge of the balcony, past the
oblivious Shipmaster, and headed for the door.

And as they reached it, Nicole looked over her shoulder.
Beyond Fievj, clearly the object of his full attention, was a ten-
dril of smoke rising from the arena.

Jeff had started a fire, all right. Hopefully, he or the Wisps or
the Shipmasters would be able to put it out before it burned the
place down.

From the confrontation Nicole had briefly heard when they'd
first crossed the balcony earlier she'd been afraid that Fievj had
sent the Q2 Wisps back to their proper section of the ship. He
had indeed done so; but to her relief she found that he'd only sent
them as far as the central corridor and the heat duct beyond it.
They came at her summons and carried their two passengers
across the duct without interference from either the Shipmasters
or the Q1 Wisps.

Nor, it appeared, had the Shipmasters managed to take control of the rest of Q2 as Nicole had feared they might. They traveled through that section toward the rear of the ship, again without
any encounters or problems.

"What do we do now?" Kahkitah asked when they were finally
back in Q4.

"We go find the person I need to talk to," Nicole said, looking
around her. She'd had one-way communications with the *Fyrantha*'s Caretaker from various places on the ship, but the only place
she'd ever talked to him face-to-face—well, face-to-hologram,
anyway—was that animal medical center the Wisps had taken
her to once.

"Is it far?"

"You don't have to come," Nicole said, turning toward the centerline heat duct.

"No, I'll come," Kahkitah said. "I fear for you, Nicole, and wish to watch over you. But only if you don't refuse, of course."

Nicole sighed. A lumbering bodyguard who had to have everything explained twice. Terrific.

Still, she'd been pretty much on her own since leaving the hive. It might be nice to have some company. Especially company who could toss Wisps around if he had to. "Sure, come along," she told him. "Let's go see what Caretaker Ushkai can do for us."

twelve

They found Ushkai in the exact same place where Nicole had last left him: standing in the long room lined by barred, twenty-foot-square cages that he'd told her had once been animal treatment areas.

Ushkai's human-looking image remained motionless as Nicole and Kahkitah walked toward it. Nicole kept her eyes on it, wondering if she was going to have to wake up whatever section of the *Fyrantha*'s computer ran the thing.

Kahkitah, for his part, seemed fascinated by everything except the image. The Ghorf's head and shoulders swung back and forth continuously as they walked, his eyes taking in everything, little bits of untranslated birdsong mutterings whistling through his gills.

"What is this place?" he asked at last as they approached the waiting hologram. "Is it a prison?"

"No, it was where they kept sick animals," Nicole said. "The *Fyrantha* used to be a zoo."

"Really?" Kahkitah asked. "Where are the animals now?"

"Probably dead," Nicole said. "No, no—that's not what I meant," she added hastily as he gave off a horrified whistle. "I mean it was a long time ago. The animals would have died of old age."

"Oh," Kahkitah said, sounding only slightly less outraged. "Is that why all the arenas have such different landscapes?"

"I guess," Nicole said. She hadn't really thought about that aspect, but now that Kahkitah pointed it out it was obvious. Different areas to show off different types of animals. "Okay, now, Ushkai is just a hologram, so let me do the—"

"What is a hologram?"

"He's just an image that the *Fyrantha* is projecting here," Nicole said. "When he talks, it's a part of the ship talking through him."

"But the image is human," Kahkitah objected. "If this is the *Fyrantha* speaking, why doesn't it speak from a Wisp image?"

"I don't know," Nicole said, feeling a flash of frustration. They were facing possible death for Jeff and the others, with the enslavement or destruction of Earth to follow. This wasn't something she wanted to talk about right now. "Probably so he wouldn't freak me out. Let me do the talking, okay?"

"Of course."

"Greetings, Protector," Ushkai said as they came up to him. "How may I serve?"

"The Shipmasters are trying to get two of the human groups together to fight," Nicole said. "I want to make it so that neither side can. On Earth animal doctors sometimes have to put the animals to sleep or keep them from moving. Are there any drugs aboard the *Fyrantha* that can do that?"

For a couple of seconds Ushkai didn't move or speak. "Ushkai?" Nicole prompted.

"You wish to put them to sleep?"

Nicole pursed her lips. Actually, now that she thought about it, that wouldn't really do the job. The Shipmasters would just wait until everyone woke up. "No, not to sleep," she said. "Something that . . . I don't know. Something that won't let them fight."

"Something that will prevent them from focusing on things around them, perhaps?" Kahkitah suggested.

"Right—something that'll confuse them," Nicole agreed. "Can't focus, or can't see straight. Maybe something that weakens their muscles?"

"There were once such drugs," Ushkai said. "There may still be some aboard."

Nicole let out a huff of relief. "Great," she said. "Where are they?"

"If such still exist, they will be in the *boultho*-three section of the ship."

"Great," Nicole said again, searching her memory. She couldn't remember ever hitting a section with that particular label. "Where is that?"

"In the forward-left-hand part of the *Fyrantha*," Ushkai said. "*Boultho* is the fourth section from the front."

Nicole's relief vanished. Forward-left-hand part of the ship. In other words, Q1.

Wonderful.

"Is there anywhere else the drugs might be?" she asked, pretty sure she already knew the answer.

"Or the instructions for making more of it?" Kahkitah suggested.

Nicole looked at him in surprise. Of course—they didn't need the drugs themselves if they could mix up a batch of their own.

"There are no other places," Ushkai said. His eyes turned to Kahkitah, and it seemed to Nicole that there was an odd look in them. "You speak of instructions, Ghorf. Do you wish the formula?"

"Yes, that's the word," Kahkitah said. "*Formula*. Can you give it to us?"

"No, wait," Nicole said. She'd seen all the stuff Trake's people had to do to make meth or get other drugs ready for the street.

"No, Kahkitah was right the first time. We need the formula, but we also need all the instructions of how to make it."

"Surely Dr. Allyce can do that with only the formula," Kahkitah suggested.

"It'll be a whole lot easier if she's got everything," Nicole said. "And we'll also need to get all the ingredients," she added, the sudden image of her grandmother putting together cookie dough popping into her head.

Followed instantly by an image of her grandmother standing in a battle line with enemy greenfire guns blasting into her.

She snapped away both images. "*Are* all the ingredients still aboard?" she asked.

"Yes," Ushkai said, his voice suddenly sounding reluctant. "Are you certain you wish to travel this route?"

Nicole frowned. Travel this route? "You mean convince Fievj and the others that Earth people can't fight? Sure. You got a better idea?"

Again, Ushkai sent Kahkitah an odd look. "There are always other ideas. There are always other ways."

"I said a *better* idea," Nicole growled. "Where do we get the formula and the instructions and ingredients?"

For a moment Ushkai stared at her. Then he gestured behind him at a console tucked between two of the cages. "The instructions can be obtained there," he said. "Ask for Setting Sun."

"And the *Fyrantha* will give it to me?"

"Of course," Ushkai said.

Nicole sighed. Only the *Fyrantha* never gave her anything unless she used her inhaler.

"The *Fyrantha* will also direct you to where the proper ingredients may be found," Ushkai continued.

"Yeah," Nicole said between stiff lips. Which meant even more puffs on the inhaler.

And of course, that was only the beginning. The instructions were bound to be long and complicated. With jobs that tricky, she always relied on Jeff or Carp or Levi to take notes while she dictated them, knowing she wouldn't be able to hold on to all the older details while she was listening to and rattling off the newer ones.

Except that Jeff and Carp weren't here. All she had was Kahkitah, who'd never had to do that job before. "Is there any place in Q1 where I can get the instructions?" she asked. If she could sneak Carp out of the arena and over to some medical center there, they'd have a much better chance of getting everything clearly written down.

"No," Ushkai said. "Only here, where the Shipmasters have no authority or command, can the instructions be offered."

Kahkitah laid a big hand gently on Nicole's shoulder. "I can do this, Nicole," he said. "I've watched and listened to the others. I can do it."

Nicole took a deep breath. If she could get Carp out of Q1 and bring him here . . . but that would mean having to go through the Q1 Wisps again. Two more times, actually, in and out, plus a third to get back in again once they had everything they needed. Right now, she wasn't even sure she and Kahkitah could run that line one more time, let alone three. "Fine," she said, reluctantly. "Do you have a pad?"

"Right here," he said, pulling the cell-phone-sized device from one of his jumpsuit's pockets. "And I have the pen, too," he added brightly, holding it up.

As if those massive fingers could write anything without it. "Okay," she said. "If you're sure."

"I'm sure." Kahkitah lowered his hand back to his side and drew himself to his full height. "And *you*, Caretaker. Are *you* certain this will have the desired effect on humans?"

"It will," Ushkai assured him.

"Because humans aren't the animals of the *Fyrantha's* zookeepers," Kahkitah went on. "We don't wish the Protector's people to be harmed."

"They won't be."

"And there are no other sources of the medicine itself?" Kahkitah persisted.

"There are not."

Kahkitah nodded and settled back to his normal posture. "Very well." He turned to Nicole. "Whenever you're ready."

Nicole looked at Ushkai. There was still that strange look on his face, as if he was trying to say something else, if she would only ask the right question.

Or, perhaps, trying *not* to say something else?

But right now she couldn't think of any more questions, and they were running out of time. "Yeah," she said, cringing a little as she pulled out the inhaler Wesowee had given her. "Let's do it."

It was every bit as bad as Nicole had expected. Maybe even a little worse.

The instructions for making Setting Sun were incredibly complicated, involving ingredients, amounts, orders of inclusion, temperatures, and even the length of time between procedures when the mixture had to simmer or cook or whatever. A lot of the words weren't familiar, making her stumble over them and then having to hurry to catch up as the *Fyrantha* continued without any consideration for the fact that she was falling behind.

In the end, it took four doses from her inhaler to get it all down, followed by three more to get the locations of all the ingredients Allyce would need.

Nicole had no idea how much of her life she'd burned away in those few minutes. But whatever that damage, she was pretty sure she couldn't really afford it.

But she had no choice. That image of her grandmother being cut down by greenfire weapons was firmly set in her mind now, haunting her thoughts. There were a lot of people she knew, mostly Trake's gang and the other gangs in the neighborhood, who she would be happy to see die that way. They deserved it. But not her grandmother.

At least Kahkitah didn't add to the problem. Through all her stumblings over strange words and her frantic attempts to catch up with the *Fyrantha*'s recitation he stood in front of her, rapidly scribbling down the words—or at least the sounds she was saying—without comment or complaint. In the end, there were only a few places where he'd failed to get exactly what she'd said, and in all of those they were able to figure out the correct words together.

The next step was to go around Q4 gathering up the materials. The *Fyrantha* had given them the locations, but Nicole had no idea how easy they would be to identify. If she was lucky, everything would be in neatly labeled bottles or jars. If they weren't, the whole thing might turn into a weird sort of scavenger hunt. All the more reason to get started right away.

To her surprise and frustration, Kahkitah had other ideas.

"You're hungry, and you're tired," he said firmly, holding the pad with the screen pressed against his chest where she couldn't see it. "You need food and sleep before we continue."

"There's food back at the arena," Nicole growled, trying to grab the pad away from him.

She might as well have tried to lift him off the floor. He resisted her pull for a moment, probably just to prove she didn't have any hope of prying off his fingers, then raised the pad up over his head, putting it a good foot out of her reach. "The arena features a mix of food granules," he said. "It may be nourishment in the strictest sense, but it's hardly satisfying."

"It's what Jeff and the others eat," Nicole bit out, starting to get angry.

Probably mostly because he was right. Her eyes felt like a spoonful of the beach sand was in them, and her stomach was growling regularly with reminders that she hadn't eaten anything in more hours than she cared to count. A meal at the hive's dining room, followed by a couple of hours of sleep in her own bed, sounded wonderful.

But everything depended on her. Until she got the chemicals and instructions to Allyce, no one else could do anything except sit on their hands. Taking time to eat or even sleep—"Come on, Kahkitah, we don't have time for this."

"You're going to eat, and then you're going to sleep," the Ghorf said calmly. "That is truth. Arguing will merely further delay our return."

Nicole wanted to hurt him. She *really* wanted to hurt him. But as she glared at his calm shark face and bumpy body, she realized she had no idea how to do that.

Besides, he was right. Fumbling around in her groggy state would probably cost more time and lead them down more dead ends than it would gain. A couple of hours of sleep, and she'd be ready to tackle the next part of the job.

"Fine," she bit out. "But if someone dies because of you—"

"Then they die because of me," he said firmly. "Not because of you. Because of me."

She tried one more glare. But even that was becoming too much effort. "Fine," she said again. "Let's get back to the vent, grab some Wisps, and get down to the hive."

And come to think of it, the trail mix back at the Q1 arena *had* looked pretty pathetic.

As usual, the Wisps—at least those in Q4—were prompt and efficient. A few minutes later, Nicole and Kahkitah were back in the hive.

Now that Nicole wasn't fighting so hard against her fatigue, it had surged in like one of the waves in the Q1 arena, threatening to knock her out with every step. Luckily, Kahkitah was there, and with his help she made it to the dining room without actually falling over.

Just the same, she ended up dozing with her head on the table for the ten minutes it took him to get the food preparation up and running.

She ate two trays' worth, rather surprised she was that hungry, then let Kahkitah escort her to her old room. She left strict instructions for him to wake her in two hours, took off her boots, and climbed into bed. She barely got the light off before falling asleep.

Six hours later, she woke up.

For a minute she just lay there, propped up on one elbow, blinking at the clock as her still-fogged brain tried to figure out what was going on. She'd told Kahkitah to wake her in two hours—how could she possibly have slept for six?

Because Kahkitah had ignored her instructions, of course.

Damn him.

Snarling, she hit the light switch, shoved off the blankets, and started to get out of bed—

And jerked back as she realized suddenly that she wasn't alone. Kahkitah was in her room, lying on the floor across the doorway with one arm folded under his head as a pillow. His eyes were closed, his breathing slow and steady.

Nicole took a full double lungful of air. *"Kahkitah!"* she barked.

She'd expected him to jump to his feet, or at least jerk violently. But he merely opened his eyes and blinked once at her. "Ah, you're awake," he said calmly. "Do you feel rested?"

"I feel damn angry," Nicole snarled. "I told you to wake me in two hours."

"I tried," he said. Stretching, he got leisurely to his feet. "I was unable to bring you to consciousness."

"Really," she said icily. "How hard did you try?"

"You needed sleep," he said. "More than two hours would have provided you."

"Wonderful," Nicole bit out. "Great for me. Pretty damn rotten for Jeff and the others. Now we're six hours behind on collecting all the stuff we need for the drug—"

"It's all collected."

"—and if Fievj and his buddies—" Nicole broke off as Kahkitah's words suddenly penetrated the haze. "What did you say?"

"The materials are all collected," he said, his voice calm. "I did it while you slept."

Nicole opened her mouth. Closed it again. "We were supposed to do that together."

"You needed sleep," Kahkitah said again. "I didn't."

Nicole took a deep breath, feeling like a complete fool. "Why didn't you—? Never mind. You're sure you got everything?"

"Yes," Kahkitah said. "But returning to the arena may be difficult. Do you have any ideas how we'll do that?"

"Yeah, I think so." Nicole took another couple of breaths, trying to force her brain to function. Still an uphill battle.

On the other hand, as long as that particular task was now done . . .

"I'm going to take a quick shower," she said, climbing the rest of the way out of bed. "Go make sure everything's packed as tightly together as you can make it."

"I will." Kahkitah pointed to Nicole's jumpsuit. "May I suggest you also change into clothing that isn't marked with yellow paint?"

"Oh. Right," Nicole said. With everything else that had happened, she'd completely forgotten about the Ejbof paintball gun. "I'll get one of my others. Oh, and if there's room inside whatever bag you pack the drug supplies into, toss in a few meal bars and water bottles."

"We aren't going directly back to the arena?"

"We're going back," Nicole said. "But the route I'm thinking of might take a little extra time."

"I understand," Kahkitah said, touching the door release. "I'll await you in the dining room."

"Okay. And Kahkitah?"

"Yes?"

Nicole swallowed hard. "Thanks."

Nicole hadn't spent much time in the Q1 section. But she *had* spent a lot of time in Q4, and while the arenas themselves weren't lined up exactly the same way between the four sections, many of the areas above and below them seemed to be laid out alike.

The last time she and Kahkitah had gone into Q1 Nicole had tried to get as close to the arena as possible before crossing the heat-transfer duct from Q2. That hadn't gone very well. On the other hand, the Shipmasters only had so many Wisps they could use to block her path. If they were focusing their attention and their Wisps in the area around the arena—and if Nicole was in charge that was certainly where *she* would put them—maybe a more roundabout approach would work better.

So this time when they left the hive she headed straight sideways to the heat-transfer duct and ordered the Wisps to take them to the very top of the ship.

They came out of the duct in the same general area Nicole had been to once before, back when the *Fyrantha* had been under attack and she'd been summoned to fix a problem with a broken defense console. The corridors here weren't laid out as straight or as conveniently as those below, but she'd been to the area a couple of times since then and mostly knew her way around. Midway through her zigzag path they passed another familiar spot: the staircase leading up to the observation room where that particular console cluster had been located.

She glanced at the stair as they passed, feeling a twinge of re-membered emotion. This was where she'd first seen proof that the *Fyrantha* was, in fact, a huge ship traveling through space . . .

"What's up there?" Kahkitah asked.

Nicole hesitated, freshly aware of the time pressure squeez-ing in on her. But Kahkitah had been aboard the *Fyrantha* longer than she had, and had probably never seen the stars from any-where on the ship. For that matter, maybe he also had doubts about where they were. "I'll show you," she said, doubling back to the stairs and leading the way up.

The last time she'd been here the *Fyrantha* had been sitting in the middle of a million bright stars. This time, to her surprise, the stars weren't there. All she could see was the hazy blue of the ship's outer hull, now wrapped in complete blackness. "What the *hell?*" she muttered. "Where'd all the stars go?"

"We're in hyperspace," Kahkitah murmured. "There are no stars there."

Nicole blinked at him in surprise. "What are you talking about? Where'd they go?"

"They're still there," Kahkitah said. "We just can't see them. Look there." He pointed in front of them. "You see that dot?"

Nicole craned her neck. Almost lost in the blue haze was a bright blue-white dot. "Is that a star?" she asked.

"That's *all* the stars," Kahkitah said. "Or rather, all the stars whose light can reach us. The ones behind us are there." He pointed behind them, where a dim red spot was shining. "Those on the sides can't be seen."

An eerie sensation tingled at the back of Nicole's neck. "How do you know all that?" she asked carefully.

"I don't, personally," Kahkitah said. "But some Ghorfs have thought a great deal about such things. Some have written those thoughts down. Others have read those words. I have spoken to some of them."

"Oh," Nicole said, feeling both relieved and a little disappointed. "I thought . . . never mind."

"That perhaps we were not as slow as you thought?" Kahkitah said gently. "I'm sorry if I disappointed you."

"Not your fault," Nicole assured him. Actually, the thought of a Ghorf Einstein would probably have been more disturbing than helpful anyway. "But you can see now how big the *Fyrantha* really is."

"I already knew," Kahkitah said.

Nicole frowned. "You did?"

"We've spent a great deal of time walking through it," he reminded her.

"Oh. Right." Nicole took one final look out through the windows, trying not to think about the sheer size of the task that Ushkai and the *Fyrantha* had dropped into her lap. To protect this whole thing from the Shipmasters . . .

"Nicole?" Kahkitah asked. "Are you all right?"

"Sure." She took a deep breath. "Break time over. Let's get out of here."

thirteen

The transition from Q4 to Q2 was easy. Nicole kept going forward until she got to what she hoped was the right place, then changed direction toward the middle and the centerline heat-transfer duct. Three Q2 Wisps came at her call, and carried them across to Q1.

There were no Q1 Wisps waiting when they arrived. That part of the plan, at least, had worked.

Now came the tricky part.

"Where are we going?" Kahkitah asked as Nicole led them through the zigzag corridors toward the center of the section.

"This used to be a zoo, remember?" Nicole said. "Before that it was a battleship or something. Either way, they had to be able to get big machines or supply containers to the arena."

"Or big animals?"

"Or big animals," Nicole said. "So I'm thinking they may have some kind of elevators or at least bigger corridors leading down there."

Kahkitah seemed to ponder that. "But we've seen the arenas," he said slowly as their path zigged again. "I haven't seen any openings in the ceiling or walls. Maybe the supply elevators come up from underneath."

"Some of them might," Nicole conceded. "But I figure there

have to be ways to get stuff in from both directions. Maybe the ones from above open through a section of wall instead of the roof."

"That could be," Kahkitah agreed. "Nicole?"

"Yes, Kahkitah?"

"You don't mind all these questions, do you? I know I'm sometimes slow."

"No, I don't mind," she said. "What do you need to know?"

"I'm confused," he said. "The creature we spoke to—you called him Ushkai?"

"The Caretaker, yes."

"He said this drug will work on humans like you and Jeff," Kahkitah said. "How does he know?"

"He told me the *Fyrantha*'s original owners set things up so that only humans can fix it when something goes wrong," Nicole said. "Don't ask me why. Anyway, I figure that means they've been snatching people from Earth for a long time, so they'd know how our bodies work."

"But what would that kind of drug be used for?"

"No idea," she admitted. "Something medical, I suppose. Doesn't sound like the *Fyrantha*'s big on recreational drugs. I mean, they don't even have beer."

On the other hand, Sam *had* been able to get their hive's food processor to create whiskey once. If Setting Sun or some other drugs had once been used for recreation, maybe some earlier group of slaves had figured out how to make it.

"Something medical would make sense," Kahkitah murmured. "A sleeping potion, perhaps?"

"Maybe," Nicole said. "Though they work us hard enough that most people probably don't have trouble sleeping. I sure don't."

"Setting Sun," Kahkitah repeated softly, an odd new tone to his voice. "Perhaps it means the final setting of the sun?"

"What do you mean? Like when the ship finally gets to wherever it's going?"

"Or the setting sun for each individual," Kahkitah said. "Perhaps the drug's purpose is to ease the pain or fear of passage from this life."

"Oh," Nicole said, wincing. That one hadn't even occurred to her.

But it made sense. A lot of people had lived and died on this ship, and she'd seen enough death to know it could be scary and painful. Something to help them through it might have been good to have around.

Too bad there weren't any more supplies of the stuff. If she kept using the inhaler the way she had in the past couple of days, she might be needing some herself soon.

"I still don't see any larger passageways, though," Kahkitah continued.

"Or elevators, either," Nicole said, looking around as she worked her mind away from thoughts about her own death. If her calculations were right, they should be over the Q1 arena. Whatever the original owners had used to move big stuff in and out, they should be seeing it by now. "Maybe all the places they would have gotten their supplies from are farther down. You see any regular staircases?"

"I think we just passed one."

"Let's try it," Nicole said. "If we don't find something else, we might have to try coming up from under the arena like you said."

She'd estimated they would need to go down twenty-five to thirty levels to reach the arena. Every few levels she took a quick look outside the staircase at the surrounding corridors, looking for the supply levels that had to be *somewhere*. But wherever they were, they weren't in this part of the ship.

On the other hand, there'd been no sign of Wisps, either. The situation wasn't great, but at least it wasn't as bad as it could have been.

They were still a couple of levels above the arena floor when the staircase unexpectedly ended.

"Where now?" Kahkitah asked as Nicole moved cautiously back out into the corridor.

"I don't know," she said, looking around. As near as she could tell, they were no more than a corridor or two away from the observation balcony where the Shipmasters could look down into the arena. If any of them or their pet Wisps were wandering around, the last thing she and Kahkitah wanted to do was sit here holding a long conversation.

"The floor is thicker here," Kahkitah said. "What does that mean?"

"What do you mean, it's thicker?"

"It's thicker." He tapped his foot on the deck, as if that move told Nicole anything. "I can feel the difference. It's much thicker. What does that mean?"

"No idea," Nicole said, frowning as she tried to visualize the ship. She hadn't been in this exact part back in Q4, and anyway things in Q1 might be completely different.

Ushkai had said the arenas used to be hangars for space fighters. So there would have been fighters down there, and maybe crew quarters and repair shops.

And missiles and fuel and explosives?

She looked at the floor. Assuming Kahkitah was right about the deck being thicker, maybe that was to protect the rest of the ship from an explosion. Was that why the stairway they'd just been in had ended? Because this deck and others like it were isolating the arena area from everything else?

"That slab of floor ahead," Kahkitah said, pointing. "It looks different."

Nicole frowned. He was right. At first glance, the section had
the same soft red flooring as every other corridor aboard ship.
But everywhere else the flooring was unbroken, as if it had been
poured onto the floor like syrup and let dry. Here, she could see
definite breaks, about three meters apart, in the red.

As if that part of the floor maybe opened up?

"There are more," Kahkitah said. "Up ahead."

"Got it," Nicole said. Now that she knew what to look for, she
could see at least two more broken sections of floor. "I'm thinking
maybe they open up."

"And lead downward?" Kahkitah started forward. "Let's find
out."

"There has to be a control somewhere," Nicole said, eyeing the
walls as they arrived at the nearest section. As far as she could
tell, the walls were the same smooth metal they were everywhere
else.

"Maybe they're only for emergencies," Kahkitah suggested. "In
that case, the control might be in a central location elsewhere."

"Like in the observation balcony," Nicole said, scowling. "So
much for *that* idea."

"Do you think so?"

"Why, don't you?" Nicole countered. "I'm pretty sure we've already used up all our luck with that balcony."

"I wasn't suggesting we go back in there," Kahkitah said. "But
even if they're normally controlled from elsewhere, surely there
would be an additional control nearby in case the main system
failed."

"Maybe," Nicole said, studying the floor. Though if the local
control was on the other side of the floor from where they were
standing, they would still be out of luck.

"One thing I don't understand," Kahkitah said, stooping down
and poking around the edges of the flooring with his fingers.

Just one *thing?* The unkind thought flicked through Nicole's mind. "What's that?" she asked instead.

"You're the Protector," he said, still probing the flooring. "Can't you just order the *Fyrantha* to do what you want?"

"We've already been through this," Nicole said. "I can ask the Wisps and the Caretaker to do things in Q4 and a little in Q2. Q1 is under Shipmaster control."

"But you said this was an emergency door," Kahkitah said. "That should always have a control nearby."

Nicole sighed. "It's probably on the other side of the floor," she said. "Something people down there could use to get away from a fire or explosion or something. Or maybe there's a code or word they had to use."

"The *Fyrantha* should certainly recognize the voice of its Protector," Kahkitah said, his birdsongs sounding a little huffy. "Can't you simply order it to open?"

"What, like *Simon Says* or something?" Nicole scoffed. "'Protector says open the floor'? That would be—"

She jerked back as one edge of the section suddenly popped up from the rest of the floor. Even as Kahkitah scrambled to get out of the way it continued angling upward, and Nicole could see a similar section of floor beneath it angling the other way, unfolding and extending something as it swung downward. Their side of the floor continued turning, flipping up and over and finally flattening out on the section of corridor beside it.

Nicole waited until she was sure everything had stopped moving. Then, she eased carefully to Kahkitah's side and looked down.

The section she'd seen extending downward had become a set of stairs. A set of stairs, moreover, that led right up to—

"Is that the stairway we used to get from the balcony to the arena?" Kahkitah whispered, pointing past the new stairs to another stairway a couple of meters away from the end.

"Looks like it," Nicole agreed.

Kahkitah gave a plaintive whistle. "I don't understand."

"Keep it down," Nicole warned, trying to look toward the observation balcony. But the thickness of the deck below them blocked a view of anything in that direction. "The usual stairs—those over there—are for the people up here to go down to the arena. Probably not too much traffic going that direction. But if something goes wrong, you want everyone down there to be able to get out as fast as they can. That's what these stairs are for."

"And those?" Kahkitah asked, pointing to the other broken sections ahead.

"Probably the same," Nicole said, feeling her heart speeding up. A bunch of other ways in and out of the arena that she'd never known were there.

And could she really open them just by identifying herself as the Protector and asking the *Fyrantha* to do it?

Maybe that was all it took. She'd called on the Wisps any number of times. She'd called for Ushkai a couple of times when she wanted information, though getting an answer had then required her to use her inhaler.

Was this all it took? Could she just ask the *Fyrantha* to do something and it would?

Even here in the Shipmasters' stronghold?

If that was true, she might have a new weapon that she'd never dreamed of. Definitely something she needed to explore.

But not now. Now, there were other, more urgent matters to attend to. "Come on," she said, painfully aware that her legs would be visible to Fievj or anyone else in the balcony long before she would even know if they were looking in her direction. "Let's get this stuff to Allyce."

———

There were no shouts of surprise or discovery from the balcony as she and Kahkitah crept down the steps, hurried across the short open area, and continued down the permanent staircase. Nicole glanced through the entrance as they passed, but didn't see anyone.

Unfortunately, enough of the balcony was out of view from her angle that that didn't mean anything. She and Kahkitah would still have to be as quiet as possible once they were in the arena, and get to cover as quickly as they could.

The cloth strip blocking the door open was still where they'd left it. They slipped through the doorway and headed through the trees toward the hive.

They were halfway there when Nicole heard a quiet call from somewhere ahead. A moment later, they circled a pair of tall bushes to see Duncan walking toward them. "Noticed the breeze and figured that was probably you," he said quietly, glancing around. "Hopefully, the Shipmasters didn't notice, or else don't know what it means."

Nicole winced. "The Shipmasters are *here*?"

"Two of them, yeah." Duncan's lip twitched. "They came to give us our weapons."

"Hell," Nicole breathed. "What are they?"

"Three-pointed spears—they called them *tridents*—and a kind of square net weighted at the corners for throwing."

"Sounds pretty easy to use."

"Yeah," Duncan said. "But don't worry—Jeff's got everyone playing stupid, like we don't know which end of the trident goes where. But I don't suppose Bungie's crowd will go along with the gag."

"Do you know if they've been to that side already?"

"I don't think so," Duncan said. "He said they weren't going to get theirs until tomorrow."

"Handy," Nicole said, looking toward the hills that divided the arena. That gave them a little more time.

But to do what? There was no way they could prevent Fievj from delivering Bungie's weapons, not without Jeff and the blue group using their own. No, their best bet was still to go with Setting Sun and hope the Shipmasters would conclude that, even if humans knew about weapons they were no good at using them. "Okay," she said. "I need to talk to Allyce. Let me know when the Shipmasters leave, and we'll—"

"Whoa," Duncan interrupted. "Allyce isn't here. She's been on Bungie's side since yesterday."

Nicole felt her mouth drop open. With Jeff's injuries still healing, she'd just assumed both Sam and Allyce would be watching over him. "Someone sick over there?"

"They're gearing us up for a fight, remember?" Duncan said sourly.

"And they still need all of you to help fix the ship," Kahkitah reminded her. "That would suggest that they really don't want any deaths."

"Or at least no more deaths than they need to prove their point," Nicole gritted. "Okay, fine—I'll go over there. Come on, Kahkitah—I need you to help me across the river."

"You talking about the way you came over before?" Duncan asked.

"Yes," Nicole said. "Why, did the Shipmasters find it or something?"

"Don't know," Duncan said. "I'm more worried about how secure you made your end of the tubing. Even with Kahkitah holding this end, if the other end breaks free you might find yourself white-water rafting without the raft."

"I wedged it pretty good."

"She'll be all right," Kahkitah said. "I'll be with her."

"No, you won't," Nicole said firmly. "You'll be here helping Jeff get ready."

"I thought you didn't want us to fight," Duncan said, frowning.

"I don't," Nicole said. "But if we can't get this stopped, I want to make sure Bungie loses."

"Preaching to the choir, sister," Duncan said. "Just one other problem. If you leave the line up, what's to stop Bungie from finding it and coming over here? We're having enough trouble guarding the ocean route. We don't need a flanking move down the hills on top of it."

"Don't worry, he won't come back that way," Nicole said. "Once I'm across, I'll toss off my end."

Kahkitah trilled sharply. "No!" he said. "If you do, you'll be trapped there."

"I can always swim back."

"Under the very eyes of the Shipmasters?" Kahkitah's gill slits fluttered. "They'd capture you before you could even dry off."

"And if you *do* try it, you'll need to do it soon," Duncan warned. "In about an hour it'll start being open enough to cross, and everyone—from both sides—will be at the extra food dispenser."

"I thought Bungie's side didn't need more food."

"They don't," Duncan said. "But they don't want us to have it, either."

Nicole caught her breath. "So you're *already* fighting them?"

"No, no, Jeff's playing it cool," Duncan said. "We go in just when the dispenser first starts to get clear, when the biggest wave crests still put it underwater but the troughs leave it clear."

"You have to be pretty fast, don't you?"

"Oh, yeah," Duncan said, making a face. "Even if you are, half the time you end up with soggy food. Water's pretty damn cold, too."

"Sounds tricky," Nicole said.

"Tricky and a half," Duncan agreed. "The upside is that none of the Greenies want to get in any deeper than they have to."

"Especially when they don't need the food?"

"Right," Duncan said. "We get about half of it out before the water's low enough that they're willing to come in to stop us. When that happens, we just back off and let them stand there and keep us away."

"Shivering the whole time," Nicole said. "Only this time, you'll have weapons and they won't."

"So what? Oh," Duncan said, his eyes narrowing as he suddenly got it. "So we should be able to march in, point our tridents at them, and make them back off. Only we don't want to do that, do we?"

"Not if we want to prove we're not fighters," Nicole said. "You need to tell Jeff to run your usual trick and leave the weapons in the hive."

"Pretty sure he's already thought of that, but I'll tell him," Duncan said. "You still going across?"

"I have to," Nicole said. "I don't know how long it'll take Allyce to mix up this stuff, and I need to give her all the time I can. Actually, getting to her while Bungie and the rest are chasing you away from the dispenser is probably my best shot."

"I guess that makes sense," Duncan said. "Be careful."

"I still don't like you being trapped over there," Kahkitah said.

"You got a better idea, I'd love to hear it," Nicole said. "If not, I'm going. You going to come and help, or not?"

"I'll come," Kahkitah said firmly. "And I *will* find a better way."

To Nicole's complete lack of surprise, he didn't.

There was little conversation possible with the river roaring beside them. But Nicole wasn't in a mood for talking anyway. She took the pack of ingredients from Kahkitah and slung it over her shoulder, made sure she had the full list of instructions that they'd copied from his pad to hers, then watched as he fished the end of the tubing from where he and Carp had wedged it near the river's edge. He tightened the line, looped it once around one of the trees, and nodded.

Giving him a small wave—which seemed both childish and stupid, she realized an instant later—Nicole locked her left arm firmly over the tubing and stepped into the river.

The water was just as cold as it had been the last time, and the buffeting and churning possibly a little worse. But this time she was ready for it, and managed to maintain her balance the whole way across. She reached the far side; and as Kahkitah stood on the opposite bank, his whole body a single hulking mass of unhappiness, she unhooked the crutch top from the branches where she'd wedged it and threw it back across to him. He caught it and, still watching her, coiled the tubing into a tight knot. He laid it at the base of one of the trees and gave her a little wave of his own.

He was still watching as Nicole turned and started down the slope.

Duncan had said it would be another hour before the ocean route became passable. Nicole found a nice spot where she could look down on the hive entrance without being immediately visible and settled in to wait.

She'd been there about half an hour when the green group made their move.

Bungie was first out, naturally—he'd learned his leadership techniques from Trake, and Trake always led the way, at least until they got close to where the danger was. He was followed by Iosif and Miron, the two men normally in charge of the team who should by all rights be in charge here, too. Behind them came the other five men, striding through the bushes like they owned the place.

Nicole watched them, a lump forming in her throat. Of course they were determined. Fievj had promised to send them home if they won. Distantly, she wondered what they would think when that turned out to be a lie.

What they would *think*. Not what they would *do*. There would be absolutely nothing they *could* do.

She waited until the last of them was out of sight beyond the tree canopy, then gave it another two-hundred count just to be sure. Then, keeping as quiet as she could, she headed down and slipped through the entrance into the hive.

She found Allyce in the corresponding room to the one where Sam had set up Jeff's treatment and recovery over in the blue side. The other woman looked up, her eyes widening as Nicole stepped in. Allyce opened her mouth, her lips starting to curve into a smile—

And closed it again as Nicole hastily put her finger to her lips. "Keep it down," Nicole warned quietly. "The Shipmasters have a listening ear a few doors down."

"I know," Allyce said, just as quietly, as she ran a quick, measuring glance over her. "I heard you'd come back. Are you all right?"

"As all right as any of us are," Nicole said. "But that's going to change real fast if we don't do something."

"Yes, I heard some of the others talking," Allyce said. "You told them that the Shipmasters like watching people fight?"

"Actually, it's worse than that," Nicole said grimly. "Here's the deal."

Allyce listened in silence while Nicole gave her the full story. "That's . . . incredible," she said when Nicole had finished. "Where exactly did you hear this?"

"The Caretaker told me."

"And this Caretaker is reliable?"

"He's part of the *Fyrantha* itself," Nicole said. "So, yeah, I'd say so."

Allyce shook her head. "I'm sorry, but I just can't believe it. Slaves—even military slaves—no. Creatures advanced enough for space travel wouldn't be that unenlightened."

"What does enlightenment have to do with it?" Nicole demanded. "As long as there are wars, people are going to want people to fight and take bullets and die for them."

"Again, that doesn't make sense," Allyce said. "Surely advanced people don't need to fight anymore."

Nicole clenched her teeth. "Allyce, listen," she said as calmly as she could. "I've seen them fighting. All sorts of aliens, all sorts of weapons. The Shipmasters set them up, watch them fight, and figure out who they're going to sell the winners to."

"And then send everyone home?"

"I really don't know. I know they leave, but that's all."

"They send everyone home," Allyce said firmly. "That's what Fievj said. They send them home. If they can send *them* home, it means they can send *us* home, too."

Something cold ran up Nicole's back. "This isn't about us, Allyce," she said carefully. "It's about Earth. It's about the whole human race—"

"I have a husband, Nicole."

Nicole blinked. "What?"

"You heard me. I have a husband. Back in Denver." Allyce's throat worked. "I haven't seen him in twelve years."

"Allyce—"

"He doesn't even know if I'm alive or dead," Allyce cut her off. "I'm sorry—I really am. But this is my chance to get home. Even if Fievj is lying, it's my only chance. I have to try."

For a long moment Nicole just stared at her, trying to think. She'd hoped that once everyone knew the full stakes they were playing for, only Bungie and Sam would be selfish enough to risk the whole world for what they personally wanted. But if she'd lost Allyce, too, who knew who else might be ready to fight for real? "What did Fievj say?" she asked. "What words exactly? What did he want you to do?"

"He said the winners would be sent back to Earth," Allyce said. "I know you believe that's a lie—"

"Any rules on how you win?" Nicole cut her off. "Does anyone have to die, or bleed, or get carried off the field? Or is the loser just whoever runs away first?"

"I—" Allyce broke off, frowning. "I don't know. I don't think Bungie said anything about that."

"Okay," Nicole said. "So you just have to win." She unslung the bag from her shoulder. "Here are the ingredients for a drug that's supposed to make people sleepy or confused or something. Make them so they can't fight, or at least not very well. I need you to mix me up enough for everyone in both groups."

"All right," Allyce said slowly. "But if no one can fight, how can anyone win?"

"Like I said, whoever doesn't run away," Nicole said. "As long as they don't look like they'd be worth anything in a real war, they can poke at each other all they want."

"I don't know," Allyce said, still not sounding convinced.

"At least mix up the stuff while you're thinking about it, okay?" Nicole said. "We can talk more later if you want. But Fievj's already starting to pass out weapons. We have to get moving."

"I suppose I can do that," Allyce said. Gingerly, she took the bag. "I assume some instructions came with this?"

"Right here," Nicole said, pulling out her pad. "Got your pad?"

"Here."

Allyce watched in silence as Nicole transferred the instructions. Then it was Nicole's turn to wait as Allyce skimmed through them. "You think you can do it?" Nicole asked when the doctor looked up again.

"I think so, yes." Allyce hefted the bag. "From the feel of this you've got plenty of ingredients, so I could probably even mess up the first batch and still have enough to work with."

"Well, *don't* mess it up," Nicole warned. "I don't know if there's enough stuff there, and I *know* there's not enough time. Speaking of which, any idea how long it'll take?"

"A day or two at the most," Allyce said. "Though I'm going to have to come up with something to tell Bungie about what I'm doing. Any idea on delivery system?"

"What?"

"You need a way to get the drug into the body," Allyce said. "Injection, ingestion, or inhalation. Do you know which one this needs?"

"Not a clue," Nicole confessed. She didn't remember anything like that being mentioned in the instruction list. "Which is easiest?"

"You don't get to choose," Allyce said, a little impatiently. "You need to find out. And you'd better hope it's not injection, because I hardly think Bungie and the others will line up for shots."

"Yeah, I'll find out," Nicole promised. "You just get some put together, okay?"

Allyce sighed. "Sure. You'd better go before they all get back."

"Right," Nicole said. "Thanks."

The area past the hive door was deserted as she slipped through. Instead of heading left toward the river, though, this time she turned right and headed toward the side wall. One of the arena's main doors was back there, but she had no doubt the Shipmasters and Wisps had a close eye on it.

But if all the broken flooring spots Kahkitah had seen were really emergency exit stairs, and if that same pattern was repeated on this side of the arena, she might have a secret bolt-hole the Shipmasters didn't know about. She kept an eye on the branches above her as she walked, hoping she could make the trip without coming into view from the observation balcony—

"You!" a voice came from somewhere behind her. "Stop!"

Fievj's voice.

Nicole broke into a run, her heart thudding. The branches and grasses swished loudly as she pushed through them, announcing her presence to anyone listening, but there was nothing she could do about that. At all costs she had to get away before he caught up with her.

And as she ran the chilling thought struck her that if the hidden door didn't open—or wasn't there at all—she would be trapped against the arena wall.

She glanced over her shoulder, wondering if Fievj was gaining. But she couldn't see anything back there except trees and shrubs. If he would bark another order she might have a clue as to where he was, but after that first shout he'd remained silent.

Maybe he was listening, tracking her through the noise she was making. Forcing back her panic, Nicole concentrated on running, wondering belatedly if Fievj wasn't trying to catch up because he knew there were other Shipmasters or Wisps in front of her and his job was just to drive her into their arms. For a moment her pace faltered as she tried to decide whether to keep going or to veer off at an angle or even abandon this plan and head toward the ocean—

And then, suddenly, she was there.

There was a narrow strip of open ground between the forest and the wall. The wall itself was the usual metal, unbroken by any cracks or other hints that there might be a door there. "I'm the Protector," Nicole said, trying not to gasp for breath. "Open the door."

Nothing. "I'm the Protector," she said again, trying to think. What exactly had she said before? "Protector says to open the door."

Still nothing. She could hear someone moving through the brush behind her now, Fievj or one of the other Shipmasters. There was a whiff of moving air from her right—

As if the main door on this side had just opened.

Nicole clenched her teeth. That was *not* what she wanted, at least not right now. "Protector says"—she had a flash of inspiration—"open the *emergency* door."

And three feet to her left, a door-sized section of the wall swung open.

She was there before it had even finished its swing, ducking through the opening and leaping up onto the stairs. "Protector says close the emergency door," she said. She glanced down to see the door swinging shut again, and then focused on the stairs. As on the other side of the arena, the stairs ended at the level of the balcony. "Protector says open the floor."

Above and in front of her, the floor dropped open, the stairs unfolding down to her deck. She climbed past the thick section of floor, then did two more flights just to be safe. Then, with a heaving sigh of relief, she opened the door into the corridor and stepped out.

And instantly ducked back again as she spotted a Wisp gliding down the corridor barely ten feet away.

The Wisp was heading the other direction, and Nicole had no idea whether or not it heard the door open. But she had no intention of finding out the hard way. She continued up the stairs, pausing only when her legs refused to go any farther, and started up again as soon as she could force the fatigued muscles back to work.

Midway to the top of the *Fyrantha* she once again risked going out into the corridor, stealing to the center line and calling for a Wisp. But there was no response. She tried again, then returned to the stairs. The Wisps who'd brought her and Kahkitah across from Q2 had been told to wait there for her. She'd find out in a few minutes whether or not they'd obeyed those instructions.

Finally, she was there. Wearily, she opened the door and dragged herself out into the corridor, almost not caring anymore if the Shipmasters had gotten there ahead of her. To her relief, she could see the three Wisps waiting patiently by the center-line wall fifty feet away.

Limping on aching legs, she walked over to them. "Take me across to Q2," she ordered, turning and backing into the closest one. Q2, then a walk back to Q4, and her own bed. The arms folded around her—

Will your companion be traveling with us? the voice came in her head.

No, Nicole answered with an unexpected sense of loss. She hadn't realized until that moment how much better and safer she'd felt with Kahkitah beside her. But there was nothing she could do about it now.

Actually, there was nothing she could do about much of *any-thing* right now. Allyce needed to mix up the drug, Jeff needed to stall Fievj's battle until the stuff was ready, and until that was all done Nicole's job was mostly to stay out of sight. Q4 would be the best place to do that.

On the other hand, Q4 was way back at the rear of the ship, and Nicole's feet and legs were already hurting. Even the thought of her own room and bed wasn't enough to make the difference.

Besides, the Wisps in Q4 might be under her control, but there wasn't anything to stop Fievj or another Shipmaster from marching back there and grabbing her, at the point of a gun if necessary. And if they decided to take that kind of action, her old hive would be the first place they'd look.

Do you wish to go straight across?

Nicole hesitated, feeling the rush of hot air as the door into the heat duct opened up. Her own bed. Her own dining room, and real food.

The Shipmasters hunting for her.

No, she needed someplace where Fievj wouldn't look. Ideally, a place where he and his Wisps couldn't sneak up on her.

Fortunately, there was such a place. *Not straight across,* she told the Wisp. *Take me down to the Q2 arena.*

Very well.

The Wisp turned her toward the wall and the open door. Distantly, Nicole wondered if the young Ejbof she and Kahkitah had run into earlier was still on guard duty.

And if he was, whether or not she would have to make him eat his paintball gun.

Fourteen

Nicole had hoped her new Protector Says routine would get her into the arena without having to use her inhaler to ask the *Fyrantha* for a code. To her relief, it did. For the first time, she was able to simply tell the ship to open the door.

Still, even if she never used the inhaler again, whatever damage the drug had done to her body was still there. As she pulled open the door, she wondered who Ushkai would pick as the *Fyrantha*'s next Protector after she died.

There were no shouts of challenge from the close-packed forest as Nicole pulled the arena door closed. Nor, luckily, were there any sudden paintball shots. Nicole thought about calling out to the Ejbofs to let them know she was here, decided the hell with it, and headed down the path into the woods.

From the open area by the door, the trees looked pretty much impassable. Now, as she walked through the middle of the forest, she could see that it wasn't quite that bad. There were a lot of places where she had to walk sideways to get through, but most of the trees were far enough apart that she could walk straight through the gaps.

But the most important point was still there: Fievj in his centaur armor and Wisps with their outstretched arms would find their way seriously blocked, which was exactly what she'd hoped for. Picking a likely-looking spot, she walked a dozen steps off the path, found a leaf-filled dip where she could stretch out, and lay down. An hour of rest, maybe two, and her legs should be recovered enough for her to head back to the edge of Q4 and see if she could get Ushkai to tell her how Allyce's drug had to be delivered.

She was dreaming about ghosts and monsters and sharp sticks when she started awake.

To find herself surrounded by a dozen Ejbofs, four of them standing over her on the ground, the others hanging off the surrounding trees.

All of them looking at her.

The nearest of them poked her in the side with the muzzle of his paintball gun. "You. Awake," the words came through Nicole's translator.

"You. Poke me again and lose some teeth," she growled back. She lifted herself up on one elbow. "Hey—you—Shooter—the guy who was watching this door last time I came in. Did you forget to tell them you weren't supposed to mess with me?"

"No one has shot you." A voice came down from above her.

She peered up. Alien faces were hard to distinguish, but that was Shooter's voice and it was more than likely his face looking down at her. From a safe distance, she noted with dark humor. "Yeah, well, *not messing* also means *not poking*," she said. "What do you want?"

"We need your help," Shooter said. "*I* need your help."

"Sorry," Nicole said. "I'm kind of busy right now."

"But—"

"Silence," the Ejbof who'd poked her said, staring up into the tree. He looked back down at Nicole. "The truth is that we'll all die without your help."

Nicole felt her stomach tighten. Since when did being the

Fyrantha's Protector translate into being mother hen for every-one and everything aboard? "I'm not going to help you in your hunt," she said. The faces of Mispacch and her family flashed up from her memory; ruthlessly, she forced them back. Helping the Micawnwi had been what had gotten her, Jeff, and her whole world in trouble in the first place. "My job is to keep the—"

"We don't need you to help the hunt," the Ejbof leader cut her off. "The hunt is over."

"—keep the *Fyrantha*—" She broke off. "What?"

"The hunt is over," the leader repeated. "We know how to catch the beasts. We need merely to know how to hold them."

Nicole shook her head. "You lost me."

"Come with us," the leader said. He gestured at the woods with his gun and then hoisted it up onto his shoulder. "We'll—"

He stopped as a distant grinding sound drifted through the woods. Nicole had just figured out the direction it was coming from when it changed to a sort of crunching noise, then quickly cut off and was followed by silence. "What was *that*?" she de-manded.

"Our quarry," the leader said. "Come, we'll show you." He led the way back to the path, then headed along it deeper into the arena.

Nicole hesitated. She had no intention of getting involved in their war. Still, going along to find out what the noise was didn't count as a promise that she would do anything about it. Getting up, she followed the three other Ejbofs who'd been standing over her. The other aliens stayed in the trees, moving nimbly from one to another like ugly monkeys.

The grinding noise had started again, much closer this time, when the leader motioned for them all to stop. "It lurks on the other side of this line," he said. "Stay back, and beware of its teeth."

He circled the nearest tree and disappeared behind it. Wishing even more that Kahkitah was here, Nicole followed.

She'd expected to find a nasty-looking animal, maybe something like a lion or tiger or at least a big snake. To her surprise, the creature on the other side of the trees was more like a giant slug, five feet long and three feet wide. It had no arms or legs, but she could see hints of lots of little feet underneath the edge, rippling as the creature moved along, like some insects she'd seen running around the Philadelphia alleys. The thing was mostly brown and gray, but there was a big yellow splotch across its back.

She nodded to herself. So that was what the paintball guns were for. The creature's colors would make it very hard to see as it moved across the forest floor, but tagging it that way made it much easier to find and trap.

In fact it looked pretty much trapped right where it was, crowded in by close-set trees in front and on both sides. The only open space was behind it, and the way the feet moved she wasn't sure it could even walk backward. The grinding noise was coming from somewhere near its front—

With a sudden crackle of torn wood, one of the two trees blocking its path suddenly tipped over. It fell a few feet before its top jammed between the trees nearest it, the impact knocking the bottom of the tree off its base and to the side. The creature lifted itself slightly, walked over the miniature stump that was left, and continued its slow but steady progress.

"You see the problem," the leader said. "We can catch and trap them, but they easily break free."

Nicole pursed her lips as she watched the slug move on to the next tree in its path. Some weird combination of beaver and buzz saw, plodding through the forest knocking it all down. "Can you pick it up?" she asked. "Turn it over onto its back, maybe?"

"The teeth go around the entire edge," the leader said. "We cannot pick it up without severe injury."

"So how did you trap it?"

"We dug a cliff edge in its path and concealed it with tree branches," the leader said. "When it reached the edge, it toppled down the slope to the circle of closely packed trees that we hoped would hold it." He gestured toward the slug. "As you can see, the beast is not trapped."

"Can you dig a pit, then?" Nicole persisted. "Not just an edge, but a hole in the ground. Get it to fall in, and you're done."

"Sadly, they're now alerted to that tactic," the leader said. "We tried the same edge technique with one of the others. It detected the woven branches, and turned away."

"How many of them are there?"

"Six."

Nicole winced. Six buzz-saw beavers, who could learn *and* could talk to each other across the arena. Terrific. "Is there something in the hive you could lure them on top of?" she asked. "Like part of a door or something that you could lift without getting in range of their teeth?"

"We've searched," the leader said. "There's nothing."

"We tried to use a tree branch to tip one over before the teeth could cut all the way through," one of the other Ejbofs offered. "But they're too heavy."

Nicole nodded, eyeing the creature. The thing certainly *looked* heavy. Still, if tipping it onto its back was all it took, Kahkitah could probably do it.

Only Kahkitah was busy with a more important job: helping Jeff and Allyce and making sure Bungie's team didn't hurt them or the others. The minute she dragged the Ghorf in here, that would probably be the moment the Shipmasters ordered the attack.

In fact . . .

She gave the Ejbof leader a sideways look. Could that be exactly what Fievj was up to? Could he have found out she was here and ordered the Ejbofs to stall her while the battle got started?

She clenched her teeth. Damn them all; and she didn't have time for this.

"Their goal is to reach the food dispensers," one of the other Ejbof put in. "When they reach one, they demolish it."

"There were twenty dispensers in different parts of the forest," the leader said, sending a sharp look at the one who'd spoken, just like the one he'd given Shooter earlier. Maybe he was the only one who was allowed to talk to the stranger. "There are now only fourteen."

"Are there any rivers you could—Wait a second," Nicole interrupted herself. "They're demolishing the *dispensers?*"

"Yes," the leader said. "We were told their goal is to deny us food and cause us to starve."

"Before they demolish them—or maybe *while* they're doing it— do they eat any of the food?"

"Why would they?" the leader retorted. "I told you: their goal is simply to deny the food to us."

"Yeah, like the Shipmasters never lie," Nicole muttered. "Give me that." She snatched the paintball gun from the leader's grip. It was heavier than she'd expected, all metal and heavy plastic—

Eleven other guns instantly snapped around to point at her.

"Oh, stop it," she growled. "I'm not going to shoot anyone. You want to fix this? Then get those things out of my face. You—up in the tree—Shooter. Tell them."

"She means it," Shooter said. "Point them away. Leader?"

Reluctantly, Nicole thought, the leader gestured, and the others lowered their weapons. "Fine," she said. "Let's try something." Sidling her way through the trees, she caught up with the slug.

She stepped in front of it, making sure to stay clear of grinding teeth that could take down a tree, and lifted the gun high over her head. She held the pose a moment, picking her spot—

And jabbed it down with all her strength, burying its barrel in the ground right in front of the creature.

She took a step back, holding her breath. The slug reached the gun, bumped into it, and the forest once again came alive with the sound of grinding.

But this time, nothing happened. Teeth that could take down a tree apparently couldn't make any headway against gun-barrel metal.

The slug tried twice more, with no greater success. Then, backing away a few inches—so the thing *could* go backward—it started to change direction.

Only to once again come to a sudden halt as another Ejbof stepped forward and rammed his gun into the ground in front of it.

As if that was a signal, the rest of the Ejbofs came to life, dropping from the trees with guns ready. A moment later, the slug was penned in by a fence of gun barrels.

"You have saved us, Sibyl," the leader said, bowing low in front of Nicole. "When we sing of this day your name will be lifted high—"

"I'm not finished," Nicole interrupted him. The slug was still moving, shifting direction over and over as it tried to find a way out of the cage. "How much food do you have?"

"How much—*what?*"

"How much food do the dispensers provide?" Nicole asked.

"The ones our enemies have destroyed provide nothing," someone bit out.

"I mean the ones they *didn't* destroy," Nicole growled. "Do they give you enough to eat, not enough to eat, or more than enough to eat?"

"That's of no matter now," the leader said. "We now can trap them—"

"More than enough," Shooter spoke up.

"Good," Nicole said. "Bring me some."

For a moment the only sound was the grinding sound as the slug tried his luck with yet another of the paintball guns. Then, Shooter stepped up to Nicole. "I have some," he said, pulling a handful of the familiar granola-like nuggets from a hip pouch. "Are you hungry?"

"Not me." Nicole took the nuggets and walked over to the slug. "But he might be."

"Are you mad?" the leader demanded. "Are you now our enemy?"

"Shut it," Nicole ordered. Picking a moment when the slug had backed up and was starting into another turn, she dribbled the food into a small pile in front of it.

The slug paused. For a moment it didn't move. Then, it moved forward a few inches, running its front edge over the pile. Another pause, and then it resumed its turn.

And as that section of ground came into view, Nicole saw that the food was gone.

"You see that?" Nicole said, pointing at the ground. "And you see *that*?" she added as the slug stopped its rotation and started back the other way, as if searching for any food it might have missed. "It's not trying to destroy your food dispensers. It's just hungry."

"Yes, I see," the leader said. "But the point is that, once we trap them this way, *we* won't go hungry."

Nicole glared at him. "You—Shooter—what's your name?"

Shooter looked at the leader. "My name?" he prompted.

The leader seemed to glare. "Aiden," he said.

Shooter—Aiden—looked back at Nicole, and it seemed to her that he stood a little taller. "I am Aiden," he said.

"Nice to meet you, Aiden," she said. "Go to the nearest dispenser and bring back all the food you can carry. And *you*"—she jabbed a finger at one of the others—"you go with him. Same orders."

"You cannot—" the leader began.

"*You*: go," Nicole said to Aiden. "*You*: shut up," she added to the leader. "You want to know how to trap them or not?"

The leader looked at the slug, still hemmed in. He looked at Nicole as if he very much wanted to say something. Nicole folded her arms across her chest and looked straight back at him, and he remained silent.

It took Aiden and the other Ejbof less than five minutes. From the direction they returned from, Nicole guessed they'd gone to the dispenser that the slug had also been aiming for. "Go ahead," Nicole said, gesturing to the slug. "Feed it."

The second Ejbof looked inquiringly at the leader. But Aiden didn't even hesitate. Stepping boldly to the paintball gun fence, he dribbled the nuggets off his palm and fingers the way Nicole had done.

The slug was faster on the uptake this time, swinging immediately around to the growing pile. "More," Nicole said. "Make piles on either side of its nose."

Aiden obeyed. The slug moved back and forth, eating one pile completely down to the ground before turning back to the next. Aiden ran out of food, and at Nicole's order the other Ejbof added his collection to the piles.

Finally, the slug slowed its movements, then stopped completely. "There," Nicole said. "Congratulations. You've trapped it."

"But we'd already trapped it," the leader said, sounding completely lost.

"Really?" Stepping to the ring, Nicole pulled out the paintball gun directly in front of the slug.

It made no move to escape. It didn't move at all, in fact, as Nicole pulled all the rest of the guns out of the ring and tossed them back to their owners. "You gave it what it wanted," she said quietly. "No; what it *needed*. Keep it fed, and it won't attack the dispensers anymore. Do the same thing with the others, and you've won your little war."

"I don't think that's what the Shipmasters meant for us to do," the leader protested.

"Do I look like I care?" Nicole countered. "You have food, they have food, and they're not attacking. That's as good a win as it gets."

"We shall see what they say," the leader said, still sounding doubtful.

"I guess you will," Nicole said. "And I need to go."

"How can we thank you, Sibyl?" Aiden asked.

"I don't . . ." She paused, eyeing the paintball guns as a sudden thought struck her. The Shipmasters and the Q1 Wisps were out to get her. But they seemed to operate on sight instead of hearing or smell or something else.

What would happen if she put a smear of yellow paint across a Wisp's face?

All sorts of things might happen, none of them good. The paint might injure the Wisp, or blind it, or even kill it. The very act of firing a weapon, even just a paintball gun, might be all the proof Fievj needed to convince him that humans would make great war slaves.

But she had to risk it. She and Ushkai held control over barely a quarter of the *Fyrantha*, and if the Shipmasters got rid of her she had no idea whether Ushkai could hold on to that part alone. Anyway, Fievj had already seen her use the greenfire weapon in the Q4 arena, and was at least partly convinced she wasn't a typical human. Seeing her shoot a paintball gun probably wouldn't change any of his opinions one way or the other.

Most important, Nicole didn't want to die.

That was really the bottom line here. She could scheme and plot and rationalize all she liked, but the cold hard truth was that she didn't want a Wisp to pick her up and throw her down a heat-transfer duct to her death. Whatever she had to do to keep that from happening, she'd do it.

Even to the point of sacrificing her world?

She winced. She'd been contemptuous of Allyce's wish to return to her husband. She'd had nothing but contempt for Bungie and Sam and their single-minded determination to get back to their lives.

Was she really any better than they were?

She didn't have an answer. Hopefully, it wouldn't come to a point where she needed one.

If it did, she could only hope she would make the right decision.

"Yes," she said to Aiden. "I need one of your paintball guns."

"Of course," he said, handing her his.

"Thanks," she said, slinging it over her shoulder by its strap. "Oh, wait. You said earlier you needed my help with something else. What was that?"

"You've already done it," Aiden said, again drawing up to his full height. "You have redeemed for me my name."

"Ah," Nicole said. If only it was always that simple. "You're welcome. Good luck, and don't forget to keep feeding them. Everybody gets grumpy when they're hungry."

Earlier, Nicole hadn't been up to heading all the way back to Q4 and the Caretaker. Now, after her nap, it still wasn't fun, but it was at least possible.

She might as well have saved herself the trip.

"The drug may be administered any way you wish," Ushkai said helpfully. "It may be injected or swallowed, or the aroma may be inhaled. The effects will be the same."

"Yeah, great," Nicole growled. "The instructions could have mentioned that."

"They did," he said. "You merely had to read with understanding."

Nicole glared at him. Trake had been like that, too, minus the flowery language. He liked to hide information so that people would have to ask. That let him not only make them come to him, but gave him the chance to mock the fact they hadn't seen the answer the first time.

She always figured Trake did it because he liked watching people flounder and grovel. Why the ship's Caretaker did it she couldn't guess.

Though now that she thought about it, the computers at her school had been a little like that, too.

"You intend to make them incapable of fighting, then?"

So Ushkai wouldn't offer any answers, but he was fine with asking useless questions. "We've already been through this," she reminded him.

She frowned. Or *was* it useless? Her mind flashed back to their last meeting and her sense that there was a question he wanted her to ask . . . "Or do you have a better idea?"

Again, there was that look. But no answer. Apparently, that wasn't the right question. "You are the *Fyrantha's* Protector," was all he said.

"Yeah, I got that," Nicole said. The hell with this. She didn't have time to stand around playing Twenty Questions. "Okay, one more thing. Do you have a"—she paused, trying to remember what Jeff had called it—"a schematic of the Q1 arena area?"

"The *Fyrantha* can guide you where you wish to go."

"If I'd wanted the *Fyrantha* to guide me I'd have said so," Nicole growled. "I want something I can look at and show other people."

For a moment Ushkai just stared at her. Nicole stared back, a creepy feeling running up her back. It was almost like he was having a quiet conversation with someone.

The rest of the ship, maybe? Maybe even the part Fievj and the Shipmasters had under their control?

For a second she wondered if she should tell Ushkai to forget it and just drop the whole idea. But it wasn't like Fievj didn't already know she'd be coming back to Q1. Besides, even if one of the Shipmasters was listening in on the conversation it didn't tell him what she was planning.

"You have your pad?" Ushkai asked.

"Yes," Nicole said, pulling it out.

"Go to the console and—"

"I already told you I don't want to use the inhaler."

"And lay it down on the blue glow."

Nicole frowned. There hadn't been any blue glow on the console the last time she was here. "Okay," she said cautiously, watching Ushkai out of the corner of her eye as she walked to the console.

To find that there was indeed a soft blue light coming from a flat part on top, a section that had looked like normal metal the last time she'd seen it. Pursing her lips, she laid the pad down on the glow.

For a moment, the blue light pulsed gently, just visible around the pad's edge. Then, the light turned bright green. "Pick it up," Ushkai said.

Nicole did so, and the green light disappeared. She punched for the pad's data records.

There they were, stacked right above the carefully scrawled

instructions Kahkitah had written down for making Setting Sun: ten pages of diagrams of the Q1 arena, covering the arena itself, the surrounding decks, plus a couple of extra decks above and below it.

"Will that be sufficient?"

Nicole pulled up the deck she wanted and peered at it, a small part of her brain noting the fact that a few months ago she would have been completely overwhelmed by something this complicated. Now, after watching Jeff and the others trace through dozens and dozens of wiring layouts, she knew how to break things like this into little pieces.

There it was, exactly where she'd expected it.

"Yes," she told Ushkai. "This will do just fine."

"Then go. Protector."

She looked up at him again. There was still that feeling that he was expecting something else from her.

But she was on a tight schedule right now. Later, maybe, she'd have time to figure out what was going on here. "Yeah," she said. "Thanks."

A few minutes later, she was back in Q2. So far she'd tried coming in right beside the Q1 arena and from way above it. Fievj had seen both, and he'd be ready for her to try one or the other of them again.

This time, maybe she could do something he absolutely wouldn't expect.

And if he did, and if he or the Wisps got in her way . . .

Nicole winced, freshly aware of the weight of the paintball gun slung over her shoulder. If anyone of them got in her way, she would do whatever she had to.

FiFteen

She started again from the top of the ship, having a Q2 Wisp carry her across the heat duct to Q1. This time, though, she crossed much farther back from the arena, with the goal to come up on it from behind.

And not only from behind, but through one of the horizontal air vent levels.

She'd heard about them from the Q4 Wisps when they were first showing her around that part of the ship. But there was so much else for her to see and learn she'd never bothered to figure out how to get to them. Now, with the Q1 schematics in hand, it was time to see how useful they would be.

The vents were similar to the vertical heat-transfer ducts she used to get up and down, with the same idea of mixing air through the whole ship, except that these were aimed front and back instead of up and down. Unlike the vertical ducts, though, the horizontal ones were narrow and low ceilinged, too small for the Wisps to travel through.

Which, considering the situation in Q1, was a definite plus. As Nicole worked open one of the access covers and dropped into the vent she wished she'd thought of this sooner. It would have made her last couple of trips to Q1 so much easier.

It took her fifty feet to realize that *easier* was the com
wrong word for this.

It wasn't just the narrowness of the tunnel, or the low ceiling, or the bits of equipment and occasional thick cable that jutted out into her path at odd places. She'd been smart or lucky enough to pick one of the tunnels where the wind was blowing at her back, pushing her toward the arena, instead of directly into her face, which would have made the trip almost impossible. But even there, the extra wind assist often betrayed her as it created eddies around some of the protruding equipment that jostled her around, sometimes right into something solid that she'd been trying to avoid. The vent was much darker than the rest of the ship, too, with only a few lights spaced along the ceiling. There were also none of the segment or level markings that regular corridors had to tell her where she was.

Worst of all, she realized that she wasn't any safer here than she was anywhere else. While the Wisps couldn't get through the vent, there were plenty of access covers spaced along the ceiling that they could open whenever they wanted to. Once they did that, all they would have to do was reach down and grab her as she passed by. Even if she saw that coming in time to keep away, their next move would be to simply open the two covers on either side of her, trapping her between them. Once they'd done that, they could just sit and wait until she either surrendered or starved.

Still, even if Fievj caught on afterward, this should be the last time she needed to sneak into the Q1 arena. As long as he didn't spot this back door until she was inside, she should be all right. Assuming, of course, that once she was there she could dodge the Wisps long enough to get this over with.

According to the schematic, the vent she was in was supposed to end in a T-junction at the edge of the arena, branching off to both sides. There was also supposed to be a service door into the arena at that junction. Unfortunately, the schematic had been a little vague on how big the door was. If it wasn't big enough for her to get through, she would have to come back up into the regular corridor and dodge Wisps while she figured out something else.

The end of the vent and the service door were visible a hundred feet ahead when she began to hear the sound of rushing water.

She picked up her pace. As best as she could figure, the pipes carrying the water into the river were directly below her. Depending on how narrow the river was at that point, she should hopefully be able to leap across to either Jeff's or Bungie's side.

The hatch was much smaller than a regular door, but to her relief it was more than big enough for her to get through. She opened it—it swung outward into the arena—and leaned cautiously out.

And with the water now thundering in her ears she discovered to her dismay that she'd miscalculated.

The river was indeed directly below her, close enough for the spray to reach her hands and face. But it wasn't the three or four feet across that she'd hoped for, with the riverbanks within easy jumping distance. Instead, it was a good twenty feet across, wider even than the section Duncan and Kahkitah had helped her across earlier, and flowing nearly as fast as it was farther down.

Worse, there were no pathways along the wall to either side: no ledges, stairways, or even handholds. Clearly, no one had ever expected anyone to come into the arena this way.

At least, not while the river was flowing.

Nicole chewed at her lip. She'd only done this a couple of times, and there was no guarantee it would work. Still, at this point she was going to have to back out and try a different door anyway. She

might as well give it a try. *"Fyrantha!"* she called, wondering if the
ship could even hear her over the noise. "Protector says turn off the
Q1 arena river."

For a long moment nothing happened. Nicole studied the wall
and riverbanks, trying to figure out what her next move would
be if the ship couldn't or wouldn't obey. Probably go down the
branch of the T-junction toward Jeff's side, try to find another
access door there, and hope it wasn't too high for her to drop down
without breaking something.

And then, like someone had turned a faucet somewhere, the
water flow began to ease. The edges of the riverbanks came into
view as the pressure and volume decreased and the water level
went down. The banks here weren't the same dirt-covered slopes
she'd seen in the riverbed separating the Thii and Ponng in Q3, but
were made of a bare white ceramic that sloped a bit inward. The
slopes seemed to be the same angle as the sections she'd climbed
across, which might mean the whole channel was that way.

Except with rocks. She remembered the roiling of the water
where she'd crossed, the twisted currents and little whirlpools
that had marked hidden boulders. She watched as the level kept
going down, wondering when she would start seeing them.

To her surprise, no rocks appeared. The white swirling water
bubbled away as the level continued to drop, showing nothing but
more flat ceramic beneath it. Barely thirty seconds after her command, there was nothing left but a wet, tapered channel leading down from the pipe like a water slide. It disappeared under
the tree branches and continued on its way toward the ocean at
the other end of the arena.

There was no time to wonder where the rocks had gone. If the
Shipmasters overhead in the balcony hadn't noticed what had happened, they'd figure it out soon enough, and Nicole had to be
under cover on Jeff's side before they sent someone to check it

out. She pulled herself the rest of the way through the hatch-way, eyeing the six-foot drop and the angled slope beneath her as she maneuvered the paintball gun barrel through the opening. The slope was pretty steep, and there was no way to know how slippery it was, and the last thing she needed right now was a pair of broken ankles. Hanging from the edge of the hatch, she took a deep breath and let go, shoving the hatch closed behind her as she dropped. She hit the ceramic, bent her knees to absorb the impact—

And promptly fell flat on her back and butt and started slid-ing down the channel, the gun bouncing noisily along behind her.

For that first horrible second she wondered if she would be able to slow down, or whether she would careen at full speed around the next curve and slam full-speed into a stack of rocks. But to her relief the channel started flattening out almost imme-diately, and by the time she'd gone fifty feet and was under the cover of the tree branches the slope had become something she could handle. She dug in with her elbows and managed to coast to a stop.

She scrambled to her feet and looked around. The channel was only waist high, but from this angle it was hard to tell exactly where she was. Still, the slope of the riverbanks seemed sharper than it had been where she'd crossed earlier, so that spot was prob-ably still downstream. Keeping one eye on the branches above her, watching for gaps the Shipmasters might be able to see her through, she headed down.

Still no boulders. She wondered about that as she half ran, half leaped down the slope until she spotted a set of small openings low on the channel sides at one of the curves. She couldn't tell for sure without stopping for a closer look, but they looked like the jets from the hot tub in that hotel she'd gone to once for a swim-ming party. If that's what they were, maybe the white water she'd thought was rocks was just extra water and air being squirted into the main stream.

Which made sense, now that she thought about it. Having boulders that might break loose and damage the channel as they tumbled down the river could be pretty risky. The only problem that jets might cause was if they clogged up.

Almost to the crossing spot now. She was still waist-deep in a pit, but without the flowing water battering at her she should be able to get a grip on the plants along the riverside and pull herself up once she got there.

And then, from above and behind her, she heard the sudden roar of the water starting up again.

For a horrified second she just stood there. No—the water couldn't be back on. She was the Protector, and she'd ordered the *Fyrantha* to shut it off.

In a part of the ship where the Shipmasters held their strongest control.

A wave of cold water washing across her feet and ankles snapped her out of it. Cursing, she took off, loping down the slope as fast as she could.

But it was already too late. The rushing water had risen to the level of her calves, and her mad dash began to falter as the current threatened to sweep her feet out from under her. She unslung the paintball gun as she fought for balance, watching the trees above her in hopes there might be a root or tree branch sticking out that she could loop the gun's sling around and pull herself out of the river before she was overwhelmed. The water reached her knees, and then midway up her thighs—

And then, suddenly, she was there.

Too late. Already she was going too fast to stop. A sudden wave rose up and slapped her in the middle of her back, throwing her into a forward stumble. Reflexively, she tossed the paintball gun

up onto the bank to free her hands as she fought for balance—
caught a glimpse of the top of Kahkitah's head as he hurried
toward the river—lost her battle for stability as another wave hit
her back—

And suddenly she was on her stomach in the river, her hands
splashing frantically to try to keep her head above water, riding
the current helplessly down the channel.

The foam and spray were all around her, splashing up into her
face, threatening to choke her as it washed into her nose and
mouth, sometimes rolling completely over her head. She gasped
and coughed and fought, her old fear of water filling her mind and
freezing any chance for clear thought. She curved around each
corner in terror that she would hit the side or that there might still
be rocks down here that she would slam into with bone-shattering
force. A horrible thought bubbled up through the rest of the terror: that if the tide was out, the river would throw her face-first
into the sand of the beach. She tried to swivel around, trying to
position herself so that she might at least land with her feet forward instead of her head. But the current was too strong. Ahead,
barely visible through the water slapping into her face and dripping into her eyes, she saw the twin bluffs that marked the end of
the river—

She barely had time to register that when there was a final
surge and the river threw her into the ocean.

Her first reaction was relief that she'd hit water instead of getting dumped onto hard sand. The current continued to push her
outward, the chaotic white water of the river fading into the calmer
ocean waves. She sputtered the last bit of water from her nose
and mouth and turned herself upright, letting her feet down
toward the ocean floor.

An instant later she dropped completely underwater again as

her head dipped below the waves without her feet ever finding the bottom.

She flailed her way back to the surface, a new wave of panic sending her heart pounding. Fighting to keep her head clear, she managed to turn around enough to look back toward shore.

She was way farther out than she'd realized. Thirty, maybe even forty yards from the bluffs and the shore.

Three or four feet deep, Jeff had said the water was. But that was only near the bluffs. Clearly, it got a lot deeper a lot faster than she'd expected it to.

She clenched her teeth. She'd never learned to swim, but she'd better figure it out, and fast. Still splashing awkwardly, she managed to work herself all the way around to face the beach. At least now the waves coming in from the end of the ocean were hitting the back of her head instead of slapping her in the face. She tried changing the angle of her splashing hands—was there something about kicking her feet, too?—and started moving toward the shore.

At least, she hoped she was moving. Between the washing movement of the waves and the fact that her eyes were barely above the water she couldn't really tell if she was making any progress. But all she could do was try.

And then, directly ahead of her, between her and the shore, something dark surged briefly above the waves.

Nicole froze, forgetting to keep paddling until she dunked herself underwater again. She clawed her way back to the surface, swiping one hand across her eyes and looking frantically around. Had it been a trick of her eyes? A fish? Jeff hadn't said anything about fish. A really big fish?

A shark?

Too frightened even to curse, she raised her eyes back to the shore.

The shark was suddenly forgotten. Gliding across each of the beaches, moving along the water's edge from the arena's sides toward the river, were six Wisps.

Each group accompanied by a centaur-armored Shipmaster.

And with that, it was over. Nicole could drown out here, or get eaten by a shark, or make it back to land and be killed by the Shipmasters. How it happened didn't matter. She was dead, and the Shipmasters had won, and the *Fyrantha* had lost.

And suddenly, directly in front of her, the object she'd seen again surged out of the water.

Nicole gasped, catching half a mouthful of water in the process. But before she could do anything, it dropped back out of view. She felt something glide past her legs and come up behind her—

And a pair or arms or tentacles or something snaked around her waist, locking her in an unbreakable grip against a hard body pressed against her back. The arms and the body lifted her upward, bringing her face fully out of the water for the first time since she'd been thrown into the river.

With her ears full of water, and her brain full of panic, she didn't hear the birdsong. But in her head, the translation came through.

"Relax, Nicole. I have you. You're safe."

"Kah—?" Nicole sputtered out some water. "*Kahkitah?*"

This time, she heard his birdsong, sounding strangely bubbly as the water surged up around his neck gills. "Yes," the translation came. "I have you."

"Yeah, thanks," she gasped, sucking in lungfuls of air. "How did—? Never mind. They're on the beach. You see them? They're on the beach."

"I know," Kahkitah said, his tone going grim. "There's only one way now to escape, Nicole. Do you trust me?"

Nicole looked back at the beach, her mind racing, Kahkitah's words barely registering. If they could get to the bluffs before the Wisps closed the gap . . . but no, they were already too close. Could she and Kahkitah go up the river? Not a chance, not against the current that had tossed her here. What if she stopped the water again—could they climb up the channel? But the Shipmasters knew how to turn it back on. The emergency exits? But even if there were any that opened up above the ocean the Shipmasters had already seen her use one of those.

Besides, the centaur armor meant a stash of greenfire weapons. Long before she and Kahkitah could haul themselves up from the water into a doorway the Shipmasters could pull out the weapons and shoot them down.

"Do you trust me?"

"What?"

"Do you trust me?" the Ghorf repeated.

Nicole shrugged, or did the best she could with her arms pinned to her sides. She had no idea what he was talking about, or what he might be thinking. But whatever it was, she had nothing better to offer. "Sure," she said. "What do you—?"

"Brace yourself," he said. "Breathe in and out quickly and deeply—many times—to empty your lungs of carbon dioxide. When I tell you, take a final deep breath and hold it."

Nicole frowned. Crisp, clear orders, plus some words she'd never heard him use before. Was this really Kahkitah?

But even as she wondered she was obeying, inhaling and exhaling as deeply and quickly as she could. They were heading away from the beach now, Kahkitah swimming far faster than Nicole could ever have managed. She watched the Shipmasters tensely, waiting for one of them to reach behind him and pop the cover on his little arsenal. But both aliens just stood there, watching the Ghorf and the *Fyrantha*'s Protector swimming

away from them. Probably also wondering what the hell Kahkitah was doing.

The waves washing around Nicole seemed to be getting
stronger. She turned her head, still breathing deeply like Kahkitah had told her, trying to see where they were. They had to
be getting close to the end of the arena by now. She could hear a
new sound over the waves, a sort of rhythmic thumping like some
of the *Fyrantha's* pumps.

"Now!" Kahkitah ordered. "Deep breath, and hold it."

Nicole did so, her heart thudding again. The pump sound was
getting louder . . .

And then, without warning, the ocean seemed to drop out from
under them. Kahkitah fell backward, still clutching Nicole to his
chest, as the water closed around them. She squeezed her eyes
shut, fighting back the urge to gasp or scream. Something slammed
hard against Kahkitah's back, half turning them over and sending them skidding down at an angle. The water pressed even
harder against them, swirling across Nicole's face and tearing at
her hair and jumpsuit. One of Kahkitah's hands let go of her waist
and wrapped around her face, protecting her and keeping her from
exhaling. There was a roar in her ears . . . small white spots
danced in front of her closed eyes . . .

And then everything went dark.

The first thing she noticed as she drifted back to consciousness
was that she could breathe again. The second thing she noticed
was that she wasn't wet anymore. The third was that she was lying
on something soft, a little stiffer than the mattress in her room,
but comfortable enough.

The fourth was that there were Ghorf birdsongs coming from
somewhere in the distance.

More than one set, too. They were too soft for her translator to pick up, but she could tell that there were at least three or four different voices. And she wasn't completely sure, but she didn't think any of the voices belonged to Kahkitah.

Darkness seemed to be pressing against her eyelids. She opened her eyes, only to find that wasn't much help—the room she was in was large, featureless, and only dimly lit. Above her, maybe a dozen feet away, was a ceiling made of corrugated metal. She frowned at that pattern, wondering why it looked familiar.

Abruptly, it clicked. It was the same ceiling as in the lower-most level of the *Fyrantha*, the one just above the recycling area, where she'd found Wesowee wandering around.

She rolled over onto her side and pushed herself up on one elbow. Sure enough, that was where she was. The open space stretched out in all directions around her, the widely separated lights creating small islands of visibility in the gloom. Beneath her was the metal grating of the floor, with the dark and odd-smelling mass beneath, while the lights showed the familiar pattern of pillars stretching from floor to ceiling as if they were holding up the rest of the ship.

She frowned. Unlike the Q4 basement, though, something new had been added here. Filling the space between the support pillars to her left, stretching out as far as she could see, were neat rows of slender, waist-high cylinders, each about as big around as the tubes of red-and-green paper her grandmother used to wrap Christmas presents in. The cylinders were standing upright on the floor grate, with just enough space between them for a person to walk. It reminded her of the fields of corn she'd seen on TV, except that these were just tubes instead of big green corn plants.

The Ghorf voices were coming from the opposite direction, and she turned to look. About a hundred yards away was a clump of lights moving among what looked like a group of chairs, couches, tables, and consoles.

She frowned. In Q4, anyway, this part of the ship wasn't set up for people to live in. Could these be more lost Ghorfs who'd given up any hope of escape and set up housekeeping?

She rolled off the mattress and got to her feet. Her clothes and hair were dry, as she'd already noted, but there was a hollow feeling in her stomach that felt like she hadn't eaten in a while. How long had she been asleep, anyway?

The Ghorfs with the lights didn't seem to have noticed she was awake. She thought about calling to them, decided that would be a bad idea if there were any Wisps around. Better to walk over herself. A wave of dizziness ran through her, and she grabbed one of the tubes beside her for balance.

Abruptly, a head appeared, floating in the air above the tube.

Nicole snatched her hand back, twitching back in reaction as the head vanished. For a moment she stood there, catching her breath, staring at the cylinder. Now that she was standing, she could see there were two sets of tiny letters etched into the top of each cylinder: one set made up of the kind of letters the *Fyrantha* used, the other something she'd never seen before. Cautiously, she reached out and again touched the top of the cylinder.

The head reappeared. It wasn't a real head, she saw now, but a hologram like Ushkai. Except that while the Caretaker's whole body was there, this was just a human head. "Hello?" she murmured toward it.

The head didn't change. She let go of the cylinder—the head vanished. She touched it again—the head reappeared. "Hello?" she tried again.

Still no answer. She pressed a little harder on the cylinder . . .

The head suddenly shrank to a quarter of its size and rose higher into the air. Lines of writing appeared below it, in both sets of letters, and the head and the words began scrolling slowly upward.

A soft birdsong came from directly behind her. She twitched, spinning around—"Welcome, Protector," the translation came as she found herself facing yet another Ghorf. "I trust you are recovered?"

"Yeah, I think so," Nicole said, feeling her lip twist. Up to now she'd tried to keep her new title private. But Kahkitah had heard Ushkai call her that, and apparently he'd blabbed. "Where's Kahkitah?"

"Returned to your people in the Q1 arena." The Ghorf gestured to the rows of cylinders beside her. "To your *other* people, I mean."

"What do you mean, my other people?"

The Ghorf waved at the cylinders again. "I assumed you were paying your respects to those gone before."

"To those gone—?" Nicole broke off, a sudden horrible feeling in the pit of her stomach. Was he saying—? "Are these *graves*?"

"Memorials," the Ghorf corrected. "The images and life stories of those who long ago served aboard the *Fyrantha*."

Nicole gazed across the field of cylinders. Not rows of corn, like she'd first thought, but rows of tombstones. "That's . . . a lot of slaves," she managed.

"Slaves?" The Ghorf shook his head. "No, these weren't slaves. The slaves' memorial is in Q2." His tone turned darker. "That one includes the fallen Ghorfs, as well as humans. This memorial is for the workers who served alongside the Lillilli as they rebuilt the *Fyrantha* into a zoo."

"So, the original slaves."

"No, not slaves at all," the Ghorf insisted. "Fellow workers. The Lillilli invited them aboard some thousands of years ago to work alongside them on the renovations."

"Wait a second," Nicole asked, frowning. "So they were—? No.

Why would they get *invited*? And how would you know that, anyway?"

"We can read." The Ghorf reached over and touched one of the other cylinders. Another image appeared, this one the head of a woman. "The life stories listed make their relationships with the Lillilli very clear. We thought you would be able to tell us more."

"You thought I could—? Is *that* why you brought me here?"

"Along with saving you from the Shipmasters," a new Ghorf voice added from behind her.

Nicole turned as another of the big aliens came up behind her. To her surprise, this one was familiar. "*Wesowee*?"

"Indeed, Protector," Wesowee said, bowing his head toward her. "A long way from the Q3 arena, is it not?"

"I don't know," Nicole said, looking back and forth between the two Ghorfs. "Because I don't have the faintest idea where I am, or how I got here."

"You are in the deepest part of the Q1 section," Wesowee said. "As to how you got here, that's simple. The ocean flow took you over the spill water, from which Kahkitah took you through the guide, around the filters and sifters, into the reservoir and aerator, and out through the maintenance level. From there he brought you here." He gave the sort of whistle Nicole had always associated with a Ghorf shrug. "Along the way your oxygen level unfortunately dropped to where you became unconscious."

Nicole huffed out a breath. They'd done all *that*? "I guess I'm lucky to be alive."

"Luck had nothing to do with it," Wesowee said. "Kahkitah knew exactly what he was doing. We've long explored all of the *Fyrantha*'s waterways."

"What, all two of them?" Nicole scoffed. "Unless you want to count the streams in the Q4 arena."

The two Ghorfs looked at each other. "The *Fyrantha* has

precisely one hundred twenty-eight water passageways large enough for a Ghorf to travel through," Wesowee said. "I would have assumed the ship's Protector would know—"

"Wait a second," Nicole cut him off. "A hundred and—you guys can *swim?*"

"We swim quite well," the second Ghorf said, a bit stiffly. "Why don't you know these things? Kahkitah said you were the *Fyrantha's* Protector."

The best defense is a good offense. "How many Protectors have you known?" Nicole shot back. "Hmm? How many? Just me, right? So get off my back and let me do this my way."

"Of course, Protector," the Ghorf said with that same stiffness.

Nicole looked at Wesowee, ready for more argument. But he remained silent. "Okay," she said. "Let's start from the top. Who's this *we* who you say have explored the *Fyrantha?* You two, you two plus the ones over there, or someone else?"

But the moment had apparently passed. "I think that conversation should be handled by Kahkitah," the second Ghorf said. "Our main reason for bringing you was the hope that the old hospice facilities might include a supply of the Setting Sun drug Kahkitah said you need. But so far our search has been unfruitful."

Nicole looked over at the Ghorfs with the lights. *Hospice.* She'd heard that word before, connected to one of her grandmother's friends. Something to do with dying, she vaguely remembered.

Was this where the old human workers had come to die, and then to be buried?

"Fine, I'll ask Kahkitah about it," she said. "How do I get back to the Q1 arena?"

"I'll guide you," Wesowee said. "Indeed, we may have lingered too long. Kahkitah wanted you back as soon as you awoke, and you slept longer than we anticipated."

"He *did* warn us that you were overtired," the other Ghorf added. "But I don't think he expected you to sleep for twenty hours before you—"

"Twenty *hours*?" Nicole cut in. "Why the hell didn't you tell me? We have to get going, right now."

"There is no rush," the Ghorf said calmly.

"Like hell there isn't," Nicole snarled. Like he would have the slightest idea what was going on upstairs. "Come on, come on."

"I'm ready," Wesowee said with equal calmness.

"Then let's go," Nicole said, her empty stomach tightening even further. The Shipmasters could be kicking off Jeff's war at any minute. Could already have started *and* finished it, in fact. If she'd missed it because Wesowee had let her sleep in . . .

"Follow me," Wesowee said, and headed along the edge of the graveyard.

"We'll let you know if we find any of the Setting Sun," the other Ghorf called from behind them.

"Yeah, you do that," Nicole called back, frowning at the cylinders. Hospice, death, and burial, she'd thought . . . but there wasn't nearly enough room in those cylinders for a body. Had they been—what was the word?—cremated? "Wesowee, these aren't the actual bodies, are they?"

"No, just the memorials," Wesowee said. "The bodies, like everything else aboard, were reclaimed."

"Reclaimed?"

"Returned to the *Fyrantha's* resources," Wesowee said. "Broken down into basic components—"

"Yeah, yeah, I got it," Nicole interrupted, her gaze dropping to the grating they were walking on, and the dark mass beneath it. "So, like . . . compost?"

"Yes," Wesowee said. If the idea bothered him, it didn't show in his voice. "Come. Kahkitah and the others await you."

sixteen

Nicole had hoped the route back into the arena wouldn't follow the same path as the one Kahkitah had used to get them out in the first place. She really wasn't looking forward to swimming back through the Q1 ocean.

Fortunately, there was no water involved. Wesowee took her along a maze of service passageways, barely big enough for him to squeeze through, with no swimming or dunking or even wading. Twenty minutes after leaving the basement, they emerged through a final door into an all-too familiar corridor.

"This will lead you into the arena inside the tree line," Wesowee murmured in a subdued birdsong, pointing to the stairs going down.

Nicole nodded. And going up, those same stairs would lead into the Shipmasters' observation balcony. Something a little less risky might have been nice.

Still, no ocean swimming was the important part. "Thanks," she murmured back.

"Good luck," he said, and disappeared back through the door into the service areas.

Keeping half an eye on the stairs above her, Nicole headed down.

The arena door was no longer blocked open the way she and

Kahkitah had left it. But as she eased it open she spotted the cloth strip they'd used lying nearby in the sand. Perhaps the Shipmasters hadn't spotted it, but had merely kicked it away accidentally during one of their trips into the arena. She stepped through the doorway, used the strip to again block the door open, and headed toward the hive.

Levi was standing guard at the entrance, holding a sort of spear with three points at the top instead of one. One of the trident things Duncan had told her about earlier, presumably. Wrapped around Levi's waist was the folded-up net Duncan had also mentioned.

Levi spotted her, glanced around, then gestured her urgently toward him.

"About time," he said as she reached him. "Where've you been? Never mind—not important. Jeff and Allyce are almost ready with the gun, but we're about out of excuses and the Shipmasters are getting twitchy."

"Jeff was able to stall them off this long?" Nicole asked, wondering what gun he was talking about. The only thing she'd left was the paintball gun. Had Kahkitah sneaked upstairs and gotten hold of a greenfire weapon?

"No, Jeff's game is played out," Levi said. "But Bennett bit the bullet and twisted his ankle to buy a little more time. Figured it would be another week before he was ready. But those pressure bandage things are damn good, and he's almost back to speed."

Nicole nodded. So the Ghorfs down in the cemetery had been right about there not being any hurry for her to get up here. "What's the new timetable?"

"The Shipmasters have handed out the weapons to the Greenies—"

"Same ones as ours?"

"Yeah," Levi said, frowning. "Why? Were you expecting Bungie to get something different?"

"They sometimes do that," Nicole said. "So when is it?"

"They told us the battle will start at sunrise, about ten hours from now," Levi said. "Jeff figures Bungie will try to jump the gun—the tide will already be on the way out by then—but he doesn't think he can have the gun ready until a little before sunrise."

"So if Bungie moves early we have a problem," Nicole agreed grimly. "What exactly is this gun you're talking about?"

"The one you left for us," Levi said, frowning. "That *was* you who left the gun, right? Kahkitah said it was."

"Sure," Nicole said, her faint hope that Kahkitah might have snagged them a better weapon fading away. "Where are they?"

"Where you left the gun," Levi said, nodding toward the path leading up into the hills. "Jeff thought it would be safer not to bring it out where the Shipmasters might see it."

"He's being careful in the hive, too, isn't he?"

"Oh, yeah," Levi assured her. "We just do drills with the tridents and nets in there. Never anything that's secret." He gave her a tight smile. "And we're pretty freaking useless at the drills, too."

"Good," Nicole said. "I'm heading up. Shout if you see Bungie coming."

"Don't worry, Jeff's got a whole system set up," Levi said. "You just get up there and see if you can make things go a little faster."

Nicole found the little group just downstream from where she'd tossed the paintball gun up onto the riverbank. Jeff and Allyce were hunched over a set of medical containers, while Kahkitah sat at the edge of the river with a collection of paintball balls on the ground beside him.

Kahkitah spotted her first. "Nicole!" he called excitedly, his voice barely audible over the roar of the river. "Are you healed? Are you well?"

"I'm fine," she called back as she worked her way through the trees to them. "More than fine. You shouldn't have let me sleep that long."

"You probably needed it," Jeff said, waving her over. "He said you were exhausted."

"No more than any of the rest of you," Nicole said. "So . . . Allyce. You're here?"

"I'm here," Allyce said. Her expression wasn't exactly unfriendly, but it wasn't friendly, either. "Jeff asked me to come and treat Bennett's ankle."

"She's been terrific," Jeff added. "She mixed up the drug, and has been helping me load it into the paintballs."

"Great," Nicole said, keeping her eyes on Allyce's. "So you're on board?"

Allyce's eyes dropped away from Nicole's gaze. "I don't want anyone to get hurt," the other woman said. "Let's leave it at that."

Nicole pursed her lips. Not exactly an answer. Still, for now it was probably good enough. "Okay. What's the plan?"

"Allyce figured out that the drug can be either administered orally or inhaled," Jeff said. "Since we probably can't talk Bungie and his team into drinking the stuff, we figured we need to get them to breathe it."

"I already said I could get it into their food," Nicole reminded him.

"And I wasn't ready for you to take that risk," Jeff said, his forehead creasing in a frown. "I'd assumed you left the paintball gun because you'd come up with something better."

For a split second Nicole thought about lying. *Sure, of course, that was the plan all along.*

Trake would probably have lied. Bungie certainly would have lied. Pretending she knew what she was doing was the best way to keep them listening to her and doing what she told them to. The best way to keep them believing in her as the ship's Protector.

But she wasn't Trake or Bungie. And she sure as hell wasn't much of a Protector.

"I hadn't really thought that far ahead," she said. "I mostly brought it to fend off the Wisps if I had to."

"Really." Jeff's lip twitched. "You know, that one hadn't even occurred to me. Sometimes great minds think together; sometimes they run in parallel."

"Okay." Nicole wasn't exactly sure what that meant, but at least he wasn't mad at her. "How can I help?"

Jeff nodded toward the paintball gun, hanging by its strap from one of the tree branches. "Let's start with whether you've ever fired one of these before."

"I shot that greenfire weapon back in Q4," Nicole said, wincing at the memory. "Probably not the same."

"Not much," Jeff confirmed. "A projectile gun has a kick—means it recoils into your shoulder—and the slug also drops with distance. You didn't have to worry about either of those with the greenfire gun. Kahkitah, how many hollow balls do you have?"

Kahkitah peered down at the ground beside him. "Approximately thirty."

Jeff wrinkled his nose. "Eight men in Bungie's team, and we need to budget at least four per in case of misses. Not enough for us to use any of them for practice shots."

"Hold it," Nicole said as a sudden, horrible thought struck her. "Are you saying *I'm* going to be the one who shoots them?"

"Why not?"

"Why *not*?" Nicole retorted. "We just settled that I've never shot something like this before, remember?"

"We're not talking sniper levels of marksmanship here," Jeff soothed. "You just need to hit their chests or cheeks."

"Oh, is that *all*?"

"Actually, you want their chests," Allyce spoke up. "The gas is slightly lighter than air, and you want it to float up into their noses and mouths."

"So just their chests," Jeff said, nodding to her. "Even easier. You hit their chests, the balls pop, the liquid evaporates, they breathe it in, and we're good to go."

"Okay," Nicole said. "But you're the soldier. You're the one who knows how to shoot straight."

"I'm the *Marine*," he corrected her. "And I'd be happy to do it, except that I'm also the one who's supposed to be leading the blue team charge. I can't very well do that *and* sit up on the riverbank shooting at the Greenies."

Nicole looked at Allyce. But the doctor had her full attention on her work, clearly intent on staying out of the conversation. "Kahkitah?" Nicole asked, turning to the Ghorf. "Help me out, will you? You know I can't do this."

"On the contrary," Kahkitah said. "I know deep in my soul that you *can* do it. You've done so many other remarkable things since coming to the *Fyrantha*. All you need is some practice."

"Which is going to be a problem," Jeff said. "Our gimmicked balls are about the same weight as the ones with paint in them, so that part should be all right. The problem is that if the Shipmasters get a look at a whole bunch of yellow trees and rocks they're likely to get suspicious. This whole thing depends on them not figuring out what we're doing."

Nicole looked past Kahkitah's shoulder, to where the upper edge of the river could be seen churning through the channel. "Why don't I just shoot into the river?" she asked. "That's where Kahkitah is dumping the paint from the empties, isn't it?"

"Well . . . yes," Jeff said, frowning in thought. "How are you going to see where you're hitting?"

"She could hang a small weight from a tree branch," Kahkitah suggested. "If it moves after she fires, then she'll know she hit it."

"If she does that, she'll be shooting downhill," Jeff pointed out. "That's a little different from shooting up or on the level."

"But she'll be shooting downhill during the actual battle, won't she?" Kahkitah asked.

"Well . . . yeah, I guess she will," Jeff conceded. "Okay, then. Let me find a stone and some tubing. I'll pace off a course and set you up a target."

"Unless you're too tired," Kahkitah said, looking at Nicole.

"Thanks, but I've had all the sleep I need," Nicole assured him.

Or at least, she told herself grimly, she'd had all the sleep she was likely to get.

Jeff set up the range, gave her some basic instruction, fired off a couple of shots, and then watched as she did the same. After that, he turned the gun over to her and headed back to Allyce and Kahkitah to finish work on the drug balls.

Shooting was easy. Shooting accurately wasn't. Jeff had pulled out fifty of the balls to use with the Setting Sun drug, leaving about a hundred for Nicole to practice with.

It took every single one of them, and she probably could have used another hundred. Still, by the time the gun was empty she felt reasonably confident that she could shoot with the accuracy Jeff said she needed.

Of course, the only movement her target rock exhibited was a slow rhythmic swinging in the light breeze, with the occasional jerk if it caught an extra-high splash. Bungie and the green team would be moving a lot more than that as they headed into battle. Worse, the minute they realized someone was shooting at them, they would be running and dodging and ducking and doing everything they could to throw off her aim.

Which meant she would have to deliver the drug as quickly and accurately as she could, and hope no one caught on until it was too late.

Night had fallen by the time she finished her practice and rejoined the others. They were still working to fill the balls, but Jeff took a few minutes to carefully load what they had into the tubular paintball magazine.

The Q1 arena night was about six hours long. Luckily, it wasn't a complete darkness, which meant Jeff and Allyce could continue to work without having to do everything by touch. It would be easier if they moved to the hive, where there was plenty of light, but Jeff didn't want to risk taking the work into the more populated areas where the Shipmasters or Wisps might walk in on them.

It was an hour before dawn when they finally finished.

"Okay," Jeff said as he loaded the last of the balls into Nicole's gun. "You sure you can get across on your own?"

"Sure," Nicole assured him. Now that she knew there weren't any dangerous rocks in the river, she could probably find a good spot near the bluffs at the river mouth. If that didn't work, she could always have the *Fyrantha* turn off the water again for a few seconds.

"Because Kahkitah can go with you if you want."

"No, you'll need him if this goes sideways," Nicole said. She looked at Kahkitah. "That's all right with you, isn't it?"

"I will certainly protect them as best I can," Kahkitah said hesitantly. "But we Ghorf aren't really made for fighting."

"We've already been through this," Nicole reminded him. "Fighting in front of Fievj would be as bad for you as it would be for us. All I'm thinking is that you could get between Jeff and anyone who wants to stab him. Maybe grab the other guy's trident and take it away from him. You can do that, right?"

"Yes," Kahkitah said, more confidently this time. "You'll be careful, won't you?"

"Trust me," Nicole said. "When are you going to dose everyone on our side?"

"About fifteen minutes before we head to the ocean," Jeff said. "Allyce says the stuff should work pretty fast when it's inhaled."

Nicole thought about the cemetery in the *Fyrantha's* basement, and the implication that people had once used Setting Sun to ease them into death. "Yes, I'm sure it does," she murmured. "Any idea how long it lasts?"

"A couple of hours, probably," Allyce said. "Possibly as long as three or four."

"And you're not taking any, Jeff. Right?"

Even in the darkness, Nicole could see Jeff's scowl. They'd had this discussion—Jeff had called it an argument, but Nicole didn't consider a conversation an argument unless it involved drawn weapons—two hours ago. Jeff's point was that he needed to react the same way as everyone else, while Nicole had insisted he could just as easily fake it and that *someone* needed to be fully functional and ready to defend everyone if something went wrong. "Still not sure that's the best plan," he said. "But no, I won't take any."

"Okay." Nicole took a deep breath. "I guess I'll see you all at the battle."

A minute later she was headed downslope, the paintball gun slung across her back, straining her eyes in the gloom as she tried not to hit any rocks or tree roots. Jeff had warned that Bungie might jump the gun, and she needed to find a good spot and be in position as soon as she could.

The slope became less steep as she got closer to the ocean, but it was still pretty challenging the whole way. She kept an eye out for a place where she could get to the other side, but the river never really got any narrower. Halfway down an idea occurred to her, but it wasn't until she was nearly at the twin bluffs that she found the right setup for what she had in mind.

The setup consisted of a slender tree on her side of the river-bank. She checked it first by tugging at it, confirmed that it was flexible, then tried climbing a few feet up. It bent under her weight, just as she'd hoped it would, leaning her over the edge of the river. She climbed down, tossed the paintball gun carefully into a bush on the far side, then started back up the tree. It continued to bend as she moved along it, until she was hanging almost horizontally over the churning water. She kept going, belatedly wondering if the tree was thin enough to break under her weight and drop her into the river.

But it didn't break, and its roots held, and a minute later she was over the far bank. She unwrapped her legs from the trunk, hung by her hands for a moment, then dropped the final five feet to the ground, landing in a crouch beside a bush. The tree, with the tension suddenly gone, snapped back upright, bouncing loudly against the trees and bushes around it.

Nicole froze. If any of Bungie's men were in the area, they might have heard that.

Nothing. Though, really, as she thought about it, how anyone could hear anything over the river noise she couldn't imagine. She straightened and walked to where the paintball gun hung by its strap on a couple of branches. She tried pulling it off, discovered the strap had gotten hung up on some kind of twig clusters—

Directly in front of her, someone pushed between a pair of bushes and stepped into view.

Nicole dropped into a crouch again, cursing under her breath. Luckily, the man's face had been turned away from her when he emerged from cover, which meant there was a fair chance he hadn't spotted her. She held her breath as he looked around in the gloom, mentally urging him to turn his back on her and head upriver.

For a moment she thought he was going to do exactly that. He peered up the slope, swinging his trident back and forth a little, stepping right up to the river's edge. He shifted his eyes upward as the trident caught on one of the overhanging branches, pulled it free, and leaned over the river, looking upstream and then downstream.

And then, angling the trident in front of him where it would stay out of the way of the tree branches, he turned and started downslope toward Nicole.

Nicole winced. Squatting beside the bush she was partially hidden, but that wouldn't last long. If the man kept going, he would pass no more than five steps away from her. She had maybe ten seconds before a casual glance to his right would nail her to the ground. At that point a quick poke with his trident would be all it would take to end her life right there.

And all she had to stop him with was a paintball gun.

She tore her eyes away from him and focused on the gun. Freeing it from the twig cluster would take a few seconds, seconds she didn't have to spare. More critically, getting it free would shake the bush, which would almost certainly draw his attention.

But right now, and for the next two seconds, it was pointed nearly straight at his chest.

There was no time to think. No time to consider the fact that she was barely able to hit a target when she had the gun pressed against her shoulder and was looking along the barrel. No time to wonder how much all that would change with a gun that was hanging upside down from a branch. The gun was there, the target was there, she was there, and the only other choice was to get captured or die.

Reaching up, sighting as best she could down the barrel, she wrapped her hand around the grip, hooked her little finger onto the trigger, and squeezed. The gun gave its usual little burp—

The man jerked to a stop, snapping his trident into a two-handed grip pointing in front of him. Nicole fired again. Again he jerked, this time looking down toward his chest. Nicole clenched her teeth . . .

Some of the tension seemed to fade from his shoulders and arms. He looked around again, but this time he seemed more puzzled than alert, more confused than determined. He looked at his chest again, then looked up. Shifting his trident back into a one-handed grip, he leaned it back over his shoulder like he was carrying a baseball bat. He looked around one last time, and started back down along the riverbank.

But casually. Not like a soldier getting ready for battle, but like someone out for a nighttime stroll. He passed Nicole without even looking over at her—now, with him this close, she could see that it was Fauke, one of the men Bungie had set to watch over her the first time she came to this side of the river—and continued down the bank.

Nicole watched him go, keeping her body still and moving only her head, waiting for the twist. There *had* to be a twist. He would turn suddenly and run back, or just throw the trident at her, or he was distracting her while someone else sneaked up behind her—she spun back around, tensing, but there was no one there—

She turned back to see him disappear from sight among the trees and bushes.

So that was it. The damn drug actually *worked*.

She took a shaky breath. That was it? Hardly. She'd neutralized one of Bungie's men, but there were seven more to go, including Bungie himself.

Untangling the paintball gun from the bush, holding it close to her body to keep it from snagging on the bushes, she headed downslope.

Somewhere down there, she knew, Bungie would be waiting.

It wasn't much farther to the bluffs. Still, in that short distance she spotted two more green-jumpsuited men walking along the river. One of them was peering across the water, while the other poked and prodded at the nearby trees with his trident. For a moment Nicole wondered what the second man was up to, decided he was looking for trees he could bend over and use to get across the river the way Nicole had done half an hour ago.

That second man never turned around toward her long enough for a clear shot. But the other man did, and she managed to fire four drug balls at him before he turned away again. She was pretty sure at least one of the shots hit his chest, but he started back along the river and disappeared from view before she could tell whether or not the drug had taken effect. She waited until the second man followed him, then continued her own way down the slope.

Trying to watch all directions at once. If one of the men had spotted her, or if Fauke had said something to someone, Bungie might have set up a trap. With all the trees and bushes crowded along the riverbank, there were lots of places he could do that and practically no way Nicole could escape. Even jumping into the river wouldn't gain her anything—if Jeff was right about the ocean level starting to pull back, the river would just dump her onto the beach, probably right in front of Bungie's team.

But no one leaped out at her, or dropped from the trees onto her, or threw a trident into her. She came around a final bend in the river . . .

And there they were. All of them, the whole team, grouped around the bluff on their side of the river. Crouching down where they would be hidden until Jeff's team waded through the river and came around the bluff.

Nicole wrinkled her nose. That was Bungie, all right. He was great at talking big, but he would never take on Jeff face-to-face if he could do something sneaky like an ambush instead.

But this time he'd outsmarted himself. With his whole team bunched up that way, they were in perfect position for Nicole to hit them with everything she had.

Carefully, quietly, she lay down on her stomach on the ground, positioning her gun barrel between two bushes as she sorted out the best way to do this. The clearest shot she had of the bluff was above their heads, but that wouldn't do—the vapor would float up into the sky without ever getting to them. The lower parts of the bluff, unfortunately, were partly hidden by the green team's bodies and legs.

But that was where she had to put her shots. Aiming carefully between the bodies down there, painfully aware that hitting someone's back or leg would alert them to her attack, she started shooting.

Jeff and Allyce had made up fifty drug balls, roughly six for each of the eight men in the Green team. Nicole had already used six, which left her forty-four. She sent thirty-six of those against the bluff, then paused to evaluate.

It wasn't easy. The men were still a good hundred feet away, and the shifting of back and shoulders she'd seen with Fauke wasn't nearly as visible at this distance. Still, the sky was brightening as the arena's fake sun started coming up, and the view was becoming clearer every minute. She could pick out individuals now: there was the man she'd shot while his buddy looked for a way across the river; there was Fauke at one end—so now he'd gotten a double or even triple dose, and Nicole wondered briefly if that much of the drug would hurt him—with the other five men still clumped together behind the bluff.

Her trick had worked. She could see now that all seven of them were showing signs of confusion and uncertainty like she'd seen with Fauke—

Abruptly, she stiffened. Seven men in green jumpsuits. The original green work group the Shipmasters had brought her to fight.

Only there should be *eight* men down there.

Bungie was missing.

She was counting again, desperately hoping he was simply hidden from her view behind one of the others, when something swished through the bushes and branches behind her and landed across her back and legs. Something filmy, something that seemed to grab at her jumpsuit like sticky tape—

"*There* you are," Bungie's voice came from behind her over the roar of the river. "Welcome to the war."

seventeen

Nicole's first reflex was to drop the paintball gun and roll quickly to her right.

That was a mistake. She'd barely gotten up onto her side when whatever had landed on her legs tightened like a blanket around her and yanked her hard to a stop, pinning her in place.

But at least now she could turn her head far enough around to see him. He was about twenty feet back, striding downslope toward her with the sort of arrogant swagger he used to use on the Philadelphia streets.

Unlike Philly, though, here there was a hint of hesitation, and he seemed to be watching the ground as much as he was watching Nicole. Maybe he was worried about tripping over a branch or root.

Maybe the slight limp he'd picked up as a result of getting an arrow through the leg in Q4 gave him good reason to worry about his footing.

Nicole looked down at her legs and hips. She was being pinned to the ground, she realized now, by one of the nets she'd seen the others carrying along with their tridents. The net seemed to be shaped like a big square, with disk-shaped weights at the four corners. Probably thrown like a Frisbee, with the weights keeping it open as it flew.

Gingerly, she touched it. To her relief, the material didn't seem to be actually sticky, like she'd first thought. But even though it didn't stick to her skin, it definitely grabbed at the material of her jumpsuit. Parts of it had also hung up on the bushes beside her, which was how it was holding her stuck here. There were only two ways out: break the net loose from the bushes and push it off her, or else roll back to where she'd started and hope that gave her enough slack to get out from under it.

Unfortunately, neither way would get her free before Bungie and his trident could reach her.

Unless . . .

Her eyes flicked to the paintball gun lying in the grass between the bushes. Had he spotted it yet? If not, and if she could get back to it before he got in stabbing range, she might still have a chance.

Abruptly, Bungie jerked to a stop. "What the *hell?*" he growled. "Where the hell did you get a gun?"

Nicole clenched her teeth. *Damn.* "Where do you think?" she countered, thinking furiously. Bungie was arrogant, nasty, and not nearly as smart as he thought he was. With all those weaknesses, there must be something she could use against him.

"Because if it was Fievj and his buddies, he and I are going to have a problem," Bungie added darkly.

And he was also paranoid. Maybe that would be enough. "You don't *really* think they want your side to win, do you?" Nicole asked, putting as much scorn into her voice as she could. "Then they'd have to send you home, and they can't afford to do that. They still need everyone here to fix the *Fyrantha* for them."

Bungie swore. "Bastards."

"You just figuring that out?" Nicole said, frowning. He was still standing there, his trident pointed sort of toward her. His eyes were on the paintball gun, but he was making no move toward it. What was he waiting for? "I could have told you they were bastards weeks ago."

And then she got it. He wanted the gun, but he wanted her to go for it first.

Because rolling over in that direction would put her back to him. Not only that, but it would also let him claim afterward that he'd stabbed her in self-defense. That probably wouldn't mean anything to Fievj, but it was important back in Philly, and old street habits died hard.

A ripple of contempt ran through her. Not only didn't he want a straight-up face-to-face with Jeff, he didn't even want one with her.

The more immediate problem was how she was going to avoid getting stabbed. If she was going to get to the gun first, she had to find a way to distract him.

"Speaking of bastards, I hope you don't think that ambush is going to work on Jeff," she continued, nodding her head toward the bluff below them. "The way they're all bunched up—come on; even *I* know better than that."

"They'll do fine," Bungie said. Just the same, he took a step to the side and craned his neck, apparently trying to see his team through the trees.

Which was exactly what Nicole had hoped he'd do. "I wouldn't count on it," she said, studying the ground in front of him. One more step and he would be right behind a slight hollow in the ground that had nearly sent her tumbling on her own way down the slope a few minutes ago. If she could get him to charge at her across that, he might fall flat on his face and give her the extra edge she needed to get to the gun. "But, hey, not my problem," she added. "Not Jeff's either. He's all set to stomp your guys into the sand."

"Like hell," Bungie said, a malicious grin spreading across his face. "Jeff's the one who's gonna get stomped. Allyce's got that covered."

Nicole frowned. "What does Allyce have to do with anything?"

Bungie's grin turned smug. "You'll find out."

"So you're just blowing smoke, like usual," Nicole said, ramping up the scorn a little higher. Had he just pulled Allyce's name at random, or did he know something about their plan? "Doesn't really work here, you know."

"The hell it's smoke," Bungie growled. "She said the whole blue team's gonna be high as a kite, and we can just walk in and bounce 'em around."

"Oh, so now it's *Allyce* who's blowing smoke," Nicole said, a cold knot forming in her stomach. Was he saying the Setting Sun drug Allyce had mixed up for them was no good?

But Nicole had seen it work on Fauke. Hadn't she?

"What the hell is it with you and smoke?" Bungie growled. "She says you and Jeff don't want to fight. So she fixed it so you won't."

"I don't want *any* of us to fight."

"Yeah, you already said that," Bungie said. "You think anyone gives a damn?" He shrugged. "Don't worry, I'll say hi to Trake for you when I get back to Philly."

"You're not going back," Nicole insisted. Could Fauke have been faking it? But how could he even have known what to fake?

Because Allyce had told him, of course. She'd told the green team exactly what Setting Sun was supposed to do.

And in the process had suckered Jeff into wasting all the time he would otherwise have had to come up with another plan.

Allyce had seemed completely sincere about helping them. And Nicole, focused on the paintball gun and their oh-so-clever Setting Sun plan, had blindly taken the other woman's word for it.

Damn her.

"So what's the gun supposed to do?" Bungie asked, jabbing his trident toward it. "It's not one of those fancy green laser things Fievj gave you before, is it? Doesn't look like one of those. Not that it matters. Not after Allyce fixed everyone up."

Nicole opened her mouth to answer—to say *something*, though she had no idea what—when the tree branches behind Bungie parted.

And Jeff slipped into view.

A very *wet* Jeff, she saw. Wet and trembling slightly with suppressed shivering in the breeze, his face and plastered-down hair as wet as his jumpsuit. Nicole felt a sympathetic shiver run through her—she knew how cold the river was.

But there was nothing distracted about the expression on his face. An old image flicked across Nicole's eyes: an alley cat she'd once seen, inching its way toward a rat.

"Never mind—I can figure it out for myself," Bungie said. He took a step to the side, veering around the dip Nicole had hoped he might fall over, and started toward the gun.

"Stop!" Nicole snapped. He was moving toward her and away from Jeff, and she had to stop him from doing both.

Bungie paused in midstep, a small frown touching his forehead. The sheer strength of Nicole's outburst had stopped him for the moment, but that wouldn't last long. She had to come up with something else, and fast. Bungie started to take another step—

And in desperation Nicole pulled the sealing strip of her jumpsuit partway open and jammed her right hand inside. "I mean it," she bit out. "Stop or I'll kill you."

Bungie barked a laugh, not even slowing down. "What, with what you've got *there*?"

"You have no idea," Nicole shot back. Out of the corner of her eye she saw Jeff moving forward, the sounds of his footsteps masked by the river's roar. "Did you *really* think that's the only weapon Fievj gave us? Remember your gun, the one you killed Jerry to get?"

Bungie stopped, a sudden crazy look in his eye. He'd had that stolen gun on him when the Wisps first brought him aboard, and he'd been trying to get it back ever since. His eyes narrowed, and Nicole could see him studying her jumpsuit, looking for an extra bulge or sag, trying to see if she really had it or was blowing smoke herself. She'd seen him do this visual search thing a lot on the Philadelphia streets, but as usual with Bungie he wasn't nearly as good at it as he thought he was.

He got three seconds to stand there, looking and thinking, before Jeff's arms snaked around his shoulders and neck and locked him in a choke hold.

Bungie might have snarled or cursed. Nicole couldn't hear him. He almost certainly struggled. Nicole didn't wait to see. The instant Jeff's arm went around Bungie's throat she rolled back toward the paintball gun.

She got only halfway there when part of the net caught another branch. She swore and tugged, finally tearing it free. She reached the gun and snatched it up with her right hand, grabbing at the net with her left and pulling it partially away from her jumpsuit. She rolled over onto her back and brought up the gun.

Just in time to see Jeff lower an unconscious Bungie to the ground.

"Come on," Jeff called, beckoning with a quick double twitch of his fingers. Kneeling beside Bungie, he started fiddling with something on Bungie's jumpsuit.

By the time Nicole finished untangling herself and made it over to them he had two strips of cloth torn from Bungie's sleeves. "Grab that net," Jeff said, jerking his head back toward it. "The better he's trussed, the better I'll like it."

"I thought he was out," Nicole said, reversing course and

pulling the net free of the bushes. A quick look downslope showed the green team was still huddled around the side of the bluff. Were they *all* faking it?

"Not for long," Jeff said. "I didn't want to risk crushing his windpipe, so I just cut off blood to his brain for a few seconds."

"Not like that's something he uses very often," Nicole said. "What do you want me to do?"

"Wrap up his legs," Jeff instructed. He rolled one of the cloth strips into a ball, then started fastening it and the other strip around Bungie's face as a makeshift gag. "As tight as you can— we don't want to leave him any extra slack he can use to get out."

"What about his arms?" Nicole asked as she levered his legs up off the ground and started wrapping her net around them.

"We'll use my net for that," Jeff said. "Snap it up—he could wake up any time."

That wasn't what Nicole had seen in movies and TV. There, if you knocked someone out, they stayed that way for minutes or even hours. But Jeff was right. She'd barely gotten her net wrapped once when Bungie's eyes fluttered open. For a second he just looked confused, then his eyes widened—

He was starting to reach for the gag around his mouth when Jeff's grip on the side of his neck sent him back under.

A minute later they had both nets wrapped snugly around him. "Find me some sticks," Jeff ordered as he finished up the last part. "Sturdy, but thin enough to fit through the holes in the net."

"What are they for?" Nicole asked as she got to her feet and looked around. One of the nearby trees had a few broken branches on the ground at its base, and she scooped them up.

"Can't have our guest wandering off," Jeff said, taking the branches from her with a nod of thanks. "We don't have any padlocks, so we'll have to improvise."

"Ah," Nicole said. She watched as he wove the branches in and out of the holes in the two nets, fastening the nets' outside edges to the layers beneath them.

Bungie woke up again midway through the process. By then it was far too late to struggle, but that didn't stop him from trying. After a few useless attempts, he gave up and glared at the two of them instead. Jeff finished his work, checked everything one final time, then tapped Bungie's chest. "Here's the thing," he said. "You're wrapped like a Fort Knox gold delivery, the tree canopy will keep the Shipmasters from seeing you, your team isn't likely to come hunting for you—I don't think they really like you all that much—and you're lying in a nice little dip so you aren't going to roll out on your own. If I were you, I'd take the opportunity to have a little nap. Don't worry, we'll come back and get you before you starve."

He stood up and took Nicole's arm. "Come on, let's go someplace where we can talk."

"What are you doing here?" Nicole murmured as he led the way upriver. "How did you get across?"

"Kahkitah brought me over," Jeff said. "I didn't know he could swim that well. Did you?"

Nicole shook her head, thinking about what Wesowee had said about the Ghorfs and their exploration of the *Fyrantha*'s waterways.

It was interesting, though, that he'd implied earlier to Duncan that if Nicole crossed the river she'd be trapped on Bungie's side of the arena, when it was clear now that the Ghorf could easily swim over and get her anytime he wanted to. Did that mean he was trying to keep his swimming abilities a secret?

"No, I didn't," she murmured. "Not until he charged out into the ocean after me."

"Yeah, that was really something," Jeff said, shaking his head. "I always thought that shark face of his was just decoration. I guess not."

"So you saw him swim out?" Nicole asked. "Were any of the others with you?"

"I don't think so," Jeff said. "Oh, and when he came back he asked me to keep it a secret, so you probably should, too."

"Already figured that out."

"I figured you had." Jeff looked back at Bungie. "Okay, I don't think he can hear us."

"If it's about Allyce screwing us, he already knows," Nicole said. "What exactly did she do?"

"She made up two different batches of the drug," Jeff said. "The one she made for us will last two or three hours. The batch she made for the paintballs and Greenies only lasts about twenty minutes."

Nicole squeezed the barrel of the gun. So that was why she'd seen Fauke react the way she had. "How did you find out?"

"Kahkitah again," Jeff said. "He followed you downriver, just to keep an eye on you. He saw you drug one of the Greenies, but then saw the guy start to come out of it only fifteen or twenty minutes later. He came back and warned me, and I leaned on Allyce until she cracked."

Nicole sighed. "Thinking about her husband."

"Yeah," Jeff said darkly. "Still buying into Fievj's lie about going home."

"People usually believe what they want to," Nicole said. "What are you going to do to her?"

"Do?" Jeff shrugged. "Not much we *can* do. Humans aren't warlike or vindictive, remember?"

"I'm serious."

"So am I," Jeff said. "Anyway, the damage is already done. Punishing Allyce won't fix that."

"I suppose you'd already drugged our side?"

"Yeah," Jeff said sourly. "High as a California commune, all of them."

"Do you have any more of that batch?"

"Some. Probably enough for the Greenies if we're careful with it."

"So how do we get it to them?"

"That's the question," Jeff agreed. "Any thoughts?"

Nicole craned her neck, looking toward the bluff. The rest of the green team wasn't completely visible from where she and Jeff were standing, but she could see enough glimpses of color through the trees to tell her they were still there. "You have it with you? And what's it in, a jar?"

"A squeeze bottle," Jeff said, pulling a water bottle–sized container from his belt pouch. A mostly empty bottle, she saw, with only an ounce or two of liquid at the most sloshing around inside. "Capped so it won't evaporate too fast."

"How fast *will* it evaporate?" Nicole asked. "Like if I squirted it on someone's chest, how long would it take to get enough of it into his nose and lungs?"

"A few seconds' exposure ought to do it," Jeff said, eyeing her closely.

"And how long before it was completely gone?"

"I'd say two to three minutes," Jeff said. "Maybe four. What have you got in mind?"

Nicole chewed her lower lip. Two or three minutes . . . yes, that ought to work. "I'll show you," she said.

She reached for the bottle, but he twitched it back out of her reach. "Tell, then show," he said firmly. "If you're pulling something crazy, I want to know about it."

"So you can stop me?"

"So I can back you up."

Nicole made a face. But he was right. "Okay, but no arguing," she warned. "I want to do this before the stuff I already hit them with wears off."

She hadn't expected him to like her idea. He didn't. But he also didn't have anything better to offer. A minute later, she headed toward the bluff and the green team, Jeff's belt pouch clutched in her arms. *It'll work,* she told herself firmly as she hurried down the slope. *The last thing big men are afraid of is helpless little girls.*

She didn't try to conceal her approach. Still, with the green team's focus on the beach beyond the bluff and the roaring of the water masking all other sounds, she was nearly on top of them before anyone spotted her.

"Hey!" someone shouted, spinning around to face her. It was Fauke, she saw, his eyes clear and wary and hostile, his hands with a white-knuckled grip on his trident as he swung it around to point at her. "Hold it right there, little lady."

Little lady. Insulting and dismissive and unafraid.

Perfect.

"You need to see this," Nicole called back, ignoring his order and loping the last few yards down the slope. "You all need to." Bracing herself, she walked straight toward Fauke's weapon. If he didn't move it . . .

To her relief, he did, twitching it aside. Not very far aside— he clearly didn't trust her. But far enough. *Little lady.* "I stole this from Jeff," she continued, dropping to her knees and setting the pouch on the ground in front of her. "He said Fievj gave it to them. I guess Fievj wants to make sure you don't win."

"What is it?" Iosif asked, stepping closer.

"You're not going to believe this," Nicole said, mentally crossing her fingers as she started to pull out the mass of twigs and leaves she and Jeff had stuffed into it. Iosif leaned down for a closer look . . .

And in her peripheral vision Nicole saw feet appearing as the rest of the group gathered around. Clearly, despite Bungie's enthusiasm—or maybe because of it—none of the green team really trusted the Shipmasters not to pull a fast one.

Jeff had argued that she should mix the Setting Sun liquid into the leaves in the pouch. Nicole had insisted that a pouch sitting on the ground would be too far away to ensure enough of the drug reached them. She'd also pointed out that handing the pouch to Iosif or Fauke wouldn't guarantee the rest of the group would get close enough to breathe in the stuff.

Besides, with the drug flowing from the pouch past her face Nicole would have to hold her breath for the crucial minute or two. Even if she could do that—and she had no idea if she could—it was bound to look suspicious.

Jeff had reluctantly accepted her arguments.

Which made it all the more satisfying that she'd been right on all of them.

The package and its implied threat had them worried enough that they'd gathered around for a look. The fact that Nicole was a harmless young woman meant they'd gathered closer than they probably would have if Jeff, say, had tried this. Even though they were all leaning over, none of them was close enough to the pouch for the drug to reach them, just as she'd anticipated.

But they were all close enough to breathe in the fumes now rising from Nicole's hair.

"Don't get me wrong—I don't want you to leave the *Fyrantha* either," she said as she continued digging stuff out of the pouch. "I already told you that. Remember, Fauke? I told you it would be bad for us to fight. But I don't want anyone hurt, either. I know Allyce told you some stuff, but Allyce doesn't know everything.

I guess Fievj wants both ends of the deal—he wants to see us fight, but he doesn't want to let you go home like he promised. I've known guys like that. Bunch of weasels. Okay, wait a second . . ."

She finished emptying the pouch, pausing as if in confusion. "That's weird—I *saw* him put it in here. Hold on." She pawed through the pile of leaves, spreading them out as if looking for something small that might have gotten lost inside. "Damn it, I *know* I saw him put it in."

She ran to the end of her chatter and paused, still looking down at the ground, focusing on the feet and legs gathered around her. If they hadn't gotten enough of the drug, *someone* ought to be grabbing her by the collar about now and demanding to know what the hell she was doing.

But there were no hands and no voices. Bracing herself, she turned her head and looked up.

Fauke was staring at the empty pouch and pile of leaves, a thoughtful look on his face. Iosif was looking at the bluff, apparently studying the pattern of the rock. Two of the others were gazing out at the ocean, fascinated by the waves. The rest were just looking around the area, their tridents held loosely in their hands, all but forgotten.

It had worked.

Nicole picked up the pouch and began to carefully back out of the circle. No one tried to stop her. She headed upslope, still walking backward so she could watch them, still half-afraid it was all a trick or a joke and that they would suddenly turn and charge at her.

But none of them moved. Or at least, none of them moved toward her. One of them squatted down and picked up an odd-shaped leaf from her pile, but as far as she could tell his only interest was in the leaf, not in the con she'd pulled on them.

Halfway back toward the nearest clump of trees she risked a glance behind her. Jeff was there, waiting in backup position just as he'd promised. He stepped half out of concealment and beckoned her toward him. She nodded and turned her gaze back toward the green team, still not sure she believed it had actually worked.

A small voice in the back of her mind pointed out that this Setting Sun was one hell of a drug. If Bungie ever got back to Philadelphia with a sample . . .

She shook her head. He wasn't getting back. *None* of them were. Even letting the thought pass through her mind was a bad idea.

She reached Jeff's hiding place. "I think it worked," she said.

"I think so, too," he agreed. "They reacted the same way our side did when Allyce and I dosed them, anyway."

Nicole took a deep breath, feeling a terrible weight lifting from her shoulders. "So that's it?" she asked, almost afraid of his answer. "We just run them all together, let them mill around a little, and Fievj will send everyone back to work?"

"I assume so," Jeff said. "I'll probably do a little half-hearted poking and cringing to help sell it, but I think we're about clear."

Nicole took another deep breath, huffed it out. Suddenly, she was very tired. "Thank you," she murmured.

Jeff snorted. "I think it's *us* who need to thank *you*," he said. "Us and everyone back on Earth. Too bad they'll never know how you saved all their lives."

"Yeah," Nicole said, wincing as her life on the Philadelphia streets rose like a ghost in front of her eyes. "If they don't just kill themselves and each other."

"That's not your problem," Jeff said firmly. "You've done all you can to—"

"*Protector!*" a voice boomed through the arena.

Nicole felt herself tense up. *Fievj.*

"Protector!" Fievj called again. "Come to the beach. I will speak with you.

"I will speak with you *now.*"

eighteen

Nicole looked at Jeff. "What do I do?"

He was facing the beach, his eyes narrowed. "I guess we go see what he wants."

"He only asked for me."

"Well, he's getting a bonus," Jeff said grimly, picking up Bungie's trident. "Let's go."

They walked down the slope, passing Iosif and the rest of the still-oblivious green team. They reached the beach—Nicole noted as they passed the bluff that the ocean had receded enough for easy passage—and looked around.

"There," Jeff said, pointing toward the green side of the arena. "Near the wall."

Nicole peered that direction. Pushing his way through the reeds onto the beach was one of the Shipmasters in full centaur armor. Fievj, probably. Behind him, appearing out of the tree cover, were a pair of Wisps.

Clutched in the arms of each Wisp was an alien—a *big* alien—of a type Nicole had never seen before.

"Who the hell are those?" Jeff muttered.

"No idea," Nicole muttered back. "But I don't think I like them."

The aliens were huge, for starters: each of them a good seven feet tall, with the chest, arms, and legs of prison weight lifters.

They wore full-head helmets made of shiny metal that covered everything from their chins up. Nicole couldn't see the backs, but the front parts bulged out into half spheres and were dotted with small holes that ran from mouth to forehead level.

In contrast, the aliens' chests and arms below the helmets were completely bare, with no armor or even shirts, showing the bulging muscles beneath their pale red skin. At their waists they wore thick brown belts, with loose purple trousers beneath, the bottom ends tucked into heavy brown boots.

Hanging from the right side of their belts were brown scabbards holding two-foot-long swords.

The group left the reeds and walked through the loose sand onto the wet sand along the ocean. The Shipmaster turned to stay out of the lapping waves and led the way toward Nicole and Jeff. Jeff touched Nicole's arm and nodded, and together they walked to meet them.

The Shipmaster walked to within ten feet of them and stopped. "Protector," he said stiffly as the two humans also stopped. It was, as Nicole had suspected, Fievj's voice. "Your warriors seem unfit for battle."

"We don't have warriors," Nicole said. "Like I told you before—and like Plato and everyone else told you—humans don't fight."

"*You* have fought," Fievj said, leveling an armored finger at her. "As have you," he added, shifting the finger to point at Jeff.

"I'm a Sibyl," Nicole reminded him. "My brain was already damaged when you brought me here. That's what being a Sibyl means. The drug in the inhaler has only made it worse."

"And him?" Fievj asked, the finger still leveled at Jeff.

"His brain is also damaged," Nicole improvised. "Just not the same way."

"Yet we've heard him say he was once part of a military group called the Marines."

Nicole felt her breath catch in her throat. Hell—how had Fievj found that out? An overheard conversation? Allyce?

"You misunderstood," Jeff said calmly before Nicole could come up with anything. "I'm not a warrior."

"You were a Marine," Fievj countered. "Marines throughout the galaxy are warriors."

"You've got some kind of mistranslation going," Jeff said, shaking his head. "On Earth the people with my mental problems are sent to an island so they won't be a danger to anyone else. The word for that is *marooning*. The group of people who are marooned are called *maroons*; the singular form of that is *marine*."

"Why would the Wisps have brought someone mentally un-sound to serve the *Fyrantha*?" Fievj demanded.

"Why not?" Jeff countered. "I mean, really, what do Wisps know about Earth?"

For a long moment Fievj stood silently. Nicole held her breath, wondering if he was actually buying into that ridiculous story.

Still, Trake had always said that if you told a lie with enough confidence people would believe you.

"You carry a weapon," Fievj said.

"What, *this*?" Jeff hefted his trident. "I picked it up because I didn't want anyone tripping on it and poking himself." He took a step forward and held it out in front of him. "I figured you'd prob-ably want to collect all of them before you sent us back to work."

"Perhaps there will be no more work." Fievj stepped partially to the side, and gestured back toward the Wisps and their bur-dens. "Behold your enemies."

Nicole threw a quick look at Jeff. "Behold our *what*?" she asked carefully.

"These are the Koffren," Fievj said. "They've been taken force-fully from their homes. That's made them angry."

"They can join the club," Jeff muttered.

"They've been told you humans are the reason for their abduction," Fievj continued. "They've been told your defeat and destruction will be the price for their return to their homes."

A shiver ran up Nicole's back. "That's crazy," she said, silently cursing the sudden tremor in her voice. "You can't let us get killed. You need us to fix the *Fyrantha* for you."

"There are plenty more humans," Fievj said. "A world full of them. The Wisps may not know much about your world"—he paused, his helmet faceplate turning pointedly toward Jeff—"but they can easily bring more if the *Fyrantha* so requires."

He looked back at Nicole. "Whether it requires more this day will be your decision. Either you will kill the Koffren, or they will kill you."

"But we don't fight," Nicole protested, trying one last time. "You said yourself that none of the others can do anything."

"Then they will all die," Fievj said. "Or perhaps you and your brain-damaged companions will teach them, or will fight on their behalf. The choice is yours. You have two hours."

"Two hours until what?" Jeff asked.

"In two hours the Wisps will release them, and the battle will begin," Fievj said. "Decide well. Decide quickly."

He turned and circled around the silent Wisps and their frozen burdens and headed back the way he'd come.

Nicole looked at the Koffren. She could just make out the outline of their heads through the perforations in their helmets, with their actual faces completely hidden. Not that she would have been able to read their expressions even if she *could* see them. But if her own experience was any guide she had no doubt they were fully conscious and fully aware of the situation.

She also had no reason to doubt Fievj's statement that they were mad as hell about being here.

She lowered her gaze to their swords. Resting in their sheaths, their blades were hidden. But the hilts looked pretty solid. Way too solid to be part of the toy weapons the Shipmasters had given the Thii and Ponngs back in the Q3 arena.

Still, no matter how sharp the swords were, they were still a lot shorter than the humans' tridents. If she and Jeff could gather everyone together, they could easily surround the Koffren and keep them back.

Except that every human in the arena was doped out of his mind with Setting Sun.

Jeff had said the drug would wear off in two or three hours. If it was only two hours, they might be functional enough by then for her idea to work.

If it was *three* hours, the Koffren would slaughter them where they stood.

Unless she and Jeff got to them first.

An unpleasant thrill ran through her, crinkling at the edge of her soul. She was talking murder here, pure and simple. She could call it self-defense—she could even call it defense of the others—but it boiled down to killing creatures who had no way of defending themselves.

Unless the Wisps let go at the first sign of any attack. Fievj hadn't said they would do that, but he also hadn't said they wouldn't. On top of that, she had no idea where Koffren hearts were located inside those bulky bodies.

Furtively, she looked at the trident in Jeff's hand. As long as the Wisps held the Koffren steady, poking enough holes through all that muscle would sooner or later hit something vital.

And even if the Wisps let go as soon as she or Jeff attacked, they would at least have cut the enemy's numbers in half.

But *murder?*

"Come on," Jeff said quietly, touching her arm. "We need to talk."

Nicole braced herself. She suspected he wouldn't take well to her idea. But someone had to make the suggestion. "Jeff—"

"I said we need to talk," Jeff said, his touch becoming a soft but unbreakable grip around her upper arm. "Inland—under the trees—where the Shipmasters can't watch us."

He turned his back on the ocean and started walking, towing her along beside him. "Okay," he said when they had made it through the reeds and were under the tree cover again. "What were you going to say?"

"I was going to say that we have to do something," Nicole said, bracing herself. No, he *definitely* wasn't going to like this. "If we don't, they'll kill all of us."

"And you think slaughtering them right there on the beach is the right thing to do?"

Nicole stared. "How did you know I was thinking that?"

"Please," Jeff said with a snort. "Aside from you looking at their swords and then looking longingly at my trident?"

"Well—uh—"

"More importantly, I think it's exactly what Fievj is *hoping* we'll do," he interrupted. "It's a classic games theory ploy: hold a big fat threat over us, with a big obvious solution staring us in the face."

Nicole closed her eyes, feeling like a complete fool. Of *course* that was what Fievj wanted. They'd messed up his plan to make the humans kill each other, so now he wanted to see if humans would kill aliens.

And especially if they would kill *helpless* aliens.

"You're right," she said. "I'm sorry."

"Skip the regrets and embarrassment," he said grimly. "We've got two hours until the Wisps turn them loose on us, and it's two of us small fry versus two hulking behemoths. We need to work out a strategy, and fast."

Nicole looked back at the ocean, trying to push her shame out of her mind. What in the world had she been thinking? Killing helpless people was—

Was like something Bungie would do.

In fact, they'd gotten caught up in this whole *Fyrantha* thing in the first place because Bungie had murdered someone and gotten shot in response. The realization that she was thinking like Bungie was somehow worse even than the thought of murder itself.

But the fact remained that Bungie was here . . . and unlike everyone else in the arena, he hadn't been drugged.

"*Three* of us small fry," she corrected. "We've got Bungie, too."

"No," Jeff said flatly. "I don't trust him. I *especially* don't trust him with something pointy in his hands."

"But—" Nicole gestured toward the beach.

"Besides, we're trying to prove we're not warlike, remember?" Jeff reminded her. "Bungie staying wrapped up like a Christmas turkey is the best contribution he can make to the cause."

"I suppose," Nicole said with a sigh. To be honest, she didn't really want to work with Bungie, either. "Then the only thing we can do is get everyone out of here. Take them back to Q4 where the Shipmasters don't control the Wisps."

"But where they *can* just walk around?" Jeff countered pointedly. "Remember, that's where you first met Fievj. Not just walking, but lugging a rack of greenfire weapons behind him."

"Oh," Nicole said, wincing. "Right."

"Anyway, running won't solve anything. Fievj will keep at us until he knows one way or the other whether Earth can be sold into slavery. No, we need to end this here and now. One way or the other."

Nicole's stomach tightened. "Are you saying we let the others die?"

Jeff's expression was tight, but his nod was firm. "I don't like it any better than you do. But I don't see any other way. In warfare, you sometimes have to sacrifice the few to save the many. And with the whole world on the line . . ." He gave a small shrug. "I don't see any other way."

Nicole closed her eyes, her teammates' faces flashing in front of her eyes. Carp, Tomas, Levi. Men she'd worked with. Men she'd shared a hundred meals with. Men she'd sometimes even laughed with.

Men who'd trusted her when she first came up with this insane Setting Sun drug idea.

Could she just stand by and let the Koffren kill them?

"No," she said, opening her eyes again. "We can't."

"Nicole—"

"Besides, like you said, it doesn't fix the problem," she cut him off. "Sooner or later Fievj will try again, and the next time there won't be anyone mixing up a drug to keep everyone peaceful. The next team they put together *will* fight, and then we'll lose everything."

"Maybe not," he said. "They've gone this long without suspecting anything."

"That was before I came along and screwed up everything."

"Not your fault—the whole thing was unstable to begin with," Jeff said. "Let's focus on the here and now. Do you have a plan?"

Nicole shrugged helplessly. "I don't even know where to start."

Jeff pursed his lips, then gave a small shrug. "You start by assessing the enemy. Make a list of his strengths and weaknesses. Once you have that, you figure out your own assets and work up a strategy."

"Yeah. Right," Nicole said, thinking back to the aliens frozen in the Wisps' grip. "*What* weaknesses?"

"Well, for starters, limited protection," Jeff said. "Only their heads are armored. That may suggest their heads are especially vulnerable."

"You mean like they're soft or they bleed easily?"

"Or they can't handle bright lights," Jeff said. "They've got a lot of eye holes, but you saw how small they are. Or maybe it's loud noises—the helmets will block a lot of sound, too."

"And a lot of the view," Nicole said, her brain starting to get into this. "Lots of holes, but metal in between them. And the holes don't go very far around the sides."

"Limited peripheral vision," Jeff said, nodding. "Good point. On the down side, it would be hard to get into one of those holes with a weapon. A single prong of our tridents would probably fit through, but the other two prongs would be blocked by the rest of the helmet."

"Maybe that's why Fievj gave us tridents instead of spears."

"Maybe," Jeff agreed. "That's another good point—he came up with a Plan B awfully fast after we drugged everyone. Maybe he was always thinking about throwing the Koffren at us."

"Or maybe Allyce told them about Setting Sun in time to change their plans."

"Again, we can leave the blame game for later," Jeff said. "What other strengths and weaknesses do they have?"

"They're not wearing any shirts."

"Is that a strength or a weakness?"

Nicole frowned. "What do you mean?"

"Well, it's a strength in that we can stab through without anything getting in the way," Jeff said. "It's a weakness in that there's no cloth to grab onto in a fight."

"Oh," Nicole said. She hadn't thought about that. "Oh, and the nets, too. They grab on to our jumpsuits pretty good, but not onto our skin."

"Right—I'd forgotten about that. And of course, their swords are shorter than our tridents. Anything else?"

"I can't think of anything," Nicole said. "You?"

"Nothing significant," Jeff said. "They should be easy to sneak up on from behind, but that comes under the general heading of limited vision. Our turn. What are *our* assets?"

"You," Nicole said, her stomach tightening. "Me, I guess."

"How about Kahkitah?" Jeff suggested. "The Ghorfs swim better than any of us knew. Maybe they do other things better, too."

"You mean like fight?"

"They're certainly built for it."

"Maybe they fight good enough for the Shipmasters to want their planet?"

Jeff hissed out a breath. "Yeah. Point. Okay, so Kahkitah's out. Then you're right—it's just you and me, and tridents and nets." He lifted a finger, his face suddenly thoughtful. "And one paintball gun. You sure you used up all the paintballs when you were practicing?"

"Yeah. I wish now I hadn't."

"Any chance we can get more?"

Nicole thought about the Ejbofs and the tree-eating slugs. "I don't know. Maybe. But Fievj knows I got it in Q2. He's bound to have all the ways across watched. Isn't he?"

"Probably," Jeff conceded. "Frankly, if I were him, I'd watch *every* exit from this arena, to Q2 or anywhere else. Someone as good at throwing monkey wrenches as you are needs to be contained."

Nicole felt her throat tighten. "Or killed."

"We've already shown we're not going to kill each other."

"That's not what I meant," Nicole said. "Never mind. What about—?"

"Whoa—wait a second," Jeff cut her off. "If that's not what you meant, what did you mean?"

"We'll talk about it later," Nicole said, her stomach churning with an echo of the utter helplessness she'd felt as that Wisp carried her toward the heat-transfer duct and her death. "What about the drug balls? We still have a few of those left. Can we use them?"

"I don't know," Jeff said doubtfully. "The balls themselves are too big to fit through the eye holes. Breaking a paintball against the helmet would throw some of the stuff inside, which could be useful, but I doubt there's enough Setting Sun in the drug balls to bother them. There's not that much liquid in there to begin with, and it evaporates pretty quickly. Most of it would just splash against the helmet."

"And that assumes the drug affects Koffren the same way it does us."

"Which would be way too convenient," Jeff agreed. "No, if we can't get real paintballs, I don't think there's anything we can do with the gun."

Nicole looked back out toward the ocean. The ocean, where she'd almost drowned before Kahkitah rescued her and took her to the Ghorfs' special hideout.

The Ghorfs had secrets, all right. Big secrets. One of those secrets could very well be that they could fight.

But she couldn't put them in that position. Not after they'd saved her life. She and Jeff and her whole team were walking the razor's edge, and at this point it looked like it would get them all killed. She couldn't do that to the Ghorfs, too.

She frowned. Kahkitah and Ghorfs. Ejbofs and paintball guns. *Assets.*

"You've got something," Jeff said softly, peering closely at her face. It hadn't been a question.

"Maybe," she said slowly. "You said the Shipmasters and Wisps were probably guarding all the exits from here."

"They are if they've got any brains at all."

"But if I *did* get out, would they be watching for me to come back in?"

"If they saw you leave, probably," Jeff said, his forehead wrinkled in thought. "If they *didn't* see you leave . . . hard to tell. But the typical sentry line tends to work better in a single direction, either keeping people out or keeping people in. Are you saying you have a way out that they don't know about?"

"I think so," Nicole said, trying to think it through. Would two hours be enough? She had no idea. But she also had no choice. "I need to go find Kahkitah."

"No, *we* need to find Kahkitah," Jeff corrected. "I'm going with you."

"It won't be pleasant," she warned. "It's pretty dangerous, actually."

"Danger's my middle name," he said. "Come on—we're wasting time."

They headed back toward the beach and turned toward the blue team's side of the arena. "One more question," Nicole said as they waded across the river now streaming across open beach.

"Yes?"

"How good are you at holding your breath?"

nineteen

Finding Kahkitah was easier than Nicole had thought it would be. He was waiting in the river just upstream from the twin bluffs, keeping a watchful eye on Nicole. He joined them midway through their walk across the stream, and together the three of them stood in the cold water as Nicole explained her plan.

Neither of them seemed very enthusiastic. But both were willing to help.

There really had been no reason to assume the water systems of the Q1 and Q3 arenas were connected in any easy way, Nicole realized later. But to her relief, it turned out that they were. Kahkitah somehow got word to one of the others, and a few minutes after leaving the Q1 arena she and the two Ghorfs were waist-deep in water, heading toward the rear of the ship.

She'd been secretly terrified that the journey would be a repeat of her earlier, lung-crushing trip through the Q1 ocean all the way down to the *Fyrantha*'s basement. To her relief, this trip was much easier. She and Jeff were never submerged for more than maybe half a minute at a time, and with her new knowledge of Ghorf swimming abilities it was much easier to trust Kahkitah to bring her through safely.

Her other fear—that the two tridents Jeff had insisted they bring along would get hung up on something or, worse, accidentally jab one of them or the Ghorfs—also turned out to be wasted worry. Her trident did a lot of bouncing against her side and leg, especially in a couple of long chambers that seemed to be made up completely of waves and foam. But aside from a bruise or two there was no damage.

More importantly, they never saw either a Shipmaster or a Wisp along the way. If the Shipmasters even knew about these passageways—and Nicole was starting to think they didn't—it apparently didn't occur to anyone to watch them.

Finally, they were there. One last dip in the stream, ten more seconds of holding her breath, and they were floating down the river that flowed through the middle of the Q3 arena.

"Nice place," Jeff commented as he shook water from his hair.

"Not really," Nicole said, trying to orient herself. From the direction of the water flow . . . "That side," she said, pointing. "Kahkitah?"

Kahkitah trilled an affirmative and swam her to that side. He caught some of the plants lining the river's edge, holding them steady while she tossed her trident up into the grasses and then climbed up herself. Jeff was already at the top by the time she scrambled to her feet, both tridents in his hands. "What now?" he asked.

"We find the Ponngs," she said, wincing as a sudden thought belatedly struck her. "And hope that the Shipmasters haven't already sent them home."

There was a log-fire sound from the grass in front of them. "Sibyl?" the translation came in her mind.

And to her relief, a familiar figure popped up out of concealment.

"Yes, it's me," Nicole confirmed. So the Ponngs *were* still here. "Hello, Moile. How are you and your people doing?"

"Very well, thank you," Moile said. His gaze flicked to Jeff, then sent a lingering look at the tridents. "We have food, and the Ship-masters assure us they're making preparations to return us to our homes."

Nicole's stomach tightened. Homes that might soon be under siege by alien armies, Moile's friends and relatives scooped up to be thrown casually to their deaths in some far-distant war. "I need your help," she said.

Moile stiffened to a sort of attention. "Your slave will provide whatever you need," he declared. His eyes flicked again to the tridents. "You have brought us new weapons. Do you wish us to destroy the Thii?"

"No, no," Nicole said. "No destroying. But I *will* need you and Teika to come with me to the Thii side."

"And once we're there?"

"I have a question for them," Nicole said. "You and these"—she nodded at the tridents—"are to make sure they listen."

"I understand," Moile said. "Shall I fetch Teika?"

"Please."

Moile nodded and hurried away through the grass.

"So you have slaves now?" Jeff asked quietly.

"Long story," Nicole said. "He and Teika volunteered to be my slaves if I chased the Thii off their backs and got them more food."

"Have they kept up their end of the deal?"

"Don't know," Nicole said. "I haven't asked."

"Ah," Jeff said. "That kind of commitment could come in handy."

"*If* it's real," Nicole said sourly. "I knew a lot of people in Philly who would promise you anything. But it was just words. As soon as they got what they wanted, they were gone."

"Yeah, I've seen my share of those," Jeff said. "But there must have been *some* real friendships in all of that."

"If there were, I never saw them," Nicole said. "Not in my group. Not since I was ten or eleven. Even then . . ." She shook her head.

"I'm sorry," Jeff said quietly.

"It's okay," Nicole said. "I got used to it. Anyway, it probably made it easier for me when I got brought to the *Fyrantha*. I didn't miss anyone, because I never had anyone to miss. Anyone or anything."

"Unlike Sam or Bungie."

"Or Allyce," Nicole said with a sigh. Allyce had betrayed them . . . but she couldn't really blame her. "Speaking of Sam, how did you get him to go along with the Setting Sun deal?"

"Oh, we didn't tell him," Jeff said, a hint of humor in his voice. "He'll be spitting nails when he comes out of it."

"Yeah, so what else is new?" Nicole said with a sniff, glad to get off the subject of Allyce. "How are we doing on timing?"

"Well, assuming it takes as long to get back as it took to get here," Jeff said, "and adding some time to get everyone set once we're back . . . it'll be a little tight, but we should be okay. There won't be time for any long-winded speeches, though."

"I wasn't planning any," Nicole assured him. "I just . . . I don't know what we'll do if the Thii refuse to help."

"That's why I wanted the tridents along," Jeff said grimly. "Pointy things can be great persuaders."

"Well, be careful," Nicole warned. "The Shipmasters watch this arena, too."

"I know," Jeff said. "Don't worry. The great thing about weapons is that if you can convince someone you're willing to use them, you often don't have to."

There was another rustling in the grass, and Moile reappeared with Teika at his side. "We stand ready, Sibyl," Moile said.

"Okay," Nicole said. "We're going to cross the river—the Ghorfs will help—and go talk to the Maven. *I* will talk," she added. "*You* will stand and be quiet. Understood?"

"Understood," Moile said. To Nicole's ears, he sounded a little disappointed.

"Good," Nicole said. "Let's go."

After the ordeal of pipes, slip ramps, churners, and aerators that had brought them here, a simple swim across a mostly quiet river was a piece of cake.

At least it was for Nicole and Jeff. Not so much for Moile and Teika. They climbed into the Ghorfs' arms without complaint, but it was clear as they were ferried across the water that they weren't at all comfortable with this mode of transportation. It wasn't until they were back on dry land that they finally relaxed.

Nicole had no idea how they would react when they found out how they were getting to the Q1 arena. It would, she suspected, show how truly committed they were to the whole slave thing.

"Do you wish us to go with you?" Kahkitah asked from the water when the humans and Ponngs were standing on the bank.

"No, that's okay," Nicole said. "If we need extra persuasion we'll call you."

She turned and headed into the tall grass. "What next?" Jeff asked.

"We find someone to take us to the Maven—"

From their right came a sound like a DJ turntable scratching. "You will stand and not flee," the translation came.

"—which I guess won't be too hard," she finished, coming to a halt.

"You will stand and not flee," the Thii repeated.

"We're standing and we're not fleeing," Nicole called back. "I'm the Sibyl. I want to talk to the Maven."

"You've brought our enemies with you," the Thii said accusingly.

"That's not all I've brought," Nicole said, gesturing their unseen company toward the tridents in Jeff's hands. "You see these?"

A pause. "Those are weapons."

"That's right," Nicole said. "Much better weapons than you've got, too. So. Are you going to take me to the Maven, or do we have to find her ourselves? Because if we have to go looking I'm going to end up in a *very* bad mood."

There was a short pause. Then, from that direction, two Thii stepped out of hiding. "I am the Maven," one of them said calmly, raising all four arms to show off the thin blue bands on her upper-arm wrists. "What do you wish, Sibyl?"

"Hello, Maven," Nicole said. "Let's start with a little history. I gave you food when you needed it, and I stopped the war between you and the Ponngs."

"And now you bring them to begin the war anew?" She jabbed two of her arms at the Ponngs.

"No," Nicole said. "I'm here because I need your help. I need the assistance of two or three—"

"We need to borrow eight of your warriors," Jeff put in.

Nicole spun around, feeling her jaw drop. "*What?* Jeff—"

"That is unacceptable," the Maven said.

"Yeah," Nicole said between clenched teeth. "Give us a moment."

Grabbing Jeff's arm, she dragged him a few steps away. "What the hell are you doing?" she demanded softly.

"You can't start bargaining at the number you want," he explained. "You have to start higher and let them talk you down."

"That's not how the Thii think," Nicole bit out. "You haven't dealt with them before. I have. Keep your mouth shut and let me handle it, okay?"

Jeff's eyes gave a flash of annoyance. But he nodded. "Fine. Do it your way."

"I will." She let go of his arm and strode back to face the Maven. "Okay," she said. "Ignore what Jeff said about eight warriors. I just need two of them."

The Maven twitched her hands in some sort of gesture. "I cannot give you any."

"I need three of them," Nicole said.

The Maven seemed taken aback. "I already said I cannot give you any."

"I need four of them."

The Maven shot a confused look at Jeff. "You—other Sibyl. Explain please to her that if I cannot give two I cannot give four."

"Don't look at *me*," Jeff said mildly. "She's the one talking to you. But it looks to me like the number goes up each time you refuse. A couple more rounds, and you'll be right back to the eight *I* asked for. You'd better make a deal before we clean you out completely."

"But it's not safe to take so many from us," the Maven protested. "Our enemies may attack."

"Why?" Jeff countered. "You've got food, they've got food, and there's a big river between you. Why would they bother you?"

The Maven looked at the two Ponngs, standing stiff and silent, then at Jeff's tridents. "There may yet be scores to be settled," she muttered.

"And they're not going to be settled now," Nicole said firmly. "*Or* maybe they will."

"What do you mean?"

"You see those weapons?" Nicole asked, waving at the tridents. "The plan is for us to take them with us when we leave. We'll also be taking Moile and Teika. If none of your warriors come with us, I'll have to think up a new plan. In that case, there'll be no point in lugging the weapons back with us. There'll also be no time for us to take the Ponngs back to their side of the river."

The Maven's arms twitched. "You threaten us with death?"

"Not if you help me," Nicole said. "I need six Thii warriors."

For a long moment the Maven stood motionless. Then she folded both sets of arms across her chest. "I can give you four. No more."

"Good enough," Nicole said. "Send someone to get them. And make it fast—our timing is tight enough already."

The Maven turned to the other Thii and murmured something too low for Nicole's translator to pick up. The Thii made a three-handed gesture and disappeared back into the grass.

Nicole stepped to Jeff's side. "Sorry," she said.

"No apology needed," he assured her. "You were right—it was your play, and I was out of line. How did you know that raising the number each time would work better than shooting high and then letting her talk you down?"

Nicole shrugged. "I don't know. Because I spent time with them before, I guess. It gave me a feel for how they think."

"Did you do other negotiations with them then?"

"Not *negotiations*, really," Nicole said. "Nothing like this, anyway."

"But you knew how to do it," Jeff said. "Interesting."

"What do you mean, *interesting*? Good interesting or bad interesting?"

"Not sure," Jeff said. "For now, just interesting."

They heard the rustling in the grass before the Thii appeared. Four of them, as promised, each carrying a bow, a quiver of light-weight arrows, and a blunt sword.

"They are here," the Maven announced, as if Nicole might

somehow have missed that. "They are Nise, Sofkat, Iyulik, and Misgk. Misgk commands."

"Yes," Nicole said. She'd met the first three the last time she was here, though she hadn't heard Nise's name, but Misgk was new to her. Maybe he'd been in the background before, ready to guide the rest of them into battle. "Thank you. If all goes well, they should be back in a few hours." She gestured at the warriors. "You can leave the weapons here. You won't be needing them."

"You requested warriors," the Maven said. "Warriors carry weapons."

Nicole pursed her lips. Pinprick arrows and blunt swords against creatures the size and bulk of the Koffren would be about as useful as beating against their chests with bare hands. Worse, really—the sharp points of both weapons would leave just enough damage to make them mad.

But there was no time to argue the point. If they wanted to lug extra stuff through the *Fyrantha*'s waterways, that was up to them. "Fine," she said. "Let's go."

"And the weapons?" the Maven added, pointing at the tridents.

"They'll come with us," Nicole confirmed. "As will the Ponngs."

"Who will wield them?"

Jeff stepped close to Nicole. "I think she thinks you're going to re-create their fight somewhere else," he murmured.

Nicole clenched her teeth. With her four Thii holding useless weapons and the two Ponngs holding the tridents? Probably. "They're not going to fight each other," she told the Maven. "They're going to help us defeat a new enemy."

"They're to protect you?"

"Yes, I guess so."

"As they would protect their comrades and their Maven?"

"Ah . . . yes," Nicole said cautiously. There was an air of formality and ritual in the Maven's tone, the kind of thing she'd heard in movies where someone was giving an oath of allegiance or something.

Which was fine as far as it went, except they *really* didn't have time for this.

Luckily, Jeff had picked up on that, too. "They'll protect the Sibyl, and they'll tell you all about it when they get back," he said. Shifting both tridents to one hand, he took Nicole's arm with the other and started gently pulling her back toward the river. "We're leaving now. All of us."

Nicole expected the Maven to keep going. But she remained silent. Either the ritual was over, or she'd figured out that she wasn't going to get to do the whole thing.

"I just hope Kahkitah was able to get word to the rest of the Ghorfs and get us some extra help," Jeff said as they pushed through the tall grass. "It'd be a real chore to get this lot back to Q1 with just two of them."

"I'm sure Kahkitah's on it," Nicole said. "Are we going to make it in time?"

"I don't know," he said. "I guess we'll find out."

The Ghorfs had indeed gotten the message to come to Q3. Unfortunately, they'd decided that meant to meet Nicole outside the arena itself, out where the river passed through the wall and started into the filter cycle.

Which meant that instead of them all heading out together, Kahkitah and the other Ghorf had to ferry Nicole's group in shifts, first taking Jeff and two of the Thii, then the two Ponngs, then Nicole and the last two Thii.

The Ponngs didn't trust the Ghorfs. The Thii were terrified at the thought of going underwater, though all four tried to hide it. In the end Nicole was just barely able to persuade them, and had to invoke both the Ponngs' slave promise and the Maven's loyalty ritual before the two groups of aliens would agree.

Fortunately, after that first rocky start things settled down a little. Once the Thii survived their first underwater experience they took the rest of the trip more calmly, and as long as Nicole stayed within view of the Ponngs while the Ghorfs were swimming with them they were willing to go along. But neither group was particularly enthusiastic, and Nicole couldn't help but wonder if they would be willing to do what she needed once they arrived in Q1.

They'd reached the very last stage of the journey when the revolt she'd half expected happened.

"No more," Misgk said firmly, holding two of his thin hands up in a sort of double-fist gesture. The other two hands, Nicole noted uneasily, were gripping his sword hilt and one of the arrows in his quiver. "No more. If you wish us able to fight at the end of this path, you must not take us through any more water."

"I understand," Nicole said, eyeing the flowing water disappearing through an opening in the wall ahead. If the Ghorfs' calculations were right, ten feet past the wall the stream emptied out into the Q1 river.

The extremely *fast* Q1 river. If Misgk and the other Thii couldn't handle one of the slower underwater passages, they sure as hell wouldn't hold up to this one.

There was the service corridor system above the river, of course, the one Nicole had already used once. But that route just dumped them in the river again, with the same problem they were already facing. Going around to the corridor and door Wesowee had taken her through after her little ocean dip would take time they didn't have, and would probably run them into a Wisp or two as well.

Which left only one option. It hadn't worked so well the last time Nicole had tried it, but time was running out and it was all they had.

Mentally crossing her fingers, she took a deep breath. "*Fyran-tha*," she called into the cramped space. "Protector says turn off the Q1 arena river."

Out of the corner of her eye she saw Jeff give her an odd look. "Protector says turn off the Q1 arena river," she repeated. A sudden thought—"And keep it off until *I* say to turn it back on."

"Nicole—"

"Shh," Nicole hissed. Something was happening. She could hear it—maybe *feel* it was a more accurate word. There was a set of deep and rapid clicks, barely audible over the swooshing of the water—

Abruptly the swooshing stopped, and the water level dropped like a bathtub draining away. Someone gasped—from the sound, one of the Thii—and then the water was gone, leaving a low-ceilinged tunnel into the arena.

"Come on," Nicole said. Dropping onto all fours, she crawled into the tunnel, trying not to think about how the Shipmasters had been able to turn the water back on earlier and nearly drown her. This time, she'd told the *Fyrantha* not to let them do that, but she had no idea if she had that authority here in the Shipmasters' stronghold.

"Wait!" Kahkitah called softly from behind her. "We can't fit through that opening."

Nicole grimaced. No, of course they couldn't. She should have spotted that right away.

Which meant that until the Ghorfs could get around to one of the arena's other entrances she, Jeff, the Ponngs, and the Thii would be on their own.

Which was really how it had to be anyway. She and Jeff had already decided that the Ghorfs had to be kept out of any fighting.

But Nicole had hoped at least to have them hanging around, being all big and threatening, when the Koffren started moving. Trake always said that intimidation was the first half of any battle.

"That's okay—you've done enough," she called back. "Anyway, you need to get everyone back to their jobs before they're missed. Jeff?"

"We're right behind you," he confirmed. "You just get to the beach and figure out where you want everybody."

"Okay." Nicole was at the end of the tunnel now, with just a one-foot drop to the bottom of the river channel. "Time?"

"I make it five minutes," Jeff said. "You still want me to gather everyone on our side and get them over to yours?"

"Yes," Nicole said. She climbed out of the tunnel and turned to look behind her. The Thii were moving briskly toward her, looking even more like insects than they usually did when they walked on all sixes. With their smaller size, the passage was a lot easier for them than it was for Nicole. "Everybody, follow me," she ordered. "And watch your step—the channel floor can be slippery."

She had a bad moment as she passed the spot where the river came back to life the last time, wondering if history was going to repeat itself. But the water remained off. Two minutes later she led the way around the bluff and onto the wet beach sand.

The Wisps and Koffren were still standing where she and Jeff had left them, but the ocean's water level had receded visibly since then, leaving them standing in a wide strip of wet sand. Iosif and the other men were no longer grouped around the bluff, having apparently gotten tired of waiting and wandered off. She spotted two green jumpsuits where the reeds met the edge of the tree line, and there were three abandoned tridents lying on the beach, two on the loose sand, the other half-hidden in the reeds.

The Thii spotted them, too. "Weapons!" Sofkat said, pointing excitedly. "Should we retrieve them?

"Yes, of course," Nicole said. She had no intention of letting the Thii use them—in fact, given their slender build and thin arms she wasn't even sure how well they could handle something that long and heavy. But she also had absolutely no intention of letting the Koffren trade up, either. "Grab them and head through the reeds into the forest. We'll figure out where to hide them up there."

"Where to *hide* them?" Iyulik asked with clear disbelief. "The Ponngs have such weapons. Why can we not?"

"You know why not," Nicole said. "Get the tridents and stash them among the trees. Then all of you get in position *there*, about midway from the water line to the reeds. I need the Thii lined up in the middle, with the Ponngs at either end."

"With *their* weapons," Iyulik muttered.

"Their weapons are there to protect you," Nicole reminded him. "Anyway, you've got your bows and arrows. We decided that's where this is going to start, remember?"

"Yes," Nise murmured, looking pointedly down the beach at the Koffren.

"Don't let their size worry you," Nicole said, wishing fleetingly that she could take her own advice on that one. "The bigger they are, the better targets they make."

"I think he was concerned more about the uselessness of the arrows we all were given," Moile put in.

"Nothing that can hurt them is completely useless," Nicole assured him. "And they'll hurt a lot more on bare Koffren skin than they did against that grass armor all of you were using."

"And what of their swords?" Moile asked. "I doubt they're as flimsy as ours."

"I doubt that, too," Nicole conceded. "You just get in position. I'll see what I can do about the swords."

She was on very close timing, she knew as she hurried down

the beach, her feet dragging on the loose sand. She hit the wet section and picked up her pace, watching the Wisps closely. There might be a hint of movement just before they released the Koffren, which might give Nicole enough warning to reverse course and get back to the others before the big aliens attacked.

Then again, there might be no warning at all.

The Wisps and Koffren were still standing motionless as she reached them. So far, so good. Watching the Wisps closely, she reached over and carefully drew one of the Koffren swords from its sheath.

It was heavier than she'd expected. Far heavier than the Thii's swords; nearly as heavy, in fact, as the humans' tridents. It was gleaming in the morning sunlight and probably very sharp. Heart still thudding, she reached over and pulled out the other Koffren's sword—

And gasped as a huge hand suddenly came to life and locked itself around her wrist.

The Wisps had released their prisoners.

There was a grinding noise like a coffee maker—"So, young one," a deep voice said in Nicole's brain. "Have your companions chosen you to be first to die?"

twenty

"I'm not here to die," Nicole said, the words stumbling over each other as the two aliens took their swords back from her. "Not here to hurt you, either. I just came to talk."

"Do you begin all conversations by stealing your enemies' weapons?" the Koffren countered.

"You don't have to be our enemies," Nicole said, feeling her face screwing up with pain. His grip felt like it was about to break her wrist. "Fievj is lying to you."

"To *us*?" The alien ground out a laugh. "That was not Fievj. Fievj deals with the slaves, and the testing arenas. That was Nevvis. Nevvis deals with the buyers. And it was *you* whom he lied to."

"What do you mean?" Nicole asked cautiously. "What did he lie about?"

"We aren't another test to be studied," the Koffren said. "We're the ones testing *you*."

"Testing us for what?"

"Your value in battle," the Koffren said. "You were the first. You demonstrated courage, though also foolishness, in attempting to disarm us." He lifted his head to look over Nicole's shoulder. "He will be the second."

Nicole turned around. Jeff had appeared around the farther bluff, herding the rest of the blue team across the empty riverbed.

Most of them were carrying their tridents, though in a loose, casual way. Jeff got them around the other bluff and, using the blunt end of his trident like he was guiding sheep, got them turned and moving up the slope.

It clearly wasn't easy. With their minds still confused, they all seemed to want to head off in different directions, and it was all Jeff could do to keep them bunched up and moving toward the trees.

"What do you think?" the Koffren said, pointing with the tip of his sword. "That one?"

Nicole looked at the second alien. But he remained silent. Maybe only the boss was allowed to speak? "That one what?" she asked, looking back.

"That one—Ah, I was right," the Koffren said. "Here he comes now."

Nicole tensed. With Jeff's attention momentarily elsewhere, Bennett and Tomas had slipped past his trident barrier and were strolling down the beach. Bennett caught sight of Nicole, said something to Tomas, and they started loping toward her, idly swinging their tridents like kids carrying hockey sticks home from the rink.

"Our second subject," the Koffren said, hefting his sword.

"No!" Nicole bit out, desperately grabbing for his arm with her free hand.

It was no use. He was bigger, he was stronger, and he had much longer arms. He evaded her attempt without even trying, lifting the sword high over his head and completely out of her reach. He looked at her, his head cocked as if he'd suddenly had an idea, and he twisted her around until she was facing the two approaching men.

And as she watched in horror, he sent his sword spinning through the air to bury itself in Bennett's chest.

"*No!*" Nicole shrieked.

But it was too late. Far too late. The sheer unexpectedness of it, the utter insanity, had taken her by surprise.

The impact threw Bennett backward, slamming him to the ground with a small splash and leaving him stretched out motionless on the wet sand. Tomas took a couple more steps, his eyes on Bennett, slowly trotting to a confused halt. He gazed at the body, then looked at Nicole and the Koffren, then back at the body. Stepping over to it, he prodded it gently in the side with the end of his trident as if expecting his friend to get up.

He was still standing there when the Koffren gave Nicole a violent shove toward them and let go of her wrist. "Go," the alien ordered. "See to your defenses and your strategy. We shall be there shortly to test them."

Nicole spun toward him, her hands clenched into fists tight enough to hurt, her anger and anguish and fear and hatred boiling like hell itself inside her.

But there was nothing she could do. Nothing she could say. Her rage meant nothing to these creatures. Life meant nothing. Only force meant anything. Force, and the freedom that their overwhelming strength gave them to do whatever they damn well pleased.

Suddenly, it was like she was back on the Philadelphia streets.

She took a deep, shuddering breath. No. There, she'd had no one and nothing. Here, she had allies and friends.

And she had a plan.

She nodded, not daring to speak, and hurried away from them. She grabbed Tomas's arm as she passed, dragging him away from the body. Jeff, she saw, had stopped just outside the tree line, his face carved from stone, the rest of his drugged charges still milling about in their carefree oblivion. Still dragging Tomas, half expecting to feel the other Koffren sword cut through her own back, she kept moving.

Jeff was still standing there when she reached him. "You saw?" she panted.

He nodded, his eyes flicking to her and then back to the beach. "You all right?" he asked, his voice as stony as his face.

"Yes," Nicole said, feeling as terrified and miserable as she'd ever felt in her whole life. "I'm sorry. I couldn't—"

"There's nothing to be sorry about." He cut her off, his voice dark with grim fury.

But as Nicole gazed into his face, she could see with a small flicker of relief that the fury wasn't directed at her. He'd seen everything, and he knew as well as she did that there had been nothing she could have done to stop it.

But the pain and the guilt remained.

"But I swear if they start a full autopsy I'm going to kill both of them," Jeff continued.

Nicole turned. The two Koffren were kneeling by Bennett's body, poking and prodding at it with thick fingers. "He said they're testing to see how useful we'd be in battle," she said, shivering. "They're probably seeing how we're put together. Bones and muscles and stuff."

"It's still desecration," Jeff ground out. "But we'll fix that later. Looks like we've got a couple of minutes. See if you can get the men a little farther inland—I don't want them wandering into the battle zone."

"What about you?"

"I'll deal with the spare tridents and make sure the Ponngs and Thii are ready."

"Okay." Forcing herself to turn away from the ghoulish scene by the ocean, she got a fresh grip on Tomas's arm and pulled him up the slope to where the rest of the group was standing around. Most of them had already lost their tridents—she could see a line of them in the reeds where their owners had abandoned them— and it was mostly a matter of sternly ordering them all to keep moving. It seemed easier than it had looked when she watched Jeff herding them up from the beach, maybe because they were used to taking orders from a Sibyl. Possibly that was why Jeff had given her the job.

Or else he just wanted her to be as far away from the battle line when the Koffren launched their attack.

She scowled. Like hell. This whole thing was her idea, and there was no way she wasn't going to be there when it went down. She would just have to get her charges out of the way before that happened—

"Hello there, babe." A growl came from behind her.

She froze. *"Bungie?"*

"Anyone else around here call you *babe*?"

She clenched her teeth. How the *hell* had he gotten out of those nets? "You need to get out of here," she said. "It's about to get *very* dangerous."

"Sure is, babe," he said.

Nicole winced. It was never a good sign when he called her *babe*. "I'm serious," she said. Bracing herself, she turned around.

He was standing between a pair of tall bushes, a trident swing- ing gently in his hand. It was a casual pose, about as nonthreat- ening as Bungie ever got, a pose that invited her to come closer for a chat.

Nicole wasn't fooled. This was his version of Trake's negotia- tion stance, the one he used when he was trying to sucker some- one into thinking no one was even dreaming about violence.

Bungie didn't do it nearly as well as Trake did. But he did it well enough. He also had a weapon in his hand and was blocking the quickest route back to the beach. He was looking for trouble, and he was looking for payback.

"Sure, you're serious," he said. His voice was the same untroubled tone that Trake used, but there was a hard edge underneath that sent a fresh shiver up Nicole's back. "See, *I'm* serious, too. I'm serious about getting the hell off this damn ship and back home."

"Bungie—"

"And if I get to make your boyfriend bleed, hey, that's an extra bonus."

"Bungie, this isn't going to work," Nicole said, taking a slow step forward. If she could get close enough . . .

Not likely. Even with just that one step she saw his eyes narrow and his grip tighten on the trident. Long before she got within jumping range the weapon would be up and ready and pointed at her.

But she had to try. If she screamed or shouted for Jeff, she risked distracting him and the battle line they'd set up. If the Koffren picked that moment to attack, it would destroy everything. "They're not going to send you home," she said, taking another cautious step forward.

And as she set her foot down, she felt it land on something thin and hard.

Another trident.

She looked closely at Bungie. If he'd noticed anything—the clink of metal, or a change in her expression—he wasn't showing it.

So she had a weapon now. But that might not help her much. Bungie was bigger and stronger, and he was a hell of a lot meaner. There was no way she could stand against him in a fair fight.

She would just have to make sure the fight wasn't fair.

"And they also—*aren't going to let you win.*" She babbled the words out in a rush as she ducked down and snatched up the hidden trident. Hefting it like a spear, she lined it up on Bungie with the three prongs horizontal, and charged.

He didn't sidestep, or take a step back. He didn't even flinch. He just rotated his own trident so the prongs were vertical and caught the front of her weapon on his.

The jolt as the tridents slammed together was more violent than Nicole had expected, nearly breaking her grip on the shaft. Probably it was harder than Bungie had expected, too, as the impact forced him to take a small step backward. Leaning forward, putting her full weight into it, Nicole pushed.

She might as well have tried to knock over a tree. Bungie leaned toward her, his feet braced against the ground. He held that position for a moment, then started to push back against her. Nicole resisted as he slowly forced her out of her forward crouch and back to an upright stance. For a second she fought for balance; and then, with a final shove, he broke her stance, making her take a couple of quick steps backward to keep from falling.

"*Damn* it," she snarled under her breath as she regained her balance. Resettling her grip on the trident, she again leaned forward and charged.

The result was the same. Again, Bungie caught her trident on his with a muffled clank. Again, he held her in place, then slowly pushed her back. This time, though, instead of letting herself be forced into a retreat, Nicole held her ground a second longer and ended up falling backward onto her rear.

"*Ow*," she bit out. She scrambled to her feet, grabbing the trident with one hand and rubbing her butt with the other. With her eyes narrowed in supposed pain, she watched Bungie's face closely.

There it was, exactly as she'd expected and hoped: a small,

superior, sadistic smile. He'd shown her his strength, he'd proved she couldn't win, and he'd made her look foolish.

Now, finally, she was ready.

She got her other hand on the trident, once again leaning forward and bracing herself for a new charge, clenching her teeth as she glared at Bungie. He gave her an amused smile in return and leaned forward again into his own stance. Revenge against Jeff was still in the cards, but humiliating Nicole was satisfying in its own way and he was in no hurry for this part of the fun to end.

Taking a deep breath, leaning even farther forward, Nicole charged.

Bungie leaned forward in anticipation, his rear foot pressed against the ground. Once again, their tridents smashed together with a thud.

But this time, instead of continuing to push forward, Nicole let go of the trident and threw herself forward, ducking and twisting around as she went.

Bungie was caught completely off guard. With his full weight already leaning forward, the sudden loss of pressure against his trident sent him stumbling helplessly toward her. He swung his trident down, but Nicole was already past the shaft.

And with a half rotation that put her back to him, she slammed full force into his legs.

There might have been a soft crack as she knocked his legs out from under him. If so, it was swallowed up in his bellowed curse and the crash of small branches as he fell over her to land flat on his face on the ground.

Nicole didn't wait to see any more. She scrambled back to her feet, ducked around the trees, and ran through the undergrowth toward the beach. Heart thudding, she cleared the last line of trees and came into view of the battle line.

To her relief, there was no sign yet of the Koffren. The Ponngs and Thii were still standing ready in the positions Jeff had assigned them in the open area past the reeds.

But while their bodies might be facing the beach, all six of the aliens were peering over their shoulders back toward her. Maybe her brief fight with Bungie hadn't been quite as quiet as she'd thought. Jeff himself, she noted uneasily as she slowed to a trot, was nowhere to be seen. Still gathering up the tridents?

If so, he'd better hurry. The Koffren were still on the beach; but where they'd been crouched down earlier examining Bennett's body one was now standing and the other was in the process of pulling the sword out of the dead man's chest. Another few seconds, and they would be heading upslope.

There was a rustle of reeds behind Nicole. She half turned, expecting to see Jeff—

And twisted away barely in time as something hurled past her side.

She stumbled, falling to one knee in the reeds, wincing as her back and knee spasmed in pain from the sudden wrenching movement. Through the trees Bungie appeared, his face contorted with fury and pain, a trident held close to his side like a crutch. "Yeah, run, bitch," he bit out as he limped toward her. "Run, and keep running, because you're dead. You're *dead*."

Nicole looked at the beach. The Koffren were both standing now, watching the drama. Not attacking, not charging, but just standing there, looking up the slope.

Waiting to see what Nicole would do.

She looked back at Bungie. She could fight, she knew. The Shipmasters had already seen her and Jeff fighting in the Q4 arena, and they'd already heard the brain-damage story she'd spun for them. The rest of the humans were still doped up, unlikely to even know what was going on, let alone come to her aid. She could fight without endangering anyone else.

But she couldn't win. She'd had one trick, and she'd already used it. If she waited for Bungie to get to her, she would die.

But if she ran, would the Ponngs and Thii still be willing to fight? Moile and Teika had pledged themselves to her, and only her, and the Thii seemed to be likewise under the Maven's orders to obey her. If Nicole left, would they, too?

She took a deep breath. Maybe the Ponngs and Thii understood the concept of *martyrs*. Maybe they honored them. Maybe they didn't.

But she didn't doubt for a moment that they understood the concept of *cowards*.

She would do her best to survive Bungie's attack. But whether or not she succeeded, here was where she would stay.

Bungie was halfway to her now, still limping but showing no sign of slowing down. Nicole glanced behind her at the trident he'd thrown, wondering if she had time to run and get it. But he'd thrown it hard, and even at his reduced speed she knew she'd never reach it in time.

She turned back, eyeing the trident in his hand, trying to plan out her move. Assuming he stopped when he got within range and lifted it up for an attack, she would rush forward and try to duck past the prongs and grab the shaft. If she succeeded, she would throw herself against him and hope that his knees and shins had been injured enough that she could bowl him over onto his back. If she got that far—

There was the sound of a scratched record. "Stop."

A *Thii* voice? Frowning, Nicole looked at the battle line.

The Thii were no longer facing the beach and the Koffren. Instead, all four had turned to face Bungie.

And all four were holding their bows, the strings pulled back with arrows ready to fly.

She felt her muscles tense. A brave move; except that she knew the arrows were all but useless. Their pointed tips would hurt, but they would barely penetrate Bungie's skin. They certainly wouldn't slow him down.

Only he *was* slowing down, she saw as she turned back. He slowed to a cautious halt, his face and his burning rage now directed at this new threat. "Back off, bugs," he snarled. "You shoot those things and I'll pull your damn legs off."

And only then did the truth belatedly hit her. The Thii arrows were indeed useless.

But Bungie didn't know that.

"I wouldn't push them if I were you," she warned, putting as much scornful confidence into her voice as she could. "I assume you haven't forgotten the last time you had to have an arrow dug out of you?"

Bungie turned his glare back on Nicole.

But there was some fear there now behind the rage and pain. He remembered, all right.

And as he stood there, hating everything and everyone, out of the corner of Nicole's eye she saw Jeff burst into view through the trees. He got two steps into his sprint before his brain caught the whole scene and its significance, and he switched abruptly to a slower and much quieter jog.

Bungie, with his full memory tied up with the arrow Sam had dug out of his leg and his full attention tied up with the four arrows currently pointed at him, never even heard Jeff coming.

Nicole waited until Jeff was two steps away. "They're watching," she warned quietly.

Bungie had just enough time to turn a puzzled look on her before Jeff reached around him from behind, wrapped both arms around his chest, and twisted him to the side and onto the ground.

Nicole ran toward them. She'd been worried that Jeff would use some fancy Marine move on Bungie, like the kind he'd used to knock him out earlier, something the Koffren might recognize as military. But Jeff had apparently anticipated that risk and had instead gone with a simple bear hug to take him down.

Of course, the downside of that was that Bungie was alive, alert, and still mad as hell. Right now, Jeff's arms wrapped around him was all that kept him from trying to kill everyone.

Or maybe not. Even as Nicole reached them Bungie suddenly went limp in Jeff's arms. "You okay?" Jeff grunted as he shoved Bungie away from him.

"We're fine," Nicole assured him. "What did you do to him?"

"Don't worry, there's no permanent damage," Jeff said as he got to his feet. "*Damn* it. I should have been here."

"It's okay," Nicole said. "It worked out. Thanks to them," she added, turning to the Thii and lowering her head in a small bow. "Thank you."

"It was our privilege, Sibyl," Misgk said, bowing in return.

And only then did it occur to Nicole that, while Bungie hadn't known the Thii were bluffing, the Thii themselves had been perfectly aware of it.

Challenging Nicole's attacker had been courageous in and of itself. Challenging him knowing they might die if he called their bluff was a whole step more so.

She still didn't know if the aliens understood the concepts of martyrs and cowards. But she knew now they absolutely understood the concept of heroes.

"Here they come," Jeff grunted. "Everyone, get ready."

Nicole looked at the beach. With the sideshow over, the Koffren were on the move, their swords swinging idly in their hands as they walked briskly toward Nicole and the battle line. "What about Bungie?" she asked, looking down.

"I've got it," Jeff said. He'd rolled Bungie over onto his stomach and was tying his wrists together with pieces from one of the nets. "And watch it. The only way he could have gotten free was with help."

"One of the green team?"

"Or one of the Shipmasters," Jeff said grimly. "The netting was cut, and as far as I know we don't have any tools here that could have done that."

Nicole nodded and stepped to the left end of the battle line beside Moile. "Everyone ready?" she asked, looking them over. Ponngs on the ends, tridents in hand. Thii in the middle, bows and arrows ready. A four-foot gap between each of the aliens, allowing them room for action and maneuver while preventing the Koffren from taking out two with a single sword slash.

"The Ponngs are ready," Moile said.

"The Thii are ready," Misgk added. "Do you still wish us to begin with arrow flights?"

"Yes," Nicole said, fighting to get the words out through a mouth that had suddenly gone dry. This was it. "Make sure to fire some at their helmets—we want them to know for sure that the arrows can't get though the holes."

"And the rest of the flights to their bodies?"

Nicole nodded. "We want them to know they've got nothing to fear from you."

"But only from *them*?" Moile asked.

Nicole winced. A good point. Once the Koffren realized the Thii weren't a threat, they would presumably shift their focus to the Ponngs at the ends of the lines. "If we do this right, it won't come to that," she said.

The Koffren were still walking casually, making no effort to hurry. Extreme confidence, or else giving themselves additional time to observe their enemies.

Either was all right with Nicole. The delay gave Jeff time to finish with Bungie and take his place at the far end of the line beside Teika, Bungie's trident now in his hand.

Nicole had no idea whether or not his presence would make a difference. Given the attackers' size, she sort of doubted it. Just the same, she felt better just knowing he was there.

The Koffren reached the range she and Jeff had decided on . . . and it was time. "Archers: *fire*," Nicole ordered.

The words were barely out of her mouth, which put the translation still a fraction of a second away, when the four Thii sent their first volley on its way: two arrows into each of the Koffren, one chest, one helmet.

The attackers didn't even break stride. One of the arrows lodged briefly in the spokesman's upper chest; a quick swipe of his hand brushed it away. Both of the arrows that hit the helmets, as Nicole had expected, bounced harmlessly off the metal.

The first volley had barely gone spinning off into the sand when the second was in the air. The arrows sped into their targets with the same lack of effect. Nicole couldn't see the faces inside the helmets, but she had the sense that the casual Koffren stride was now taking on a note of arrogance. They had nothing to fear from the defenders, and they knew it.

They kept coming, ignoring the arrows that continued to rain uselessly on them. They were thirty feet away . . . twenty feet . . . ten . . .

"*Now!*" Nicole snapped.

The four Thii tossed their bows aside and spun around to put their backs to the Koffren. They dropped into low crouches, balancing on their lower arms—

And digging their upper arms and feet into the ground, they began throwing sand behind them.

Back in the Q3 arena, Nicole had been amazed at how fast they could go through the ground. But that had been packed soil, and without any particular urgency driving the action. Now, dealing with dry, loose sand and facing enemies who intended their deaths, it was like someone had opened four fire hydrants filled with pressurized grit.

The Koffren were caught completely by surprise. They staggered back as bucketfuls of sand streamed into their helmets, passing through the holes with ease, blasting straight into eyes and noses and mouths. For a moment their forward movement turned into a confused halt as they twisted to their sides, swinging their swords uselessly against the onslaught, trying to turn their faces away from the blasts.

But the move gained them nothing. As they twisted away, and as Nise and Iyulik kept up the barrage from their original positions, Sofkat and Misgk scampered around to the sides to where the Koffren were now facing and restarted their attack.

Again, the Koffren tried to turn away. Again, the two Thii switched positions to compensate.

Some enemies, half blind and half smothered, would probably have retreated. But she'd seen the Koffren spokesman's attitude, and heard his words, and seen his casually cruel actions. These creatures were far too arrogant to ever admit even temporary defeat in front of an enemy they knew to be inferior.

Given enough time, they would overcome the Thii attack. Nicole had no intention of giving them that time. "Ponngs: prepare!" she shouted, watching the Koffren closely as she backed up toward the trees.

The Koffren might not be able to see, but they could clearly still hear. Spinning toward her voice, ignoring the continuing flood of sand into their faces, they raised their swords and charged.

The Ponngs were ready. They gave way before the aliens' charge, staying between the attackers and Nicole. Nise and Iyulik likewise ended their sand barrage, dodging to the sides to get out of the way as the Koffren ran through the spots where they'd just been digging. "Ponngs: prepare!" Nicole shouted again, noting the small shift in direction as the Koffren again homed in on her voice. Blind, all right, relying entirely on sound. "Ponngs: prepare!" The Koffren stumbled a bit as they left the sand of the beach and came up onto solid ground. They regained their footing and continued on.

And in perfect coordination Moile and Teika stopped their retreat, dug the blunt ends of their tridents into the ground behind them, and dropped the prong ends to about a foot above the ground facing the charging Koffren. The attackers' legs slammed into the tridents between the prongs, wedging them against the prongs' bases.

Once again, the attackers were taken completely by surprise. With one leg abruptly jammed to a halt, they fell in the same unison as the Ponngs' attack, toppling forward to land flat on their faces with painful-sounding thuds and the crushing of reeds and grass. One managed to get one hand beneath him in time to partially break his fall; the other didn't even get that far.

For a moment they lay there, probably dazed, certainly with the breath knocked out of them. But Moile and Teika weren't finished. The two Ponngs had danced out of the way as the Koffren fell, disengaging their tridents from the attackers' ankles as the creatures slammed into the ground. Now, dodging around to the sides, the Ponngs lifted their tridents high and jabbed them downward, catching the attackers' sword-arm wrists between the prongs. The prongs dug about halfway into the ground; holding on to the shafts, the Ponngs jumped up into the air and landed on the base of the prongs, burying them the rest of the way into the ground and trapping the Koffren's wrists. Even as the aliens bellowed again, Jeff stepped up to the one at his end of the line and pinned down the alien's other wrist.

"Sibyl!"

Nicole looked up. Misgk, with the Thii part of the battle over, had run over and retrieved the trident Bungie had thrown at her earlier. He threw it to her, putting the full weight of his slender body behind the toss. She caught the weapon and stepped over to the other fallen Koffren. It was the spokesman, she saw, Bennett's blood still red on his sword.

For a stretched-out second she gazed down at him, lying helpless on the ground before her. Nearly as helpless as Bennett had been.

The plan had called for the defenders to merely immobilize the Koffren. But there was no reason that plan couldn't be changed.

It wouldn't be murder. It would be justice.

Justice.

Nicole wanted to kill this creature. She wanted desperately to kill it. She was the *Fyrantha*'s Protector. She could make decisions like this.

But it wasn't what her grandmother would do. It wasn't what Jeff would do.

It was what Bungie would do.

Snarling under her breath, she lifted the trident high and jammed it into the ground around the Koffren's other wrist. She jumped on the base twice, making sure to bury the prongs completely. For another moment she gazed down at her enemy, feeling her hands starting to shake with reaction, then looked up.

Jeff was standing silently to the side, watching her. A relieved smile touched his lips, and he gave her a small nod. "What now, Protector?"

Nicole took a deep breath. *Protector.* "Fievj!" she called toward the sky. "Fievj, answer me!"

There was a moment of silence. One of the Koffren started trying to pull free, stopped as Jeff put a warning foot on the back of his neck beneath the edge of his helmet.

There was a rustle of bushes from behind them, and Nicole turned to see an armored centaur emerge from the trees.

She scowled. Jeff had been right. The Shipmasters *had* had someone on the ground back there to mess with them. "I am Fievj," the centaur said. "What do you wish?"

"Your experiment is over," Nicole said. "We didn't fight. We *don't* fight. Do you finally get that?"

"We understand now," Fievj said.

"Good," Nicole said. "So you'll return all the humans to Q4 and give up this nonsense?"

"We will."

"I expect to see them back in their hives within the hour," Nicole warned.

There was a short pause. Possibly he was wondering if he should ask what she intended to do if they *weren't* returned that promptly.

But he passed on the question. "They will be," he said instead.

"Good." Nicole nodded at the spread-eagled Koffren. "Once they've been returned you can come and get your soldiers. One other thing."

She braced herself. Probably this was a waste of time. But she still had to try. "The Koffren have committed murder against the people of the *Fyrantha*," she said. "I expect you to punish them for their crime."

This time the pause was longer. Probably, Nicole thought darkly, Fievj was wondering how stupid or naïve she was.

But again, he passed up on the obvious comment. "We'll deal with them," was all he said.

"Good," Nicole said again. "Then we're done." She turned to Jeff. "Can you take the Ponngs and Thii back to the Q3 arena? I want to make sure they get back to their people all right—"

"Their people are gone," Fievj said.

Nicole turned back. "What?" she asked carefully.

"Their people are gone," Fievj repeated. "They've been returned to their worlds."

"When exactly did this happen?"

"Thirty minutes after you left the arena."

"Really," Jeff said, his voice unnaturally calm. "How very convenient for someone."

"The transport was already scheduled," Fievj said. "It was unrelated to your own activities."

"Of course it was," Jeff said. "I guess the Wisps will just have to make a couple of extra trips."

"Impossible," Fievj said.

"No, I think you'll find it's not," Jeff said quietly. "You made a deal with them: they fight, then they get to go home."

"These six weren't in place when the time came," Fievj said. "They will therefore not be transported home."

"That is unacceptable—" Nicole began.

"It's all right, Sibyl," Moile said.

Nicole turned to him. He and Teika had come up behind her, their backs stiff, their faces as usual unreadable. Behind them the four Thii stood silently together, their postures much the same as the Ponngs'. "We can't let them get away with this," she said.

"Can you force them to obey you?" Moile asked.

Nicole looked at Jeff. But there was no answer in his eyes. "No," she admitted.

"It will be all right," Moile said. "The Ponngs have often been pressed and beaten down. But we've survived. We'll survive this, as well."

"Moile and I offered ourselves as your slaves," Teika added. "We're bound by honor to continue in your service, if you wish it."

Nicole unclenched her jaw. Great; except she *didn't* wish it. She had enough trouble taking care of herself without having a pair of aliens underfoot. On top of which, the whole concept of slavery made her skin crawl.

And even if she found a way to force Fievj to send them home, what then? Had the Shipmasters already sold the Ponng world to some warmonger? If so, would Moile and Teika really be better off there than they would be aboard the *Fyrantha*?

She focused on the Thii. "Misgk?" she asked. "What does a commander of the Thii say?"

"We wish very much to return home," Misgk said. "But Moile of the Ponng speaks reason." He made a double popping noise. "And I dare say that if the Ponngs can survive captivity aboard this vessel, so can the Thii."

Moile half turned and bowed to him. "We accept your challenge."

Misgk returned the bow. "Very good."

"Hold it," Nicole said, some of the challenges she'd seen within Trake's group flashing through her memory. Most of those challenges had ended in pain or injury. A few had ended in blood. "We're not doing challenges here."

"Yet we're as yet ill-equipped to function alone aboard this vessel," Misgk continued, ignoring her comment. "We would therefore ask to be permitted to accompany you until such time as we can manage our own lives and activities."

Nicole made a face. So now it wasn't just two aliens under-foot, but six. Terrific. "Jeff? What do you think?"

"I don't see what else we can do right now," he said. "But I think we'll walk back to Q3 first, just to make sure Fievj isn't lying about everyone else being gone."

"Good idea," Nicole said, eyeing Fievj and wondering if he would protest the implied insult. But he remained silent. "Every-one all right with that?"

"We are," Moile said.

"We are," Misgk added.

"All right," Nicole said with a sigh. "Take Kahkitah with you. Just in case you need some muscle."

"No problem," Jeff said. "Where do you want to meet after-ward? Our Q4 hive?"

Nicole looked back at the beach. Four Wisps had appeared from somewhere and gathered around Bennett's body. As she watched, they lifted him gently in their arms and glided across the sand toward the far arena wall. "Yes, take them to the hive," she said. "And then . . . gather everyone together, or everyone who wants to come. Kahkitah can show you the way."

"The way to what?"

Nicole swallowed hard. "The place where Bennett will be laid to rest."

twenty-one

The Q2 memorial area was smaller than the one Nicole had seen at the bottom of the ship in Q1. But it was just as somber, and carried the same weight of remembrances, and of loss, and of sorrow.

Or maybe it carried more. Nicole had never known any of the people whose lives were recorded in Q1. But she'd known Bennett. Others of their little group had probably known more of the people here.

"I'd always wondered what happened to people who died aboard ship," Levi murmured to her as they stood in a loose group by the narrow cylinder with Bennett's face floating above it. "But Plato would never talk about it. So this is where everyone's buried?"

"Yes," Nicole said. It wasn't entirely true, but it was close enough. Certainly everyone Levi had known was here.

Including Plato himself. Briefly, she wondered if she dared try to find his cylinder.

Probably not. Aside from the painful memories it would bring back, his biography might also mention the fact that Nicole was the one who'd killed him.

"I suppose you noticed Tomas didn't come," Levi went on.

Nicole nodded. She'd headed here straight from Q1, without

going to the Q4 hive first. Part of that was wanting to give the blue team enough time for the Setting Sun drug to wear off, part of it was to make sure the Wisps had Bennett's pillar set up properly before everyone else arrived.

It had also given her a lot of quiet time to think. By the time the rest of the blue team arrived, three hours later, she'd come to a decision.

"I don't think he blames you," Levi continued. "Not completely. But . . . you know."

"Yeah," Nicole said. "How much . . . I mean, could you . . . ?"

"How much did we know about what was happening?" Levi shrugged. "Pretty much all of it. We could see and hear everything, but we couldn't really do much. For me, it was like I was sitting back watching someone else working my body. Someone who didn't know what he was doing and didn't much care."

"And maybe easily distracted?" Nicole suggested. "I saw some of the green team staring at the rock pattern in the river bluff."

"Yeah, I got a little of that, too," Levi agreed. "Though I could usually drag myself back when I noticed what was happening. I couldn't feel much, either. Carp sliced his arm on a thornbush— he told me afterward that he saw it and knew he'd hurt himself but he couldn't feel any pain. Weird stuff."

Nicole nodded. Which fit pretty well with the idea that Setting Sun had been used at the end of someone's life. Easing the pain, while still allowing him or her to say good-bye to friends or family.

If there *had* been families. She really didn't know how things had worked back then.

But really, why not? Maybe once the *Fyrantha* had been more like a big city than a collection of slave groups.

"I think he'll come around," Levi continued. "But right now, he's hurting. You don't make many friends here—you know that as well as I do. But Tomas and Bennett got along pretty well."

"I'm sorry it happened," Nicole said. "I wish there was something I could do. Wish there was something I could have done."

"I know," Levi said. "We all do."

"So how bad is it?" Nicole asked. Having watched Tomas's moods over the months she'd been aboard the *Fyrantha*, she was pretty sure she knew the answer to this one. But she still had to ask. "Does he want me dead?"

"He's . . . mostly right now it's the pain talking," Levi hedged.

"So he does."

Levi shrugged uncomfortably. "If it helps, he wants Bungie dead more."

"Is that why you're over here talking to me right now?" Nicole asked. "Does he want you to find out from me where Bungie's hiding?"

Levi huffed out a sigh. "Yeah, pretty much. I'm sorry."

"It's okay," Nicole assured him. "I don't really blame him. To be honest, if Bungie walked outside the ship right now I wouldn't shed any tears, either."

"Do you know where he is?"

Nicole shook her head. "The Shipmasters took him along with the Koffren. I don't know what they did with him after that."

"Nothing good, you can bet on that," Levi growled. "Maybe we should have killed him when we had the chance. Him *and* the damn Koffren."

"We were trying to prove humans don't fight or kill."

"Yeah, I remember," Levi said. "Did it work?"

Nicole shrugged. "The whole battle was carried out by the Ponngs and Thii, who the Shipmasters already knew could fight. Speaking of whom, are you and the others going to be able to accept them as our guests for a while?"

"I don't see why not," Levi said. "They didn't do anything to us that anyone can be mad about. And it's not like we don't have acres of room and tons of food. We'll barely even have to look at each other if we don't want to."

"Good," Nicole said. "We'll try to get them their own areas as soon as they're up to speed."

"No problem." Levi touched Nicole tentatively on the shoulder. "Anyway . . . thanks for setting this up. This memorial, I mean. Bennett was important to all of us."

"I know," Nicole said. "You're welcome."

"At least he didn't die for nothing," Levi said. "He'd be pleased to know that at least Earth is safe now."

He nodded a farewell and walked over to where Carp and Duncan were talking quietly together. Nicole watched him go, an ache in her stomach. *At least Earth is safe now.* Levi believed that. Probably the rest believed it, too. And Nicole had no intention of saying anything to the contrary.

She'd already decided that the truth wouldn't gain them anything.

There was a movement of air against the back of her neck, and Jeff stepped to her side. "How are you doing?" he asked quietly.

"Tired," she said. "Sad. Relieved." She hesitated. "Angry."

"Yeah, there's a lot of that going around," Jeff conceded. "So what are you going to do about it?"

"What do you mean?"

"You can let your anger churn around and tear you up inside," Jeff said. "We need to watch Tomas and make sure he doesn't go that route. Or you can channel it into action."

"Any action in particular you have in mind?"

"No." Jeff peered closely at her. "But it looks like you do."

"Is it that obvious?"

"To me. Probably not to anyone else."

"I've got a couple of ideas. I was going to follow up on them once everyone else was back in the hive."

"Sounds good," Jeff said. "Speaking of the hive, I've got the Ponngs and Thii settled in. I also picked up samples of the food they were getting in Q3 to make sure we can feed them something safe here."

"Oh," Nicole said, feeling her face warm with embarrassment. "Sorry—that never even occurred to me. Wouldn't have done to bring them over just so they could starve to death. Thanks."

"No problem," Jeff said. "Just because you're in charge doesn't mean you have to think of everything personally. That's what you have staff for."

Nicole raised her eyebrows. "'Staff'?"

"Maybe more aide-de-camp," he said with a shrug. "Titles don't matter much here. I don't suppose I get a cool uniform?"

"Afraid a blue jumpsuit's the best I can do."

"In that case, never mind—I've already got one of those. So where do we start?"

"We start with someone called the Caretaker," Nicole said. "And some very important questions."

Jeff had never been to the animal treatment room before. Nicole found herself watching his face out of the corner of her eye as the two of them walked down the wide corridor between the cages, Kahkitah lumbering along behind them. Probably Jeff was thinking the same thing she and Kahkitah had their first times here, that the treatment areas were the *Fyrantha*'s version of prison cells.

But while he looked back and forth between them as they walked—and looked up and down, as well—he made no comment. For the moment, anyway, he seemed content to follow her lead, and to let her do things her way.

Though there'd been a moment down below, when the Wisps were heading toward them with outstretched arms, that she thought he was going to bail right there and then. At that point, it was only her reassurances that had made the difference.

Or possibly it was the fact that Kahkitah had stepped into the Wisp's embrace without any hesitation. Nicole didn't see Jeff as the type who would do something purely so as not to be shown up by someone else, but with guys that was always possible. But right now the *why* of it didn't matter. He was here, and that was what she needed.

Back at Bennett's memorial, she'd let Levi believe a lie. Unlike him, and unlike the others in the hive far below, she needed Jeff to know the truth.

Ushkai was waiting at his usual spot as they approached. "Greetings, Protector," he called.

"Hello, Caretaker Ushkai," Nicole called back. "I have some questions."

"Certainly," Ushkai said. "Speak them."

"So who is this again?" Jeff murmured.

"He's a hologram of someone who used to be aboard the *Fyrantha*," Nicole said. "He's sort of like the ship talking, or at least this part of the ship."

"Which part? Q4?"

"It's a little more complicated," Nicole said. "There's the part that controls him, the part that controls the Wisps, the part that talks to the Sibyls, and the part the Shipmasters control."

"Which I'm guessing is most of Q1?"

"Not sure how big their area is," Nicole said evasively. "Ushkai told me that they fly the ship and run the daily functions. It looks like they've also taken control of the Q1 Wisps, and maybe partial control of the ones in Q2 and Q3."

"But this Ushkai is his own section?"

"That's what he told me."

"So you can trust that when he talks he's telling you the truth?"

Nicole felt her throat tighten. "That's what we're here to find out."

They reached the hologram and stopped a few feet away. "Speak your questions, Protector," Ushkai invited.

"Let's start with a simple one," Nicole said. "How much of the *Fyrantha* do the Shipmasters control right now?"

"Most of the Number One section," Ushkai said. "That includes—"

"You mean the Q1 section?" Nicole asked. "The forward-left quadrant?"

"We may designate that as Q1 if you wish," Ushkai said. "That area includes the flight controls and the day-to-day functions for most of the *Fyrantha*."

"How about the Wisps?" Nicole asked. "You told me once they were run by a different part of the ship."

"For the most part they are," Ushkai said. "But those in Q1 are subject to the Shipmasters' commands."

"How about the ones in Q2 and Q3? They were afraid to go into areas they weren't assigned to."

"The Wisps are simple creatures," Ushkai said. "Such fear is perhaps understandable."

"Perhaps," Nicole said, keeping her voice steady.

"But fear should not interfere with their function," Ushkai continued. "Did they refuse to obey your commands?"

"There were some problems," Nicole said. "You said the Shipmasters mostly run the ship's functions. Does that mean they can see and hear everywhere on the ship?"

"No."

"Can *you* see and hear everything?"

There was just the slightest hesitation. "I can see many things."

"Can you see into Q1?"

Another hesitation. "I can see parts of that quadrant."

"So what do the Shipmasters say about what happened in Q1?" Nicole asked. "Have they decided Earth and humans are useless to them?"

"Yes."

Nicole closed her eyes, a sort of numbness creeping over her mind. She'd hoped that wouldn't be Ushkai's answer. She'd hoped it desperately.

But there it was. And with that, everything had gone to hell.

"Glad to hear it," she murmured. "Thank you. Come on, everyone."

She turned and headed back toward the heat-transfer ducts and the Wisps waiting for them there, Jeff and Kahkitah on either side. "What's wrong?" Jeff murmured. "Nicole?"

"I don't understand," Kahkitah added, his birdsongs sounding confused.

"Later," Nicole said. The numbness was gone, replaced by a swirling despair that threatened to strangle the breath and the hope out of her. "We need to find someplace private."

Ultimately, there was only one place she could think of.

The image of Bennett's face that had been floating over his marker earlier had disappeared, though Nicole knew that a touch on the pillar would bring it back. But she had no interest in reminding herself of her past failures.

"Why here?" Jeff asked quietly.

"This is like the *Fyrantha*'s basement," Nicole said. "It's the only place where I specifically called for the Caretaker and didn't get an answer. I'm hoping that means he can't listen in on us here."

"Is Ushkai now our enemy?" Kahkitah asked.

"He's not Ushkai," Nicole said with a tired sigh. "The hologram—maybe that whole section of the ship—has been taken over by the Shipmasters."

"How do you know?" Jeff asked.

Nicole looked closely at him. But there was no doubt or skepticism in his face or voice. He wasn't disagreeing or distrusting her, but simply asking for her reasoning. "A couple of things," she told him. "First of all, he started talking about the Number One Section and seemed surprised that I called it Q1. But he's the one who told *me* to call it Q1."

"Could he have forgotten?" Kahkitah asked.

"He's part of a computer," Jeff reminded him. "If computers start forgetting things you're already in trouble. Anything else?"

"Yes: the Wisps," Nicole said. "I suggested they were afraid to go into other sections of the ship, and he agreed. But that wasn't true. The Wisps I brought from Q2 to Q1 said they couldn't see anything past the corridor by the heat duct. But they never said anything about being afraid to go there."

"Could he have misunderstood?" Jeff asked.

"Maybe," Nicole said. "But here's the big one. Did you ever let Allyce get within range of the Oracle part of the Q1 arena hive? Or could anyone else have mentioned our Setting Sun plan where the Shipmasters could hear?"

"No," Jeff said. "I was *very* careful about that."

"And the paintball work was all done under tree cover where they couldn't see from their observation balcony?"

"Every bit of it."

"I'd have heard if they'd come within view through the trees," Kahkitah added.

"You and your spies?"

Jeff frowned. "His what?" he asked, frowning at Kahkitah.

"We'll get to that in a minute," Nicole said. "So there should have been no way they would know about the plan. Yet they had those Koffren all ready to go before we even reached the deadline for our battle. That means they must have known for at least a while. How did they find out?"

"The Caretaker said the Shipmasters could hear most of the ship," Kahkitah pointed out.

"No," Nicole said. "When I first met the Caretaker he said the Shipmasters controlled very little of the ship. I think whoever was speaking through the Ushkai hologram just now guessed where I was going with my questions and had to pretend they could see everything."

Kahkitah gave a startled-sounding whistle. "You obtained the formula from him," he said. "If he was under their control, then they knew."

"Or if he wasn't completely under their control, they could at least listen in." Nicole hissed out a curse. "I've had the feeling ever since that meeting that there was something odd about him. I thought maybe there was some question he wanted me to ask, but now I'm thinking we were watching a battle between his control and the Shipmasters'."

"Maybe it was both," Jeff said thoughtfully. "Maybe he wanted you to ask if he was still free and independent."

"Which suggests he might not have been fully under their control?" Kahkitah asked.

"Or maybe it isn't that way even now," Jeff agreed.

"None of which matters," Nicole said. "The point is that if they can hear what we say to him, he's useless. We can't get information, and we certainly can't ask him to do anything for us."

"But how could this happen?" Kahkitah asked, sounding puzzled.

"We've made a lot of repairs in Q4," Jeff said, rubbing his cheek thoughtfully. "Maybe some of that work got those two parts of the ship hooked up together again."

"Which brings us to you," Nicole said, looking at Kahkitah. "You and the rest of the Ghorfs."

"The spies you mentioned a minute ago?" Jeff asked.

Nicole nodded. "We can start with Wesowee. He wasn't really lost down in the Q4 basement, was he? He and others were searching for me. At your orders?"

"I give no orders to anyone," Kahkitah said, his birdsong sounding studiously neutral.

"You're splitting hairs," Nicole said. "Okay, so maybe all you do is send a message and alert and someone else gives the actual orders. But then there was the whole Setting Sun thing. I wondered how you were able to collect the ingredients all by yourself while I was sleeping. But you didn't, did you? You called in your buddies to help."

"There was need," Kahkitah said. "And you *are* the *Fyrantha's* Protector."

"And suddenly a whole bunch of other things make sense," Jeff murmured. "Big, dumb, happy Ghorfs . . . only sometimes you have these flashes of insight or observation or deduction. Who are you, anyway?"

Kahkitah lifted his hands. "We are merely the Ghorfs—"

"No," Nicole cut him off. "No more. Everything has changed, Kahkitah. We're in for the fight of our lives, and we have to know where everyone stands."

For a moment Kahkitah gazed at her. Then, he nodded. "We are an army," he said, his birdsongs suddenly hard and cold and confident.

Nicole felt herself straighten up. "An *army*?"

"A small one only," Kahkitah said. "And largely self-taught, with the guidance of those few who'd seen military service before being brought to the *Fyrantha*."

"And your mission?" Jeff asked.

"To survive," Kahkitah said. "To endure, and to watch, and to prepare. And, ultimately, to return home."

"And your communication system?" Nicole asked.

"Our daily duties are to different work groups, as you know," Kahkitah said. "But we've developed a private communication system that runs throughout the ship."

"Something the Shipmasters can't tap into?" Jeff asked.

"We believe so," Kahkitah said. "We've been able to isolate it from the rest of the *Fyrantha*'s systems."

"Really," Jeff said. "That's very interesting."

"Why?" Nicole asked.

"Because whenever Bungie sabotaged things, the *Fyrantha* always told you about it so that we could fix it," Jeff said. "If the Ghorfs isolated some system that's supposed to connect to something else, the ship should have noticed and told someone to fix it."

"Unless it didn't *want* it fixed," Nicole said.

"Why would it do that?" Kahkitah asked.

Nicole took a deep breath. "Because I think that, on some level, the *Fyrantha*'s on our side."

"Against the Shipmasters?"

"Yes," Nicole said. "I can't help thinking about what Ushkai told me before, that the ship set things up so that only humans can fix it. Why do that?"

"Because it's comfortable with us?"

"No," Nicole said, a shiver running through her. "Because of the other lie Ushkai told just now. The one that convinced me that the Shipmasters were controlling him. Remember I asked him if Earth was safe?"

"He said it was," Kahkitah said.

"He lied," Nicole said. "I saw it in the arena. But I didn't realize what I'd done until everything was all over and it was too late to fix it."

"What did we do wrong?" Jeff asked.

Nicole closed her eyes. "The Shipmasters are looking for slaves to run ahead of armies," she said. "Slaves that can fight, or at least cost the enemy ammunition while they die."

"But you didn't show that you could fight," Kahkitah said.

"No," Nicole said. "We showed we can get others to fight for us."

For a long moment no one spoke. "We don't just run and die," Jeff said at last. "We motivate. We persuade."

"You lead," Kahkitah said quietly.

"We lead," Nicole agreed, wincing. "That's got to be at least as valuable to the people the Shipmasters deal with."

"Or more so," Jeff said. "That changes things, doesn't it?"

"Yes," Nicole said. "It means we're running on borrowed time. I don't know how much the Shipmasters know about Earth, but I get the feeling it's not very much."

"Oh, they don't know squat," Jeff said with a snort. "Five minutes looking through a newspaper would have proven how violent we were. In fact, I doubt they even know where Earth is."

"Yet they send the Wisps to bring more of you," Kahkitah reminded him.

"*They* don't send the Wisps—the *Fyrantha* does," Jeff said. "As long as the ship has the coordinates it can send the Wisps to pick up new people more or less automatically."

"Maybe," Nicole said. "But even if that's the case, it won't last much longer. Now that they know Earth is worth something they'll start looking, and sooner or later they'll find it. We can't let that happen."

"So we stop it," Jeff said. "You, me, the Ghorfs, and maybe a few others. We stop it, and we stop them."

Nicole took a deep breath. This was happening way too fast.

Or maybe it wasn't. Maybe she'd known this day was coming from the moment Ushkai first declared her to be the *Fyrantha's* Protector. This day, and this decision.

The word the *Fyrantha's* translator used for *protector*, he'd told her then, had two shades of meaning. There was Protector against danger from within, and Protector against danger from without.

Caretaker . . . and Warrior.

She gazed over the rows and rows of memorial pillars. Men and women who'd died so that the Shipmasters could once again turn the *Fyrantha* into a warship.

"Yes," she said. "It's time to fight back against the Shipmasters.

"It's time to take over the *Fyrantha*."

TIMOTHY ZAHN is the Hugo Award–winning author of more than thirty science fiction novels, including *Night Train to Rigel, The Third Lynx, Odd Girl Out,* and the Dragonback sextet. He has also written the all-time bestselling Star Wars spin-off novel, *Heir to the Empire,* and other Star Wars novels, including the recent *Thrawn.* He lives in coastal Oregon.